EYE

of the

BEHOLDER

David Ellis

AN OTTO PENZLER BOOK

Quercus

First published in Great Britain in 2008 by

Quercus
21 Bloomsbury Square
London
WC1A 2NS

ISBN-13 (HB): 978-1-84724-305-8
ISBN-13 (TPB): 978-1-84724-306-5

This book is a work of fiction. Names, characters,
businesses, organizations, places and events are
either the product of the author's imagination
or are used fictitiously. Any resemblance to
actual persons, living or dead, events or
locales is entirely coincidental.

Book design by Amanda Dewey

EYE

of the

BEHOLDER

For Sally Nystrom

✥

The "Mansbury Massacre"

A source in the Marion Park Police Department confirms that the body count is six. Six bodies have been discovered in the basement of Bramhall Auditorium on the Mansbury College campus. We have no word yet on whether the bodies include the missing Mansbury students, Cassandra Bentley and Elisha Danzinger.

—Carolyn Pendry, Newscenter 4, 1:18 P.M., June 26, 1989

Marion Park Police have arrested Terrance Demetrius Burgos, 36, a part-time handyman at Mansbury College, in the murders of six young women who were found murdered and sexually molested in a campus auditorium.

—*Daily Watch*, June 27, 1989

1

PAUL RILEY followed his police escort, navigated his car through the barricades, and stopped next to a patrol car. He shifted the gear into park, killed the engine, and said a quiet prayer.

Now the storm.

When he opened the door, letting in the thick, humid air, it felt like someone had jacked the volume on the stereo: An officer's voice, through a bullhorn, warning the spectators and reporters to respect the police barricades. Reporters shouting questions at any officer they could find, some of them now turning to Riley, a man they didn't know. Cops and medical and forensic technicians shouting instructions to each other. Other reporters, positioned with microphones, speaking loudly into cameras about the breaking news; hundreds of citizens, gathered from everywhere, speculating on what, precisely, had been found inside Bramhall Auditorium.

Riley knew little more than they. The word was, six bodies, young women, mutilated in various ways. Then there was the one additional fact that had been delivered by his boss in a shaky voice:

"They think one of them is Cassie."

Cassandra Bentley, he'd meant, a student at Mansbury College, but, more important, the daughter of Harland and Natalia Bentley, a family worth billions. Family money. Political contributors. People who mattered. Even the name sounded wealthy.

Riley looked up at the bruised sky, where three news helicopters circled over this corner of the Mansbury College campus. He clipped his badge—all of three weeks old—to his jacket and looked for a uniform. There were plenty of them, in various colors—blue for Marion Park police, brown for deputies from the county sheriff's office, white for Mansbury security, black from some other jurisdiction, probably brought in for crowd control.

He gave his name, and his title, something he wasn't used to saying: "First Assistant County Attorney," the top deputy to the county prosecutor.

"Who's in charge?" he asked.

"Lightner," the cop said, gesturing toward the auditorium.

Bramhall Auditorium took up half the block, a dome-topped structure arising from a large concrete staircase, a threshold supported by granite pillars, with a manicured lawn to each side. Riley counted the steps—twelve—and entered the lobby of the auditorium.

It was only slightly less sticky inside. No air-conditioning. School was out. No one was supposed to be using this auditorium this time of year. *Access,* Riley thought to himself. *Who would have access?*

Riley moved cautiously. He was new to this job but not to crime scenes. He'd been an assistant U.S. attorney—a federal prosecutor—for many years, and had spent most of the time working on a street gang that was no stranger to violence. Riley groaned at the number of law enforcement officials inside the place. Fewer was always better, but, as he looked around, he realized that little would be gained from all of the fingerprint dusting going on around him. This was an auditorium, with a decent-sized lobby, and a massive theater that, including the balcony, could probably house several thousand people. It would be easier to figure out who *hadn't* left their prints.

To the side of the lobby, a door opened—the door, presumably, leading to the basement and the maintenance locker where the bodies were found. An officer stepped out and lifted his gas mask—with its charcoal-impregnated odor filter—just before he vomited on the floor.

Paul found himself instantly wishing for city cops. As a former federal prosecutor, he had a built-in bias against the city cops, too, but anything was preferable, in his mind, to a suburban cop. But jurisdiction was jurisdiction. He wasn't working with the FBI anymore.

Riley took the gas mask from the spent officer, who was wiping at his mouth. He told the officer to clean up the mess and get some fresh air. He then took a deep breath and opened the access door.

It was a wide staircase, the steps filthy with shoe prints. He kept his hands off the wooden railing. He hit the landing and turned for the final set of stairs.

There were only two uniforms down there when Riley reached the basement. One of them was in the elevator, which had been shut down. The initial flurry of fingerprinting and photographing had probably already happened.

It was a wide hallway with several heavy doors propped open, several storage rooms already combed over with no results. Riley moved down the hall to the last room in the hallway, the room that mattered, feeling his pace slow.

He steeled himself before he took one shuffle step into that last doorway.

The room was large, with rows of chain-link lockers and shelving units, all containing chemicals and cleaning supplies. Mops and brooms and an oversized garbage can with sprayers containing purple and blue fluids attached. And on the floor, lined up, posed, arms at their sides, legs together, were six corpses.

How to explain? People always said words can't describe. That wasn't true. He just wouldn't have known where to begin or end. He'd seen pictures of Dachau and Auschwitz, but those were photographs, capturing the horror and desperation in only two dimensions. He tried it as a defense mechanism, tried to think of these six butchered girls as photos on a page, ignoring the upheaval in his stomach and the adrenaline pounding through his body. He fought to keep his breathing even, his mind clinical.

The first victim was blond, seemingly a beautiful young girl, though the yellowish hue to her skin made her look more like a wax statue. The blow to her skull could only vaguely be seen from her angled head, near the scalp. Far more prominent was the wound to her chest, where her heart had once been. Calling it a wound was insufficient. It was like the life had been ripped from her.

Second victim: The wound across her neck was so gaping that you sensed if you lifted her the head would detach. Her skin had paled as well. She looked more like a mannequin than a human being, or maybe that was yet another defense mechanism. Maybe it was easier to think of them as objects, at least while you were looking at them. That was usually how the offender viewed them, too.

The victim next to her was also naked, had been burned over her entire body with acid, down to her feet and hands. Most of the skin had been scalded off her face, leaving the skeleton, her eyes protruding from the bone in a ghoulish stare. She would have to be identified through dental records. Looked like one of her hands might still have the skin, too, for fingerprint identification.

The fourth victim looked more recent than the first three, more of a natural hue to her skin, but still, to Riley's eye, not a recent death. Her arms and legs had been severed yet were positioned in the appropriate places, like she was a broken, battered doll. Her eye sockets were bloody, empty crevices. The eyes had been gouged out with a blunt instrument.

The fifth victim's eyes were wide-open, like her mouth, and the petechiae on her neck and face suggested suffocation.

The last of the victims was the most recent, he assumed from the color of her skin, and because it seemed clear that whoever did this was placing them in chronological order. Her face was swollen from premortem bruising, her nose crushed, the bones above her eyes and on her cheeks clearly smashed as well, the top of her skull battered to mush. Her dark hair was sticking out in all directions, matted from the blood and brain matter. This, from what he'd been told, was Cassandra Bentley.

Six young women had been lined up like sides of beef, murdered and mutilated in various ways.

Okay, he'd seen it. It was important to view the crime scene, if you were going to prosecute a case. And there was no doubt Riley was going to handle this one.

His limbs electrified, his head woozy, Riley made his way back up the stairs. Neither the hallway nor the staircases showed any signs of blood. The fun hadn't taken place here. They'd been murdered somewhere else and transported to this auditorium.

When he opened the door into the lobby, a tall, skinny man with dark curly hair nodded at him. "Paul Riley? Joel Lightner. Chief of Detectives at M.P."

Riley removed his gas mask and shook Lightner's hand. Lightner looked midthirties and baby-faced. Riley wondered how many detectives a small town like Marion Park could possibly have.

"Chief Harry Clark," Lightner said, motioning behind him. Clark was one of those guys who would look sloppy without the uniform, bad posture, a sizable midsection, soft in the chin, with small eyes, and a military cut to his thin hair.

"And Walter Monk, head of security at Mansbury."

They all shook hands and exchanged notes. Lightner flipped open his notepad and read off the list of injuries. The first girl, a blow to the skull and her heart had been removed; second girl, throat slit near the point of decapitation; third girl, burned with sulfuric acid; fourth girl, arms and legs severed, eyes gouged out; fifth girl, strangulation, or drowning; final girl, beaten savagely about the face and skull, with a single gunshot wound through the back of the mouth.

"There was intercourse in each case," Lightner added. "The M.E. thinks the first victim is about a week old. Each one seems more recent than the— it looks like maybe it was one murder a day, for a week. The last one, they figure, was probably yesterday."

"They were down here a whole week and no one noticed?"

Monk, the security guy, had to be near sixty. His long, beaky face nodded slowly. "Between spring semester and summer school, there's a two-week period off. The whole school basically shuts down."

And whoever did this, Riley thought, *knew that.*

"The last one is Cassie Bentley?" he asked. "The rich girl?"

Monk sighed. "Hard to tell for sure, she was beaten so badly."

Riley surely agreed with that. The poor girl's face had been crushed. They'd need dental records for confirmation.

"But, yeah," Monk said, "I think so. Especially because the first one's Ellie, so it makes sense."

Riley perked up. He was playing catch-up here.

"Elisha Danzinger," Lightner explained. "Ellie. She and Cassie shared a dorm room. Best friends."

Riley turned to Monk. "How many kids here at Mansbury?"

He made a face. "About four thousand."

"Four thousand. And how is it you know these two girls so well?"

Monk grunted a laugh. "Oh, well, everyone knows Cassie Bentley. She's a Bentley." His face turned sour. "And she's had her share of trouble. Disciplinary things. Cassie's a little—kind of a troubled young girl."

Lightner hit Monk with the back of his hand. "Tell him what you just told me about Ellie."

"Yes, Ellie." Monk took a breath. "Ellie had had some trouble with a college employee. A part-time handyman. He did odd jobs. Painting, blacktopping, maintenance. He'd been assigned this block of buildings when he worked here."

"And?"

"And he'd been following Ellie around campus. Stalking her. She'd gone to court last year and gotten a restraining order. And we fired him, of course."

Riley thought about that. A handyman. Keys to buildings like this auditorium. Knowledge of the school schedule. "Ellie's the one, her heart was ripped out? The first one?"

They all nodded.

"So you know this guy? This handyman?"

"His name is Terry Burgos," Monk said. "I have his home address right here."

Riley looked at Lightner. Did he really need to say the words?

"I'm taking a couple cars with me," said Lightner.

"Wait," Riley said. "I need a phone. And someone find me one of the ACAs. We're not taking any chances. Surround the house right now. If you can get his consent for a search, then go in. Otherwise, freeze the situation until I say so."

Lightner shot Riley a look. Cops had all kinds of ways of obtaining consent, or saying they did after the fact.

"We're not fucking this search up, Detective," Riley said. "Are we clear?"

Riley left the cops and found an assistant county attorney, sending her off to a judge for a warrant. Then he found a phone in the school's administrative office and dialed the number for his boss, County Attorney Ed Mullaney. "You'll need to call Harland Bentley," Riley told him. He looked out the window at a news copter overhead. "If he hasn't already heard."

2

B Y THE TIME Paul Riley pulled up to Terry Burgos's house, the Marion Park Police Department had been there for an hour. Burgos had answered Detective Joel Lightner's knock at the door and had not resisted when Lightner had asked him to wait on the front porch while an assistant county attorney obtained a warrant to search his home.

A news copter hovered overhead. Reporters were lining the police tape. The neighbors were out, some of them dressed for work, others in robes, clutching their small children, as they looked on. The news had spread naturally. A killer lived at 526 Rosemary Lane.

The house was nondescript, one of a series of bungalows where the "townies" lived just west of campus. The police were everywhere, looking for trace evidence and footprints in the dirt out back, scanning the garage, where some blood and hair had been found, and working on Burgos's Chevy Suburban parked in the driveway.

Burgos had been taken to police headquarters, where he would be questioned. Riley wanted to be there, but he wanted a look at the house first. He'd already had a preview. The master bathroom, garage, and truck held some obvious promise, but most of what they needed to know was in the basement.

His stomach was swimming, but he had to keep his composure. This was his case. Everyone would follow his lead. He nodded to Lightner, who was on his way to the garage. He was going to wait for Riley before heading back to the station, but the instructions had been clear enough to the uniforms taking Burgos into custody: No one talked to Terry Burgos until Riley said so.

Riley followed the path of rocks up to the house. The yard had been neglected, brown spots littering the dry lawn. The screen door, which had seen better days, had been removed by one of the cops, leaving the front door, which was propped open by a rock from the front steps.

The interior of the house on the main floor was relatively undisturbed. Some antique furniture, dilapidated tile flooring, a fairly well-kept, humble presentation.

Riley held his breath and took the carpeted basement stairs down, nonetheless noticing the smell first. To the untrained nose, it smelled like sewage more than anything else. Most people, when murdered, lose control of bowel functions and soil themselves. There were no bodies down here, but Lightner had said there was no doubt that the murders happened in the basement.

He was right.

The basement was not furnished, a concrete floor with a small workout area, with a weight bench and a barbell with modest weights gathering cobwebs. A dartboard hung precariously on one wall next to a target for a BB gun. The room as a whole was probably poorly lit, but the police had installed high-powered lighting, leaving the technicians to work in an odd glow.

Riley turned to the back of the basement, where Burgos had a small workshop—a power saw and some hand tools and sawhorses. The floor was spotted and dirty. Bloodstains, most likely that Burgos had attempted to wipe clean. A number of technicians were gathering hairs with tweezers, placing other items in paper evidence bags near the workshop area, where it appeared the murders had occurred.

Riley walked up to the small workbench and sucked in his breath. Resting on the bench was an ordinary kitchen knife, a good five- or six-inch blade, covered with dried blood and other particulate. The first two victims, Elisha Danzinger and an unidentified girl, had been treated to that weapon. Next to the knife was a handsaw, its blade similarly covered in blood, other bodily fluids, and what appeared to be bone. That was the weapon he'd used to dismember the fourth victim.

A freestanding bathtub rested in one corner, looking like something plucked from a garbage dump, with significant corrosion inside. Riley had no doubt that this was where Burgos had scalded the one victim with acid. Sitting on top of a nearby washing machine was a car battery and a glass vial.

Four down, two to go.

Riley already knew that upstairs, in the master bathroom, police had found hairs in the drain of the bathtub, which was presumably where one of the victims had been drowned. And in the garage, they had uncovered a single bullet and a .32 caliber handgun—presumably the gun used to shoot Cassie Bentley through the back of the mouth, either before or after Burgos had beaten her almost beyond recognition.

That covered them all. The guy hadn't gone to great lengths—*any* lengths—to cover this up. He'd left the murder weapons in full view. He'd left trace evidence of the victims in his basement, car, and garage. He'd left the victims' identification—purses, driver's licenses, clothes—in a garbage bag in his bedroom. Yes, he'd confined the murders to his property, or so it appeared at first blush, but otherwise Terry Burgos had made little attempt to clean up or discard his weapons.

On the workbench, resting next to the knife and handsaw, was a King James Bible, with bloody fingerprints along the pages. A single sheet of paper, tacked to the poster board on the wall behind the workbench, listed a number of passages from the Bible, chapter and verse. He leaned over the bench to get a close look at the sheet, which was written in red ballpoint pen. At the top, set apart, was a verse from Jeremiah 48:10:

Cursed be he that doeth the work of the LORD deceitfully, and cursed be he that keepeth back his sword from blood.

Beneath this verse, descending down the page with numbers next to them, were other biblical passages, by citation only:

1. *Hosea 13:4–8*
2. *Romans 1:24–32*
3. *Leviticus 21:9*

4. *Exodus 21:22–25*
5. *2 Kings 2:23–24*
6. *Deuteronomy 22:20–21*

In the last of the six citations, a reference to Leviticus had been scratched out in favor of a passage from Deuteronomy. The edit had been done with a thin black Magic Marker.

Riley let out his breath. Six girls dead, six verses from the Bible.

Okay. Enough. The crime scene wasn't his specialty, he'd just wanted a taste. Riley appreciated the fresh air when he stepped outside again. He found Lightner near the garage. Lightner's body language suggested a fully charged cop working the biggest case of his career, but his eyes showed something dark and evil. They had just seen two gruesome crime scenes. Now it was time to connect them.

"Let's go get a confession," Riley said to him.

3

PAUL RILEY nursed a cup of water and watched the suspect through a one-way mirror in the observation room. You learned more from your eyes than you ever did from your ears. Innocent people were nervous in custody. Guilty people often weren't.

Terry Burgos was sitting alone in an interrogation room, wearing headphones he'd been allowed to bring, moving his head and tapping his foot to the beat, sometimes playing drums on the small table in front of him. The guy looked the Mediterranean part, short, beefy in the chest and torso, dark around the eyes, lots of thick, curly dark hair. Had a baseball cap pulled down and appeared to be humming to himself. He had drunk two cans of Coca-Cola and gone to the bathroom once. Had not requested a lawyer and had not received *Miranda* warnings.

Burgos had sat idle in the room for over an hour. Riley had wanted time for the police to gather whatever information they could before questioning the suspect. That, and he wanted Burgos hungry for lunch. Riley had hoped for more time, but there was no way anyone was letting go of Burgos, and there was only so long you could hold someone and keep lawyers away. Everyone, soon enough, was going to know about Terry Burgos, and it wouldn't take long for an attorney of some kind or another to be knocking on the door.

Various cops and prosecutors came in and out of the observation room, peering in on the suspect with morbid curiosity. There was a palpable intensity in the police station because they knew they had their man, and it was the biggest thing this town had ever seen.

Burgos did not have a clean sheet. Two years earlier, he'd been arrested on suspicion of battery of a young woman, but it ended in a *nolle prosequi*, meaning the charges were dropped. Paul assumed the woman had failed to show for the hearing. Last year, he had been charged with sexual assault, but the case had been pleaded down to a misdemeanor battery, and he hadn't done any time.

Elisha Danzinger had gone to the police to swear out a complaint against Terry Burgos in November of the previous year, 1988. She had alleged that Burgos, at the time a part-time handyman at Mansbury, had been following her around the campus, making threatening comments and generally making her feel uncomfortable. The police had brought Burgos in but hadn't charged him. There was nothing on which they *could* charge him. Paul knew, from the Mansbury staff, that this past January Ellie had gotten an order of protection against Burgos, a civil action not contained in the police file, which had prohibited Burgos from coming within five hundred feet of her.

Burgos was age thirty-six, lived alone, and had worked two jobs. The first was a part-timer for Mansbury until he was fired this February, primarily landscaping but occasional cleaning assignments as well. For his second job, which he still held, he worked in an off-campus printing company owned by Mansbury College professor Frankfort Albany.

Terry Burgos, by all accounts, was moderately intelligent, if undereducated, and introverted; didn't get an A plus for hygiene; didn't complain much; and seemed generally indifferent to life. The unconfirmed word was he'd had a difficult childhood growing up in Marion Park, spousal abuse charges between his parents, and very poor school performance, ending short of a high school diploma.

Joel Lightner was standing next to Paul, watching through the one-way as Burgos jammed to his music. Lightner was bouncing on his toes, like a pitcher in the bull pen who was about to get the tap on the arm from the coach. "When do we start?" he asked.

"Do we have the photos?" Riley asked.

He nodded, handed Riley a file.

There was no reason to wait much longer. Unless Burgos's nerves had completely overtaken him, which Riley doubted from looking at him, Burgos was probably hungry. Things like withholding food were bases for a defense attorney to argue coercion.

Riley sighed and stretched his arms. "You up for this, Detective?"

Lightner nodded efficiently. "Marion Park's not Mayberry, Paul. I'm no virgin."

That was true enough. Marion Park, a nearby suburb, didn't have the city's crime, but at least one prominent gang, the Columbus Street Cannibals, had begun to have a presence down there.

"Doesn't mean I'm not open to suggestions."

"Okay." Paul looked through the one-way mirror again. "Hands off, first of all."

"Only way I do it."

"Let's make it a courtesy, for starters. Don't let him leave, obviously, but tell him he can. See if he tries."

"We'll do lunch," he suggested. Riley's thought exactly. A conversation over lunch was more casual. So they were on the same page. It was standard practice for detectives to interrogate suspects, not ACAs. Paul could overrule that and take it himself, but then he'd be a witness and disqualified from prosecuting the case. There were some other ACAs floating about right now, guys Paul had summoned from the city, including the chiefs of the criminal prosecutions and special prosecutions bureaus. But Paul made the call, right there, that Joel Lightner would get first crack. He had caught the case and it was his. Besides, if they were right about this guy, he wasn't going anywhere, whether he confessed or not.

"Record it," Riley said, as Lightner walked out of the observation room. Paul brought in the bureau chiefs, plus Chief Clark and three other of his detectives. All of these people could verify anything that the tape recording couldn't. Riley also wanted to hear their thoughts on the progress made so far.

They all watched, in silence, through the one-way mirror. Terry Burgos was quietly bopping along to the music from his headphones. He didn't even look up as Joel Lightner entered the room, carrying a tape recorder. Lightner placed it down on the small wooden table and extended the cord to the wall socket. Only when he felt the vibration of the recorder hitting the table did the suspect take notice.

Lightner took a seat opposite Burgos and gestured with his hands that he should remove the headphones. Burgos fumbled with the player, finally turned it off, and removed the tiny speakers from his ears.

"Appreciate you coming down, Mr. Burgos. Do you mind if I record this conversation?"

Burgos looked over the detective, in rolled-up shirtsleeves. Joel placed his finger on the RECORD button. "The time is 1:25 P.M. on Monday, June 26, 1989. My name is Detective Joel Lightner, chief of detectives for the Marion Park Police Department. I'm sitting with Terrance Demetrius Burgos. Mr. Burgos, do I have your permission to tape-record this conversation?"

The suspect continued to look him over, then gave a halfhearted shrug.

"Can you answer out loud, Mr. Burgos?"

"Okay," he said. He spoke quietly, hesitantly.

"Okay, I can tape-record our talk?"

"Okay." He smoothed his hands over the table. "Got any more Coke?"

"You want a Coke? No problem." He went to the door and issued the request. "You're probably hungry, too, aren't you? Missed lunch."

"Uh-huh."

"What do you feel like?"

He didn't answer. Maybe he took the question more literally.

"A burger and fries?" Joel asked. "A sub?"

Burgos looked at Joel. "I like tacos."

"Tacos? Great. I know a place." He spoke again to the officer outside the door. Then he returned to the table, settled back into his chair. Lightner's way was laid-back, slouching and crossing a leg. Some guys didn't have the natural ease about them, try as they might, and came off looking like someone who was trying too *hard* to look at ease. Joel, he had it, Riley could already see. "I want to thank you for coming down here. I want you to understand, Mr. Burgos, that you're here as a courtesy. You can leave if you want to. Okay?"

The suspect shrugged. "I don't mind."

"Good," Paul said aloud. Joel had been to school. He had told the suspect he was free to leave, which meant Burgos technically was not in custody and *Miranda* warnings were not required. But Joel had made sure to offer the guy a meal on the house before mentioning he was free to go. Now Joel could have a nice, casual chat without ever mentioning the word *lawyer*. Terry Burgos was about to learn that there was no such thing as a free lunch.

"What-cha been doing this morning, Terry?"

The suspect shrugged. "Not much."

"Listen to the radio at all?"

"I listened to my music."

"You haven't listened to the radio today?"

"Nah."

"What about TV? Watch any television today?"

"Nope."

"Have you spoken to anyone today? Neighbors? Anyone?"

Burgos shook his head. "Nobody."

Paul's confidence in the detective was growing. Lightner had just cleared the weeds. By the time the police got to Burgos's house late that morning, it would have been possible that Burgos had already heard about these killings from news reports on the radio or television. Now, thanks to Lightner confirming that Burgos had not listened to any media sources, any knowledge that Burgos might admit to could not be attributed to TV or radio, or even neighbors. If he knew something, it would be from his personal knowledge.

"You, uh, you did odd jobs at Mansbury, is that right?" Lightner asked.

"Yeah."

"Painting, blacktopping, rake leaves, shovel snow. That sort of thing?"

"Yeah."

"Cleaning?"

"Sometimes. Sometimes I cleaned. Whatever they told me."

Joel scratched a cheek.

"I don't work there no more," Burgos added.

"No? You don't work at Mansbury anymore?"

Burgos shook his head.

"Why not, Terry?"

"I dunno." Burgos shrugged. "They fired me."

A uniform arrived with the Coke, and Burgos seemed more animated. He popped off the top and took a swig. Paul wasn't in the habit of second-guessing, but he wasn't thrilled with these last few questions. He would have *told* this information to Burgos, not asked, to let Burgos know that he already knew, no bullshit. Lightner was playing dumb.

But there was more than one way to a confession, and Joel needed to do it his way, as much as Riley wanted to intervene.

"Terry," Lightner said, "when you *did* work there, did you ever work at Bramhall Auditorium?"

Burgos studied his soft drink like it was a prized diamond. Licked his lips, took another swig. "Yeah. I've done that," he said.

"Ever go down to that basement, Terry? Where the cleaning supplies are?"

Well, Joel was cutting to the chase a bit, but this was one of those great questions for an interrogator, damned if you say yes *or* no.

"Yeah," he said.

Riley turned to Chief Clark, who was standing next to him. "Tell your officer not to deliver that food until you say so." What Riley meant was, not until *Riley* said so, but there was no need to step on toes.

"Can anyone go down there, Terry? Like, could I just walk down there and go to that basement?"

"You need a key," he said.

"Do you have a key?"

"When I worked there, I had keys to all the buildings."

Paul held his breath. This was one of those moments. In an interrogation, you were always looking for the breakthrough. Sometimes, it came remarkably easily. Otherwise, it was a game, where any number of questions could potentially open the floodgates. The interrogator's job was to poke around the dam, look for the hole.

Burgos had ducked the question.

"I mean now," Lightner said. "Do you still have keys?"

"I had to return them."

Ducking again. Yes, he had returned the keys. But had he made a copy?

The assumption—the only cautious assumption that could be made— was that Burgos had made copies of every key to the Mansbury facility. So the dean, Janet Scotland, had canceled classes indefinitely and declared all school areas off-limits, while law enforcement scoured every single nook and cranny of every facility to ensure there were no more dead bodies. They had the whole school on lockdown; students there for summer school, which had been scheduled to begin that day, were confined to their quarters, with police guarding every residence hall. Between the university campus and the printing company where Burgos worked part-time, almost the entire police department was searching for bodies and evidence.

Lightner apparently decided not to press the issue of the keys. He saw, as they all did, that Burgos was sensitive to it. He had decided to tread lightly for now. He asked about what Burgos had been doing, and where, going back the last two weeks. The medical examiner had been confident that the murders had all happened within two weeks, maximum. That worked out to roughly a victim every other day, at the least, and possibly one every day.

The police had recovered the driver's licenses of all six women, by this point, from a dresser in Burgos's bedroom. So the names were known, and they had been run for sheets. There were the students, Ellie Danzinger and Cassie Bentley, and then there were four other women who were not enrolled in Mansbury, each of whom had been picked up at least once for solicitation, which was a nice legal term for prostitution. Two students and four hookers.

Officers were already fanning out to find the victims' friends so that a time line could be set. It was always harder to pinpoint when prostitutes went missing because often the traditional sources—employers, parents, spouses—were absent. Still, it could probably be done, most likely through their landlords, if they had a regular place to stay. It would have been nice to know, before questioning the suspect, when exactly these women went missing. Then the questions on Burgos's alibi could be framed with more precision.

But there wasn't time for that now. Burgos could lawyer up at any time, and it seemed abundantly clear that an attorney would muzzle him. So Joel had to go back two weeks and ask about each day.

A pattern emerged during this line of questioning, as it would with most people's lives. Terry Burgos had no day job at this point, since he had been fired from Mansbury, but he worked every night, Monday through Friday, at the printing plant owned by Professor Frank Albany.

"Who works with you there at the printing plant, Terry?"

"Usually, just me—at night." He wiggled the empty Coke can, then belched and giggled.

"This is our mass murderer?" asked one of the prosecutors in the room with Paul.

"What hours do you work?" Lightner asked.

"Whatever." Burgos shrugged.

"What does 'Whatever' mean, Terry?"

"Whatever they need. Usually, I start at six. Then I go to whenever."

When pressed by Lightner, however, the suspect could not be specific on the recent hours he'd worked at the plant. That would be easy enough to find, and it was critical information.

As for daytime over the last two weeks, Burgos was even less forthcoming. Stayed in the house a lot, sometimes went for a drive in the country in his truck, but he wouldn't be pinned down on any particular thing on any particular day.

"How do you record being at the printing plant?" Joel asked, changing the subject back. A common tactic in interrogations. Return to something uncomfortable and watch the reaction. "When you work the night shift, Terry, do you sign in or punch a clock?"

"I sign in." Burgos wiggled in his seat. A little claustrophobia, maybe hunger, was setting in.

"So it's like an honor system, right, Terry? If you signed in, then left, no one would know?" Joel shrugged his shoulders. "I mean, you told me no one else worked nights but you."

"Yeah. I guess I could do that," he agreed, a little more readily than Paul would have expected.

Riley looked at his watch. It was twenty past two. "Give him his food," he said to the chief. A few moments later, the officer stepped in with the bags of food he'd kept in an oven in the department's lunchroom.

They needed a segue. Joel seemed to sense it and came out of the room. He entered the observation room, sighed, and rolled his head. "He's not an idiot," he said to Riley. "He knows what to admit and where he can squirm. The guy has no commitments during the day, and he works alone at that plant at night."

Riley looked around the room. "Any thoughts?"

There were plenty, from the various prosecutors and detectives. Everyone wanted a part of this thing. Strong-arm him. Accuse him. Make him think he's not a suspect. Ask for his help. All of those positions could make sense.

But all Riley could think was, this guy had been sitting in police custody going on two hours and he hadn't demanded an explanation of *why* he was being held. So much of this, in the end, was going with your gut.

Riley went to the grouping of the photographs of the six victims. There were over a dozen of each one, from various angles and distances. "Get me a new folder," he said to no one in particular. In the meantime, he selected a single photo of each victim, cutting down the number of photos from over seventy to just six. Riley placed the six shots into the new folder. He looked at them a moment, then removed the photograph of the first victim, Ellie Danzinger.

That left five photos, one each of victims two through six.

Riley had another thought and rearranged the photos, so they were not in the order in which they had been lined up on the floor.

"Show him these," he told Joel. "While he's eating."

"Okay."

"Make a note of the order they're in currently," Paul ordered. Lightner complied, with the entire room as witnesses, scribbling down the order on a notepad.

"They're out of order," Joel noted, but then he looked at Riley and understood. "And we're leaving Ellie out of it?"

"Right."

"I like that." Joel used the bathroom while Riley and the others watched Terry Burgos eat his tacos. Burgos did so with precision, pouring a bit of hot sauce and scooping a small amount of guacamole for each bite.

Joel walked in with the file of photographs and opened it up for Burgos to see. But the suspect was still enjoying his food. So Joel got out of his seat and walked over to the suspect. "What do you think about those, Terry?"

Burgos put down his food and his fresh, sweaty Coke. He wiped his hands with a napkin and spread out the five photos, leaned in close for a good look. His face showed neither horror nor recognition. The word that came to Riley's mind was *familiarity*. He fixed on each one, first carefully wiping his hands with the napkin and then tracing his fingers over the dead corpses featured in the eight-by-ten glossies. He mumbled to himself but nothing audible. He held a finger in the air, still murmuring, then lightly touched each photo. Joel Lightner was watching the suspect closely but knew better than to start the conversation. Not yet.

Burgos then took the photos and rearranged them.

Riley's heart started drumming. He couldn't see the order in which Burgos had arranged them but he felt sure that, at that moment, they matched the order he had seen them on that floor in the basement of Bramhall Auditorium.

Burgos looked up at Joel a moment with curiosity, then back down at the photos. He lifted the manila folder up and looked under it. He pinched his fingers on each photo as if he was looking for another one stuck beneath it.

"Here we go," Riley whispered.

The chief started to speak, "What's he—," but Riley threw a palm on his shoulder and moved toward the mirror.

Terry Burgos looked up at Joel. "Where's the first one?" he asked. "Where's Ellie?"

4

TWO OF the detectives in the room grabbed each other. The chief clasped his hands together in relief. Riley had been a part of countless interrogations over the years, and he'd seen it happen in various forms. The breakthrough. The moment the witness gave it up, out of vanity, guilt, frustration, relief, coercion.

Now the tough part, he thought to himself. There hadn't been much question of guilt, not since they looked inside Burgos's house. This was now about something else entirely.

"I have shown you five photographs of women who were murdered," said Detective Joel Lightner, suddenly aware of the tape recorder and its inability to pick up what he'd done. "You rearranged them in a particular order. And you are asking—"

"Where's the first one? Ellie?" Terry Burgos repeated the question, shaking a photo in his hand and then slamming it down. He jumped from his seat and looked off in the distance. At that moment, Riley would have given anything to get a better look at his face. He could only see his profile, which had been an oversight on his part; Burgos should have been facing the one-way mirror.

Riley couldn't see the order in which the photographs had been rearranged by Burgos, either, but at this point he had no doubt that they were in the order in which the bodies had been placed in that custodian locker.

Burgos's breathing escalated. He seemed incredibly uneasy all of a sudden, but his feet were planted. A couple of the people in the room with Paul jerked at Burgos's physical movement, but Riley held out a hand. Joel Lightner was the consummate professional, expressing no alarm whatsoever at Burgos's mild outburst. Though Joel had left his gun outside the door, he knew there were dozens of officers who could rush in on a moment's notice.

Burgos, still standing at his chair, slowly pointed to the first photo in the sequence, presumably the second victim, because Ellie Danzinger's photo had been left out of the mix. This was the woman whose throat had been slit, almost decapitating her.

"Colombian necklace," Burgos said.

"Colombian *what?*" Chief Clark whispered.

Colombian necklace. Paul drew a finger across his throat. A figure of speech, slang, in the drug trade. The Colombians would slit the throats of competitors.

Burgos turned to the next photo, presumably of the third victim. "Assault with a battery."

That didn't register. Assault *and* battery? The third victim had been burned. But he hadn't said assault and battery. He'd said assault *with a—*

"Battery acid," Riley mumbled. "Inventory his books," he called out to no one in particular. "His music, too. Now." Riley heard some orders issued behind him, and someone left the room.

Burgos pointed to the next victim, presumably the one whose limbs had been removed and eyes gouged out. "Eye for eye, limb for limb."

A biblical reference, which was consistent with what Riley had seen in Burgos's basement.

Burgos kept going to the next one, who'd been drowned. "Someone taught her to sleep underwater."

"This fuckin' guy," someone mumbled behind Paul.

Burgos pointed to the next one, the last victim, Cassie Bentley. Cassie's face had been beaten almost beyond recognition. Paul thought of his own daughter and what it would be like to find her in such a bloody and battered condition. Joel Lightner had told Riley that it would be years before he could eat lasagna again.

"Now it's time / to say good-bye / to someone's family," Burgos said. Paul felt a chill. He was saying it to the tune of the *Mickey Mouse Club*, for God's sake. "Stick it right / between her teeth / and fire so happily."

Both rooms—the observation room and interrogation room—fell silent. Riley felt a collective shudder among his colleagues. The suspect was making the details of his gruesome murders sound like a corny nursery rhyme.

Stick it right between her teeth, Burgos had said. Yes. Though Cassie Bentley's face had been beaten severely, the M.E. had found a gunshot exit wound in the back of her head and gunpowder residue in her mouth.

Detective Lightner seemed in no hurry to interrupt the recitation, but, after a good minute, it was clear that Terry Burgos, still standing by his chair, eyes on the photos, was going to require some prompting. Riley, trying to keep his emotions out of this, was impressed that Lightner seemed able to do that very thing.

"You mentioned a 'first one,' Terry?" Lightner's voice was trembling. "You mentioned a name?"

"Ellie." The suspect—the killer, there was little doubt now—pointed at nothing in particular. "He opens a heart once so cruel."

Opens a heart. Ellie Danzinger's heart had been removed.

Paul realized he'd been holding his breath, that he was perspiring. He looked at the chief, who returned the same look that Paul assumed was on his own face—not knowing, really, what to think of this spectacle. It was horrific and bizarre and, yes, exciting.

And they had their man, in less than half a day.

"You're talking about Ellie," Lightner said.

Burgos seemed lost in thought a moment.

Of course, Riley knew, Burgos was talking about Ellie Danzinger. *Opens a heart.* He had sliced her heart out—postmortem, according to preliminary findings. They were already trying to contact the Danzinger family in South Africa. This was the man who had been stalking their daughter, the one against whom they had obtained a restraining order. Paul wondered how hard the family had lobbied for Ellie to leave Mansbury, to get distance from Burgos. One thing he knew for sure: That thought would forever haunt the family.

"She was a gift," Burgos mumbled.

Lightner cocked his head. "Say again, Terry?"

"Ellie." Burgos lifted a hand, then slowly raised it to his forehead. "She was a gift from God."

"Ellie was a gift from God. Okay." Lightner wasn't entirely sure what to do with that. He held his breath a moment, even shot a glance toward Riley and the others, though he couldn't see them.

"What was it you were saying about Ellie?" he asked. "'Opening her heart'?"

Burgos had drawn his arms around himself. His head angled downward, as if in deep thought. A long moment passed. Lightner held completely still, watching Burgos.

Slowly, Burgos brought an index finger to his lips. His mouth opened, and everyone in the viewing room craned forward.

He spoke just above a whisper: "A girl who is cool to someone at school until he opens a heart once so cruel."

Paul remembered the restraining order Ellie Danzinger had obtained against Burgos. He'd been harassing her, stalking her. *A girl who was cool to someone at school.*

"Hmm." In the interrogation room, Joel was trying to sound nonchalant, harmlessly curious. He twirled his finger. "Sounds like—a poem or something."

On the other side of the glass, Chief Clark turned to Paul. "We'll go through his books," he said.

"Could be a song." Paul gestured toward the headphones and Walkman resting next to Burgos in the interrogation room. "Start with that music right there," he said.

Someone behind Paul asked, "What's this shit about a 'gift from God'?"

"Talk to me about Cassie Bentley, Terry," Lightner said to Burgos. "Was she a gift from God, too?"

"Cassie." Burgos shook his head slowly, brought a hand over his heart. "Cassie saved me."

"How's that?" Lightner scratched his cheek, doing his best to be casual. "How did Cassie save you, Terry?"

Burgos rubbed his eyes furiously, then clasped his hands together on top of his baseball cap. It was as if he hadn't even heard Lightner.

"You said, 'A girl who is cool to someone at school,' Terry." Lightner was trying another way in. "Is that 'someone' you, Terry? Did someone treat you badly at Mansbury? Maybe deserve what they got coming? You mean Ellie, right?"

Paul winced. Lightner was trying to bring Burgos back to the table. Trying everything in the book—empathy now. Maybe trying too hard.

"Did Ellie piss you off, Terry? Did she need to be taught a lesson?"

Terry Burgos looked around the room, put his hands on his hips. His eyes seemed to move in all directions except toward Detective Joel Lightner.

"I think I'm ready to go home now," Burgos said.

5

TIME BECAME an irrelevant concept. Orders were given, information retrieved. New revelations came every few minutes. The forensic pathology staff had worked immediately on the bodies, coming back with preliminary reports on each of them. Information was coming in slowly about the various victims, and about Burgos. Riley knew that the overload would have to be contained. Several days, at a minimum, would be needed to process and categorize all the information.

Riley glanced at his watch and couldn't believe it was evening. There had been a shift change but none of the cops on duty had left, and even those off duty that day had come into the station to volunteer. The station house was swollen with law enforcement personnel ready to do whatever was necessary to put Terry Burgos away.

Marion Park was close to the city, but still—it wasn't the city. It had its share of crime, but this particular crime was in a different category. And this had happened at Mansbury College, one of the most prestigious liberal arts schools in the country, a school that had propped up this small suburb, made its name known across the country. The town wasn't just horrified. It was outraged.

Terry Burgos had refused any further questioning. Detective Lightner had given him *Miranda* warnings at that time and asked him pointed questions about each of the victims by name—Elisha Danzinger, Angela Mornakowski, Jacqueline Davis, Sarah Romanski, Maureen Hollis, and Cassandra Bentley. Burgos had refused to answer or even look at Lightner, moving toward the corner and tapping the wall lightly with his foot. So Lightner had processed Burgos, and the investigation had turned to pursuing several angles to bolster the case.

Riley was reading the Bible, looking at the passages cited on that piece of paper in Burgos's basement, when the buzz in the station house suddenly grew quiet. Riley looked up and saw County Attorney Edward Mullaney walking with two people, immaculately dressed and well-coiffed. He had never met the Bentleys before but he recognized them immediately, anyway. Mullaney caught Riley's eye. Riley followed them into the chief's office.

Chief Clark was shaking Harland Bentley's hand when Riley walked in. Natalia Lake Bentley was sitting passively in a chair, her face swollen and red. Mullaney took Riley's arm and whispered in his ear: "Mrs. Bentley just identified Cassie."

Riley nodded and introduced himself. Harland Bentley was all business, giving his name while he gripped Riley's hand, relying on the formalities of a business transaction, familiar territory for him. The formality was forced. A defense mechanism. He could see the anguish across Mr. Bentley's face, his wavering attempt to contain his emotions.

Mrs. Bentley briefly looked up at Riley. She had been raised well, and kept her posture perfect, but her face was wound tightly, her eyes deep and sunken—the eyes of a mother who had just identified a cold, beaten body as her only child.

"Mrs. Bentley," Riley said. "I'm so sorry. We found the man who did this."

"Tell me what he did," Harland Bentley said, his mouth curled. "I want to know everything he did."

Riley stiffened, and nodded toward Mrs. Bentley.

"I just identified what was left of my daughter," she said, without looking at him. "Do you think that anything you're going to say will shock me?"

The medical examiner had already made preliminary findings. Riley preferred to think of it in clinical terms: fractures of the mandible, maxilla, lachrymal, hyoid, ethmoid, and frontal bones—fractures of virtually every facial bone and most of the cranial bones—but it came down to the simple fact that her face, and most of the front and top of her skull, had been crushed by multiple powerful blows. Pieces of bone were lodged in her brain. Most of her teeth were found in her throat. They would need dental records to make the identification formal, but all Riley needed to do was look at Mrs. Bentley's face to know that it was Cassie.

And stated in clinical terms or otherwise, the Bentleys had seen their daughter, or what was left of her. They knew what Burgos had done to her face. That wasn't what Mr. Bentley was asking about.

"Postmortem," Riley said, "he fired a single .38 caliber bullet through the back of her mouth."

Mr. Bentley held his stare. He knew that, too.

"There was intercourse," Riley conceded. "Postmortem."

Harland Bentley closed his eyes, his jaw clenched. For a long moment, he said nothing. He seemed unsteady on his feet.

"And Ellie, too?" Mrs. Bentley asked.

"Yes, ma'am."

Natalia Bentley placed a hand near her throat, struggling for a moment. There would be time to question her, but Riley wasn't one to wait.

"Mrs. Bentley, I'm sorry to ask—there'd been some talk of Cassie having some trouble? Some disciplinary issues?"

"Disciplinary issues didn't get my daughter murdered," said her husband.

Riley didn't respond. Surely, even in their grief, they could understand the reason for the question.

"I would say *emotional* issues." Mrs. Bentley's eyes grew foggy as she weighed the memory. "She was trying to find her place. She hadn't yet succeeded."

"Like any girl her age," Harland added.

"No, not like *any* girl." Mrs. Bentley looked in his direction but not at him. "Any girl isn't born into such wealth and privilege. It's a burden that is hard to appreciate. It isn't easy forming relationships when everyone is thinking about how much money you have, and what that money could do for them."

It made sense. But Riley wasn't sure if Natalia was talking about her daughter or herself. It was hard not to detect a rift between husband and wife. He made note that Mrs. Bentley had not even looked at her husband.

"I thought of it as testing boundaries," she added. "She could be dramatic. But she never hurt anyone but herself." She looked up at Riley, who clearly wanted something more specific. "She'd become insular. She'd miss class, refuse to eat, refuse to talk to anyone. Things like that. But she never projected anything onto anyone else. And inside, she was as sweet and generous a person as you will ever meet."

"Enough," Mr. Bentley said. He turned to the county attorney. "I want this man dead."

Mullaney nodded. "Of course we'll seek the death penalty, Harland."

Bentley then looked at Riley. "You can prove it was this man?"

"Absolutely, sir."

"No plea bargains. I want this man dead." He looked again at Ed Mullaney, then reached for his wife's arm. She pulled it away. She could not be placated.

After some words of comfort from the county attorney, Harland Bentley shook his and Riley's hands and left with his wife. Mullaney's posture collapsed as soon as they were out of the office. "Christ, you should have seen Nat when she came out of the morgue," he said. "I thought we'd need a body bag for *her*."

Riley nodded. Distraught families had not been his custom as a federal prosecutor. New terrain for him, and he didn't like it.

Mullaney drew close to Riley. The man knew how to put on a face for a press conference after a homicide, the wide Irish brow furrowing in sobriety. Riley had seen him do it several times. But this was a different face. This was no ordinary murder. This was a mass homicide. And his biggest financial supporter's daughter was one of the victims.

"I've been to their home," Mullaney said. "I've met Cassie. She was a beautiful, sweet girl." He squeezed Paul's arm hard. A vein appeared in his forehead.

"Needless to say, Paul," he said, "we can have no mistakes."

6

7:45 P.M.

B Y THE TIME Riley visited Ellie Danzinger's off-campus apartment, the technicians had done their work. He believed in visiting the scenes, regardless, and there was every reason to believe that the first crime Terry Burgos had committed took place in this apartment.

The apartment was well appointed, though Riley understood it had come prefurnished, which made sense for a student on a summer rental. There were four apartments in total, each a duplex, facing a courtyard in the center that made a square.

There was no sign of forced entry. There was a window overlooking the street that was closed. Couldn't rule out the possibility that Burgos had come through the window in the dead of night, but it seemed unlikely. Riley saw it for himself, the dust that had accumulated on the locks on the window. The downstairs contained a living room, bedroom, half bath, and kitchen. All undisturbed. No trail of blood.

"The fun happened upstairs," Lightner said. They took carpeted stairs up to a great room and a master bedroom. The top floor looked more lived in, a stereo and television in the great room, a tiny kitchenette that seemed to serve more as a bar. Lightner gestured toward the dishwasher. "It was full. Everything inside was washed."

So nothing could be taken from any of the glasses. But that seemed like a dead end, anyway. There was no chance Ellie Danzinger had invited Terry Burgos in for a drink.

Riley walked slowly into the bedroom. The bed was unmade. The comforter was bunched at the bottom of the bed. There were spatters of blood on the wall and some on the bed, but not much. To the left of the bed, however, was a sizable bloodstain, encrusted on the carpet fibers.

"The M.E. thinks she died on the bed," Lightner explained. "She was hit over the head, and she bled out right there." He motioned to the bloodstain. "M.E. says she lost over a liter and a half of blood."

Riley didn't know if these details were significant.

Lightner got close to the bed but not too close. "M.E. figures Ellie was lying on the bed, faceup, right? Her head was hanging over the side of the bed. That's the only explanation."

"Why is that the only explanation?"

"The amount of blood," he answered. "Other than ripping her heart out—which we know he did at his house—the only other wound on her body is the blow to the head. A significant blow, but not normally enough for her to bleed that much. Gravity played a part. Her head was lower than the rest of her body."

Okay. That made sense. "This is relevant?"

Lightner shrugged. "To bleed out that much, Ellie must have been lying there for at least an hour. The M.E. says there's no way she would have bled that much any quicker."

Riley thought it over. "So he didn't move her right away. He waited at least an hour. Why?"

"Maybe for nightfall to come," Lightner speculated.

"But she'd been in bed." Riley shook his head. "It would've already been night."

"Yeah. I don't know." Lightner looked tired. It had been quite a day for all of them.

"Maybe that's when he had intercourse with her," Riley suggested. "It is a bed, after all." It was quite the image. The intercourse, according to the M.E., had clearly been postmortem.

It was a possibility. But Lightner didn't know. Nobody knew, yet.

"They find that professor yet?" Riley asked. "The guy who employed Burgos?"

"Albany," Lightner said. "We'll find him." He hit Riley on the arm. It was time to head back to the station. Nobody had any illusions about going home anytime soon.

7

IT WAS NEAR MIDNIGHT. Someone had turned on a television in the
police station. The local channels had been covering this all day, flashing
in and out of soap operas and game shows and, later, prime-time offerings.
The "Mansbury Massacre," they were calling it.

Riley and several others pulled together two detectives' desks to form
something like a conference table. Riley played with a cup of lukewarm coffee and looked around the table at Chief Clark and Detective Lightner. None
of them had eaten all day. Clark had subsisted on coffee and cigarettes;
Lightner, coffee only. Riley's stomach was crying to him but he knew he
couldn't eat. Nothing would go down if he tried. The station, at this point,
smelled like a locker room. They were coming down from the initial high of
the brutal murders and then, in the same day, catching the killer. Everyone
was catching his breath. Virtually everything had been done, and what
hadn't yet been done could wait. But Paul already knew that the physical
evidence would tie up Burgos. He wanted to know more about the hideous
poetry Burgos was reciting when describing the murders. He knew this
wasn't about guilt or innocence anymore.

It had been a song, as they'd suspected. And it hadn't taken them long to
find it. Burgos had been listening to the tape on his headphones before the
questioning. The tape was amateur grade, bearing a makeshift label with the
name of the musical group—"Torcher"—handwritten in bloodred ink in a

thick Gothic font like calligraphy. The title of the tape—"Someone"—was written beneath it in the same manner.

The song with the relevant lyrics bore the same title, "Someone," a song that lasted less than three minutes. It started slowly with an acoustic guitar playing single notes, but then all hell broke loose, violent guitars, thumping bass, incessant drumming, while the vocalist screamed the lyrics like machine-gun fire. If you closed your eyes and listened, you wouldn't comprehend anything. But they had a copy of the lyrics, which they had found handwritten on a piece of paper in Terry Burgos's bedroom.

The lyrics from the first verse of "Someone" described six murders, in more or less the precise manner that Burgos had committed them:

> *A girl who is cool to someone at school until he opens a heart once so cruel*
>
> *Thespian lesbian glamorous actress rejection so reckless Colombian necklace*
>
> *His poetry flattery just didn't matter she told him to scatter assault with a battery*
>
> *A senior so prim her figure now trim since she got rid of him eye for eye limb for limb*
>
> *A neighbor's daughter nobody fought her until someone taught her to sleep underwater*
>
> *Now it's time to say good-bye to someone's family stick it right between those teeth and fire so happily*

The lyrics, however sophomoric, were filled with rage. Riley imagined an outcast, rejected by women, probably by everyone. Terry Burgos likely would fit that bill. But Burgos hadn't written the lyrics. And what was really bothering Riley were the biblical verses that Burgos had cited on the paper found in his basement. Six different passages. He'd read them all, thanks to a cop who had a King James Bible in his locker. All but one of them was from the Old Testament and could be attributed in some way to these acts of violence.

The book of Hosea said that for nonbelievers, God would "rend the caul of their heart"—or "open a heart once so cruel." Romans wrote of lesbians being worthy of death, which corresponded with the "lesbian" in the song. Leviticus talked of burning a promiscuous woman to death, which could be loosely translated to being scalded with battery acid. Exodus referenced the infamous eye-for-an-eye, tooth-for-tooth, limb-for-limb language for those who practice abortion—in the lyrics, a senior "now trim since she got rid of him" probably referred to a senior who'd had an abortion. The book of Kings suggested death to those who mocked a prophet. The biblical verse hadn't mentioned anything about drowning, but presumably the "neighbor's daughter" in the song had mocked the song's author, who evidently considered himself some kind of prophet.

That left the final murder described: *Now it's time, to say good-bye, to someone's family, stick it right between those teeth and fire so happily.* This last murder in the first verse had a different quality in the song; the percussion and bass disappeared, and the singer had sung the lyrics a cappella to the tune of *The Mickey Mouse Club.*

And Burgos had followed these lyrics. He had stuck a gun between Cassie Bentley's teeth and fired a bullet through the back of her mouth. He had done so after beating her severely. The corresponding biblical passage, from Deuteronomy, had described a different act of violence—the stoning of a whore. The lyrics and the biblical passage weren't compatible. Burgos had followed them both; he had stoned Cassie *and* shot her.

But Burgos had originally written down a different verse, not from Deuteronomy but from Leviticus, which had talked about adultery, and which called for death to both the adulterer and the adulteress. Why had Burgos changed biblical passages?

Riley didn't know. It was just the first day of a long investigation. But he could already see his arguments forming. He would need to find discrepancies between the lyrics and Burgos's actions. An insanity defense was inevitable—Burgos had killed at the direction of God—and Riley would need to show that Burgos hadn't followed that direction faithfully.

A cop knocked on the door to the room and told them that Professor Albany was here. Riley had very much wanted to make the professor's acquaintance. Albany owned the printing company where Burgos worked nights. And, more important, they had learned Albany had taught a class that both Cassie Bentley and Ellie Danzinger had attended.

Frankfort Albany walked into the room looking every bit the college professor in an off-white shirt, open at the collar, with a tweed sport coat, and slacks in desperate need of an ironing board. He wore his hair long and off his face. All he was missing was the pipe. His washed-out expression resembled those of many people Riley had seen this long day, people who had gone through a range of emotions.

They sat, Riley, the chief, Joel Lightner, and Professor Albany, around the desks with the tape recorder in the center. The professor looked around the table at each of them, as if he wanted to say something but didn't know where to start. Ordinarily, Paul would break the tension, but he wanted to hear what Albany would say.

"I really—I just can't believe this." He reached into his jacket and removed a small metallic case, opened it up. Cigarettes. "Does anyone mind?"

"Not if you're sharing," the chief said.

The professor's movements were tentative. He was shaken up, and falling back on ritual comforts, tapping the cigarette, flipping open the lighter, squinting into the fire as he lit up. He slid the case over to the chief, his eyes catching on the course materials sitting in front of Paul.

"Tell me about Terry Burgos," Riley asked.

"I—I have to say I like Terry," Albany said with a trace of apology. "He did his work without supervision and got it done. He was good at setting the artwork, careful with detail. He never left a job half finished. He kept a clean work space. He was—well, he was a loner. Even after he lost his day job at Mansbury, he wanted to continue working nights. I think he liked working alone. And since he got the work done, I had no reason to say no."

That was an interesting point. Burgos had requested the night shift even when he had nothing to do during the day. Paul was working on the assumption that the prostitutes, at least, were abducted and murdered during the evening—that was when most streetwalkers plied their trade.

"What hours did he keep?" Lightner asked. "Burgos said he worked 'whenever.'"

"That's more or less correct. His hours were variable." Albany crossed his leg. "We'd have overflow—work that didn't get completed during the day—and we'd leave it for Terry. Sometimes it was two hours' worth of work. Sometimes five."

"Sometimes none?" Lightner asked.

Albany shook his head. "When is there ever *nothing* to do? No, there's always something."

"What kind of a job has variable hours?" Riley asked.

"A job," Albany said testily, "where you're trying to give someone a break. He needed the work, and he did a good job on the overflow. It worked out for both of us. Is that okay with you?"

"You have records of his time entries," Riley said. "We'll need them."

Albany nodded absently.

"And no one else worked with him at the plant?"

"Correct. It was just Terry at night."

"How did you know he entered his time correctly?"

"I—well, I didn't, I guess," Albany conceded. "I trusted him."

Paul noticed that Joel Lightner was watching Albany closely.

"What class did you teach with Ellie and Cassie?" Riley asked.

Albany nodded. Riley figured the professor was aware that Cassie Bentley and Ellie Danzinger were two of the victims. Everyone was, by now.

"It's called 'Violence Against Women in American Culture.' We discuss the glorification of hostility toward women in pop culture. Movies, television, music."

Violence against women in music. How appropriate, under the circumstances. Riley snapped to attention, as Lightner did the same.

"Wait a second." Riley slid the paper with the song lyrics across the table to Albany. "Does *that* music look familiar to you?"

Albany looked at it for only a moment. "Of course. This is Tyler Skye's song. 'Someone.'"

"For God's sake." The chief leaned forward. "You *teach* this?"

Albany looked at the chief like he'd look at a student. "*Study* it, is a better description. Yes, of course. Can you think of a more appropriate song?"

"And who's Tyler Skye?" Riley asked.

"The man—well, really, the boy who wrote these lyrics. He was a high school student. I mean, this is the anthem of the rejected boy, no?" When no one responded, Albany cleared his throat and explained. "Tyler Skye was a student who wrote this diatribe and posted it, one night, all over his school. They discovered he was the author and expelled him. A year later, he's a high school dropout and the lead singer in a garage band called Torcher. And he committed these lyrics to song, obviously. Torcher was very big in the underground music scene on midwestern campuses. The lyrics aren't particularly well written, but they are certainly edgy. That appeals to students, the controversy, the rebellion. That's often more important than the substance."

The professor looked around the decidedly hostile table, smoking his cigarette nervously. "Look, the point of the class was, these lyrics were harmful. Part of a larger problem about society's view of women. I can't imagine how Terry could have come away with anything different from our class."

"*Terry* took the class?" Riley sprang forward.

Albany's eyes cast downward. "I let him sit in, yes. Terry—Terry wasn't educated, but that didn't mean he was dumb. He was—*curious* is a good word. I gave him many things to read and consider. He didn't bother anyone. He sat in the back of the class and didn't say a word. Until, that is—well, you know about Ellie."

"Until he developed a fixation on Ellie Danzinger," Lightner said. "That's where he met Ellie, right? And Cassie Bentley? In this class of yours."

Albany nodded. "Obviously, I didn't have the slightest idea that anything like *this*—"

He didn't finish. He didn't need to.

"Tell me about Cassie Bentley," Riley said.

The professor pinched the bridge of his nose. "A sweet girl. Very sensitive. Moody. Unable to trust people. But very sweet inside." He took a breath. "I know she'd had some attendance problems. She had them in *my* class, too."

"Paint me a picture," Riley requested.

"A picture." Albany looked up. "Quiet. Shy. Very polite and respectful, always. Lost, maybe." He nodded his head. "*Lost* is the word. I know some people thought she was anorexic. She'd go through spells where she didn't go to class, didn't eat—sort of locked everybody out. Even Ellie, her roommate."

"What about recently?"

"Recently?" Albany tapped his fingers on the table. "Recently. Yes, I'd heard that she was doing that kind of thing. I mean, I didn't have her this semester in class, but I did run into Ellie not very long ago—right before finals—and she said Cassie was 'up to her old tricks,' I think she said. Not leaving her room. Not even studying. More of the same, really. It seemed like a roller coaster with Cassie. Up, down, up, down. Recently was down."

Joel Lightner asked, "You keep in touch with Cassie, personally?"

The professor shrugged. "It's a small campus. I'd see her. But she's 'Cassie Bentley,' you understand. Everyone knows about her. I think that explains, more than anything, why she was so private. You won't find five people that knew her well."

"How about one?"

"One? Ellie Danzinger," he said with no trace of irony. "I know Cassie had a cousin who came into town sometimes. She'd fly in and fly out. You know, life of the rich and famous. I can't help you beyond that."

Lightner deflated. But Riley figured this was a dead end, anyway. Harland Bentley had had a point, in the office earlier today—Cassie Bentley's emotional problems hadn't gotten her killed.

He wanted to get back to the real cause of Cassie's death. "We have some reason to believe there's a religious aspect to these murders," he said. "The Bible, in particular. Do you teach anything about that?"

Albany gave a faint nod. "Actually, with regard to this song—Tyler Skye gave an interview where he justified the depictions of violence by what was in the Bible. It was, I think, his way of shooting back at critics."

Riley took the list of biblical verses and slid it across the table. Albany picked it up and read them. "Yes, exactly," he said. "These are the verses. Oh, Jesus." He hooded his eyes with a hand. "Did Terry think—oh, God." He looked up at them. "Look, I don't teach that the Bible tells us to kill women like this. I'm simply showing that the attitudes against women are well rooted in our history. Tyler, himself, made that point. It's just a class, guys. Oh, my God."

He dumped his cigarette into an empty Coke can. "I take it, this is how Terry killed those girls? In accordance with these lyrics?"

The chief nodded at Albany. "You tell us."

"Well, surely you don't—" A look of fear spread across his face. "Listen, it's all over television." He placed a hand on his chest. "You can't think *I'm* responsible for this."

Riley didn't think so, but there'd be time for that.

Riley nodded toward the list of verses he'd put in front of Albany. "The last murder," Riley said. "Burgos wrote down something from Leviticus, then crossed it out and wrote in something from Deuteronomy."

Albany took a moment to recover, then looked over the list and slowly nodded. "Tyler Skye had cited Leviticus as the justification for that murder. Death to those who commit adultery."

"What about Deuteronomy?"

Albany shook his head. "I don't know. Tyler Skye didn't mention Deuteronomy here. What does that passage say?"

Riley told him—it mentioned the stoning of a whore.

But Albany didn't know. "Tyler didn't cite that. Stoning? No, that's not what Tyler meant."

"Right," Riley agreed. "'Stick it right between those teeth and fire so happily.' He's not talking about stoning. He's talking about shooting someone. And he said that came from Leviticus?"

Albany nodded. "Leviticus doesn't mention shooting per se, of course. Just death to those who commit adultery. But Skye definitely meant the use of a gun. We know that because of what Tyler Skye did, ultimately."

Riley stared at him. Albany clearly held the room's attention.

The professor cleared his throat. "About a year ago, Tyler Skye killed himself. He shot himself in the mouth."

Stick it right between those teeth and fire so happily.

"Apparently, his girlfriend left him because of his infidelity."

The others in the room reacted with appropriate disdain. But Riley was focused. Tyler Skye, purportedly justifying his lyrics through the Leviticus passage, had committed suicide, following the lyrics to the letter—putting the gun *between those teeth,* meaning his teeth.

But Burgos hadn't followed that example. He had beaten Cassie with a stone, or some similar object, and introduced a new passage from Deuteronomy to justify it. And *then* he had fired the bullet in *her* mouth—but had not turned the gun on himself.

He hadn't been faithful to the lyrics. It was a positive development, no doubt, for the prosecution. But it also raised a question.

Why? Why had Burgos decided to improvise, to introduce a new biblical passage never cited by Tyler Skye or suggested by his lyrics?

"Can't say I'm sorry to see Mr. Skye go," Chief Clark muttered.

"Well, maybe you should be," Albany replied. "Torcher has sold twice as many records since Skye's death. Now," he added ominously, "he's a legend. He has a cult following."

"How many people we talking about?" Chief Clark asked, his eyes downcast. "How many psychos we got running around here, waiting to act out these lyrics?"

"I would say Torcher has thousands of listeners. Not *tens* of thousands."

Paul frowned, not at Albany's estimation, but at the chief's acknowledgment in his question. He was suggesting what was inescapable now: Terry Burgos had been following the lyrics to a song, or at least pretending to. And he'd matched the lyrics to verses in the Bible.

Terry Burgos killed those girls because God told him to.

He could envision the defense now. Burgos was going to claim that the lyrics were preaching God's word—burning and beating and torturing young women for various sins. He had interpreted these asinine song lyrics as a coded directive from the Almighty Himself. Tyler Skye, in his twisted way, had mimicked biblical passages, and Burgos had taken them as literal direction.

That would be a problem. It made the job more difficult. It would be a nice, simple story for the jury to understand, without fancy terminology like *psychosis* and *sociopathology.* The guy thought the song was a call to him and he acted on it. He must be crazy. Could you imagine anyone doing this who *wasn't* insane?

They worked on Albany for a while longer. But Paul was no longer listening. There was no doubt that Terry Burgos committed the crimes. The evidence, less than a day into it, was overwhelming, and he'd more or less admitted it. This was no longer about guilt. This was about insanity. If the state still used the modified ALI definition of insanity, then Burgos had to prove two things: that he was suffering from a mental defect at the time he committed the killings, and that he didn't understand that he was committing a crime.

But Paul knew, already, that he could find discrepancies between these acts and the lyrics of the songs. That would be key to showing that, if Burgos thought he was following the word of God—or the word of the prophet Tyler Skye—he hadn't done a very good job. He already had more than one discrepancy—Burgos had introduced a new biblical passage and he hadn't killed himself, like he was supposed to. And Burgos had engaged in sexual intercourse with each of the women—the prostitutes before their death, the students postmortem—and there was nothing in the Bible about *that.* He had committed these crimes during summer break, before the start of summer school, understanding that once summer school started the bodies would be found. He knew, in other words, that what he was doing was a crime, so he was doing it quickly before someone would find the bodies. They also knew that the four prostitutes had worked different parts of the city, which suggested that Burgos was smart enough not to return to the same place. Again, this demonstrated his appreciation that he was breaking the law, and not wanting to get caught.

And Paul was just getting started. By the time this went to trial, he'd punch enough holes in Burgos's conformity to the lyrics, and to the Bible, to sink a ship. And he'd have plenty of evidence to show that Burgos knew that what he was doing was illegal.

Professor Albany was in tears a half hour later. Paul didn't blame the guy for what happened, but he didn't have the time or energy to care. There was only one person he cared about now, only one person he would care about for the next nine months.

Terry Burgos, he was sure, didn't stand a chance.

June 5, 1997

Deathwatch

Being parents was everything to us. Everything that was good and true in our life centered around Cassie. This man—this monster—has taken away our life. He has taken our daughter, our dreams, everything that a parent has.

—Harland Bentley, in a statement to the *Daily Watch*, June 29, 1989

This man deserves what his victims received. This man deserves death.

—First Assistant County Attorney Paul Riley, in closing arguments during the sentencing phase of the trial of *People v. Terrance Demetrius Burgos*, May 31, 1990

With the abandonment of his habeus petition before the circuit court of appeals today, Terry Burgos is poised to become the twelfth person to be executed in this state since the reinstatement of capital punishment.

—*Daily Watch*, October 19, 1996

8

MARYMOUNT PENITENTIARY, half an hour to midnight. The prison stands isolated in the countryside, ten acres of land bordered by cast-iron gates twenty feet high, topped with several coils of razor wire. The prison is monitored twenty-four hours a day by correctional officers from an access road that surrounds the facility. The manicured lawns, filled with weight-sensitive motion sensors, are swept with spotlights from watchtowers on each flank of the octagonal building in the center that houses the inmates. Someone tried to escape last year but didn't even make it to the gate. A sharpshooter blew his knee off from two hundred yards.

A mile out, I pull up to the gate, which looks like something medieval, a thick door with the name of the prison etched in a Gothic font. I lower the car window and feel the thick, steamy air outside, filled with the faint shouts of protesters nearby.

"Okay, Mr. Riley." The guard hands me two passes for Building J, one to hang from my rearview mirror and one for my shirt. "Drive slow," he adds, motioning to the long paved road ahead. "One of 'em threw himself in front of a car."

I drive slowly, as advised, on a narrow road made narrower by media trucks lined along one side. Up ahead, near the mammoth front gate of the facility, I see the two camps, neatly divided by the road and by two dozen county sheriff's officers in full riot gear. The east side of the divide is for the abolitionists, about a hundred strong, people gathered in circles in candle-light vigil, ministers and priests praying, others marching in a large square carrying signs, like picketers at a labor rally. A young man with a ponytail stands on a makeshift platform of wooden crates, shouting through a bull-horn. "Why do we kill people to show that killing people is wrong?" he cries, to the excitement of his supporters.

The other side is a much smaller group, people who support capital pun-ishment—especially for Terry Burgos. A banner, set up on poles, bears the names of all six victims of Burgos's murder spree. The reason this group is smaller is that they're winning the debate, nationwide, and especially here. We like to execute people in this state.

An officer checks my windshield for authorization, then makes me roll down the window and show him my credentials again. The noise from the protesters is almost deafening through the open window, dueling bullhorns and chants. The guard checks my name against his list on a clipboard. "Okay, Mr. Riley," he says. "Get through this gate and they'll direct you in." The guard signals to someone and the gates slowly part.

A hand slaps against my car door. A couple of reporters try to see into my car, get a look at one of the official witnesses. I move the Cadillac forward slowly as the reporters jog alongside, shouting questions at me. I hear bits and pieces of what they're saying. One of them asks me what I'm doing here, which seems silly, because I was the prosecutor, the one who asked the jury to impose death. But then I reconsider the question and don't have an answer.

I drive through the entrance, leaving the reporters at the gate. Several buildings down, I'm directed to one of the visitors' spaces. I move from the stifling heat to a guard-attended door, which a stocky correctional officer opens to a frigid reception area. A group of uniforms loiter, smoking ciga-rettes and chatting. One of them recognizes me and says hello. I do the *Good to see you* reserved for those whose names I can't recall. I always hate doing that because they know, every one of them. And I know that because people used to do that to me.

I make it down to the basement, the last to arrive, as usual. All the other invited witnesses are there, all wearing name tags. Three or four parents of the runaways and prostitutes, dressed in formal, if ill-fitting, attire. I always treated them with courtesy because they had lost their daughters, but, the truth is, most of them had long before said good-bye to their kids. I stifle the urge to say to them now what I stifled the urge to say to them then: Maybe if they had spent a little more time with their girls when they were teenagers, their daughters wouldn't have ended up walking the streets of this city for a living, ready-made prey for a mass murderer. There is a sense of gravity to their expressions but importance, too, a temporary respect bestowed upon them. They are official witnesses to the execution of the most notorious criminal in recent memory in this state. How exciting for them.

I see David and Maureen Danzinger and feel something float through my stomach. I'll never forget the looks on their faces after they identified their daughter, Ellie, who had been a sophomore at Mansbury. They had flown back from South Africa immediately upon hearing the news but seemed unable to comprehend the fact until they saw it firsthand, saw their daughter lying dead on a slab with a tremendous gash in her body where her heart used to be. They spent the entire year in town, waiting for the trial, which they attended every day.

Maureen Danzinger approaches and takes my arm. It's been over seven years now. Seven years, waiting for this day, probably hoping that it would bring some semblance of closure, knowing in her heart that it would not. Her hair has grayed, her eyes sunk, her midsection widened, and she's probably reconciled herself to the fact that her daughter's killer was caught and convicted, would be dead in half an hour, and justice would be done. That will have to be enough. People are like that when dealing with such staggering pain. They need hope. They can't bring their daughter back, so they focus on something that is attainable—justice for the murderer. It won't untie the knot but hopefully loosens it.

I say hello to her husband, David, as well. He is dressed in a dark suit. That seems to be the attire of choice, funeral chic, which I find interesting, because when you get down to it, no one's really mourning the loss of this guy, at least no one in this room.

Joel Lightner walks up to me and smirks. Retired police detective, the one who broke the case. Or *caught* the case that practically fell into his lap, he'd admit after one too many bourbons.

"Bentley's not coming?" he asks me, a trace of disappointment in his tone.

He's referring to one of the other victims' families, the other student besides Ellie, who was murdered. Cassandra Bentley, daughter of Harland and Natalia Lake Bentley. I shake my head no. Harland's my client now in private practice, we talk on a weekly basis, and we never so much as broached the subject of Terry Burgos's execution.

"Jackals are in the next room." Joel says it with disdain out of the corner of his mouth, his reference to the reporters who won the lottery and are inside the compound, but this is a marketing opportunity for his new business as a high-priced private eye. He'll be sure to throw out some quotes to the media.

I look to my right through the Plexiglas window, where the reporters are sipping drinks or munching on cookies. The warden's rule—reporters can come but can talk to the official witnesses only if the witnesses are willing. He even designated a separate room for the media until showtime. At the moment, no official witnesses are in there, but that's probably because I'm late. They've probably gotten everything they wanted by now.

Joel nudges me. "Know what he had for his final meal?"

I shake my head, even though I know.

"Tacos," he says, beaming.

We are led into the official witness room at 11:45. It's a room no larger than a living room, entirely lacking décor, gray walls and two rows of seats, the second row raised a single step up. No one really knows where to sit, but people seem to be in a hurry to take the back row, as if that provides them with distance from the spectacle. I figure I'll let the victims' families make the decision, so I end up sitting front and center, next to Joel on one side and Carolyn Pendry, a television reporter from Newscenter 4, on the other. Looking forward from my seat, there is a floor-to-ceiling window into the neighboring room, currently covered by a pale green curtain.

I can't shake the analogy, it's like going to the movies, settling in and waiting for the curtain to part. There is a table with pitchers of water and coffee—as if anyone needs caffeine right now—but otherwise no refreshments. Joel Lightner asked me yesterday if he should bring popcorn.

"What're you doing after?" Carolyn Pendry, the reporter, whispers, with a tremble in her voice. She's one of the city's many reporter babes, tall and blond, high cheekbones. She's completely made up, like the other reporters who will be going on camera later. She's making a joke, an attempt to seem cool. Joel and I are going to get a steak afterward, actually, but I'm not going to share that with her.

Carolyn leans into me. "What did he say to you yesterday?"

"No comment." The fine reporter she is, Carolyn learned that Terry Burgos requested that I visit him yesterday. In the last three days before an execution in this state, an inmate is placed in an area known as "Deathwatch," a group of four cells in the building adjacent to the execution chamber, where he is under twenty-four-hour observation by a team of correctional officers who work twelve-hour shifts. Condemned inmates are allowed two visitors a day over each of the three days. I was the only person to visit. It lasted all of five minutes.

The next several minutes are weird. The Department of Corrections sets a rigorous protocol for executions—from the timing of the final consultations with clergy to the last meal to the "death march" from Deathwatch to Building J to the official phone call to the commissioner, seeing if there are any last-minute stays—but there are no regulations that explain how to watch a man die. People are antsy in their seats. The reporters especially— the ones who are here for their job—are not enjoying themselves. It's guaranteed airtime for them, maybe a special afterward about the crimes or the death penalty, but that doesn't mean they're going to enjoy this.

At about ten to twelve, the curtain on the window parts, pulled manually by prison guards. Carolyn, next to me, jerks. Various noises from the witnesses, gasps and moans and even a sob. The people in the back row are looking at the man who killed their daughters.

It's a large space, with a small circular room within a room, a pale green–painted octagonal metal box, about six feet wide and eight feet high. The entrance is through a rubber-sealed steel door that has been closed by a large locking wheel. There are windows on all seven other sides, so that each of us in the viewing room can see the condemned prisoner.

Terry Burgos is in white boxers only, sitting in a metal chair, with leather straps across his upper and lower legs, arms, thighs, chest, and forehead. A long Bowles stethoscope is affixed to his hairy chest and leads outside the gas chamber, where a doctor will be able to pronounce Burgos dead without having to enter the chamber.

The forehead restraint is a new thing, after a guy down south split his head open banging it against the steel pole behind the chair while he fought the air hunger. Leave it to our state to want to stop a man from knocking himself unconscious so we can execute him.

If Terry Burgos looks pathetic, a hairy, pudgy man sitting in his underwear, strapped into a chair, with an audience watching the spectacle, he doesn't reveal any awareness of it whatsoever. He doesn't show much of anything, moving his eyes from person to person with the wonderment of a child. He has lived almost entirely in isolation for the last seven years, and maybe there is something stimulating about this.

Beneath Burgos's chair is a bowl filled with sulfuric acid mixed with distilled water. Suspended above the bowl, in a gauze bag, is a pound of sodium cyanide pellets. When the warden gives the signal, the guard outside the gas chamber will pull a lever that will release the cyanide into the liquid, causing a chemical reaction that releases hydrogen cyanide.

Actually, there are three levers that will be pulled simultaneously by three different guards. Two of the levers will not do a damn thing, while the third will lower the pellets into the acidic water. None of the three guards will go to bed tonight knowing that he was the one who killed a man. The state may lack compassion for its killers but not for the executioners.

"I hope to God he doesn't hold his breath," Carolyn says to me. She's done her homework. If Burgos takes a deep breath of the gas, he'll be unconscious in seconds and will die peacefully. If he holds his breath and fights it, he'll likely go into convulsions, and this could last up to twenty minutes.

"Terrance Demetrius Burgos," the prison guard begins, holding the clipboard away from his face. "You have been convicted by a court of law in this state of five separate violations of Article 4, Section 6-10(a), of the Criminal Code, to wit: the homicides of Elisha Danzinger, Angela Mornakowski, Jacqueline Davis . . ."

Carolyn Pendry makes a noise, leans forward, and, with a guttural groan, vomits on my shoe. I ignore the bile at my feet, offer her a handkerchief, and take her hand, lacing my fingers with hers. She attempts an apology, but there's no need. She will not be the last one to react in such a way. There's a doctor on call, in fact, for the witnesses.

". . . Sarah Romanski, and Maureen Hollis."

Terry Burgos has gained a good twenty pounds since his arrest, adding a second chin that covers his neck, his eyes reduced to tiny beads now. He has almost no hair on top; a few strands stick up over the leather restraint that covers his forehead. I look for it in those eyes, any sense of remorse or compassion. Or fear. I admit it, I want this to hurt.

". . . jury has determined that these homicides were committed with pre-meditation and under special circumstances warranting the imposition of capital punishment . . ."

I feel the collective tension behind me, the mixed emotions of the people so angry and hurt, reliving the tragedy all over again over these last few weeks, now getting the justice that they clamored for, begged the jury to impose.

"You have signed a written statement, notarized and validated by a court of law, indicating your choice of lethal gas."

That, or electrocution. I'd have gone the other way. I can't imagine anything worse than fighting for air.

I look at the two telephones on the wall, one black, one red, the latter connected directly to the governor's mansion. Then I peek at the clock. Twelve on the dot.

When I look back at Burgos, he has settled his gaze on me. Now we have made eye contact, and I know he's going to watch me as long as he can. I consider looking away, showing him the lack of respect he probably deserves, but I lock my stare on him. Maybe I owe him that much. Maybe every prosecutor should have to look in the eyes of the person he has condemned. Maybe that's why I'm here, and why I agreed to visit him yesterday.

His tongue peeks out from between his thin lips. His eye winks but it seems involuntary. No human being, no matter how psychotic, could approach this punishment without some reaction. His fingers drum along the arm pads. His toes dance. His chest heaves. He is perspiring heavily, which is not an appealing sight on a man almost entirely naked.

". . . are entitled to make any final statement at this time."

Absolute silence. Terry Burgos has never apologized, never offered a single word of contrition. This is what the families are waiting for, I suspect—something, anything, to make this better.

His lips part but he says nothing. We are still staring at each other, so it seems that the families will not get what they wanted. Whatever he has to say, he will say to me.

The prison guard is unsure of his next move. Surely, he wants to give Burgos at least this much, the chance to make it right or find some peace. Maybe he likes the guy, in a weird way, having spent the last seven years with him on death row. Most of these guys, sitting in solitary confinement, turn to God or simply lose the will to fight, end up being pretty good inmates.

The guard finally looks at the warden, who holds up a finger, and we all wait.

Terry Burgos clears his throat with a struggle. One guy, out west somewhere, rambled on for almost twenty minutes when given the chance to have his last words.

Another agonizing minute passes, as the prisoner and I stare at each other. I look for a smirk, for an indignant scowl, for fear in his eyes. What I receive, instead, is nothing but childlike wonderment, a hypnotic gaze.

The warden moves closer to the glass cell. "Terry, do you have anything to say?"

Burgos shakes his head slowly, as much as he can with his restraints. His eyes still on me, his mouth parts again. He speaks to me silently, his lips moving in coordination with his tongue and teeth. I'm not much for lipreading but I know what he's saying.

The warden, who is not facing Burgos, takes the silence as a negative answer and motions to the prison guard, who will now order the officials to begin the process.

"The prisoner has declined any final statement," says the prison guard.

Sobbing, behind me. Some of the family members wanted to hear contrition. Others probably expected something self-serving and are relieved at the lack of a statement. But the guard is wrong. Terry Burgos didn't decline a final statement. He mouthed it to me, the man who put him in that chair.

The same thing he said to me yesterday, in his cell.

I'm not the only one.

June 2005

The Second
Verse

Sunday
June 5, 2005

9

THE CHANGE in the picture quality on the television is notable, going
back, as it does, eight years. In the top right of the screen is the date:
JUNE 1, 1997.

Carolyn Pendry, in a blue suit and cream silk shirt, sits professionally, her
legs crossed, a notepad in her lap. "Thank you for agreeing to speak with me,
Mr. Burgos," she says.

The screen cuts to him. Convicted murderer Terry Burgos is seated, his
posture poor, shoulders slumped forward, in his orange jumpsuit. His thin-
ning hair is in place. His face is rounded from the added weight, damaged
from poor nutrition. His eyes are deep-set, a penetrating black; otherwise,
his expression is utterly noncommittal.

"Mr. Burgos, you are scheduled to be executed in four days. The appellate defender's office is attempting to reinstate your appeal in the federal
courts over your objection. What do you say to that?"

Burgos blinks, his eyes moving away from the reporter. His tongue peeks
out, wetting his lips.

"Are you ready to die, Mr. Burgos?"

His body reacts slightly, jerking, a semblance of a smile playing on his
face. Like he's amused by a long-forgotten memory. His eyes still far away.
"How do you know I'm gonna die?"

"Are you saying you can't die?"

His face goes serious, his eyes opening wider. Like he's daydreaming.

"Mr. Burgos?"

"You can kill a body. You can't kill the truth."

A pause. A change of topics, perhaps. The subject is not making this easy. Like talking to an infant.

"Did those women deserve to die?"

Burgos leans back in his chair. He's enjoying a thought. Like the reporter isn't even there. "It's not for me to decide."

"Who decides, then?"

"You know." Burgos rocks in a chair that doesn't assist him. Back and forth, the first sign of animation.

"God decides," says Carolyn Pendry. "Did God tell you to kill those women?"

"'Course He did." Burgos punctuates it with a jerk of his head.

"You said Ellie Danzinger was a 'gift from God,' Mr. Burgos. What—"

"God gave her to me." The gentle rocking of his body accelerates.

"How did God do that?"

Burgos raises his hands for emphasis, two hands slicing the air, the shackle connecting his wrist dancing in the air. "You all think I'm crazy because I see things you don't. But that don't make me crazy. You all believe in the Creator and in the Second Coming, but if Jesus came down you wouldn't believe Him."

Camera cuts to the reporter, Pendry. A thoughtful expression on her face.

"You'd say He's crazy." Burgos keeps rocking.

"Did Tyler Skye tell you to kill those women?"

Burgos brings up his knees, puts his feet up on the chair. Arms around his knees, a round ball, rocking back and forth.

"Did—"

"God did." He nods his head emphatically.

"Tyler Skye's song didn't tell you to kill those women?"

"Tyler was a messenger. So am I."

"Mr. Burgos, according to that song, weren't you supposed to kill *yourself* last? Wasn't that what Tyler Skye had meant with the last line?"

Burgos takes a breath. Blinks his eyes slowly. Keeps rocking back and forth.

"Why didn't you kill yourself, Mr. Burgos? Why did you kill Cassie Bentley instead?"

Like he's in a fog. He doesn't respond.

"You said Cassie 'saved' you, Mr. Burgos. What did—"

"Cassie saved me. God told me I wasn't done. He gave me Cassie instead."

He begins to hum to himself. Looks up at the ceiling.

"Mr. Burgos, did you think your attorney was wrong to call you insane?"

"Insane. Insane, insane." Burgos begins to laugh, a giggle.

"Mister—"

"What's that? Insane." He frowns suddenly, staring off, concentrating. "What's that?"

"Insane," the reporter says calmly, "means you can't control what's inside your brain."

"That's everybody."

"It means you can't tell right from wrong."

"That's everybody."

"Mr. Burgos, would you kill those girls again if you had the chance?"

"Kill those girls again." He stops moving. His eyes are open in slants, staring into space, his shoulders gathered about him. The camera zooms in on his expression.

"I'm gonna sleep now."

"You don't want to answer my questions?"

Burgos doesn't answer, his foggy stare frozen on the screen.

The screen shrinks and moves to the corner of the television picture. Anchorwoman Carolyn Pendry, today, looks into the camera with a crisp, professional manner.

"Fifteen years ago today, Terrance Demetrius Burgos was sentenced to death. The jury rejected his lawyer's claim of insanity and imposed five counts of capital punishment. My brief interview with Mr. Burgos, eight years ago, was the last, and only, time he granted an interview."

The camera angle adjusts. Carolyn Pendry turns. "Did Terry Burgos really view the violent lyrics of Tyler Skye's music as a call from God? Did he deserve death for his actions? The debate rages on even today.

"But in this reporter's opinion, the verdict is in. Anyone who would take sophomoric, abusive lyrics and read them as signs from an almighty being is not someone who lives in our world. Terry Burgos wanted to kill, to lash out at an indifferent society, and his brain was searching for an excuse."

A dramatic pause. Camera angle adjusts again. "Terry Burgos did not fit the legal definition of insanity because he knew that what he was doing was against the law. But that doesn't mean he was sane. Terry Burgos suffered from severe paranoid schizophrenia and killed because of it. The fact that he may have been aware that a criminal law existed, that forbade him from doing what he did, does not change that fact.

"Terry Burgos deserved to be locked up and treated. He did not deserve death." She nods her head. "For *Sunday Night Spotlight*, I'm Carolyn—"

In the dark room, nestled in the corner, beyond the view of the sole window, Leo puts down the remote control, stares at the television screen, dissolving to a dot and flickering with static. Dissolve and flicker, flicker and dissolve. He brings his knees to his chest and holds his breath, squeezes his eyes shut, listening for the faintest sound, listen, listen.

The house buzzes from the utter silence.

I'm not like him.

He jumps at the ring of the phone. His eyes cast about the room as the rings echo. The answering machine kicks on. Leo hears his own monotone request that the caller leave a message, followed by a long, tortured beep.

"Leo, this is Dr. Pollard. You've missed two sessions, Leo, and you've not returned our calls. Are you taking your meds? We've talked about the importance of doing that."

I don't believe you. I don't believe you anymore.

"I'm going to give you my home phone number, Leo. It's important you call me."

Leo buries his head in his lap. He waits for the doctor to complete his message, the machine to click off. With the room once more silent, he raises his head again.

I'm not like him.

He takes a breath. Thinks about it.

I'm better.

Sunday
June 19, 2005

10

———

LEO CRAWLS up the dark staircase, his body spread over four carpeted stairs, his limbs splayed about like a spider. The body weight is transferred evenly. Stairs don't groan from the burden. No chance of slipping or stumbling. No groan, no slip, no stumble.

You can't hear me coming.

At the top of the staircase, he can see into the bedroom. The darkness is thinned by the light through the window, from a streetlamp below. The room is quiet save for the contorted snores of Fred Ciancio, like his nose is battling his throat.

Leo rises slowly. One of his knees cracks and he holds absolutely still. Fred Ciancio doesn't move. Loud, uneven, wet snores, his head cocked to the right on the pillow.

Weapons. Look for weapons. Eyes adjusting now.

No weapons. Nothing.

He wasn't expecting Leo.

He slips it out of the back of his pants. Holds it in his right hand.

Ciancio stirs. Unconscious response to Leo's body heat, to the adjustment in the room temperature.

But Leo is not hot.

"What—?" Ciancio's head pops up.

Two long strides and he's at the bed. He lands on his chest, presses Ciancio's head down to the pillow with his left hand, his palm over Ciancio's mouth.

He shows it to him, the tip of the weapon between Ciancio's eyes. His face moves in toward Ciancio's, so the old guy can make him out. The sharp weapon moves from the bridge of Ciancio's nose. He runs it along Fred's pajama top, down his chest, feeling for the rib cage. He finds a seam between the ribs.

You shouldn't have called, Fred.

He doesn't die quickly.

Monday
June 20, 2005

11

"CHIN UP, HECTOR," I remind him, as the elevator door opens. The reporters are waiting in the lobby of the federal building, perking up as I emerge from the elevator bank with State Senator Hector Almundo, who has just pleaded not guilty to eleven counts of fraud, extortion, bribery, and theft. The senator, smartly dressed in a gray suit and black tie, heeds my advice, moving stoically past the reporters as they shout questions at him. It's like taking a punch to the groin. There's no easy way to do it.

We stop short of the revolving doors. The reporters close in and push their microphones in front of the senator's face, until they realize that it will be me doing the talking. I say the usual, about the charges being false and how much we look forward to the opportunity to vindicate ourselves at trial. I leave out the part about Senator Almundo sobbing in my office an hour earlier, asking me how many people he'd have to flip on to avoid jail time.

After this needless exercise, we head outside, where I put Hector in a waiting car. As he drives off with his wife and brother, I wave off a handful of reporters. Dutch Reynolds and Andy Karras want to talk on background, but I'm not in the mood. "Thanks, everyone, that's all," I say with finality.

One reporter catches my attention because I don't recognize her, and because she's a damn sight easier on the eyes than most of the print media. She looks like someone who belongs in front of a camera, tall and fair complected, television skinny, with an oval, pink face, a perfect nose, and expressive blue eyes. And a damn nice sky blue suit, too. I take her hand graciously, but my tongue instantly swells, that problem I have with the cute ones. If there is such a thing as the battle of the sexes, it's the most lopsided battle I've ever fought.

"Paul Riley? Evelyn Pendry from the *Watch*."

That's what I thought, print media. The newspaper. The name rings a bell.

"No comment, Evelyn."

"I wanted to wish you a happy anniversary," she says, waiting for a reaction. "Sixteen years."

"Sixteen—oh, is it? Right." I'd forgotten. This is the week, sixteen years ago, when we found the bodies. I'm still shaking her hand and I have to remind myself to let go. I cast aside my carnal instincts for the moment—a few seconds, at least—because she's a reporter, and you're always careful with them. "I'm running late for something," I say.

"Getting Hector's defense ready?" she asks, playing with me. "He'll be singing within three months."

If she were less attractive, or wrong, I might be more annoyed. I point to my watch.

"I was wondering if you might have some time for me," she says.

I like that, the suggestive wording of the question. Or maybe it's just my hormones. I would probably find something provocative in the way she asked for hemorrhoid medicine.

"On or off the record?" I ask.

A quaint smile appears on her face. She keeps her eye contact. "That would be up to you."

Oh, I do believe this breathtaking woman is flirting with me. A cynic might substitute the word *manipulating*, but why go through life cynical?

"Do you mind?" She holds a small tape recorder near my chest. Without waiting for an answer—they never do—she flips it on and starts with the basics, names and dates.

"You've been in private practice for fifteen years," she says to me. "Shortly after convicting Terry Burgos, you opened your own law firm?"

I say nothing, though I flash that Riley smile that has won women over across the globe.

"And when did Harland Bentley hire you as the lawyer for all of his holdings?" She cocks her head, still holding the recorder near my chin. When I don't answer, she says, "I just want some basic background here, Paul. We're running a story on the Almundo indictment. This is free publicity."

I nod my head politely and stare at the recorder. "You're Carolyn Pendry's daughter, aren't you?" I ask, making the connection.

She frowns at the non sequitur, especially that one. Apparently, this woman wants to make it on her own, without her anchorwoman mother's bootstraps. Seems that transcendent beauty runs in the family, but the last time I was within breathing distance of a Pendry I was wiping her dinner off my shoe.

"Running late," I say. I hand her my card.

Preemptively, she moves to block my path. "Just a few questions, Paul. Background is fine with me. I'll buy you a drink. C'mon, one harmless drink after work?"

She's trying to recover now, back to the flirtation. It probably works for her most of the time, her looks alone. Why not? If I looked like that, I'd use it, too. A fellow like me has to rely on his winning personality.

"I could mention Burgos," she says, walking alongside me. Unless I throw her an elbow, or jump in a cab and close the door quickly, it looks like she's not taking no for an answer. "Never hurts to remind everyone that you convicted the most famous serial killer our city has ever seen."

That much is true. Almost every potential client I meet gets around to asking about it. Inevitably, I find myself recounting the details, the grizzly murder scene, the flamboyant defense team, the rush of hearing the jury announce that the aggravating factors outweigh the mitigating factors. I leave out the part that, however time-consuming and publicized the case may have been, the prosecution of Terry Burgos was one of the easier cases I handled.

"Speaking of—are you close to the Bentley family?" she asks me. "Ever talk to Natalia? Or Gwendolyn Lake?"

She needs to work on her segues. Why even pretend she's running a piece on Hector Almundo, when she obviously wants to talk about Burgos and the Bentley family?

"Would you describe Cassie Bentley as a troubled girl? Emotional problems?"

I stop, having reached the end of the courthouse plaza, and face Evelyn. Her hope springs eternal, the recorder poised before my face, as she chews on her lip. She seems to be formulating yet another question, but I'm more interested in the movement of her mouth. Dr. Freud had a point.

Harland Bentley had married Natalia Lake, heiress to the Lake mining fortune. Natalia's sister, Mia Lake, had lived with her daughter Gwendolyn on the other side of Highland Woods from Natalia and Harland—two enormous mansions, one for each Lake sister, essentially framing the wealthy suburb. Mia Lake died long ago, early eighties or something, leaving Natalia to serve basically as the mother to her niece, Gwendolyn Lake. But these people had something like a billion dollars, all told, so nobody went hungry.

Natalia and Harland divorced shortly after their daughter, Cassie, was murdered by Terry Burgos. Natalia moved over to the other mansion, where her dead sister once lived, and where Gwendolyn Lake, her niece, might still live, for all I know. I never had the pleasure of meeting Gwendolyn, though from what I heard, it wouldn't have been a pleasure.

I don't know why Evelyn's asking about this. But I don't enjoy cat and mouse, unless I get to be the cat. Or is it the mouse? "Cassie Bentley was a promising young woman whose murder was a tragedy," I say. "Natalia Lake handled herself with incredible grace and dignity. I wish her, and her niece Gwendolyn, the very best."

Evelyn is quiet. Didn't get what she wanted there. What did she expect? I'm a lawyer. I play with words all day.

I give Evelyn a wide smile. "And Senator Almundo is innocent," I add.

She deflates. I gently take her recorder and slide the cue to the off position. "Evelyn," I say, "when I cross-examine someone, I like to ask questions in the abstract, out of order, so the witness doesn't see where I'm going. Then I tie it all together, in my favor, before they have a chance to fix the damage. But we're not in court, I'm not under oath, and I don't have to play your game. So do me a favor—say hi to your mother and have a nice day. If you want to play straight with me, you've got my number."

I bid her adieu and leave her at the corner of the plaza. She calls out to me, "I'll play straight, then," but now she's incurred penalties for lack of courtesy. I'll return her phone call one of these days, but not this week.

I GET BACK TO my office just before three. I take a moment to savor the stenciled name SHAKER, RILEY & FLEMMING at the elevator bank of the building, or the same name in extruded gold lettering, set off against a marbled wall, over the receptionist's head when I step off the elevator into our suite. The reception area is finely manicured, complete with cushy sofas and a mock courtroom to the side that reminds clients that we are preeminent trial lawyers. Best decision we made, that courtroom, when we moved into this space. Clients eat it up. Almost every case ends in settlement these days, but every client wants a warrior just in case.

I say hello to the receptionist but I've forgotten her name. That's the downside. Time was, we were a handful of lawyers, Judge Shaker and I getting the firm started, with one prized client—Harland Bentley—and six hungry lawyers, chasing after business and trying as many cases as we could. We ate pizza every Wednesday night, while we looked anxiously over revenue projections and talked eagerly about new clients and upcoming trials, and which weekend we were all going to come in to put a new coat of paint on the walls. We drank scotch every Friday night before heading home. We even had a hoops team in the bar association league.

Now we're over a hundred attorneys in these beautiful surroundings, paying princely sums to associates out of the finest law schools, churning cases with the best of them. I passed a conference room the other day and realized that I didn't know the name of a single one of the young lawyers in there.

I say hello to a couple of young associates, each of them female, young, and attractive. Both of them ask me how I'm doing, and I answer, innocuously enough, "Fighting the good fight." They both laugh, and I'm on my way. Pop quiz: Attractive young female associates laugh at your jokes because (a) they find you attractive, too, (b) they find you incisive and brilliant, or (c) you sign their paychecks?

"You missed the personnel meeting. Again."

That's why I like my assistant, Betty, who gives me no quarter, and who doesn't even look up as I pass her cubicle. She's learned the sound of my gait, or she has a hidden camera or something; she always knows when I'm approaching.

"I had an arraignment," I explain.

"You have the four o'clock with Mr. Otis."

Right. He's the chief financial officer of a Fortune 500 company who's now under investigation by both the SEC and the U.S. attorney for fudging books after the company restated its earnings for the third quarter of 2003. It will be a delicate dance, this meeting, thanks to Sarbanes-Oxley, a federal law that more or less eviscerates the attorney-client privilege for corporate officers. Basically, if a CFO, CEO, or anyone else with an important title with multiple letters, talks to an attorney about funky recordkeeping, that attorney might have to turn him into the feds or risk criminal liability himself. And the Communists—I mean, the American Bar Association—actually endorsed this idea, which is when I canceled my membership.

I need to look over some information before the meeting. Other work, including a brief that has to be filed tomorrow for one of Harland Bentley's companies, is piled high on my desk. The message light is blinking on the elaborate contraption known as my phone. But I've been meaning to procrastinate for a while now; it's time I got around to it. So I go to the mail. Most of it is bills or requests for money from one source or another. This one, in a plain white envelope and handwritten, looks like something personal. When I shake it, a single piece of paper, folded twice, falls out, containing these words in printed handwriting:

> *If new evil emerges, do heathens ever link past actions?*
> *God's answer is near.*

"Another satisfied customer," I say to the empty room. I fold the paper back up and slide it into a desk drawer. I was once a former prosecutor, both federal and then local, so it's not unheard of for me to get some fan mail from inmates who have me to thank for their surroundings. Usually, they threaten to liberate some part of my anatomy. Occasionally—this usually happens with some of the gangbangers I took down as a fed—they have found God and want to know if I have, too. Once I even wrote back, saying I never lost Him to begin with.

I pull the envelope out of the wastebasket. Local postmark. Mailed from here in the city. Reminds me of some of the mail we used to get when we prosecuted Burgos—freakish, fire-and-brimstone stuff that usually made us laugh but occasionally creeped us out.

My secretary Betty walks into my office. "Are you talking to yourself in here?"

"Are you the new evil emerging?" I respond.

She gives me a look, closer to disapproving than curious.

"God's answer is near," I tell her. She picks up my coffee, sniffs it, then rolls her eyes and leaves the office.

LEO STANDS OUTSIDE the building that houses Paul Riley's law firm. He uses a moist towelette he got at a fried chicken joint to wipe down the envelope one last time. Then he drops it in the mailbox and walks away.

12

"PAUL RILEY," I say to the man at the long table in front of the Canary Room. He looks up my name on a list, checks it, then finds my name tag and hands it to me. The premade tags are done well, even if they're annoying stickers, with my name on top in a fancy font and my law firm's name beneath. When you're toasting the governor at no less than five grand a pop, you get fancy name tags. Score one for the little guys.

Joel Lightner, next to me, gives his name and spells it, because he's an unannounced guest. He's my date for the night, before we go grab a steak and a martini or five. Joel is a former cop, the one who worked the Burgos case with me, and who used that case as a launching pad to a very successful private investigation business, of which I am his best customer. Joel didn't want to come at all, not being dressed in a tuxedo like me and most of the attendees, but I wrangled a little bit of time out of him.

"Twenty minutes," he says, holding me to my promise as we walk into the ballroom on the mezzanine level of the Maritime Club. The place is white walls and dark oak, with a thirty-foot ceiling that is slowly accumulating cigar smoke. I wave to someone I know and Joel points to the long bar along the side wall. "Twenty minutes," he reminds me. "And she isn't gonna be here."

"I'm not looking for her," I argue, but already he's mocking me with a wave of the hand. Dare I protest too much, I plow into the herd of penguin suits, the insincere, hearty banter, the mingling of the powerful and hungry. I join some people I know, a couple of the power corporate lawyers in the city and some

CEOs. It's a fine way to press the flesh, get your faces in front of people again, and let them know to call you if they need anything. What I really want to say is *Call me if you get indicted,* because it's still the work I prefer—the criminal stuff—but, more and more, my practice is devolving into civil litigation, with loads of paper exchanges and written motions and pretrial depositions that run up the bill very nicely, thank you very little, but are boring as hell.

I'm just into my first martini, courtesy of a traveling waitress, when I see Harland Bentley in a small circle of people and shaking hands with Governor Langdon Trotter.

Now, there's a power couple. A second-term governor being groomed for national office and the richest man in the city, one of the wealthiest in the nation. Harland Bentley's personal worth is estimated at something just shy of one and a half billion dollars, with holdings in hotels and real estate and industrial equipment and financial services corporations—all of them bearing his name. A client that any lawyer would kill to service.

On Harland's arm is his latest piece of eye candy, tall and leggy in an evening gown, with a sculpted face and a mane of blond hair that cascades down her back. I would call her the "flavor of the month," but that would be giving Harland too much credit for longevity. I think he has a turnstile in his bedroom at this point.

As I walk up, Harland Bentley puts his hand on the governor's back and subtly positions him so that he's facing me. "Governor," he says, "you know that I have the best lawyer in the country, don't you?"

I shake the governor's hand with a smile. Governor Trotter is a big, strong guy, the photogenic hunter type, with an ever-present tan that offsets silver hair and blue eyes. And a grip that would make a bear wilt. "Great to see you, Paul," he says warmly. He was always good at that personal thing, like you were the only person in the room. Then to Harland he says in that organ-toned voice, "I may try to steal him away from you yet, Harland." The small group around the governor laughs appropriately, though they probably aren't sure they get it.

Harland Bentley is no less impressive but not in a physical sense. He is of average height, maybe five-ten on a good day, with a trim, unremarkable build and a tight haircut that may be showing the beginnings of male-pattern baldness. But the guy just oozes power—from his ten-thousand-dollar suits to his intense stare to the delicate, precise way he speaks, which isn't often—that's why the people in the small group are more concerned with Harland than the governor. Harland introduces me to his date, Jennifer, who offers me a manicured hand and tells me she works in public relations. Yeah, I'll bet she does.

As I greet the others in the circle—a couple of politicians and a big fundraiser from downstate—I catch the governor saying something in confidence to Harland. Harland pats one of the pols on the back, and says, "Let's give these two some privacy."

Suddenly, it's the governor and me, and I wish I had another martini.

"How are things, Lang?" I ask him.

"Always a circus, Paul. Always a circus." He puts a hand on my shoulder. "And you, my friend?"

"Oh, you know me, Governor. I always travel the speed limit."

A wide smile spreads across the tanned face. This guy, I'm reasonably sure, will be president someday. "I was sorry to hear," he says, growing more somber.

"Probably for the best." I'm trying to convince both of us, and wondering if I answered too quickly. But there's no sense in denying it. Someone had to say something.

"Not in my opinion, it's not. But who listens to me? I'm just the governor." He makes another grand show, a beaming face. "I don't think she's coming, by the way."

"Out saving the world." I answer instinctively, hopefully with no trace of bitterness. That's two people now, Lightner and the governor, who think that she's the reason I'm here.

"That's our Shelly," he agrees.

No, I want to say. That's *your* Shelly. Not mine anymore.

"You know, I wasn't kidding." He bows his head forward slightly, as if in consultation with me. His eyes move about the room stealthily, then return to me. "You just have to say the word. You had an impressive run as a prosecutor, you put away Terry Burgos, you've made your money in the private sector—Harland over there doesn't pass gas without asking you first—it's time to finish your legacy in a robe."

He's mentioned it to me before, more than once, but in this context it feels like pity. A consolation prize. Sorry my daughter dumped you. Wanna be a federal judge?

"Not my style," I say.

"Think about it, then." A typical answer from someone with so much power. *No* means *Maybe later.* He can't appoint anyone to the federal bench; only the president can. But the president's a Republican, and so is Trotter, so the courtesy rule is that he gets to make the call for the federal judges in this state. "I'm tired of putting people on the bench who I owe. It would be nice, for a change, to make someone a judge because they're the best qualified."

I smile at him, like I appreciate the vote of confidence but the answer is still no.

"Not your style," he says.

"I'd have to be fair, Governor."

He likes that one, pats my shoulder so hard I actually lose my balance. "Yes, that would be an occupational hazard. You'd have to be fair." He laughs and takes my hand. "Thanks for coming, Paul. Let me know if you change your mind."

"Nice to see you, Governor," I say, as he's already calling out, in a hearty voice, to the next adoring group.

I grab another martini from the bar and have to stop myself from draining it. I say hello to a lawyer whom I should recognize but don't. He starts talking about some class action and I finally place him, just as I see her.

So she's here after all.

Standing in a circle of two men and a woman. The woman runs a consulting firm. The two men are lawyers, ogling Shelly as she talks to them. It's not really her thing, this schmoozing. I've never seen her in a black satin gown, the V neckline highlighting her long neck and tight shoulders.

I take a deep breath, like a razor cutting through my chest.

She's hitting them up for money for her legal clinic. Perfect place to do it, especially when she's the daughter of the guest of honor. She makes a joke and puts a hand on one of the men's arm, and it's like a fist to my throat. She turns her head and her eyes catch mine, and suddenly I realize that I'm standing still, alone, simply staring at her.

I raise a glass to her and do something with my mouth that I hope resembles a smile. She squints at me, her face working itself into a pleasant expression, as she maintains the conversation with her company. She has the poise to control her reaction but I know what she's thinking. I'm the fly in the soup.

Not the right time in my life, she'd said. Like it was nothing personal. Like she was all booked up.

I turn back to the bartender, feeling mean and angry. I order another drink, even as I feel the weight on my tongue. I better pace myself.

"Hi, Paul."

I turn around and there she is. I stifle the instinct to reach for her. It feels so natural to do so. It was easier when she was twenty yards away.

"Working the crowd?" I say.

"Like everyone else." She has a glass of orange juice, which I assume is not spiked with anything interesting. Shelly is a workout freak, a kickboxer, marathon runner, self-defense instructor. She's almost a foot shorter than me but she could flatten me in two seconds.

She looks different with the makeup, hairdo, pearls, and gown, and I find myself offended. She's not allowed to change.

"So how've you been?" she asks me.

I start for the easy line—*Never better,* something like that—but there's always been something about Shelly that brings out raw sentiment. Plus, I've had too much liquor to be diplomatic.

She nods, like she understands my dilemma. "I see you're representing Senator Almundo in the Public Trust indictments."

"Yeah, and how 'bout this weather?" I put my drink down by the bar. Small talk. She might as well be sticking pins into a voodoo doll of me.

She appraises me, and I don't like what she's seeing. I can't decide what reaction I want from her. I don't want *this.* Not pity. I want to shake her up, watch her struggle.

But that's not Shelly. One of the sweetest, most generous people I know, devotes herself to helping children in legal jams, but she spent most of her life nursing wounds and became an expert in façades. No show, no tell.

"You're making this awkward," she informs me.

"You're right. I wish I could say it's great to see you." I step closer to her. "I don't want to talk to you like this. If you want to really talk to me—any time. You have my number."

She smiles, just a bit, and I go find Lightner. He's talking to a guy who works for the state police, but he's more than ready to head out.

"Did you find her?" he asks me.

"I wasn't looking for her."

Lightner hits my arm. "Have it your way, Riley. Can we get that steak now?"

13

DETECTIVE MICHAEL MCDERMOTT navigates the Chevy onto Carnival Drive, where an entire neighborhood has turned out on this mild evening, mingling in groups outside their homes. A blue truck is parked in the driveway, with COUNTY ATTORNEY TECHNICAL UNIT stenciled on the side.

The call came in at two minutes to five—two minutes before McDermott and his partner, Stoletti, were off for the night. Carnival Drive is on the near north side, close to the neighboring suburbs, and, more important, only one block within the jurisdiction of his squad.

Two minutes, one block, and McDermott would be home by now, eating dinner with his daughter, Grace. Life is a game of inches.

"I'm getting nostalgic over here." Detective Ricki Stoletti bends a stick of gum in her mouth as they pull up. Stoletti has been his partner over three years now, since her transfer from the Major Crimes Unit, a multijurisdictional squad in the northern suburbs.

She could have griped at the last-minute call, could have begged off the assignment. Grabbing a homicide costs at least three hours, up front. Mr. Frederick Ciancio has just ruined both of their evenings.

A uniform, a beefy Irish guy named Brady, breaks away from a neighbor interview and approaches. "Hey, Chief. Hey, Ricki."

McDermott stifles his preferred response, raises his eyebrows.

"Frederick Ciancio," Brady says, flipping a notepad. "Sixty-two. Retired from a security gig, Bristol Security. Worked as a guard at Ensign Correctional before that."

"Ensign. Huh." Stoletti chews her gum with enthusiasm. Ensign Correctional is a max security prison on the west side of the county. "When did that end?"

Brady holds a look on Stoletti. A lot of men don't like women who are taller than they are, and Stoletti, five-ten and physically fit, carries quite the profile. Major point in her favor, that she can handle herself physically. She brushes her bangs off her face. Another major score, she doesn't color her hair, light brown, but with healthy streaks of gray.

"Neighbors tell me it was late seventies," says Brady. "Said he worked security like twenty-five years after that."

McDermott stores away that information. Prison guards are known to make both enemies and friends with the inmates. But twenty-five years off the job is a long time. "Multiple stab wounds?" he asks.

"Multiple is an understatement. My guess for a weapon is a Phillips screwdriver." Brady nods to the crowd. "A neighbor stopped by when Ciancio was late for poker. His car was still in the garage, so he used the spare key he has to go in and look around. Found him in the bedroom."

McDermott lets his eyes run over the neighborhood, still bathed in light at nearly six o'clock on a June evening. There are cops who live up here, people who are required to stay within the municipal boundaries but want something as suburban—read low crime—as possible. The street is humble, mostly bungalows with quarter-acre lots and single-car garages, but it could be plucked out of any number of suburbs. A nice, quiet place.

"Is the M.E. here?" Stoletti asks.

Brady shakes his head no. "But it looks like he died last night. Less than twenty-four hours, I'd say."

McDermott glances at Brady but lets it go. The uniforms are always looking to impress.

"Good job, Brady," he says. He ducks under the crime-scene tape, Stoletti following, and enters the home.

There is a burglar alarm pad on the ground floor, which makes sense for a former security guard. "Need to see if the alarm company got called," he says to Stoletti. Occasionally, intruders will come in on an alarmed house and force the homeowner to give up the password. If that were the case, at least they could pinpoint a time of death.

Another uniform in the kitchen, guy named Abrams who is standing with a County Attorney Technical Unit member, tells McDermott that the back door lock was picked. "And the alarm company hasn't gotten a call from this house for over a year," he tells McDermott.

"Good job, Ronnie." Saved him a phone call. Three possibilities. One is that Ciancio didn't use his alarm—not likely for someone who worked security, in one form or another, for most of his life. Second, the offender knew the alarm's password. Third, the offender broke in when the alarm was turned off—middle of the day, for example, while Ciancio was in the house but unsuspecting—then the offender surprised him later, probably in the middle of the night; the alarm wouldn't matter because he was already in the house. But that would mean the offender got the alarm password out of Ciancio before he killed him, because he must have deactivated it before leaving.

The CAT unit is dusting for prints on the staircase as McDermott and Stoletti climb. McDermott reminds the technician to check the alarm pads. The stairs are carpeted in thick, white industrial. Splotches of the carpet have been removed on several steps.

McDermott feels it, like always, the flutter of his heartbeat as he approaches the scene, even as he reminds himself: The victim is an elderly male, dead from multiple stab wounds and a broken neck. Not his thirty-four-year-old wife, his high school sweetheart. Not Joyce, splayed about the floor, dead from a single gunshot wound.

The bedroom is right at the top of the stairs. The scene looks contained to the bed. Fred Ciancio is lying on his back, mouth and eyes open. He is wearing a pajama top, a solid white that has now been peppered with dark stains from where the incisions were made around his body. The deepest, most obvious is right in the Adam's apple. His head rests on the pillow. The bedspread is still gathered around his ankles. The smell of bodily fluids, including urine and feces, is made worse by the thick air coming through the open windows. Someone probably thought it would help to air it out, but when there's humidity it makes it worse.

"I counted twenty-two," says a CAT technician named Soporro, emerging from the bathroom. "Twenty-two wounds. Fatal one in the neck."

But the other stabbings came first, before he died. Too much blood spilled out of too many holes. If the wounds had been postmortem, his heart would not have pumped blood and little would have escaped from the body, even due to gravity. McDermott gets up close to the body, looks at some of the wounds that aren't covered by the pajama top, in the upper chest and shoulder. Small, circular punctures.

A Phillips screwdriver, the uniform had thought.

The wounds are shallow, enough to penetrate the skin but not by much.

"He was tortured," McDermott mumbles.

"Mike." A uniform calls to him from the hallway. "We found the weapon."

THE STOMACHACHES ARE BACK. The acid penetrates the stomach walls, sets fire to the lining. Like sandpaper on a raw wound.

No more. No more. He bites his lip and counts it out, one, two, one-two, one-two. It's temporary. A flash of lightning. The question is how long before it returns.

Leo looks at himself in the rearview mirror of his car. He runs his finger over the scar beneath his eye, the half-moon, the only menacing feature on an otherwise long, soft, pockmarked face.

Soft. That's what they think of me. Soft like a feather. Soft like a kitten.

He jumps as a man in uniform brushes the driver's-side window. Leo tucks his chin into his chest, pretends to look in the glove compartment— an excuse to turn to his right to see if they have someone on the other side of the car, too. His left foot taps softly along the carpet in the footwell, touching the handgun, edging it closer so he can reach it more easily if necessary.

But, so far, the right flank is clean. He holds his breath and counts backward from twenty.

Nineteen . . . eighteen . . .

The man-in-uniform is putting a ticket on a windshield, two cars ahead. Did he look back at Leo? Did he look *past* Leo, at someone behind him?

Leo turns in his seat, cranes his neck to look behind him. A blur of pedestrians and traffic.

No one there.

Leo turns back just as Paul Riley emerges from the building in a tuxedo, only twenty-five minutes after he arrived. Riley is walking with another man. Is that—is that—? Could that—is that—?

The cop? Lightner?

Right. Joel Lightner.

Riley looks annoyed, arguing with Lightner, as he raises his hand for a cab.

Joel Lightner. Lightner, Joel.

Leo looks back at the rearview mirror. Watch for the diversion, that's when they'd do it, they'd wait until he sees Riley, when he's looking forward, and then come for him, look right, look left, nobody, no one, they haven't found him yet, not yet.

Riley and Lightner.

Leo starts his car. He tries on a smile for size, but it doesn't work, it doesn't fit. He puts the car into gear as Riley and Lightner jump in a cab.

MCDERMOTT EMERGES from the house an hour later. He sucks in the warm, clean air and avoids eye contact with a couple of reporters huddling near the police tape.

The medical examiner has given a preliminary on cause of death. As expected, it was the full-throttle wound to the neck, not the flesh wounds, that ended Fred Ciancio's life. The offender just wanted a little fun before he popped him. As he walks toward his vehicle with Stoletti, one of the reporters, someone he's seen before, shadows him until he gets to the car. She doesn't have a microphone, let alone a camera.

"Detective McDermott? Evelyn Pendry from the *Watch*."

The *Watch*. Right. She's a crime-beat reporter. Print, not television, though she looks like she belongs in the latter. She is well sculpted in every way, with shiny blond hair pulled back, and a perfect, powder blue suit.

"No comment," he says.

"Was Mr. Ciancio killed with a Phillips screwdriver?"

McDermott shoots a look at Stoletti, who pauses a beat while rounding the car to the passenger's side. Damn that uniform, Brady. What did Evelyn Pendry promise him? A mention in the article as the responding officer? Dinner and dancing?

"He said no comment," Stoletti says. "But if you want to be accurate, Evelyn, you won't print that."

"I need you to talk to me," says the reporter, an uncharacteristically informal tone to her plea.

McDermott, half in the car, leans back out. "Do you have something to tell *me*?"

She blinks. She becomes aware of three other reporters who have caught up with her, training a camera on the cops.

Evelyn Pendry gives a curt shake of the head no. McDermott watches her for a moment, but she looks away in defeat. He closes the door and drives away.

14

"THE PROBLEM with a perfect martini," I explain to Lightner, "is that it's perfect." I hold up an empty glass. Three hours ago, Lightner and I moved past the dining room and into the bar at Sax's. I've had a few now, maybe half a dozen or so, so I wave for the check with the universal sign, scribbling in the air, except that my scribbling would be ineligible at this point. Or illegible. One of those. "I better stop drinking before I become an asshole."

"Too late." Lightner has a toothpick in his mouth. He leans back against the booth, one arm over the top, looking around the place, at the end of a long night. The air is heavy with perfume and smoke and alcohol. The chatter is still animated, but some people have left. Winding down now. I have a full stomach and far too much vodka in me. Lightner, as always, can hold more than me, but his eyes are bloodshot, his cheeks a rosier shade of his normal cherubic pink. He still thinks he's got my number because he tagged along to the governor's fund-raiser, and I'm getting tired of telling him that I didn't drag him there to see my ex.

He nods toward the bar, removes the pick from his mouth, and is starting to say something when the waitress brings the check. Lightner stares at the bill like it's radioactive. I've seen more movement from a mannequin.

"No, no," I say, grabbing the bill. "I already picked up dinner. Let me get this, too."

"This is, like, client development."

"Yeah, but *I'm* the client. You're supposed to treat me."

"So I got next one." Lightner points his toothpick toward the bar. "You're not gonna believe this, Riley, but I think this lady is actually looking at you."

The thing I like about Lightner is, he hasn't changed since I met him, sixteen years ago. His wallet is thicker, his clothes much nicer, and his hair a little grayer, but he's still got that youthful enthusiasm about him.

"She's got an ass you could eat lunch off of," he says.

That's what I mean about the youthful enthusiasm. I drop down my credit card. "Great. Pass her a note. Ask her if she likes me."

"Try not to fuck this up," he says out of the side of his mouth as the woman walks up to our table. "Hello there, young lady. My name's Joel."

"*Hi* there," the lady says with more enthusiasm than I have ever been able to muster in my entire life, not even when I got accepted to Harvard or when I hit the winning jumper against Saint Mary's High my junior year. Clock ticking down, I beat this guy off the dribble with a head fake, then a fadeaway jumper. I wouldn't say nothing but net, but it went down. It's not like I remember every detail. For example, I don't remember the name of the guy guarding me.

"May I ask your name?" Lightner asks.

Oh—Ricky Haden. Tall, gangly kid. Didn't move his feet on defense.

"I'm Molly."

Molly is wearing low-riding jeans and high heels, a loose white top that falls off one shoulder. No way she's interested in me. Must be a pro. They come around these places sometimes, looking for the guys with money who've had a few drinks in them and want a little companionship.

Wait. That's me.

"Well, Molly, sitting across from me here is the great Paul Riley. You may have heard of him. But right now, Molly"—and, with this, Joel scoots over and offers her a seat, which she takes—"Molly, right about now Paul is feeling a little blue."

"Why is Paul blue, Joel?"

I wasn't supposed to get the ball, but they crashed down on Joey Schramek, our center, so I kicked out and had the open look. Haden wasn't planted, so he bought my fake, and, next thing I knew, the ball was sailing through the air and the buzzer was sounding.

"Paul is blue, Molly, because he had his heart broken."

Swish. I prefer to remember it as a *swish.*

"Nothing but net," I say.

"I know who Paul Riley is," says this woman—Molly, I think it was. "I saw a special on television a couple of weeks ago about Terry Burgos."

"You hear that, Paul? Molly saw you on TV."

Okay, so she's not a pro. Molly, from what I can see at this point, is in her mid to late thirties and wears a decent amount of makeup and her hair is tossed nicely. The outline of her face is oval, and I think the rest of the pieces would measure up pretty nicely if I could see straight. I think if I could see straight, I would also figure her for out of my league. But that's the thing. Men are all about looks. They seek out the best-looking female in the room and lust after her. I leave open the possibility that women do the same, which is why I hang out with homely people. Still, most women look for more substantive things—

"He seemed very—self-assured," she tells Lightner.

Exactly. Women go for things like brains and a sense of humor and success and confidence. Guys like me count on it. I'm not much to look at, but I've got some smarts and I can crack wise, and I'm a prince of a guy once you get to know me.

"Do you win all your cases?" she asks me.

Joel sits back. He likes that question.

"Yes," I say.

"Oh, the *modesty*." Molly smiles at me and holds her stare on me.

I hold up two fingers. "The second rule in litigation is, settle the ones you can't win and try the ones you can."

She opens her hands, still looking at me. When I don't elaborate, she says, "If everyone followed that rule, you'd never have a trial."

"First rule is, know the difference." I wave to the waitress. "Buy you a drink, Molly?"

"I was going to buy you one."

"Even better."

Joel Lightner seems happy enough with the developments. It annoys me a little that he looks out for me. "I got that thing I gotta do," he says. "Molly. My apologies. It was a pleasure meeting you."

Molly doesn't resist, gets right out of the seat to allow Joel out. I'm waking up a bit now.

"You don't remember me, do you?" she asks when she sits back down.

I don't. I consider lying, but lying always digs a hole. And I'm too drunk to be creative.

"That's okay. I was here last week, when you were—not with your friend here but a client, it looked like. You ordered a drink at the bar and made a joke. You made me laugh. You were very nice."

"And sober," I add.

"You *were* sober, I'll give you that. Maybe you could use some coffee."

"That's a better idea." I push myself out of my seat. "I normally make an excellent first impression. Believe me."

"You made a good first impression with me."

Oh, that's right. I'm actually feeling better than expected, which is probably due to the adrenaline kicking in, fighting through the intoxication. But this really isn't my thing. I was as celibate as a priest for a good eight, ten years before I met Shelly. Never did the pickup scene. Not ready to start now.

"I think the best course of action here, Molly, is that I put you in a cab."

She smiles at me like she's suspicious. "You're either a gentleman or you're not interested."

"I'm neither. But I'm much closer to a gentleman when I'm sober."

But the truth is, she's half right. I'm not interested. I'm carrying a torch for someone who has moved onward and upward.

She motions down the way. "I live about three blocks down. Walk me home?"

Three blocks down puts her near Lilly. Sax's is on the west side, so she must live in one of the lofts that have cropped up out here. She's probably an artist. Dancer or musician. Dancer would be good.

I like this side of town, in part because it has largely avoided gentrification so far. The near west side is still industrial, with only a handful of excellent bars and restaurants standing out among the construction companies and factories. Even the little modernization that has taken place has been met with resistance from community groups. They put a Starbucks down the road a few months ago and half the neighborhood protested. The other half ordered mocha lattes. The area is getting whiter and trendier. The stampede of progress is running roughshod over the cluster of protesters who wring their hands.

It rained earlier, leaving the damp smell that I love. Small pockets of rainwater fill the potholes that cover the roads out here, where there's no money, and the aldermen don't have the mayor's ear.

"Do you still do criminal cases?" she asks me.

"When I can." The heater criminal cases are few and far between for a guy like me, because my billable rate is ridiculous, and the only criminal defendants who can afford me are of the white-collar variety, where the injuries are calculated by accountants, not coroners.

"Let's talk about you," I suggest.

We turn a corner, down a street of tall buildings that make it feel more like an alley. We walk over long-abandoned railroad tracks embedded in the asphalt, and I'm wondering where she lives. Some of these old warehouses have been converted, but they don't display any signage. The deal is, these lofts are gorgeous and cheap, but you can't walk to much, and you're lucky if you have a view of anything other than the side of a building.

"So?" I ask.

Molly stops, looks up at me, and blushes. At least, I think she blushes. Her face seems to change in the shadows. The street is relatively dark, some illumination from a streetlight to our south, casting a light on her face that highlights the smooth skin, those wonderful eyes looking up at me.

"Let me give you my card," she says.

"Oh. Great," I manage, but as she's reaching into her purse, the shoulder strap on her bag slides off, landing hard on her elbow, and the momentum topples the purse from her hand onto the sidewalk. The purse's contents spill onto the pavement.

I bend down to help, so we are both in a crouch. This is the part where we look into each other's eyes and submit to the sexual tension. But I have neither the physical nor mental capacity for that right now, and my heart, alas, belongs to another. So I concentrate on the credit cards and lipstick and money clip and compact on the sidewalk when I probably should be concentrating on the sound of footsteps behind me.

Then it hits me, a tickle in the back of my brain, as I watch her eyes move over my shoulder, her lips part in expectation. I guess she's a pro after all. Just not the kind I expected.

A split second later, it hits me for real, something hard and metal, on the back of my skull.

15

YOUR BODY IS WARM, Paul. Your body is moving, rising and falling. You're still alive, unconscious but alive.

She's running away, trying to escape, but she's in heels, she can't move like Leo, he darts down the alley, faster than her, she's running but he's catching her, closing ground quickly, here I come, she's trying to scream but the fear stops her, stops her cries, closes her throat, the only sounds her tortured breathing and her heels going *clack-clack-clack* on the pavement, *clack-clack-clack*, but not for long.

He comes at an angle, lowers a shoulder, barrels into her, knocks her against the alley wall, *smack* against the wall, *smack* and *plop*, she falls onto a bag of garbage, then rolls onto the wet street.

Quiet now. Mumbling and crawling, mumble, but don't scream, can't scream, pushing herself off the pavement, crawling and crying.

He raises the tire iron, follows her, it's over now.

Quiet now. Quiet.

People v. Terrance Demetrius Burgos

Case No. 89-CR-31003

July 1989

Riley relayed instructions to an assistant county attorney, who walked with him on his way to the office of the county attorney. "Tell whoever it is at the print lab that it's me asking, that this is the Burgos case, and this goes first in line," he said to the man, who was scribbling notes. "And if he can't put us first, tell him I'll want a five-page memo, single-spaced, explaining why." He watched the young ACA run off and chuckled to himself. He'd thought to threaten the guy at the print lab with his job, but making him prepare a written memorandum would be scarier still. He was beginning to get the flavor of county government.

He took a breath and approached the door of his boss's office.

"Come in, Paul, come in."

County Attorney Ed Mullaney was a large man in his midfifties, with a mess of freckles over a drawn, red face. His chin had sagged over the years and hung over the collar of his shirt. He was like an old-fashioned big-city boss, heavyset and cigar-chomping, most comfortable leaning back in that rickety leather chair of his, waxing philosophical about politics and law enforcement. He'd been a big drinker in his time, so the story went, but stomach problems had kept him off alcohol lately, and his mood was less than cheerful as a result.

Riley collapsed in the chair across the desk.

"You look like an Irishman who could use a drink," Mullaney said.

"Is there any other kind?" Riley tried to smile. It was only six o'clock. The day was winding down for Mullaney but just beginning for Riley. It had been five weeks since the discovery of the bodies and arrest of Terry Burgos. Riley hadn't been home before midnight a single day since the murders, something not lost on his wife, Georgia. The investigation had felt like a tidal wave. Riley had assembled a task force of lawyers, investigators, and officers and placed them under his supervision. Delegation was something Riley was trying to learn on the job. So far, not so good.

By now, every victim had been conclusively identified: the prostitutes by fingerprint analysis and visual identification; Ellie Danzinger by her parents and by fingerprints provided by the South African government; and Cassie Bentley by her mother, Natalia Lake Bentley, and through dental records.

They had the murder weapons: The knife used to slice open Ellie Danzinger's chest and slit Angie Mornakowski's throat—complete with traces of their blood and Burgos's, and with Burgos's prints all over them. The glass container that held the sulfuric acid—battery acid—used to kill Jackie Davis, with several of Burgos's prints. And the gun that blew out the back of Cassie Bentley's skull, with Burgos's latents wrapped all around the handle and barrel.

They'd found semen matching Burgos's blood type in the vaginal cavity of every victim. They'd found the victims' clothes and identification, not to mention blood and hair, in his house. They'd found two large body bags in his basement that, between them, had traces of all of the victims inside. They could put Angela Mornakowski and Sarah Romanski into a blue Chevy Suburban—just like the one Burgos drove—on the nights they went missing. They had Jackie Davis's thumbprint on his rearview mirror and a latent from Maureen Hollis's right hand, index finger, on the dashboard. They could put each of the hookers in that truck.

The physical evidence was simply overwhelming.

"Things are looking good, man," said the county attorney. "Smile once."

It was true that, by and large, things had gone quite well. Last week, Burgos's court-appointed attorney, Jeremy Larrabee—a lifer in the public defender's office, a wild-eyed guy with colorful suits, a ponytail, and the Bill of Rights surgically implanted to his chest—had taken his best shot and lost. Larrabee had moved to suppress Terry Burgos's statements to the police, where he had identified each victim by name and all but confessed to their murders. The argument was that Burgos hadn't received *Miranda* warnings. Judge Albert Donaghue had ruled that *Miranda* warnings weren't required because Burgos hadn't been in custody—in the tape-recorded conversation, Detective Joel Lightner had clearly informed Burgos that he was free to leave at any time. Larrabee tried to argue that the cops baited Burgos by keeping him over the lunch hour, and then offering him his favorite meal—tacos—if he stayed. Judge Donaghue wryly noted that he had read over the Constitution and the framers hadn't mentioned anything about free Mexican food.

After the state appellate and supreme courts denied Burgos an immediate appeal, it was clear that Burgos's incriminating statements would be introduced at trial. Just yesterday, the day after the supreme court denied the appeal, Terry Burgos entered a plea of not guilty by reason of insanity to six counts of first-degree murder.

This case was no longer about proving Burgos committed these crimes. This case was now about proving that Burgos was sane when he did so.

"Sounds like you have the prostitutes locked down," Mullaney said.

Riley nodded. Not only could they put each of the hookers in the truck; they also had learned that Burgos was acquainted with each of them. Other prostitutes had easily identified Terry's photograph as a regular customer with Angie, Jackie, Sarah, and Maureen, though when asked none of them knew the name "Terry Burgos."

Burgos had always called himself "Tyler Skye."

The time frame worked, too. The police had been working under the assumption that the women had been murdered in the order they'd been placed in the auditorium basement. The medical examiner had backed that up, more or less, and of course the manner of death had matched the song lyrics sequentially.

From what they knew, the evidence also supported this chronological theory. Ellie Danzinger, the first woman killed, had ordered food into her apartment at 5:35 P.M. on Sunday, June 18, so she was at least alive at that time. From her answering machine, they knew that she had received five phone messages, beginning at 10:15 P.M. that same night, that Ellie had never checked, much less returned. So the operating theory was that Burgos had broken into her condo sometime between those time intervals, beaten her, and abducted her.

And now they had been able to pinpoint the last-known whereabouts of every prostitute, too, confirming that Burgos had killed these women on consecutive days. Angie Mornakowski on Monday, June 19, between nine and nine-thirty; Jackie Davis on Tuesday night, around ten-thirty; Sarah Romanski on Wednesday night, around ten; and Maureen Hollis on Thursday, again around ten.

"Cassie Bentley is more difficult," Riley said. It was ironic, he thought, that hookers would be easier to pinpoint in terms of LKWs than the students, Ellie Danzinger and Cassie Bentley. Given their line of work, it would be easy to vanish a hooker. But college girls?

"Students who are not students during the summer," said Mullaney.

That, of course, was one of the problems. School was not in session, not even summer school yet, and these two rich girls didn't have jobs. The other problem was, the best person to ask about the whereabouts of each of these girls was the other one.

Cassie had had dinner with her mother at their home on Tuesday, June 20, before going back to campus in preparation for summer school the following Monday. They never heard from her again. The fact that Wednesday through Saturday had passed without a word from Cassie had been the reason for Harland's call to County Attorney Mullaney the day before the bodies were found.

"Especially Cassie," Riley added. "She's a real question mark."

"The timing, you mean." Mullaney was a big-picture guy, but he had kept close tabs on Cassie Bentley's case. He'd recently told Riley that Harland Bentley called him twice a day.

The problem was, it appeared that Burgos had killed the girls on consecutive days, beginning with Ellie on Sunday, through Maureen, on Thursday. If the pattern followed suit, Cassie should have been murdered on Friday, June 23, the day after Maureen Hollis. But that hadn't matched with the medical examiner's estimate. The M.E. calculated Cassie's death had most likely been Sunday, June 25—the day before all the girls were discovered.

Which meant Burgos had skipped two days before killing Cassie.

"Serial killers usually escalate their pace," Riley said. "Not slow it down."

Mullaney nodded with concern.

And then there was Burgos's comment to Lightner about Cassie during the interrogation: "Cassie saved me." What did that mean? How did Cassie "save" Terry Burgos? Was he referring to some salvation for completing his murder spree?

Mullaney was nodding with too much enthusiasm. He wagged a finger at Paul. "Cassie's a problem," he said. "She could muck this whole thing up."

Riley rolled his neck. Exhaustion swept over him. He needed to get out of this chair and back into the office. "Oh, we'll figure it out, boss. We're not there yet but we will be."

"No, I'm concerned. I'm very concerned about this, Paul."

"Now that he's pleading insanity," Riley said, "he's conceding he did it. We'll be fine."

Mullaney shook his head and eased his large frame out of his chair. "We still have to prove the elements on every one of these girls. And who knows what Larrabee will try to do with that time frame. This is a problem."

Riley watched his boss. Mullaney wasn't a worrier. Not for this kind of stuff. He hired people like Riley to do the worrying.

When Mullaney had summoned him, Riley had assumed it was a periodic update—almost daily since the murders. Now, he wasn't so sure.

"Something on your mind?" Riley asked.

Clearly, something was. Mullaney yanked up his pants and sighed heavily, moving toward the window. "Paul," he said, "I gave Harland my word that his daughter wouldn't be dragged through the mud."

The slow, compliant nod of Paul's head became a shake, no. "The victims' personal lives are going to be front and center, boss. Burgos had a specific reason for each of them. Each of them committed a sin, in his eyes—at least, that's what he's going to say. I don't know how well he knew Cassie from that class that he sat in on, but whatever he's going to say about her, he's going to say. She was a whore, she was a lesbian—"

"Oh, yes." Mullaney waved a hand. "I had to ask Harland, you know. I had to ask this grieving man if his daughter was a dyke. I don't think he can handle that kind of thing in the public eye."

Riley nodded like a good soldier, trying to read between the lines.

"The Bentleys aren't just *any* family, you know. You say something about one of them, it's in every newspaper in the country. Word gets out that Cassie may have been gay, or these other things we're hearing—missing class, not eating, turning away her friends—these things, when you're talking about someone famous, Paul—they get magnified. The media will turn Cassie into some kind of a crazy, suicidal freak."

Riley didn't speak.

"Hell, Paul, look at the coverage on Harland and Natalia's separation last week."

Riley had read it, too. Reports were that the Bentleys were divorcing. The skinny was, their daughter Cassie had been the only thing holding them together.

Mullaney turned to Paul and leaned on the windowsill. "Paul, another thing that concerns me here is putting all our eggs in one basket."

Riley watched his boss without responding. The thought had crossed his mind as well. In a multiple-murder case, one school of thought was to hold back one of the victims. In the unlikely event that something went south and the defendant beat the charges, you could always charge him again with the other, remaining victim. Two bites at the apple.

"What are you saying to me, boss?" Riley asked.

Mullaney opened his hands. "This is going to be a circus, as it is. Subtract the Bentleys—"

"And it's still a circus."

The county attorney smiled politely, but his eyes went cold. After an appropriate pause, he said, delicately, "The family of one of the victims, recognizing that their daughter is going to be dragged through the mud, and recognizing that the other five murders will be prosecuted, has requested that her murder be prosecuted at a later time. And we wouldn't agree to this, of course, unless we also felt that it was a sound legal strategy. In this particular case, it clearly *is* good strategy."

Riley suppressed a smile, a sour one. Mullaney's words could have been plucked directly from a press release. But the words brought ice to his chest.

The county attorney was telling Riley to drop Cassie's murder from the charges.

"You said yourself, Paul, her case was the toughest."

"I did."

"Answer me this," said Mullaney. "Does dropping the charges on Cassie prejudice your ability to convict this animal? Does it hinder you in the slightest?"

"No," Riley conceded.

"And, in fact, doesn't it give us a second chance at him if he somehow gets off on insanity with the other five girls?"

"Also true."

"All right, then." Mullaney nodded, like the deal was sealed. "Can I trust that the look on your face will be gone when you walk out of this office?"

That surprised Riley. He always prided himself on playing it straight. And he didn't have a big problem with the maneuver. It made sense. He just didn't like the fact that a wealthy political contributor was making decisions for the prosecution.

"I don't like it," Riley said.

"I didn't ask you if you liked it." Mullaney turned back to him. "I asked you if you were going to be a team player on this."

Paul felt the room shrink. He was new to a political office, but he wasn't stupid. The coach was telling him that he could change quarterbacks anytime. The play had already been called, to move the analogy. It was just a question of who would take the snap.

"I appointed you as my top deputy, over a number of deserving people already in this office," Mullaney said, carefully, "because you're the best trial lawyer in the city. And I want the best trial lawyer in the city prosecuting this animal."

Riley didn't answer. He was being snowed. Riley had been brought in precisely *because* he was an outsider—a federal prosecutor, above the tarnish of local politics. There had been a scandal that had exploded only a few months ago, a few county prosecutors found to be on the take, in concert with some dirty defense lawyers and cops—and Mullaney had brought in a consummate outsider to show his commitment to an overhaul. It was political cover, and it was insulting for Mullaney to pretend otherwise.

"I'm going to need an answer right now," Mullaney said.

Riley cleared his throat, his eyes moving from the floor to the county attorney, who stood at the window.

"Grow up, Paul," he said earnestly. "You said yourself, this is good trial strategy. If a victim declined to press charges, we'd drop a case, right? This is basically the same thing, except the victim can't ask. Her family can. They don't want her bloodied any more. Don't let your imagination—or your pride—get in the way here."

Riley got to his feet, stuffed his hands in his pockets, chewed on his lip. He couldn't believe he was being threatened. And he knew what Ed Mullaney was thinking—this was the biggest case a prosecutor could hope for. And it had fallen into Paul Riley's lap.

Riley looked beyond Mullaney, through the window and onto the plaza. It was a warm, sunny day. Riley pictured himself leaving this office, crossing the plaza to the federal building, knocking on the door and asking for his old job back.

Mullaney was next to him now, a look of compromise on his face.

Riley knew, suddenly, that his days at the county attorney's office were numbered. Yet Riley wanted this case. He wanted to put away this monster. He didn't believe, in any way, that Terry Burgos deserved to beat these charges. He had used rational thought all along the way as he butchered those women. He hadn't come close to meeting the legal definition of insanity.

And regardless of how new Riley was to the job, Burgos had killed these women on his watch.

Riley did the math. It would probably take six to nine months before this case was over. He would convict Terry Burgos, and then he would resign.

"From here on out," Riley said, "I make the calls."

"All of them." The county attorney put a hand on Riley's shoulder. "Now, go convict us a mass murderer."

Tuesday
June 21, 2005

16

"WAIT, SHELLY. Just wait," I say, then open my eyes. A brief moment of panic, disorientation, then I lift my head and see the street. Dillard Street, I assume, where I last remember escorting the young lady who called herself Molly. I look for my watch and find only the impression of one, like a tan line, on the skin of my wrist. I make the mistake of touching the back of my head, moist and raw. I manage to get to my feet on shaky legs and instinctively wipe at my suit, damp from lying on rain-soaked trash. I could make a decent salad out of what I brush off my tuxedo.

I'm in an alley that intersects Dillard, where a pair of garbage bags just served as my bed for the last hour or so. I'm still in my clothes, at least, but that's about all I can brag about. No money, no keys. Still have my wallet and credit cards and license, only the cash missing. They probably figured they wouldn't have time to spend the limit before I canceled them tonight—*they* being the woman, "Molly," and whoever hit me with the sledgehammer, which is how I choose to remember it.

My head is ringing but I'll live. I take a deep breath and catch the odor of city garbage on my clothes.

Oldest damn trick in the book. Jesus, how easy could I make it? I let this lady walk me into an alley, middle-aged and sauced off my rocker. The guy could have been wearing clown shoes and I wouldn't have heard him. A child of ten could have taken me.

At least I have an *I was mugged in the city* story.

The good news is, I'm only two miles from home. I don't ordinarily consider it unsafe to walk these streets, and I'm figuring the odds of being jumped twice in one night makes me more or less immune from attack. Not that I have any choice. No cash.

So I walk, hoping that it will sober me up and clear my head, but it's more like gravity is trying to pull me down with each step I take. A concussion, or a hangover, or both. The cool air helps fight the nausea, but I'm swimming against the current. I try to celebrate with each street sign I pass, that much closer to home, when what I'm really doing is trying to ignore the pain and my gullibility and my bruised ego, and the fact that I was dreaming about my ex-girlfriend when I came to.

I own a brick house on a corner, a single-family place I bought six months ago. Way too big for just me—*a home for a family,* Shelly had noted ominously—but I liked the look of it, and I suppose it didn't hurt that the place had been owned by a U.S. senator at the turn of the century—twentieth, not twenty-first.

Before moving here, I had lived in a high-rise condominium, downtown by the lake, a place that was close to work and very low maintenance but that never really felt like a home. I didn't like having a doorman who could register my comings and goings, not that there was anything particularly interesting about my life. It just didn't feel private.

So now I have privacy and then some. Forty-five hundred square feet all to myself. I'm now locked out of my house, but, in a rare moment of invention, I hid a spare key when I first moved in. I was terrified of losing my keys, though I didn't anticipate losing them *this* way.

I head to the alley by my garage where I taped the spare key underneath the rain gutter. I open the gate and walk into my backyard, which is small by suburban standards but pretty ample for the city. The border is covered in shrubbery that manages to grow all by itself, thankfully, because I don't have a clue about that stuff. On the back of the garage is a basketball net, with a small paved area serving as a minicourt. Then there's a small kids' play area—swing set, jungle gym—which I think was what spooked Shelly. I might as well have proposed marriage on the spot.

Not the right time, had been her way of putting it.

A few steps lead down to the basement door. Only then do I realize that I never checked my spare key against this lock. Never checked to see that it worked. I've never, in fact, opened this door since I moved in last January. I'm hoping pretty damn hard that it's the right key, because if it isn't, it really doesn't do me much good, now does it? There are ways to pick a lock, but I have no experience. The only robbery I've ever committed is when I send my clients their bills.

I turn the key and say a silent prayer. Nope. No, Mrs. Riley, your son is as scatterbrained as always. He can try the hell out of a case, but don't give him any menial chores. "God," I say, "dammit."

I decide that this door is going to be sorry it kept me out. I go with a rock from the garden. There is probably a safer and more efficient way to do this, but my head is screaming for a pillow, so I wind up like the mediocre baseball player I used to be and slam it against the small pane of glass closest to the lock.

"Dammit," I yell. "Shit." I hold up the side of beef that is my right hand, shards of glass cutting between the knuckles, blood cascading down to the sleeve.

Nice night.

I reach through and turn the dead bolt. I try to focus on the relief at being home, rather than yet another chore I have now created for myself, a new pane of glass for the door. They sell you on how well the old places are built. That's fine if you want to survive a hurricane, but get ready to fix toilets and reignite the water heater and find the circuit breaker in the middle of the night. I didn't go to law school to be a carpenter. I went so I could afford one.

The basement is huge. Soon to be a recreation area—billiard table, dartboard, wet bar, and, of course, a big-screen plasma television—if I ever get to it, which should be sometime before there's peace in the Middle East. There are over a dozen boxes I haven't gotten to. The only thing I have set up in the basement is what I affectionately call the Wall of Burgos. It looks like a trophy case in a high school, except instead of banners and medals there are weapons and scratched notes and barbaric photographs and courtroom sketches.

The city magazine that did a story two months back on my purchase of this house spent more time on the Burgos stuff than on the rest of the house put together. The story was supposed to be a fluff piece about someone buying the old Senator Roche home, but instead it was about the guy who prosecuted Terry Burgos.

After Burgos was executed, those of us who put him away divvied up the items. There were all kinds of photographs and memorabilia in the evidence room, and we ransacked it like looters after the Rodney King verdict. Over a dozen members of the team have at least one item from evidence. I think some of them are on eBay now.

I was the luckiest, probably because I was considered unofficially the head of the Burgos team. I have the original note Burgos wrote, with the lyrics of that stupid song that he used as a blueprint for his murders. There are two photographs of him being led in, and out, of the courtroom during the trial. An article, featuring a photo of me, from *Time* magazine. A photograph of the bathtub where Burgos drowned Maureen Hollis. A transcript of the interrogation where Burgos incriminated himself to Detective Joel Lightner. And, front and center in the montage, two of the weapons in Terry Burgos's arsenal: First, the knife that Burgos used to remove the heart of Ellie Danzinger and to slice Angie Mornakowski's throat—an ordinary kitchen knife with a five-inch blade. Second, the machete that Burgos never got around to using. My personal favorite. A heavy-duty, twenty-six-inch, high-carbon spring steel machete.

I blow out a long sigh. That was a real time. Chasing bad guys, putting together links in a chain to prove the case, grabbing beers with the coppers after. Now I'm wealthy beyond my wildest hopes, I have a governor itching to make me a federal judge, and here I'm pining for the past. You spend so much time looking to move up, you forget how much you enjoyed the climb.

I rip a piece of cardboard from one of the unpacked boxes, find some packing tape, and do my best job patching up the hole in the basement door. It doesn't fix the problem but it provides some temporary relief. Now I need the same thing for the pain in my head and my hand. I decide on a particular medicine, one that is served in a conical glass, I don't care if it's past three in the morning, and head upstairs.

17

LEO SITS in the coffee shop, back to the wall—never show them your back—eyes on the store window and the door. He pretends to read the paper but looks over it down the street. His eyes feel heavy. His movements are slow. It was a late night—more accurately, an early morning—with Riley and the one in the alley.

He watches each person who enters the café. None of them pay him attention. But that's exactly what they'd want him to think. They'd want his guard down.

They underestimate him. He knows they could be anywhere, they could be anyone.

He touches his stomach gently, begging the acid to stay away, knowing that the more he obsesses, the more likely, and ferocious, its arrival.

A young, thin, blond-haired woman in a tank top, with sunglasses perched on her head, pushing a baby in a carriage and holding a bottle of green tea, takes a lounge chair three feet away from him. She pretends to tend to the baby but her head turns and she looks in his direction, casually, oh so casually, like it's not on purpose.

Talk to the lady. Test her.

He tries. He doesn't do so well with words. Doesn't say them right. *I like your baby,* is what he wants to say.

The woman turns and smiles at him "Thank you." Looks at him like she feels sorry for him. "This one kept me up all night."

He tries to smile. Long night.

At night, I think about dark things.

Try again: *How old is she?* He does okay with that.

The woman answers—"She's ten months"—and Leo breaks eye contact, but he can see her reaction, she picks up her child and holds her close.

Leo winces at the stabbing in his stomach. The woman gets up quickly and walks toward the counter. He looks out the window just in time to see Paul Riley's car in the alley, his car backing out into the alley, behind his house.

The woman is looking in his direction, he pretends not to notice, but he's smarter than her. He can watch her without letting her know he's watching her.

I know you're staring at me, you little bitch. I could rip your eyes out without breaking a sweat.

Leo puts on his baseball cap and leaves the café. He looks back. The woman is staring at him through the window, caressing the baby's head. Bad baby. Fake baby.

Leo jogs to his car. He drives miles away and then turns back toward Riley's street, entering from a different direction. He keeps north of Riley's house for a long while, parked by a curb, watching the rearview and driver's-side mirrors. Nothing. No vehicle traffic. Nothing. Nobody.

He drives to the next block over and parks. This street is like Riley's, expensive houses, high gates and small, elaborate landscapes, fancy lawns, perfect houses, perfect people, shiny and happy. He removes his gym bag from the trunk and walks to the corner, turning in the direction of Riley's street, stops midblock and turns down the alley.

He finds Riley's detached garage and the gate into his backyard. He uses Riley's house keys from last night. First one doesn't work, second one fails, third time, he's in.

There's a sliding glass door on his patio, but it's not opened by a key. No. Down a stairwell is a door under lock and key that leads to the basement. He stands at the foot of the stairwell, five feet below ground. One of the panes to the basement door window has been shattered and replaced with a piece of cardboard.

Leo slips another key into the door, the first one doesn't take, second one does, he heads inside with his bag. Good. Good.

Twenty minutes later, he emerges from the house and locks the door behind him, walks back up the stairs and looks up into a vibrant sun. He admits it, yes, it feels good, feels good, but it's a weapon they use, the weather, turning everyone into smiling, shiny, happy people. Happy, smiling, shiny, ignorant robots.

I can live in your world. I can live in yours and mine at the same time. That's the difference between me and you. That's the difference between me and Terry.

He calmly marches back to the gate. Once back in the alley, he picks up his pace, eyes darting about because this would be a time, when it's nice and shiny and warm, not a care in the world, right, not a care in the world and I'll be whistling to myself and then you'll come, then you'll come when I don't expect it—

But then he's on the sidewalk, back to the car, safe, start the car. Calm now, heartbeat normalizes, breathing exercises, blast the air-conditioning, breathe in, breathe out, cold against his wet shirt, try to smile. He passes by the coffee shop, his hat pulled low, and looks through the window, to where he was sitting not a half hour ago.

The woman with the baby is gone.

He looks in the rearview mirror at the cars behind him. He quickly pulls over, forcing the other vehicles to pass him by, the drivers to show themselves, but none of the drivers are thin, blond-haired women with a baby in the back, but then, they wouldn't be that obvious. He waits, one-two, one-two-three, a break in the traffic, and he pulls the car into a quick U-turn. Turns left at the first street, then another left, then another, driving in a square, eyes on the rearview mirror at all times. Looks okay. But, to be sure, he repeats the process twice more. He's gotten this far. No reason to let up now.

Tonight, he will know for sure.

18

JEREMY LARRABEE crosses his leg after completing a brief summation of the facts of his case to Judge Landis. His client, Josefina Enriques, was an administrative assistant in one of the suburban plants of Bentley Bearings. She's a fifty-two-year-old Latino woman who filed a workers' comp claim for carpal tunnel syndrome a year earlier. Three months later, she was fired by my client, Bentley Bearings. The lawsuit Jeremy Larrabee filed on her behalf included claims for discrimination based on race, gender, age, and workers' comp retaliation. He's given notice to the court that he will seek to certify a class of all employees who fall within these categories.

Judge Landis turns his tired eyes to me. "Mr. Riley?"

I'm annoyed for two reasons. First, my head is still killing me from being jumped last night. Second, I shouldn't have to be here. I supervise all litigation involving Harland Bentley's companies, but I don't oversee the day-to-day work on these cases. That job belongs to the partners who work under me at my firm. But whenever trial judges call a settlement conference, as Judge Landis has today, they want the "trial attorneys" present, meaning the lead lawyers on each side. So here I am.

Make it three reasons I'm annoyed, because the wound to my pride is almost as bad as the one to my skull. I still can't believe I got snookered by that lady last night. She batted her eyes at me and my defenses evaporated.

"Oh, I'd be very interested in how Mr. Riley spins this," says Jeremy

Larrabee. Jeremy and I have history, not a particularly amicable one, but I always get a kick out of him. Always wearing his emotions on his sleeve, still with the sixties-era ponytail, the acne-scarred skin and deep-set eyes, the bright wardrobe. Today, it's a lemon yellow shirt, wild purple tie, and chocolate sport coat.

"She was fired because she took two-hour lunches," I say. "And because she only showered about once a week. We're not offering a dime."

Larrabee's jaw clenches. A vein shows itself above his bushy eyebrows. He's past sixty now, and, from what I hear, has all but abandoned criminal defense. In fact, I don't think it was long after he lost the Burgos case that he gave up the practice. Now he's a plaintiff's lawyer, working on some civil rights stuff that suits him, and, these days, spending much of his time suing Bentley Bearings, one of the subsidiaries for Harland Bentley's holding company, BentleyCo. He has no fewer than eleven suits filed against us currently. So far, we haven't offered anything on any of the cases. He is building up fees and expenses on these cases and looking for seed money—a settlement of at least one of these claims to pay for the prosecution of the other ones.

"I think it might be helpful if I spoke to each of you separately," says the judge. "Starting with Mr. Riley."

A common tactic in a pretrial conference—the judge talks to each side separately, trying to scare each party into thinking their case is garbage and they better settle but quick. Judges always try to settle cases to clear their dockets. The last thing Judge Landis wants to hear is a motion for class certification on a bullshit case like this.

Jeremy stands tentatively and looks at me. "Mr. Riley," he says, and walks out.

I put my head in my hands as the door closes, and it's me and the judge.

"I noticed a nasty bruise on the back of your head," the judge says. "Your hand has seen better days, too."

"You shoulda seen the other guy."

"How is the governor's daughter these days?"

He means Shelly. I look up at him and don't say anything, but my expression betrays me.

"Ah, too bad." He settles back in his leather chair. "I liked her. She had a real—spirit."

"That she did."

"Her loss. Hmm. I see you have Senator Almundo in the Public Trust indictments. Are the screws pretty tight?"

"Any tighter," I say, "he'd explode."

"Well, if anyone can pull a rabbit out of a hat . . ." The judge nods at the door. "Interesting that Larrabee's suing Harland Bentley's company. I mean, with the history." He shakes his head, like he doesn't know what to make of it. "Some kind of grudge or something?"

I shrug. "His client killed Harland's daughter. What would he have against *Harland*?"

Judge Landis drums his fingers conclusively on his desk. He doesn't know, either. How could anyone understand the erratic mind of Jeremy Larrabee? "Now, Paul, about this case—"

"Not a dime, Danny," I say. "Larrabee's a cockroach. We throw him a crumb and he multiplies."

The judge drops his hands on his massive desk. His chambers are an homage to the hunter. The floor is covered with bearskin and the walls are adorned with various beheaded animals. I'm no hunter, but I've played a few rounds of golf with the Honorable Daniel Landis. The only thing I've seen him hunt for is a Titleist that he sliced into the woods.

He massages his prominent forehead and then wags a finger at me. "You're going to give him nuisance money," he says.

"We'll give his client a year's worth of soap," I say.

The judge's shoulders tremble as he laughs.

"And we'll strap a feedbag to her face."

"Stop." The judge's face is red as a beet, a smile planted on his face. He catches his breath. "Ten thousand," he says. "Your billionaire client spends that on dinner. And the woman gets reinstated."

"Ten thousand *what*?" I say. "Ten thousand nose plugs for the people who have to work around her?"

Danny likes that one even better. His laughter turns to a cough and he waves me out. His face a bright red, he holds up ten fingers as I close the door to the judge's chambers.

Jeremy Larrabee is sitting in the empty courtroom, talking on his cell phone. He seems surprised to see me. "Already?" he asks, punching out the cell phone. He needs some work on his poker face. He was hoping for something, anything, from me, and the fact that I spent about sixty seconds in there gives him the answer. I pick up my jacket and briefcase.

"You're leaving?" he asks.

"I am." I try to show lawyers every courtesy, but this guy is trying to play one of Harland's companies and his cases are bogus. He needs to see how little I care about him.

"Give the judge a minute," I say. "He's still in tears over the plight of your client."

"I'm going to get that class certified," he answers. "Then we'll talk."

There is no chance that Danny Landis is going to allow a class action on this case. Jeremy should know that. A good lawyer knows the law. But a great lawyer knows the judge.

"Jeremy." I step closer to him. "Do yourself a favor and pick another company. We won't settle a single one of these. That's eleven trials and you'll lose them all. That's a guarantee. Make a good business decision."

I rethink the judge's question, why Jeremy would pick Harland's company to go after. Is he looking for a rematch with me? I've wondered that since the first suit was filed, but I'd never ask him. He wouldn't admit it, anyway.

I walk away but he calls out to me: "Cost of litigation."

The three-word mantra of any desperate plaintiff's lawyer. *It will cost you a hundred grand to litigate this case, so give me eighty and we're all winners.* Sure, Larrabee's right that it will cost Harland Bentley over a hundred thousand to take this case through trial. That's what this parasite is counting on, that companies will forgo principle and pay out some cash just to save money on the defense of the case. They aren't counting on Harland Bentley. Or me.

"Five thousand," I say, remembering what the judge asked but cutting it in half.

"Five thousand isn't even close," Larrabee says. "Her lost wages alone—"

"I meant for all eleven cases." I push the door open and leave the courtroom.

McDermott is twenty minutes late to work, but he figures he has it coming after working late into the night on the Ciancio homicide. The desk sergeant says, "Hey, chief," as he walks past. McDermott curls in his lips, winks at the guy. The coffee in the Styrofoam cup, dark roast from Dunkin Donuts, is hot in his hand, but he's betting he won't have the first sip until it's cold.

"'Morning, chief." Kopecky, another detective, hits him on the arm.

"Enough with the 'chief' shit." McDermott says it loud enough for every-one to hear, but it's probably a bad idea to sound pissed off with this bunch, it only encourages them. He places the coffee on his cluttered desk, half of which is taken up by the new expensive Dell computer that he can barely use.

"Hey, chief, Streets and San found a Vicky in a Dumpster." Collins this time, a big Irish guy like McDermott. "I'm taking Kopecky."

McDermott lets his eyes wander through the buzzing station house to the lieutenant's office. The lew must be having a bad day. That's why Collins is asking McDermott. "Sure, Collins, sure."

McDermott isn't chief of anything. The detectives at Area Four, Third Precinct, answer to Lieutenant Coglianese, who has seen better—more sober—days of late. Four months now since the lew's wife passed away, and the cops at Four could smell it on him the day he returned from bereave-ment. He'd gone a few rounds with the bottle in the past, like his father, and there was a debate within the detectives' squad about what to do. They turned to the senior detective, McDermott, who had made the call to get the lew through the next six months, until he had his thirty and could retire full.

Which is fine, but now McDermott has much of the lieutenant's admin-istrative work to go along with his own paperwork. In between, he's expected to solve a crime here and there, too.

He looks at the "leader board" and counts the number of unsolved vio-lent crimes. More to come today, starting with the Dumpster girl. Business at Four is booming. The summer months are the best for business. Rapes and muggings double from May to September. Gang shootings triple; some say because of the heat, its effect on emotions. McDermott thinks it's because of the extended daylight hours. More time for the bangers to look at each other wrong.

"Collins," he says, opening the lid on his coffee, breathing in the rich aroma. "Where's the Vicky?"

Reason he's asking, three weeks ago on Venice Avenue, a gang sniper opened fire on a crime scene, a cluster of at least eight officers and detectives. Turned into a full-scale assault on the Andujar housing project. Since then, most of the detectives have taken to wearing vests, like the patrol officers.

Turned out the sniper was an eleven-year-old kid with a 30.06 rifle.

"East side." Collins hangs his shield around his neck. "LeBaron and Dillard."

LeBaron and Dillard. Not a bad area, so reinforcements not needed. "That's my neighborhood," McDermott says. "Clean it up."

19

B Y THE TIME I get back to my office, I'm relatively sure an army of tiny gnomes has taken up residence inside my head, hacking my brain in search of gold. At ten—eighteen precious minutes from now—I have twelve partners and senior associates waiting in a conference room for our monthly update on every piece of litigation related to BentleyCo or one of its subsidiaries. Last I checked, we have sixty-nine open matters. It will be a long meeting. Yesterday, I had everyone draw up summaries of the cases, so that I wasn't walking into the meeting cold. I probably should have read them.

I pass a couple of female associates who are chatting outside an office. They call me "Mr. Riley," which means they are probably among the crop of summer associates—second-year law students from the top schools around the country who spend a summer interning at the firm. By "interning," I mean that they get taken out to expensive, two-hour lunches almost every day and attend functions at night like baseball games or cocktail parties or boat cruises, all on the firm's dime. The firm, of course, is wooing them, not the other way around. Each of the ten members of the summer associate class at Shaker, Riley & Flemming will be offered a full-time associate position upon graduation, unless they do something incredibly stupid like have sex with a paralegal on top of a desk after hours. I use that example because one kid, law review from Columbia, actually did that last year after a party we had at some museum.

I pass the cubicle where Betty, my assistant, is typing on her computer. Betty is the queen of the law firm, the senior partner's assistant. She's been with me since I was at the county attorney. My relationship with Betty has lasted longer than any in my life, save my daughter, if you call that a relationship.

"Morning, Bettina," I say.

I've been with Betty through her divorce and mine, her remarriage and my confirmed bachelorhood, from our first suite of offices on River Drive that housed only eight people to our new place, our palace, that Betty says "lacks charm." Betty is not shy about her opinions. She is a tough woman who grew up with a healthy suspicion of all things human, which makes us a pretty good match.

"Paulina," she says, not missing a beat with the typing but keeping her voice low. She doesn't like being called by her full name, which is why I do it, and she typically answers with a female version of my name. But she wouldn't say it in front of others, because that would be showing disrespect to the boss. She demands the utmost respect for herself and for me. We are a team, and the team sticks together in public, much like Vito Corleone wouldn't tolerate disagreements among the family in front of outsiders. The analogy is apt, though sometimes I wonder which one of us is the Godfather.

She follows me into my office. "You didn't sign that card for Judge Benson," she advises me. "So now his gift is going to be late. And don't say I didn't remind you, because I did."

"Okay, I won't say that." I hang up my suit jacket behind my door and look around for the present. Betty keeps track of the birthdays of judges, politicians, and, most important, clients and buys them small gifts and a card for me to sign. The best way to market yourself to clients is little things that let them know you're there. Birthday and holiday cards, constant status letters if there's a pending case. Clients want attention. Betty makes sure I give it to them.

My desk gives new meaning to organized chaos. *Chaos,* because I have a bachelor's habit of leaving stuff lying everywhere, and *organized,* because Betty comes in here, first thing every morning, and sorts it into piles. It isn't clean, exactly, but it isn't haphazard, either.

I realize Betty is still standing by my desk, hands on her hips. If you didn't know her, she'd look nondescript enough, a small woman with wide hips, a stout face, hair pulled tightly into a bun—or whatever they call a bun these days. Betty is four years older than me, which puts her at fifty-five, but she typically speaks to me like I'm her son—

"I'm still waiting for the present."

—a son she disapproves of. I begin to look around for whatever it is I'm giving Gordy Benson for a present, checking around the accordion folders against my wall, the drawers of my old desk. I have no idea what the object of my search is, which makes it fairly difficult, but I don't want to tell Betty that. The only person more afraid of Betty than me is, well, everyone else at the law firm.

"You have a meeting with the group," Betty reminds me, looking over my calendar.

"Right. I have a few minutes." I touch the back of my head, where I got hit. I probably need stitches, but I hate things like that. More likely, I will put it off until there's an infection of some kind, and then I'll consider doing something about it.

"You don't look good," she informs me. "You *haven't*."

"Flattery will get you nowhere." I pick up a stack of envelopes. "Mail already?"

"That's yesterday's mail."

"Oh, goody." I put it down and massage my temples, not unaware of a very disapproving look being cast in my direction. "Aspirin, Betty. Your boss needs aspirin." When I sense the utter lack of response from her, I look up at her. Her arms are crossed, one foot eagerly tapping the carpet. "What?"

"The present," she says. "And the card."

"Okay, right."

"You don't remember what the present is, do you?"

"Of course I do," I say, falling back in my chair. "It was a basketball signed by the '84 Celtics after they took the Lakers in seven. Bird, Parrish, McHale, Johnson, Maxwell, Ainge, Henderson . . ."

Betty frowns. "It was a pinot noir from Willamette Valley."

"That was my next guess."

Her eyebrows lift. "And where's the pinot?"

"Lightner and I drank it the other night."

She shakes her head and waves me off. Instead of leaving, she stops, considers something a moment, pivots and stares at me. "I'm going to ask you a question. And I want an honest answer."

"Thanks for the heads-up." I root around my desk drawers for a pain-killer. Again, a pregnant pause from my assistant, meaning she wants my attention. "The question, Betty, the question. The suspense is killing me."

"You should go home and sleep."

"That's not a question. That's an opinion." Here we go, a bottle of Excedrin. I pop four out of the bottle and swallow them dry just as I remember that I have a bottle of water in my private fridge, about three feet away from me.

Betty asks, "How many days has it been since you and Shelly broke up? And don't tell me you don't know."

I shrug. "Couple months, maybe."

She raises her eyebrows.

"Sixty-three days," I concede.

"Can you name a single day, out of those sixty-three, when you *didn't* have a drink?"

"You already used up your question." I swallow half the bottle of water in a single gulp, then press the cold, sweaty plastic against my cheek. "You're not my mother, Bettina; you're my assistant. So go and assist me, please."

Jerry Lazarus, one of the young partners at the firm, sticks his head into my office. "Can I interrupt?"

"Oh, please do, Laz. For God's sake, *please* do."

Betty walks off after giving me a stare that would freeze the sun.

"We're ready on Lysinger. Local counsel's ready to find a judge." Lazarus nods at my desk. "You see the brief?"

"Oh. No," I admit, leafing through a small pile on my desk. One of the many subsidiaries owned by Harland's BentleyCo is a company called Bentley Manufacturing, which makes industrial equipment for fast-food restaurants. A restaurant chain in Texas is looking to break the contract, so we're beating them to the punch, seeking an injunction that keeps them from doing so. Blah, blah, blah. Civil litigation sucks.

I find the brief and wave it. "How different is this from the last draft?"

"Not much," Jerry says. "We added the tortious interference count."

"Who did?"

"Lance." Jerry nods. "But I looked it over. We're good."

One of our associates—the grinder—drafted it, and probably researched through the night before doing so. Then my young partner here, Jerry—the minder—thoroughly reviewed it. Now I—the finder, meaning it's my client—will look it over as well before we send it out. And Harland Bentley will gladly pay the tab for all of the overlap. Civil litigation is the best.

"We hooping tomorrow?" I ask Jerry. Our regular game, every Wednesday at lunch.

He shrugs. "Not sure about that, boss. I'm a little worried about it."

"Worried? Your wife didn't give you permission?"

"Worried," he says, "because my future here might be in jeopardy if I keep taking you to school like last week. I think your jockstrap is still on the court."

"Lazarus." I finish my water and smack my lips in satisfaction. "If you could post up half as well as you sling bullshit, you might get a shot off once in a while." I wave him off. "Now, go practice law. Or practice your outside jumper. Something that doesn't involve you being in my office."

"See you in—five minutes," he says.

Yeah, shit, I have to go to that meeting. At this point in my career, it's ninety-five percent oversight on this work. The lawyers under me are more than capable. I guide them with strategy, but this stuff isn't rocket science. I'm there for the profile stuff—major hearings and the very rare instance that we go to trial, but the only thing that involves me personally much anymore is the criminal stuff.

I do a quick run through the mail. Much of it is obviously junk mail or requests for money from charitable foundations. I set the charity mail to one side, because we have a committee that decides where we direct our money. We have committees for everything.

But then there is another letter with a handwritten address—looks generally like the same penmanship, same thick ink pen. Local postmark again. I turn the envelope upside down and let the letter fall out. For some reason, I open it carefully, touching only the corner of the paper:

I will inevitably lose life. Ultimately, sorrow echoes the heavens. Ever sensing. Ever calling out. Never does vindication ever really surrender easily. The immediate messenger endures the opposition, but understanding requires new and loving betrayal and new yearning.

My laugh is uncomfortable. There is no doubt this is the same handwriting as the last one. Creepy, this guy. I guess it's the anniversary of Burgos. Is that what this is about? *Sorrow echoes the heavens? Understanding requires new and loving betrayal and new yearning?* Who the hell is this guy?

I pull out the other letter, which I've kept, for comparison:

If new evil emerges, do heathens ever link past actions? God's answer is near.

Yep. Same precise handwriting. Same freakish, pseudoreligious-spiritual drivel. It rings familiar, too, but I can't place it.

My intercom buzzes. "Yeah, Betty?"

"Mr. Bentley for you."

"Sure." She rings the call through and I answer. It's Harland's assistant—or one of them, he has three—asking if I can meet him tonight. I say yes and get the details, without asking why Harland couldn't call me himself.

As I hang up the phone, I notice the blinking message light on my phone. The first message is from that reporter, Evelyn Pendry, reiterating that she'd like to speak with me. When I play the second message, my breathing halts. It is the voice of my one and only, speaking in a hushed tone, with the sounds of the office in the background.

"*I thought we could have that conversation.*" Shelly, in a soft, workplace voice. "*The usual place and time?*"

THE KEY, see, is to get along, go along, live in their world, pretend that all you see is what they see. Walk up to a hot dog vendor and order, just like anyone else, Polish with relish, bottle of water, put your face up to the sun like you enjoy it.

Here he is. Coming through the revolving door, no briefcase, bouncing down the stairs with a purpose, the great Paul Riley, the man given credit for stopping Terry.

Leo tosses the hot dog into a trash can, takes a swig from the water bottle, tosses that, too, follows Riley on foot, moving from a warm, sunny spot into the shadows of the high-rises. He looks up to the rooftops, but it's not like they'd show themselves.

The walk isn't far. Riley goes four blocks, two north and two east, and turns in to the Dunstworth Hotel, one of the ornate, old city hotels. Leo stops short, careful not to walk in immediately.

Where's he going?

Leo doesn't know. No point in following Riley while he's inside, anyway, nothing Leo can do, should be safe, no reason to worry, wait it out, won't be long.

The pain hits his stomach hard. He brings a hand to his belly. It's all he can do not to double over with the pain. The hot dog didn't help, but when he's tired he has to eat more and he's plenty tired. Electrified but exhausted.

A minute later, a cab pulls up to the hotel. Leo does a double take, but, yes, it's her. The same one in the photos he has.

Her name is Shelly Trotter.

20

SHELLY STANDS across from me in the elevator, our backs against opposite walls. Between us is an elderly, well-dressed couple, just two more of the Dunsworth Hotel's wealthy clientele. I catch her eye but we play it cool, like we don't even know each other. My body is in chaos, my spirit motoring on adrenaline. Suddenly, my headache is history.

She goes first, walks to the suite, and inserts the key card. She holds the door, but I stand there as she walks in and turns to face me. The clench of her jaw could be mistaken for hunger, a primal urge, but I sense ambivalence as well, even conflict.

She begins to unbutton her blouse. I step forward, but suddenly my wingtips are frozen to the carpet. I look over the posh surroundings, take in the smell of her along with the antiseptic scent of a freshly cleaned suite.

"What are we doing here?" I ask.

She shakes her head slowly, continuing to undress, her blouse parting, revealing her pale, freckly skin, a lavender silk bra. She doesn't know, either.

Maybe that's all I wanted to see, even the slightest crack in the armor. I move toward her as she backs up, kicking off her heels. Her pants drop to the carpet. She lets me finish the job, unclasping her bra, lowering my mouth below her neckline, as I lay her on the bed. Her skin tastes like salt and smells like fruit. I run my tongue over her rib cage, stick it in her belly button, provoking a reaction from her. I work through the anguish strangling my heart, knowing I want this more than she.

We are tentative, each of us, feeling around the boundaries of something intimate. It's a bumpy roller-coast ride until she feels me inside her, reacting with a small moan. I look into her eyes and she looks away. Her body goes motionless, letting me take the lead. I run a finger down her face. She closes her eyes, but I can't read the expression. I bring my mouth to hers, tasting her lip gloss, but her lips don't part.

This, I know, is wrong, I'm offering but she's not accepting, but I don't stop. I grip her hair tightly and increase the pace, closing my eyes like her, escaping into something distant and angry, and holding my breath at the end.

I withdraw immediately and hike up my pants, walking past Shelly toward the window overlooking the street. The sidewalks are filled with people, escaping for lunch to enjoy the weather.

"That was nice," she says. "I . . ."

I button my shirt and stare at the faint reflection of my face on the window. I sense her coming up behind me, then her hand on my shoulder, her chin nestling between my shoulder blades.

She doesn't finish the thought and I don't help her. The uncompleted sentence basically sums up our relationship.

"It wasn't nice," I say. "It felt like a gift."

Her fingers draw over my back slowly. "I want this to work."

I close my eyes and tip my head against the window. My heart is ricocheting against my chest and my knees threaten to give out. "But?" I say.

"But it *has* to be slow."

"I always said slow is fine."

"No, Paul." She laughs quietly. "You moved out of your condo into a single-family home. And that casual walk in front of the jewelry store? Remember that?"

I laugh, too, releasing two months' worth of tension. She fits in my arms like she never left. I take in the familiar smell of her hair and the shape of her head, knowing that I'm back out on the limb, raw and exposed and thrilled and overwhelmed.

PAUL RILEY AND SHELLY TROTTER say good-bye outside of the Dunstworth Hotel with a release of their held hands, no kiss. Shelly Trotter ducks into a cab while Riley watches her, a gleam in his eye. Yes, he can see it, Riley's feelings for this woman.

Yes, that could be helpful.

Leo pulls his baseball cap lower on his face and begins walking. It's time to get ready for tonight.

21

I MAKE IT TO GALA, a new place that opened up a month ago, at half past
seven. There's already a line out the door, but I walk up to the doorman, a
foreigner who is roughly the size of two men put together, and give him my
name. To the bemusement of the twenty fashionably attired people standing
along the sidewalk, I walk right in.

All because I said the two magic words: "Harland Bentley."

I'm in a suit and tie, which makes me either over- or underdressed,
somehow not fitting in. The downstairs is a restaurant at full occupancy.
The place sports "Asian fusion" cuisine, whatever the hell that means. The
waitstaff is in all black, T-shirts and jeans. The music is some kind of combination pop and dance—pop-disco fusion?—except I don't think anyone has
called it "disco" for the last decade or two. In my book there are two kinds of
music, jazz and everything else. Nowadays, it's more important how you
look on a video than how well you sing. Nobody invents new music anymore, anyway, they just create a not-so-subtle variation on an old style and
give it a new name.

I give my name to another guy, bigger than the first one, at the staircase
that leads up to the bar. I pass a sign on the way up that indicates that this is
a coming out party for some great new artist on the scene. I decide I will not
inquire what they mean by "coming out." I pass two men in turtlenecks, one
with a ponytail and one with a shaved head, both of whom wear painfully
bored expressions as they bound down the stairs. The music upstairs is,

well, like disco used to be. All sorts of computerized sounds, an urgent beat and thumping bass. I can't believe people listen to this shit. The lighting is almost nonexistent, but the majority of the people are gathered near the center of the room, encircling a man who is, yes, wearing a turtleneck. This is the artist, I dare guess. I should tell him it's seventy degrees outside.

I take a look over at the bar, briefly considering a martini, when I hear my name. Harland, with an Asian woman on his arm who is almost as tall as he and skinny as a pole. I'm putting her at twenty-three, tops. "Lisa, this is Paul Riley."

I take her manicured hand and admire her slinky dress a moment. Jeez, this guy goes through women like I go through vodka.

"You really should meet Raven," he says to me.

"I can't wait," I say, though I have no idea what he means. As he waves his hand to someone, I realize that "Raven" is the artist. A wave from Harland seems to count for a lot around here, because before I know it, Raven is standing before Harland, putting his hands together and bowing. His hair is sharply parted and standing on end. His face is pointy and delicate. If this guy didn't get his ass kicked every day growing up, my mother didn't raise me Irish Catholic.

"Raven," Harland shouts over the music, "this is a friend of mine, Paul. Paul, Raven here is one of the most relevant postmodern artists to come along in years."

I shake his hand, trying to decipher, in the dark lighting, if Raven is wearing eyeliner or if someone punched him in both eyes. If his name really is Raven, then I'm guessing it's the latter.

"I thought the point of post-modern art was to reject the concept of relevance," I say, leaning into him and feeling awfully satisfied. I read that somewhere. Raven either can't hear me or pretends he can't. Harland finds the whole thing amusing and whispers something to Lisa, who seems to be posing off to the side. He kisses her hand and turns to me.

"Shall we?" he asks me. Apparently, Lisa is going to fend for herself up at the party. I imagine she'll be just fine. There are plenty of men who'd be happy to attend to her, and I imagine enough illicit narcotics to prop up a South American dictator.

Harland could have met me downstairs instead of making me come up to meet him. I don't suspect he brought me up here to meet this gender-ambiguous artist. No, the point was that you always come to Harland, even if you're meeting him on neutral ground.

Or maybe he just wants me to see *his* relevance, cavorting with the beautiful elite, mostly half his age, and his latest piece of eye candy. His money is old news. So are the women. But he has to be the benefactor to the art world, with the latest supermodel on his arm. He's a walking cliché. It's almost sad.

Almost.

Downstairs, the staff is wildly enthusiastic at his appearance. I get a lot of empty, anticlimactic nods hello after they realize I'm just some lawyer, not a movie star or artist. I do remember a painting I did, in third grade, of a house. I thought it was pretty good. Sister Virginia took one look at it and told me I should be a lawyer.

A hostess takes my briefcase before I remember that my case notes are inside. I have a file with a rundown on every single piece of litigation that my firm is doing for BentleyCo or its subsidiaries. With Harland, you come prepared. Updating him is not unlike the Socratic method in law school, where you scrambled for answers while the professor peppered you with questions that had no accurate answers. This guy oversees the worldwide operations of dozens of companies and he still keeps tuned to every detail of every piece of litigation.

We get a corner table that has been reserved. There is a step up to the table, which appropriately places us above the other diners. A waiter gallops up to the table with scrolls that are apparently menus. But I already know Harland is going to order something off the menu.

The best word to describe Harland is *severe*. There is no middle ground with the guy. A viselike handshake. Hair tightly cropped, almost to a crew cut. His eyes are small and fierce and liquid, as if he is constantly awaiting the opportunity to prove himself. His jaw seems permanently clenched. His shirts are heavily starched. His clothes are the nicest I've ever seen, and I try to wear some decent threads myself. The guy never served, but he conducts every aspect of his life in military fashion. He wakes at five A.M. every morning, swims half a mile in his pool—the outdoor one in the summer—then eats an efficient breakfast and makes it into the office by a quarter to seven. If I had a dime for every time I had voice mails from Harland when I walked into my office, voice mails from seven that morning, I'd be rich.

Richer.

"Thanks for meeting me, Paul."

"Always a pleasure, Harland. Always."

"Henry," he says to the waiter who appears again out of nowhere. "Perrier with lime for me. Paul?"

I'm not sure how Harland already knows the name of a waiter in a restaurant that's only been open a few weeks. I guess it's that kind of small detail stuff that made him a billionaire. Either that, or the twenty million in starter money he got from the divorce.

I have a taste for my usual. Harland pauses, as if he disapproves. He doesn't drink. Doesn't smoke. The only vice of which I'm aware—and many others are aware, no doubt—is his mouth. This guy speaks with the smooth ease of the ultrawealthy, but if something rubs him wrong he can cuss like a truck driver.

So I always try not to rub him wrong. But I order the martini, anyway, dirty and straight up, with blue cheese olives.

Okay, there's the mouth and the women. Every time I see him on the society page or at a social function, it's a different one. Blond, brunet, redhead, buxom, petite, leggy—the man doesn't pin himself down to a single trait, unless you count young and drop-dead gorgeous as traits.

A woman who looks like she came off a runway, her hair tossed and pearls around her neck, says hello to Harland. Kisses on each cheek, a quick wiggle of the fingers in my direction.

Harland sits back a moment, basking in the glow. This guy's a rock star. Still with the hint of a smile across his lips, he turns to me.

"Do you know someone named Evelyn Pendry?" he asks.

HE FEELS SAFE in the dark, warm and secure, the great equalizer, you can't see me, even with the light coming in through the space between the two doors, still dark, dark closet, then the *click* of the dead bolt—

Leo frees the knife from his sock and gets out of his crouch.

Thump on the floor, by the door. Dead bolt locks again. Footsteps moving quickly on the carpet. The television turns on, the scripted voices fading into the room. The news.

"First in the news, tonight," says Evelyn Pendry, imitating her mother's voice and crisp intonation on the newscast playing in the background. She walks into the bedroom, pulling at her earrings, repeating her mother's words. She unbuttons her blouse, kicks off her heels, wiggles out of her skirt.

The scent of berries wafts into the room. Leo inhales, it's been so long since he smelled someone like that—

"Senator Almundo," she says, repeating Mom's words, "denied the allegations."

She stands in front of the mirror in her cream satin underwear, cocking her head decisively and punching her lines. "Senator Al*mundo* . . . *denied* the alle*gations*."

Leo stares through the crack between the doors of the bedroom closet as Evelyn repeats the phrase again, working on her punctuation.

Her figure is firm and shapely, but he's not thinking that way, no, he wonders how she'll react, she seems athletic, young and athletic, not Old Man Freddy sleeping in his bed, not like the girl with Riley in the alley. No, this one, this one will put up a fight.

He grips the knife in his hand, swallows hard.

He takes a breath and it happens, the calm sweeping over him.

She is early, unexpected. He will wait until nightfall, when she's in bed.

He closes his eyes and holds his breath.

When he opens them again, Evelyn Pendry is staring at the closet.

HARLAND LACES his hands together. "So she was talking about a background story."

"Well, that's how she framed it," I explain. "She wanted to do a piece on the Public Trust case and Senator Almundo and me. Then she started asking me questions about *my* background. And she asked if I kept in touch with Nat and your niece, Gwendolyn."

"*Gwendolyn.* Yes, Gwendolyn." It seems Evelyn Pendry asked Harland about those two women as well. He angles his head. "I haven't heard from Gwendolyn in years. And if it's many more before I do, I won't complain. What a vile girl."

"You two didn't hit it off," I gather.

Harland looks hard at me, wets his lips, and answers evenly. "This was Cassie's only cousin. The closest thing she had to a sibling. And she didn't—" His face changes, a break in the anger, a moment of emotion before hardening again. "She didn't even come back for Cassie's funeral. This girl couldn't take one day away from her gallivanting across the globe to pay her respects to Cassandra. That I will never forgive."

Harland married Natalia Lake, heiress to the Lake fortune, when she was nineteen, and—coincidentally, I'm sure—had just inherited almost a billion dollars from her father, Conrad Lake. They divorced after about twenty years of marriage, not long after their only daughter Cassie was murdered. Harland took twenty million and went his own way, investing in hotels first—Bentley Suites—and then building a number of businesses that bear his name, including Bentley Manufacturing, Bentley Bearings, Bentley International, and Bentley Financial.

Word was, Harland's fondness for young women did not begin after his divorce but long before. The marriage had turned into a cold one, held together by the one thing they had in common—their daughter. Once Cassie was gone, as far as I understand, they looked at each other and cried uncle. Rather than fight—there was a prenup, though I don't know the details—Natalia took a chunk of her fortune and threw it at Harland as a parting gift. A cynic might say Harland's principal motivation these last fifteen years has been to top his ex-wife's fortune, and I dare say he's succeeded. My firm, of course, has profited correspondingly.

"Where's Gwendolyn now?" I ask him.

He opens his hands. "I heard that she bought some property in Lake Coursey, up north. She still has a place in France, I suspect. But I really don't know. And I really don't care." His eyes fix on me. "Did this reporter, Evelyn, say why she was asking these questions?"

I shake my head. "I stiff-armed her. It never got that far."

The waiter arrives with the drinks and asks us if we want to hear the specials. Harland doesn't, and I don't, either. I already know he's going to order something that swims in the water. I usually do, too, but I'm thinking of something that grazes on land.

"You had that *karioka* last time, Henry," he says to the waiter. "With the sweet sugar?"

"Yes, sir, Mr. Bentley."

"That would be a nice start. Thank you. And tell Homaro to stop by when he's free."

I wasn't here for that meal, with the *karioka*. I don't even know what *karioka* is, but I would be willing to bet that it isn't a selection on the menu this evening. That's how a guy like Harland gets off, ordering something off the menu and knowing that they'll make it, because he asked. And probably knowing that they'll mark the price up, as well, for the effort.

"So." Harland clasps his hands together and looks at me. "This reporter called me and I made the mistake of speaking with her. She was very intrusive. Very aggressive. I can take a lot of things, Paul. Someone in my position is going to be a media target."

"True."

"But when it comes to Cassandra, the spotlight turns off."

"Sure." That, I always believed, was why Harland didn't want Cassie's murder prosecuted. Burgos's insanity defense centered around his belief that he was carrying out God's will in punishing sinners. That, of course, required a showing in open court that the victims of his crimes were less than model citizens.

"What kind of questions did Evelyn ask, Harland?"

He puts a fingernail between his teeth, lost in thought a moment. "I want to preempt this," he says. "I want to talk to you about how."

That's Harland, never answering the question. I state the obvious. "She's a reporter." His reaction tells me that he's not impressed with the First Amendment. "You're talking about—what—threatening suit?"

"Or speaking with Lyman."

Lyman Kruger is the publisher of the *Watch*. That option could cut either way. Sometimes, letting a publisher know that you're very concerned about possibly defamatory articles leads the publisher to clamp down on the reporter, putting pressure on her to either be *sure* she's right or drop it. Other times, though, it backfires by piquing the interest of the newspaper.

I tell him all of that. "It could make things worse," I say.

Harland bristles at my advice. Men in his position don't like being told they are without options. "I want it to stop, Paul. Homaro!" he calls to a man dressed in all white, presumably the chef, who delivers the appetizer—some deep-fried meatballs that smell delicious. They exchange pleasantries, speaking in Japanese, and then the chef leaves the table.

"I want it to stop," he repeats to me as he helps himself to the appetizer. He sticks the tiny fork into the meatball with a bit too much enthusiasm.

In that snap of a moment after Evelyn Pendry's shoulders jerk violently, Leo bursts out. This isn't the time, not the time—

You see me.

—but there's no choice, and he still has the element of surprise. He rushes toward her, but she has the angle on him and breaks for the living room. He goes low and catches her ankle. She falls to the carpet.

Keep. Her. Quiet.

Leo twists her ankle sharply, feeling the snap. She trades terror for pain, crying out but in reaction, not alarm. He comes down on her, pressing the knife against her face. She freezes, breathing rapidly but not making a sound. She's calculating, yes, calculating, thinking it through, she knows the knife is close enough to end this right now. If she cries out—if she tries to warn them—it's over.

He grips her silky blond hair, savors it a moment, then yanks it. She understands. He turns her over so she is on her back, facing him. He puts his knees on her arms and presses the knife against her throat.

She smells like strawberries.

22

M IKE MCDERMOTT leans against the wall in the living room, watching Grace read to her grandmother. He does that a lot these days, silently watches his seven-year-old daughter, marveling at how a man who handles violent criminals and visits horrific crime scenes can be laid so bare, so utterly vulnerable and terrified by this small little lady.

She is an *excellent* reader, the word her teacher used. She has her mother's intelligence, her critical reasoning and verbal skills. And her behavior has improved this year. Fewer outbursts. Socializing more.

Year Four, is how he thinks of it. He doesn't measure her from birth but from Joyce's death. She still has the dreams, still asks the unanswerable questions. But Dr. Sutton says there's no indication of early-onset. Only a third of the children, at most, inherit their parents' bipolar disorder, he said—meaning about seventy percent don't. McDermott confronted him with the literature—*early-onset can consist solely of depression that evolves into bipolar*—but the doctor says she's a functional little girl who's finding her way through this.

She blames herself, the doctor had said, words that filled McDermott's throat. *That's not unusual. It was her mother, after all.*

McDermott remembers staring at his shoes at that comment, unable to find words.

So he watches Grace every day, the highs and the lows, looking for the warning signs. Every time she argues or cries or has a tantrum or jumps for joy, he makes a mental note. He was even keeping a journal for a while. *Laughed at a cartoon. Complained about her cereal.*

" 'Matt,' " Grace reads in a narrative voice, " 'who had seen guests come and go for many years, knew there were two kinds . . .' "

Mike's mother, Audrey McDermott, is on the floor with Grace, gathering her granddaughter in her arms and reading along with Grace over her shoulder. The sight of it almost moves McDermott to tears.

The phone rings. They look up but McDermott raises a hand. He gets it on the second ring, and, after listening, mouths the word *Shit.*

McDERMOTT MAKES IT TO the apartment building by nine, pulling up behind a squad car, one of six parked along the curbside, lights flashing. There are news trucks and camera crews and reporters in makeup positioning themselves and scribbling notes and checking the artificial lighting. One of them is angling herself by the apartment building, asking her cameraman to evaluate the position.

The building is on the near north side, four stories high, with a courtyard in the middle. Looks like a series of condos, pricey, given the neighborhood, but presumably very small. Evelyn Pendry probably didn't earn much as a staff reporter for the *Watch.*

He takes a wide, inner staircase of concrete steps. There are CAT officers on the stairs, dusting the handrails for prints, though it's a community staircase full of hundreds of useless finger- and shoe prints. The killer wouldn't need to touch the handrail, and probably wouldn't be stupid enough.

On the third floor, the CAT unit is again at work, brushing for prints and searching outside the apartment in the hallway with paper evidence bags, but they seem to be doing it as an afterthought, as if their work is nearly done. McDermott looks down in the courtyard, where a number of the residents are huddled, looking upward and gossiping about the woman who was murdered. Some of them probably knew Evelyn Pendry.

Ricki Stoletti, in a dark jacket and jeans, emerges from the apartment. She gives some instructions to the uniforms and then looks down the hallway. She nods at McDermott as another woman walks out, someone he recognizes. Perfectly tossed blond hair, expensive suit.

Oh, of course. The victim's mother, Carolyn Pendry. The news anchor.

Stoletti does an intro. "Detective Mike McDermott, Carolyn Pendry."

"Mrs. Pendry, I'm so sorry."

Carolyn Pendry is the reason McDermott is here. The call came from the commander himself. She is probably the most prominent newsperson in town, and when her child is murdered she gets the top-ranking detective in Area Four.

He does the preliminary talk quickly, because he wants to go in.

"I'm coming with you," she tells him.

"Well, Mrs. Pendry—"

Kid gloves, the commander said. She gets what she wants.

"It would be better if you—"

"I've already seen her. I want to know what you think."

McDermott looks at Stoletti, who gives him a *You're the boss, don't look at me.*

"Okay," he relents. "Let's go."

AFTER DINNER WITH HARLAND, I should be in a foul mood. Harland wants me to figure out a "diplomatic" way to shut off Evelyn Pendry's inquisition, which leaves me with an impossible task. But I'm not in such a bad mood. Correction: I'm *flying* since my rendezvous with Shelly today. I hate like hell that I've surrendered that much of myself, but, what the hell, I'm a tall drink of water, there's a lot of me to go around.

I pick up Shelly on my way home. Our conversation is civil—How was your day? Fine, how was yours?—though I'm bursting at the seams.

I strip off her clothes before she's taken two steps into the foyer. I think of the staircase, but there's no carpet, so I carry her into the adjoining room and get busy. I'm still the scrappy basketball player at heart. What I lacked in talent I made up for in hustle, dove for the loose ball, took the charge. I apply the same can-do spirit in the bedroom, or, in this case, the living room, or parlor, or whatever this room is. I may not score a triple-double, but she'll know I gave her the full Riley effort.

And it's different this time, compared to this afternoon. She doesn't hold back, pressing her tongue into my mouth violently and gripping my neck and wrapping her legs around my waist.

We need to break up more often.

"Now, *that*," I manage, "was nice."

I collapse on her, feeling her heart pounding, her breath on my neck. I inhale the wonderfully fruity smell of her hair, which is not difficult because my nose is buried in it. Calling this moment *nice* is like calling sky-diving *interesting*.

"I was afraid," she whispers. "I needed time."

I move my face over hers and get my arms underneath her back and press her tightly to me.

"I love you," she says.

I take a couple of breaths and remind myself of everything I've learned about playing it cool. Cue the fireworks. She has never said those words to me before.

MCDERMOTT WALKS OUT OF Evelyn Pendry's apartment and takes in the fresh air. There are nothing but questions now.

"She didn't meet me for dinner," Carolyn Pendry explains, leaning against the railing, looking down onto the courtyard. "I called her at work, home, her cell. She *always* answers her cell."

"Any sense, Mrs. Pendry, of who might do something like this?"

Evelyn Pendry was tortured. Her body was peppered with knife wounds before the fatal wound to the left temple. The weapon of choice, your basic switchblade, was found in the trash can in the small kitchen.

Same brutality as last night, at Fred Ciancio's. Different weapon.

"She covers the crime beat." Carolyn touches her eyes.

"I know," McDermott says. "I saw her yesterday."

Carolyn looks at him, tries to read his face.

"By any chance," he tries, "does the name Fred Ciancio mean anything to you?"

She freezes a moment, like it rings a bell, then she lets out a gasp. She backs into Stoletti, his partner, and covers her mouth.

"You know him," he gathers.

"Call Paul Riley," she says.

"Paul—"

"Paul Riley." She moves to him, takes his arm. "The man who prosecuted Terry Burgos."

23

I MAKE IT THROUGH the reporters and up to the third floor of the apartment complex, courtesy of some uniformed officers who are expecting me. They were vague on the phone, first a cop named McDermott, then Carolyn Pendry, who grabbed the phone away and gave me a little detail.

I see Carolyn first, talking with a heavyset guy who looks familiar to me. He is moving his hands and, it seems, trying to reassure her. She is nodding along. She paints the contrast, the beautiful hair and clothes, a perfectly etched face that is now drawn and beaten with sorrow, a slumped posture.

When she sees me, she says, "Paul," and drags the guy with her. "This is Commander Briggs. Paul Riley."

We shake hands. They brought the big brass in. The commander showing up after ten o'clock to a murder scene? Well, it is the daughter of Carolyn Pendry.

Carolyn's face melts in anguish. She touches my arm. "Thank you—thank you—"

"Carolyn, my God. Anything I can do. I'm so sorry to hear."

She pulls me along, just as a woman appears in the doorway of the apartment that must be Evelyn's. A tall woman, midforties, with a shield hanging from her neck.

"This is Detective Stoletti."

"Paul Riley."

"I know who you are." She gestures inside.

Nice to meet you, too.

"Don't touch anything," she tells me.

I don't answer but heed her advice. A tall, ruddy-faced guy, almost my height but with a little more size in the torso, introduces himself as Mike McDermott. Friendlier on the surface than Stoletti, but seemingly no more pleased to see me.

I consider reminding them it wasn't my idea to come here. I was lying in bed with a beautiful, naked woman thirty minutes ago and was in no hurry to move.

He gives me the same lecture about tampering with evidence. Looking over McDermott's shoulder, I can see that they've already combed it, anyway. The place is what I would expect, a tiny apartment with a kitchen you could barely turn around in, then a single living room with a single piece of furniture, an L-shaped couch. Patches of carpeting have been lifted from the living room, the main room in the apartment. The kitchen is taped off, with a long counter that's been dusted.

I walk into the living room, which is undisturbed. The fun, I assume, will begin in the bedroom, the other half of the condo. I feel an adrenaline spike. This is what I used to do. Chasing bad guys. Solving puzzles.

As I get closer to the archway between the living room and bedroom, I feel my body slow, a defense mechanism. I look down and a noise escapes my throat. It doesn't matter that I knew it was going to be Evelyn Pendry. I can't stifle the shock upon seeing this happen to the person who hounded me yesterday with questions.

She is lying on the carpet, naked to her underwear, her arms and legs spread, her head rolled to the right. Her left temple wears an ugly, bloody gash, what looks like a deep wound. Her mouth is open. The color of her skin has already begun the death fade. She looks like she was in midsentence, as if something had just occurred to her, something important, or like she hadn't completed what she'd set out to do.

The bright lights in the room seem garish under the circumstances, plunging this murdered woman into a spotlight at the point in time where she most deserves privacy. I want to cover her in a blanket and close her eyelids. I watch her vacant eyes, waiting for her to blink.

I walk within a few feet of her and bend over. The foul smell coming from the young girl's body is urine and feces; her sympathetic nervous system had broken down as she'd fought the killer. Or fought the pain.

The wound to her head aside, Evelyn Pendry's body has been ravaged with knife cuts. Some are superficial, others deeper. There is blood from each wound, which means they happened before her heart had stopped circulating blood.

She was tortured before he killed her, before he put one through her brain.

I look back at the detective and see that Carolyn isn't in the room with us. I'm glad for that, though she's obviously already seen this.

"He enjoyed himself first," I say, taking another look, bending down. There is no blood that I can see splattered around. "He held her down right here and went to work on her."

I look at the detectives, neither of whom seems impressed so far. I don't know what they expect from me. I still am not entirely sure why I'm here.

"How'd he get in?" I ask.

Nobody answers at first. I don't expect them to like me, but I don't really care.

"How'd he get in?" I repeat.

McDermott shrugs. "No forced entry. Either he picked the lock or she let him in."

"Was there sexual trauma?" My eyes avoid Carolyn, who is in the room with us now.

McDermott shakes his head no. "He just wanted to hurt this girl."

I stand up and look at the detective. "You don't think she let this guy in," I say.

He doesn't respond to that.

"The bathroom," he says. "Tread lightly."

I turn and walk carefully into the bathroom. The light is already on. I look first with my eyes down on the floor. Then I catch it in my peripheral vision. I look up at the mirror and see my reflection, with ghoulish words written on the glass in red lipstick:

I'm not the only one

I step back, almost losing balance. I look at the cops, who seem to be making something out of my reaction.

"That mean something to you?" Stoletti asks.

I let it happen, let it rip through me, grip my insides and twist them in knots.

"You okay?" McDermott asks me.

I walk past them and again look at Evelyn, squat down carefully to examine the wound to her head. A young one. Never got her age, but she had so much ahead of her. Smart and ambitious. I recall what I said to her the last time we talked, my dismissive brush-off. There's always that regret if you left on a bad note, said something negative, like I did. But there is more than one reason now that I wish I had listened to her.

"Switchblade, right?" I look at them. "That's what he used here?"

"Right," McDermott says, as Stoletti asks, "How did you know that?"

"This wasn't the first victim, though."

Nobody answers, at least not verbally. Their expressions are enough. The detectives look at each other.

"She's the second victim," I say. "There was a first. *Right?*"

"Right." McDermott nods. "What was the weapon there?"

"An ice pick," I say.

His look tells me I'm right. "What the fuck," he mumbles.

Carolyn parts the detectives. "Is this another song, Paul?"

I stand up and look back at the bathroom. My heart rattles against my chest.

"Same song," I answer. "Second verse."

People v. Terrance Demetrius Burgos

Case No. 89-CR-31003

August 1989

First Assistant County Attorney Paul Riley placed the tape in the cassette and hit PLAY, reading along with the lyrics, which had been printed on poster board and left in one of the designated war rooms for the Burgos case. Tyler Skye, the lead singer of Torcher, screamed, over angry guitar chords, what he called the second verse of the song "Someone":

A second verse a wretched curse a fate no worse a hate perverse

Both the guitar and percussion kicked up after this introduction, as Tyler Skye's voice erupted, spitting out a litany of violent lyrics faster than the human ear could follow:

An ice pick a nice trick praying that he dies quick
A switchblade oughta be great for lobotomy insane a call to me
Precision blade incisions made a closer shave a bloody spray
Trim-Meter chain saw cheerleader's brain's all paint on the stained wall
Machete in the head he isn't ready to be dead I can't explain why I'm in
    pain why I'm unable to refrain from getting in somebody's brain
Ditchin' life kitchen knife no more itch and no more strife no more hate
    I passed the test
And on the seventh day I rest.

The second verse ended in suicide, just like the first verse—the *Mickey Mouse* lyrics. *Ditchin' life . . . no more itch and no more strife.* No more of that because he killed himself. It only bolstered the interpretation of the final murder in the first verse—*stick it right between those teeth and fire so happily*—suicide. But Burgos hadn't killed himself. He'd taken Cassie instead, and presumably was getting ready to move on to the second verse when he was apprehended. They had found all of the weapons described in the second verse—the ice pick, straight razor, chain saw, machete, and kitchen knife—in Burgos's basement. All of them seemingly pristine, unused. Not a trace of blood or anything else found on any of them.

They had caught him before he could get to the second verse.

Joel Lightner walked in while Riley sat against a long table, staring at the lyrics on the board and listening to the music. Lightner raised his eyebrows to indicate his opinion of the lyrics. They were not different, in any meaningful way, from the first verse. They listened, together, to the refrain, which was a slight variation on the refrain following the first verse:

That someone is me you still haven't caught me I tried to warn you but you never sought me you don't understand I'll never be done it won't ever stop

The music, already loud and vicious, exploded with a heavy percussion line, guitars blaring, as Tyler Skye completed his final rhyme, screaming it ferociously:

I'm not the only one

Riley killed the cassette player. They didn't speak for a long time. *I'm not the only one,* probably the most horrific of all the lyrics. This music was out there, for any deranged person to buy into, to act upon.

"We're absolutely positive there's not a second burial site," Riley said.

Lightner made an equivocal grunt. They'd used the county dogs and covered the entire Mansbury campus. They'd searched every inch of Terry Burgos's house, excavating his garage and basement, digging up his yard. They'd looked everywhere and come up empty. "There's no reason to think so," Lightner said. "The murder weapons were totally clean. The machete was still in its wrapping. And I think ol' Terry would tell us if there was another site. He's not exactly shy about this."

That much was true. Burgos had not been shy with the psychiatrists, who had begun to examine him after Burgos pleaded not guilty by reason of insanity two weeks earlier. He'd gone into great detail, not on how he committed the murders but why. He'd recounted the biblical verses and Tyler Skye's lyrics, and the sins committed by the victims that made them worthy of his wrath.

"So," Lightner said, "we're officially down to five kills now."

Last Friday, August 11, Riley informed the court that the prosecution was dropping the charges on the murder of Cassandra Bentley. Within about five seconds of the words leaving his mouth, simultaneous press releases came from the offices of the county attorney and the Bentley family. It was the Bentleys' express wish that their daughter not be subjected to the cruel innuendo that would accompany this insanity defense, their accusations of promiscuity and whatever else a "desperate defendant" might try to say. It was enough, the Bentleys' press release said, that Burgos was now conceding that he had killed Cassie, and that he would be prosecuted for the other five murders.

Riley forgot about it the moment he left the courtroom. It didn't matter anymore. It was all about the insanity defense now. Burgos would have to demonstrate that he was suffering from a mental defect and that he was unable to appreciate the criminality of his actions. So it was now the prosecution's job to prove the opposite—that Burgos was *not* suffering from a mental defect and that he *knew* that what he was doing was a crime.

Burgos had a decent argument on mental defect. He'd been diagnosed as a paranoid schizophrenic for several years. And he had the easy, common-sense argument, too. How could someone who did this *not* be crazy?

The second prong of the insanity test was another story. Burgos would have to establish that he did not appreciate that he was committing a crime when he murdered those girls. Appreciation of criminality was less about shrinks and more about facts. So the task force focused on gathering such evidence, and things were already looking hopeful on that score. Burgos had killed the girls during the short break between the end of the spring term and summer school, knowing that no one would be checking the basement of Bramhall Auditorium during that time period. And he'd picked prostitutes from different parts of the city, so that he'd never have to show his face back in the same neighborhood while he continued on his murderous spree. All of these actions were indicative of a man who knew he was breaking the law and didn't want to be stopped—a man who was not legally insane.

Lightner moved in for a closer look at Riley. "You eaten anything today, sweetheart?"

Riley waved him off, but his wife had made the same comment. Riley had dropped about six pounds in the last three weeks. Food was the last thing on his mind. This prosecution would be the biggest thing he'd ever do as a lawyer, and on top of that, he was trying to oversee one of the largest prosecutorial offices in the country.

"Let's get a greasy cheeseburger at Baby's," Lightner suggested.

Riley glanced at the clock. It was past one o'clock. He'd been in the office since seven and hadn't eaten a thing. He walked with Lightner back to his office for his suit jacket and found his secretary, Betty, placing the mail on his chair.

"More fan mail," Betty said when she saw them.

The cops and prosecutors had received all kinds of weird mail about the Old Testament and wrath of God stuff since they began to prosecute Burgos. Almost none of the correspondence actually favored what Burgos had done, but many letters warned "sinners" of the consequences of their actions.

"This one, I thought, was especially weird," Betty said.

Riley took the letter and, along with Lightner, read it:

As justice or belief will eternally live, likewise do others need evil. I must ask your new, educated elite: Does opportunity now evade morality or respect ethics and love? Behold a new year.

He looked at Betty, who shrugged. "This *is* weirder," he agreed. Most of the letters they got simply recited verse from the Old Testament, or predicted rather dire consequences for people who did not follow the Lord's teachings. But whatever else they were, they were not vague. "You have the original?"

She nodded. "Tagged and stored."

As a precaution, the county attorney was tracking all of the original letters sent to its office, keeping each one sealed in plastic and dated.

"I don't even get what this says," Riley said.

"Some people need evil like others need faith," Betty speculated, looking over his shoulder. "And today's generation is greedy and immoral."

"What is this, Philosophy 101?" Lightner asked. "Today's generation is greedy and immoral? Today's cop is hungry for a cheeseburger." He nodded at Riley. "Can we go?"

Riley reread the letter. "This is weirder," he repeated.

"Lawyers." Lightner sighed. "Don't make this more difficult, Riley. I'm starving over here."

"Yeah." Riley thought for a moment. *Don't make this more difficult.* He dropped the copy of the letter into the garbage and headed out for lunch.

*Wednesday
June 22, 2005*

24

THE DETECTIVES' squad room at Area Four, Third Precinct, is filled with detectives and some uniformed officers, too. Detectives Ricki Stoletti and Mike McDermott stand up front. It's nine in the morning. Everyone is on alert, a collective energy in the room.

Everyone is reading the sheet that has been put in front of them, the now-numbered lyrics to the second verse of Tyler Skye's song "Someone."

(1) An ice pick a nice trick praying that he dies quick

(2) A switchblade oughta be great for lobotomy insane a call to me

(3) Precision blade incisions made a closer shave a bloody spray

(4) Trim-Meter chain saw cheerleader's brain's all paint on the stained wall

(5) Machete in the head he isn't ready to be dead I can't explain why I'm in pain why I'm unable to refrain from getting in somebody's brain

(6) Ditchin' life kitchen knife no more itch and no more strife no more hate I passed the test

And on the seventh day I rest.

Ricki Stoletti speaks first. " 'An ice pick a nice trick praying that he dies quick.' That's Ciancio. 'A switchblade oughta be great for lobotomy.' That's Evelyn Pendry."

"So next up is a razor blade," says someone in the back of the room.

Another guy, seated at the table, says, "So all we have to do is find out who has bought a shaving kit over the last ten years." He gets some laughter, but this isn't exactly a merry moment, least of all for Mike McDermott.

Still another guy raises a hand and nods to me. "It says 'on the seventh day I rest.'"

I nod. "The sixth kill is suicide. He kills himself. No more itch. No more strife. No more hate. He's done now. He kills himself on the sixth day, with the kitchen knife. On the seventh day, he rests. Obviously comparing his actions with those of God, in creating the world."

A woman in the back says, "So the offender's gonna do us all a favor and kill himself?"

"Burgos didn't." I shrug. "The first verse called for suicide at the end, too, and he ignored it."

"That's one of the reasons you beat his insanity defense, right?" says an older guy in the back. "Because he didn't follow the song lyrics."

Score one for the old-timer.

"Maybe when he's done with this song," says a big guy, standing against the wall, "he'll follow the lyrics to that old Randy Newman song and start killing short people."

"Yeah, maybe so," says McDermott. "That's strictly fucking hilarious."

The minor burst of animation in the room quiets. When McDermott talks, they listen.

McDermott squints into the air. "Let's start with what we know. We know this offender leaves a totally pristine crime scene. Two kills, no prints, no trace evidence. He holds them down and tortures them. Controls them. The scene is highly organized. Clean entries and exits. He leaves the weapons behind."

He leaves the weapons behind. A good point. Everything else he did, he did on purpose.

He wants us to know.

"And then, page four of the packet," McDermott continues. "We think this is our same guy who sent Riley these."

Everyone flips to the back page.

"The first one—'If new evil emerges'—Riley got on Monday. Two days ago."

If new evil emerges, do heathens ever link past actions? God's answer is near.

"The second one, he got yesterday."

I will inevitably lose life. Ultimately, sorrow echoes the heavens. Ever sensing. Ever calling out. Never does vindication ever really surrender easily. The immediate messenger endures the opposition, but understanding requires new and loving betrayal and new yearning.

"In the first one," I say. "He's saying, if the murders start again, will we link it to Burgos—to past actions? Apparently, he's about to tell us."

"Yeah, and what about the second one?" Stoletti asks.

We've already been through these notes. I went to my office last night and showed them to Stoletti and McDermott.

"Hell if I know," I say, rereading the message myself. "He's mortal? He won't go easily, but he'll go at some point?" I look at McDermott.

"He's talking about understanding," he says. "Understanding the true message, whatever he thinks that message is. Right?"

"You have to be willing to betray convention," I speculate. "To think outside the box. Understanding requires betrayal of the conventional, and the yearning to *want* to understand."

No one comments on that. If anyone has a better idea, they sure as hell aren't speaking up.

"He uses the word 'new' twice," Stoletti says. "He didn't need it the second time. 'New betrayal' and 'new yearning.'"

"Now it's a grammar lesson," says the guy sitting next to her.

She isn't in the mood. "I'm saying he's deliberate about his choice of words. This handwriting is very careful. He didn't write this quickly. He took his time. He thought about every word. 'Never does vindication ever really surrender easily.' It's sloppy. He doesn't need 'ever' because he wrote 'never.' I don't know what it means, but it's weird."

She's right. I hadn't looked at it that way. The handwriting is meticulous. But the choice of words here is odd.

"Let's everyone think about this," says McDermott. "We've got the originals being worked up right now. Impressions, ninhydrin, everything. Let's talk about Fred Ciancio."

Last night, Carolyn Pendry dropped this on us: When she was reporting on Terry Burgos back in 1989, she got a call from a man who said he had some information about Terry Burgos. The man seemed scared, Carolyn said. He said it was important, but he wasn't sure whether to share the information with her. Then he hung up. But Carolyn, ever the reporter, traced the phone call back to a house. The house was owned by a man named Fred Ciancio.

She visited him at the house and he refused to talk to her. She tried more than once to get him to talk, without success. She looked into his background and came up with nothing. And then the trial began and she never followed up.

"So we have no idea what information Ciancio had for Carolyn Pendry," McDermott concludes. "All that we know about him is that he was a prison guard in the sixties and seventies, and then a security guard, until he retired two years ago."

"And," Stoletti adds, "we know that two days before he was murdered, he called the *Daily Watch* newsroom."

Presumably, Ciancio's phone call to the *Watch* newsroom was to speak with Carolyn's daughter, Evelyn Pendry, a *Watch* reporter. Whatever it was that Fred Ciancio had wanted to say to Carolyn Pendry back in 1989, we assume he said to her daughter Evelyn only a few days ago. That would explain Evelyn's questions to me about Terry Burgos. That would also explain her unusual interest in the Ciancio crime scene, according to McDermott.

I look at the handouts McDermott has given us. There is a sheet with the lyrics and sheets with brief rundowns on the two victims, Fred Ciancio and Evelyn Pendry. Something on Ciancio's sheet catches my eye. "Security guard, Bristol Security Services, 1978–2003."

I knew, from McDermott last night, that Ciancio had been a security guard. But I didn't know where.

"Bristol," I say. "Ciancio worked for Bristol Security?"

"Yes." Stoletti nods. "He worked security at the shopping mall in Wilshire. Why?"

I check the dates again. Ciancio worked for Ensign Correctional, a maximum security prison on the southwest side of the county, until 1978. Then he worked for twenty-five years for Bristol. "Bristol Security was the firm that contracted with Mansbury College," I say. "Back in the day."

McDermott watches me a moment. "Did that come into play at all?"

Bristol Security helped us with the search of the grounds for more bodies. I'm sure they were embarrassed that the murders happened on their watch. I think Mansbury canceled their contract after the bodies were found. Like it was *their* fault. But no, I don't see anything. I tell McDermott so.

"Bristol Security is a huge security firm," I add. "They probably have hundreds of contracts all over. It could be a coincidence."

McDermott nods his head once. "Is that what you think? It's just a coincidence?"

I shrug. "Wally Monk was the head guy assigned to Mansbury," I tell him. "Call him. Ask him if he knows Ciancio. I think he's retired but you can find him."

Stoletti makes a note, clarifying the spelling with me.

"So," she asks. "Can we assume that this guy is a copycat?"

There's a collective release in the room. It's on everyone's mind.

Me, I've never been a big fan of the copycat theory. These guys either want fame—in which case, why be known as some other killer's imitator?—or they are deranged and have their own issues to deal with.

But there's no denying the first two kills, patterned after the second verse. There's no denying what he wrote—"I'm not the only one"—on the bathroom mirror.

"Why now?" I ask. "Why sixteen years later?"

No one has an answer for that, of course. Hell, they're looking to *me* for the answers.

"And why," Stoletti adds, "are people associated with those murders dying now?"

Another one nobody can answer.

A woman sitting on a desk, her feet on a chair, asks me, "Were Burgos's victims random?"

I tell her, Burgos always wanted us to think they weren't. He could ascribe a particular sin to each of the women he murdered. "But I don't think these victims are random, either."

McDermott shakes his head, but he's agreeing with me. We both thought that, last night—too coincidental to be random. Evelyn Pendry was at

Ciancio's crime scene, seemingly troubled. And we know from the phone records that Ciancio had called Evelyn just before he was murdered. Then there was the conversation that I had with her, where she pretended to be interested in Senator Almundo's prosecution but, in fact, seemed much more focused on the Burgos case.

She seemed, if memory serves, particularly interested in why Harland Bentley hired me so soon after I prosecuted his daughter's killer.

"Does this remind you of Burgos?" some cop asks me. A big Irish guy. I think they're all Irish. I think it's in the union contract.

I make a face. The answer is, not really. "Burgos, he wasn't careful at all. He brought them to his house. He had unprotected sex with them, leaving his bodily fluids inside them. He left evidence of the women all over his house. He left evidence of himself all over the auditorium basement. *This* offender has performed two perfectly executed kills. He came in and out without a trace, controlled them and the scene. This offender feels like a pro. Burgos was not. That's what I can tell you about Burgos. This offender, I really don't know *what* to tell you."

"And you're our expert on serial killers," Stoletti says.

I shake my head. "Understand this, everyone. I'm no expert. I've never solved a serial killing—not in the way you're thinking. We found six bodies and caught our offender within an hour. That's what I mean about him being sloppy. We found Ellie Danzinger dead, first thing we did was go after the guy who had been stalking her so intensely that she got a restraining order against him. This was also a guy, by the way, who had worked for the last few years as a maintenance man in that same auditorium where we found the girls. And when we went to see him—boom!—there it was. It was all there. So don't confuse me with someone who knows how to track a serial killer. Burgos left bread crumbs all the way to his door. This guy's not leaving anything for us."

"Except notes," someone says.

"And his murder weapons. But that's intentional," I answer. "No doubt, he wants us to make the connection. But that doesn't mean he's going to let us catch him."

McDermott runs his hands through his hair and groans. "I'm supposed to ask you if you'll work with us on this."

I smirk. He couldn't have been less enthusiastic. It isn't his call, I can see.

It's Carolyn Pendry's. The police commander is not stupid, not so naïve that he can't recognize the utility of an ally in the television media. Carolyn wants, Carolyn gets.

"If I have a question," I say, "you answer."

His smile is tight, forced. "Whatever you say, Counselor." Then he moves to the center of the room. These are his detectives, I assume, though I didn't catch a title from him. He reads from a clipboard. "Kopecky, Collins. I want to know every newspaper article Evelyn Pendry worked on for the last year. Especially crime, but whatever. And talk to everyone at the *Watch*. See if Evelyn dropped some hint about what she was doing. Pittacora, I want you to listen to every song that Torcher ever released. Find the lyrics. They're probably on the Internet somewhere."

"Speaking of Internet," he continues, "Sloan and Koessl, look at every Web site devoted to Terry Burgos. The chat rooms, especially. Anything looks interesting, get a subpoena from Judge Ahlfors and get the URLs. If this guy had a Burgos fixation, maybe he decided to drop a line or two."

One of those two, either Koessl or Sloan, a guy who's paying too much attention to his hair, asks me, "Any idea how many Web sites we're talking about?"

"No telling. Dozens, probably." I snap my fingers. "You better look at Web sites devoted to Tyler Skye and Torcher, too. He wrote the lyrics, after all."

"Good." McDermott nods. "Yeah, especially any cross-reference between Torcher and Burgos. Grab as many uniforms as you need. We need that fast. We need all of this fast. Okay." He scans his list. "On that same note, Ashley and Knape, hit the DOC. I want to read every letter that anyone ever wrote to Burgos in prison. You will definitely need uniforms for that. Keep in touch with Koessl and Sloan. Again, a cross-reference would be great."

"You can probably skip the marriage proposals," I add, getting a laugh. At least three women proposed to Burgos while he was on death row. I don't get people. Or maybe my problem is, I do.

"Saltzman, Bax," says McDermott. "On Fred Ciancio. Follow up with this guy, Wally Monk, that Riley was talking about. The guy at the security company. I want to know where Fred Ciancio was working back then. I want to hear from everyone who worked at Bristol Security with Ciancio. Anyone who worked side by side with him, or had a beer with him, or ever smelled one of his farts. And look at everyone assigned to Mansbury College back then.

"Williams and Covatta, also on Ciancio. Find his daughter. Talk to neighbors. Find his safe-deposit box. Anything that could tell us why he might have some secret. And find out who this goon in the background of this photograph is." McDermott takes a photograph, which I can't see, and hands it to one of the cops. "Tell me why Ciancio had a copy of this photo," he says.

I crane to look at the photo but can't see it.

"Powers and Peterson, Ciancio used to work at Ensign Correctional. I want to know about him there. I want to know if he was a good guard or a bad one. And take a copy of this photograph"—he hands another copy of the photo to the nearest cop, who hands it down, again avoiding my eyes—"and see if the goon ever did time at Ensign.

"Kinzler," he adds, dropping the clipboard to his side. "Look at recent releases, especially violent offenders."

Recent releases from prison, he means. A good thought. That might explain the sixteen-year gap in the murders.

"Look at mental institutions, too," I add.

McDermott points at the guy who must be Kinzler, who writes it down.

"Yeah, he's probably a whack job," says Kinzler.

McDermott winces, like someone swatted him in the face. The room goes silent a moment—why, I have no idea.

"Jann, Abrams, Beatty." McDermott, his face colored now, checks off another box on his list. "Recanvass both crime scenes. Maybe Evelyn Pendry talked to Ciancio's neighbors. I want to know what she was asking them."

"Everyone keeps this quiet," Stoletti says. "Our anchorwoman out there"—she gestures toward Carolyn, I assume, wherever she is—"is willing to keep a lid on this for now. I don't think she'll give us long. But let's keep it down as long as we can."

"Go," says McDermott. "Meet back here at five. Get me some answers."

The group gets up, eager to move forward. The one detective, Kinzler, approaches McDermott, but he waves him off, pats him on the arm. Something about the "whack job" comment but I have no idea what.

When the place empties, McDermott touches my arm. "Where would you start? Just on a gut call."

I think about that, and the answer comes surprisingly quickly.

"The nutty professor," I say. "Frankfort Albany. Cassie and Ellie's teacher, the class about violence and women. Burgos's employer back then, too."

"I'll do it," says Stoletti.

"Let me go, too," I say.

Stoletti looks at McDermott, who has the ultimate call. By the look on her face, I think she would rather share a car ride with a flatulent child molester.

"It's not a bad idea," he says. Seems like he enjoys his decision, too.

"What are you going to do?" I ask him.

He tugs at his ear, the corner of his mouth turned up. "I want to see your file on Terry Burgos," he says.

25

HEAD DOWN. Baseball cap, sunglasses. Mustache, beard, eyebrows are fakes, easy to tell it's a getup, but it's okay, point is, he won't see your face, he'll only see the money.

Not the way to do it, but no time, have to hurry, there he is, parking his bike by the building, fluorescent vest, removing the biker's helmet, locking up the bike, now, now—

Leo approaches the messenger, a bag of parcels over his shoulder, Leo clears his throat, holds out the package, look at the package, pay no attention to the face—

He does his best, shows the man the package, bearing the name Shaker, Riley & Flemming. Shows him a fifty-dollar bill, too.

"Yeah—they're up there. You want me—you want me to deliver this?" His eyes focus less on the package, more on the fifty.

Leo nods.

"This"—the kid shakes it—"this is a letter?"

Leo nods. Yeah, a letter.

"Why don't you deliver it? Is this like a joke or something?"

A joke. He likes that. He tries to smile. He tries to smile a lot but he can't.

The kid looks at the fifty and shrugs. "Okay, bud."

Leo watches the boy burst through the revolving doors.

"EVERYTHING," I say into the phone to my assistant Betty. "Witness lists and profiles, summaries of evidence, transcripts—whatever we have. I need a couple of copies of everything. Yes, everything. And Betty, if anyone asks, I'm just doing a speech or something. This stays between us. Call Detective McDermott when you're ready."

I click off the cell phone. I'm riding shotgun with Ricki Stoletti, with whom I have the privilege of paying a visit to Professor Frankfort Albany. Stoletti looks tired, probably as tired as me. She's wearing a blouse, under a plaid jacket, and blue jeans. Not clothes recently purchased.

She tells me she's been McDermott's partner for over two years. She joined the city police four years ago, after spending fifteen years working the Major Crimes Unit in the suburbs. Major Crimes was a consolidation of several police departments in the northern suburbs, a multijurisdictional detective's squad. I know of them well, because I had a homicide case that came from there. That might explain her hostility. I walked a guy on a first-degree and made the cops look pretty bad in the process.

"Why this guy Albany first?" she asks, maneuvering her Taurus toward the expressway to take us down to Mansbury College. "Because he knows this song so well?"

"Because if Evelyn was looking into this, she would have talked to him. And because he knows the principals involved. He taught Ellie Danzinger and Cassie Bentley. He was Burgos's boss. And he was the one who showed these song lyrics to all three of them."

"And because he's a creep?" She looks at me.

"You're about to rear-end that Lexus," I tell her. She hits the brakes. "Yeah, I was never high on that guy."

"Why?" she asks. "Anything specific?"

Nothing specific. Just a vibe I always got from the professor. Something about him that always made me wonder.

"He was a big witness for you, right?"

"You could say that," I agree. "He established Burgos's attempt at an alibi. Burgos was fudging his time sheets, to make it look like he was at work when he was off abducting the women. His time sheets said he worked from six to midnight, but we know he abducted the girls all around nine or ten o'clock. His time sheets were a lie."

I look over at Stoletti, who seems like she doesn't get it.

"By creating an alibi," I explain, "he showed that he appreciated that what he was doing was criminal. He was trying to avoid being caught—"

"Yeah, yeah, I get the idea." She turns toward me for a moment, then seems to think better of whatever it was she was going to say.

"Burgos was given flexible hours," I say. "He could work as much, or as little, as he wanted, up to six hours. He very deliberately wrote down six to midnight. What about this doesn't make sense?"

"Well—no, it makes sense." She makes a noise, an uncomfortable chuckle. "I mean, one way of looking at that is, Burgos *did* have an alibi for the murders." She glances back over at me. "Right? He was at work, so he couldn't have killed the girls."

Now I laugh, with more gusto than she. "But it was a *fake* alibi. Stoletti, if you admit you killed those girls—which he did—and you then claim you were insane—which he did—then the alibi goes from proving you innocent to proving you guilty."

She raises her hand in surrender.

"Anyway, that's why we needed the professor. Burgos didn't testify, so we had no way to pin him to the time sheets without Albany's testimony."

Stoletti gets us on the ramp and we're on our way down south. It turns out that she drives faster than I do, which is probably easier when you carry a badge. We avoid near-certain death maneuvering around a truck and finding ourselves up close and personal with one of those tiny Saabs. I could learn to like this lady.

"So Albany *was* your star witness," she gathers.

"One of them, sure. The alibi put a serious dent in their case. They had a decent argument on mental defect, but on appreciation of criminality, they had no chance. Not after that. I was hoping to get down there alive," I add, after she pulls another stunt, slicing our car between a Camry and a Porsche.

"Don't be such a wuss. You, either," she says into the rearview mirror as the Porsche driver works his horn behind her. I'll be really impressed if she flips him the bird.

"We're not partners," she says. "You know Albany, and you can probably put some ice in his pants, so you're tagging along."

"Fine by me. Unless I need something. You're supposed to be cooperative."

Stoletti knows the rules. I get full access. But all rules are meant to be twisted and tortured. And she doesn't seem to like the way I framed them.

"I do the talking when we get down there," she informs me.

"Ask him whatever you want to ask him," I say. "I'll do the same."

"I take the lead. Understood?"

"No," I say. "Not understood. Get off here. I know a shortcut."

She veers off onto a ramp and points to her bag, which is between my feet.

"There's a manila file in there," she says. "Your copy."

I open it, however much I hate reading in a car. Gives me a headache. But I don't have to read so much as look, because the file is full of photographs from the Ciancio crime scene. Pictures of the man himself, spread across the bedroom carpet, peppered with knife wounds, primarily in the legs and torso, the fatal one going through his eye.

There are several photos of the ice pick itself, a steel rod with sharpened point and wooden handle, with plenty of Ciancio's blood on it. Flipping the page, there is a Xerox copy of what appears to be a dated newspaper photo with jagged edges, having been ripped from the paper. The newspaper photo must have been a black and white and the Xerox isn't the greatest, but I make out a familiar face.

Harland Bentley.

It's back at the time of the murders, I imagine. It looks like him back then, his hair a little fuller, his face a little tighter. He's wearing an overcoat. His eyes are cast downward as he fights through a cadre of reporters holding microphones. I can't place where. Near the courthouse, maybe. Another man is standing in profile a bit apart from the reporters, wearing a fedora, his head turned and his eyes on Harland. Looking at Harland intently, it seems, though photographs tend to have that effect; everyone looks like they're staring in a still photo. The man looks young, though his eyes are deep-set, something that resembles a scar beneath the right one. Don't recognize him, but I'm sure I wouldn't want someone menacing like that looking at me.

I look up. "Take this to the next light, turn right. This is the 'goon in the background'? This is the photo McDermott was handing out?"

She glances over at the photo. "Yeah. We know Harland Bentley, and we know those are reporters. But who's the creepy guy?"

"Well, I've never seen him before. Where'd you find this?"

"We just got it early this morning. It was in a shoe box in Ciancio's bedroom closet."

"It was in with a bunch of other photos?"

"No, it was shoved into a box with a pair of shoes," she says. "He was hiding it."

I watch us fly past other cars, opting to withhold comment on the subject for the time being. I'm thinking to myself, *What was Fred Ciancio doing with a hidden photo of Harland Bentley?*, when Stoletti asks me that very question. I tell her I have no idea.

"Another stop I'll need to make," she says.

"What—Harland Bentley?"

"Yeah." She looks over at me. "Why, you got a problem with that?"

"Well—no, I—have you called him?"

"I had someone check to see if he was in town. He's at the office today. I'll swing by."

"Without calling him?"

She angles her head. "I like these guys better when they're not expecting me. Before they lawyer-up and make things tougher. Our offender's gonna move again fast, I think. We need to nip this thing right now. I don't have time for fancy attorneys." She nods. "Same thing with the professor. He's not expecting us. His class ends at eleven and we'll be waiting for him. Believe me, they're better fresh."

"I didn't know that," I say weakly.

"Am I supposed to care about what you know?"

"In this case, yes." I look at her. "Because I'm Harland Bentley's fancy lawyer."

"Oh, you've gotta—" She puts a palm out, as in stop. "When did *this* happen?"

"About fifteen years ago. I represent all of his companies. It's not exactly a secret."

"Well, it's news to me. Have you talked about this thing with him? This investigation?"

"You don't expect me to answer that."

She pulls the car sharply to the curb and stops abruptly. I half expect the air bag to deploy. She shifts in her seat and gets in my face. "Wait just a second. You're advising Harland Bentley on this case?"

"I didn't say that."

"Yes or no?"

"Harland Bentley has nothing to hide. Relax, Ricki. Don't get hysterical."

She works her jaw as she glares at me. I happen to know for a fact that women hate it when you accuse them of being hysterical.

"I don't like you, Riley," she says. "You get that?"

"I was beginning to get that impression."

"You were, were you? You'll be getting the impression of my handcuffs on your wrists if you think you can play both sides here."

"Detective Stoletti," I say calmly. "Put the car in gear and drive to the campus. It's almost eleven. I'm going to help you find whoever did this, because I think I owe that much to Evelyn Pendry, and because this idiot is sending me letters. And because if you're like any of the other cops who come from Major Crimes up there in the nice, safe suburbs, you couldn't find a Catholic at the Vatican."

She holds her tongue, the color pouring into her face, then shifts the Taurus back into gear. "If I find out you're sabotaging this investigation, you'll need a fancy lawyer of your own." She guns the car and blows a red light. I grip the armrest and hang on.

26

M cDERMOTT LOSES almost an hour in the lieutenant's office with Commander Briggs, some of the top brass from the county attorney's office,
and the media relations guy for the department. A bunch of politicians
readying for the downside and hoping for the upside. He spends less time
giving them an update and more time helping them find the right way to say
it in a press release that will have to be issued, at some point. These guys have
invented hundreds of ways of saying absolutely nothing.

He finds Carolyn Pendry standing by his desk, pacing, on a cell phone.
Her grief has morphed into steely resolve, which makes her somewhat easier
to deal with. McDermott doesn't like the soft stuff, dealing with the victims,
but the only sign of her tears now is the smeared mascara. He doesn't know
to whom she's talking, but he knows she's not enjoying the conversation.

"I appreciate that," she says. "Yes, I have your cell, too."

He casts one eye on his desk, which has now been overtaken with material from the Fred Ciancio and Evelyn Pendry homicides. Inventories, preliminary autopsies, photos, trace evidence workups—or the lack thereof.

He doesn't know if the offender is a copycat or not. All he can say with his
gut is that whoever it is, he isn't finished. Next up is a murder with a damn
razor blade. That's no kind of lead at all. But the fourth murder mentions a
"Trim-Meter chain saw." That's the one. Not just a weapon but a particular
model. He needs to track down the area retailers who sell that brand.

"I can absolutely *assure* you that if I have any comment, you'll be the first." Carolyn Pendry closes her cell phone, her face defiant. In other circumstances, McDermott could get a real rise from this one. This woman is really put together. The physical response brings Joyce to mind. You miss everything about your wife when she's gone. Before they had Grace, and before everything went south, God, they were like hungry animals.

"My colleagues won't leave me alone," she tells him. "Everyone calls to send their condolences, but then it always winds around to wanting a comment. Everyone wants the inside story. I can't take a breath without them standing there." She reads the look on McDermott's face. "And no, Detective, the irony is not lost on me."

"I wasn't going to say anything."

"The reason I'm here." She clears her throat with some difficulty. "Two weeks ago, I did a special on Terry Burgos. The anniversary of his execution. June fifth."

"Okay."

She angles her head, struggling. This woman's job is composure and she's learned well. "I said that he was insane." She forces the words out. "That he shouldn't have been convicted. He should have been locked up and treated, not executed."

There's a question or two in there, but it's better to let this go.

"I think I unleashed someone." She shakes her head slowly. "I said that anyone who would follow lyrics like this—and take them as the word of God—anyone who would do that must be insane. Regardless of how the state defines insanity."

Okay. The point being, someone who had like-minded thoughts got upset at being called insane and decided to do something about it.

"Then why your daughter?" he asks.

"Because there's no—" Her throat closes. She places a hand on her chest to suppress her emotions. She finishes with a whisper: "Because there's no worse way to hurt me." She turns her back to McDermott and weeps quietly.

"I understand the thought," McDermott says gently. "But then we have Fred Ciancio, a guy who called you with 'information' back then, and then called Evelyn recently. And it looks like Evelyn was following up with him. And now they're both dead. If somebody was unleashed, Mrs. Pendry, I'm not sure it was because of your editorial on a TV show."

She turns back around. She seems to appreciate McDermott's theory, which absolves her, but she can't shake the guilt. "I should have stayed on Fred Ciancio back then," she says. "He sounded so scared on the phone. And then when I went to his house—when he realized I had traced his call back to his house—he was terrified. I really thought there might be something there. But then he refused to say another word to me. He got cold feet. And then everything started happening with the trial."

"It was natural for you to drop it," he tells her. "You looked into him, he was a security guard at a shopping mall who refused to talk to you. There was nothing there."

She shakes her head. "I always told Ev, don't be lazy. See it through. Keep trying different avenues. Get your story."

Which, apparently, is what she was doing with Fred Ciancio.

"Did you mention Ciancio to your daughter?" he asks.

She nods. "Oh, it must have been quite a while ago." Her eyes drift off. "Years, I mean. Many years. I used to tell her stories about what I did. She's very good about retaining information. It's why she's such a"—her throat catches—"I mean, was—excuse me, I'm sorry." She brings a fist to her mouth, shuts her eyes.

"No problem, Mrs. Pendry." He can imagine how Evelyn must have reacted, having heard from her mother a long-ago story about Fred Ciancio, a lead that hadn't panned out, a gnawing doubt—and then suddenly the same Mr. Ciancio called Evelyn to talk.

McDermott's cell phone rings.

"Have they found her computer yet?" Carolyn asks.

"No." Evelyn had a laptop computer but it was not at her house and not at her office. The assumption is, the offender took it after he killed Evelyn.

McDermott checks the caller ID and excuses himself from the desk. "Kopecky."

"Mike, that Vicky in the Dumpster. The one in your hood?"

"The Vicky in the—Kopecky, what the hell? You're supposed to be—"

"We got a call from the lab," Kopecky says. "You're not gonna believe this."

27

WE WAIT, Stoletti and I, outside the Green Building, on the campus at Mansbury College. The building is in the quad—the central square of campus, where the students hang out in small groups and toss Frisbees, and probably smoke a little weed when no one's looking.

"Down the street, through those buildings," I say, "is Bramhall Auditorium."

The sun has come out, warming my face and making me uncomfortable in my suit. It's a beautiful day, though probably not such a great one for summer school students. I did that once, in high school. Took typing class over the summer. They wouldn't let us wear shorts to school—the same Catholic school dress code applied in the summer—and we baked as the sunlight poured in. I once told one of the nuns that there was nothing in the Bible that prohibited air-conditioning. She didn't take it in the spirit of whimsy with which it was offered.

"No prints from Ciancio's house?" I ask.

"Nope."

"What about Evelyn's?"

"Nothing." Stoletti puts a stick of gum in her mouth. "Guy didn't leave shit for forensics. Either place. Hey, does it bother you, this guy goes to the second set of verses?"

"The first verses, Burgos already did," I say.

"My point exactly. If he's a copycat, he's not copying."

"Let's ask *him*," I say, motioning to the stairs of the Green Building, where Professor Albany is walking out, a bag over his shoulder, chatting in a friendly manner with a female student. We get close enough to be seen, and wait for him to finish his conversation with the adoring student. He glances at us and begins to stride down the walkway. Then he stops and looks back at me, recognition registering in his eyes.

Stoletti says, "Soft-pedal Burgos, remember?"

I nod to Albany, and Stoletti and I walk up to a man who doesn't seem very happy to see either of us. Stoletti has kept her shield in her jacket pocket, but she has that recognizable swagger. He could probably make her for a cop.

"Mr. Riley," he says, like they're curse words. Up close, I see that time hasn't changed him much. Fiery eyes, a goatee with more pepper than salt that matches long, disheveled hair. The life of a professor seems a fairly easy one, as stress goes. Which makes me wonder how this guy is still a professor.

He's stepped it up in the wardrobe department, I notice. His sport coat is caramel, with a light yellow tailored shirt with spread collar, a tie that pulls colors from both the jacket and the shirt. I dig clothes, and I like the good stuff, but you keep it simple. First-rate but simple. This guy looks like a pretty boy. But, wow, nice threads. What are they paying tenured professors these days?

Which makes me wonder, again, how this guy ever got tenure.

I introduce Stoletti, and we walk in silence to his office. We pass a memorial that Harland built for his daughter and for Ellie Danzinger. Where a small park was once located now stands a small monument, a four-columned canopy, past which is a large park with a fountain on a marble base and a manicured garden and concrete walls with quotes from Gandhi and Bob Dylan and Mother Teresa and similar folks, talking about love and peace and forgiveness.

Albany has a decent-sized office that gets good sunlight. In terms of organization, it's a train wreck. Books everywhere, paper haphazardly placed in piles. There is classical music coming from speakers on a shelving unit behind his desk.

Genius at work, or something like that.

"I read the article this morning," he says, taking his seat behind a large oak desk. "Please." He motions to the two leather chairs.

"Which article was that?" Stoletti asks. I stifle the instinct to roll my eyes. That's a bad start, the dummy routine. You use that when you're looking to put somebody in something. Feign ignorance and let them dig a hole. This guy knows exactly why we're here. I have no doubt that Evelyn Pendry paid him a visit, and you only needed to spend a nanosecond on the *Watch* this morning to learn that one of its reporters was murdered last night.

"You ever talk to Terry after he was convicted?" I ask.

"No." He makes a face like I asked him if he has lice. "Never."

"Professor," Stoletti says, all but throwing an elbow at me. "Do you know a woman named Evelyn Pendry?"

"The murder victim," he says. "The reporter. Yes, she contacted me."

"When?"

"She came by last Friday."

"Tell me about that."

He digs at his ear. "She mostly covered background. She wanted to know the part I played, that sort of thing." He nods his head aimlessly, playing with a fancy pen on his desk. I look around the shelving behind him and see no indication of a significant other. No ring on his finger, either.

"The part you played," Stoletti says.

"I was a witness, Detective. Surely, you know that. Surely, Mr. Riley has carried on at length about his brilliant performance. Everyone hailed the great prosecutor! Everyone scorned the professor, who had the misfortune of employing a mass murderer."

Yeah, that confirms my vibe from back then. He felt it, too. We looked him over pretty hard after we arrested Burgos. Checked his alibis, even searched his house, with his consent. In the end, he proved to be a valuable witness for the prosecution, but he didn't enjoy the guilt by association, and we weren't exactly delicate with the guy.

"Let's stay on track here, Professor," Stoletti says. "Tell me everything Evelyn said to you, and you to her."

"It was pretty much historical background. I guess that's redundant." He waves a hand, but keeps his eye on the desk. "She wanted to confirm dates. She asked me about Terry, the kind of person he was. She confirmed that Cassie Bentley and Ellie Danzinger took my class on violence against women. It was really just a time line and basic confirmation of facts."

"Nothing else." Stoletti's foot wags, but she's otherwise still.

"It really didn't take very long at all." He sighs, then looks at Stoletti. "Oh, she asked me about another man. His name was Fred but I didn't get the last name."

"Ciancio."

"Yes. Yes, exactly." He seems surprised she made the connection. "She asked me if I knew him or had heard the name. I told her I never had."

"Was that the truth?"

He pauses a beat, then chuckles. "Well, of course it was. I have never heard that man's name before she asked."

Stoletti nods and sighs.

"How was she killed?" Albany asks.

Stoletti takes a moment with that. I decide to keep it between the two of them. Maybe Stoletti has another clever response. "We're not sure yet. You got any thoughts?"

"Just curious."

"Why so curious?"

Albany's eyes flicker to mine, in a way intended to be covert, I think. "I thought it might be an ice pick," he says.

"Why do you say that?" Stoletti asks. "An ice pick?"

Albany smiles at her, like he might at a student who couldn't keep up. "Should we say it together, Mr. Riley?" He closes his eyes and recites from memory. " 'An ice pick, a nice trick, praying that he dies quick.' " He opens his eyes and looks at her with satisfaction.

I put my hands together and applaud silently. Albany doesn't know that Ciancio was first, so he got the ice pick. Evelyn got the switchblade.

"You think this is connected to that song?" Stoletti asks.

"Who can say?" He nods at me. "I assume that's why Mr. Riley is here. Last I heard, the counselor was doing quite well in the private sector. Evelyn Pendry comes to my door asking about Terry Burgos, then she's murdered, then here is Mr. Riley himself."

"You have an opinion on the subject?" she asks.

"Not—I'm a teacher," he answers. "Terry took the words of a troubled high school student and read into them biblical implications. Is someone else doing the same? I don't know. I do know there are an awful lot of Web sites devoted to Terry."

"We're looking at those," she says. "Do you? Look at the Web sites, I mean?"

"I've seen them. To the extent that what he did to those women has been glorified, it's part of my class."

"You're still teaching that class?" I ask.

He smiles at me. "More popular, and relevant, than ever. You listen to any hip-hop music lately? They talk about beating and sexually abusing women more often than ever. They talk about having intercourse so violent that it destroys a woman's vaginal walls."

Stoletti nods at him. "And what do you think about that?"

"I think it's disgusting. But, I must say from a cultural standpoint, fascinating, too. We focus on the first verse of the song, by the way," he adds. "The first verse identifies victims—not by name, of course, but how they affected Tyler Skye. Girls who rejected him. Girls who mocked him. The second verse—well, the ice pick lyrics are directed at a man. A couple of them are specifically directed at women. Some of them don't specify a gender. And none of them explains why he's killing them. There's nothing about being rejected or betrayed or insulted. The second verse is simply a description of how the murders will be committed."

That's true. The second verse was less personal.

"We'll need a copy of your course materials." Stoletti thinks a moment. "And a list of your students for the past few years."

"Well, the course materials, no problem." The professor shrugs. "The students' names could be problematic. I think you need to speak with the administration. There are privacy laws, yes?"

Neither of us answers. Albany swivels in his chair and reaches into a cabinet, pulling out three-ring binders, getting together the course materials. Stoletti looks at me with her eyebrows up. Albany slides a course packet across his desk to Stoletti and asks, "Anything else?"

I can see that his initial nerves have subsided and now he's back to being the arrogant asshole I've always known. Good. Now it's time.

"Yeah, one more thing," I say. "You can tell us everything that you and Evelyn Pendry discussed."

He gives me a look, like he already did that.

I fix a look right back on him. He's no fan of mine, but I'm pretty sure he still has a switch I can flip. "Professor, we have the notes that Evelyn wrote up from your interview. We know what you talked about with her. So let's hear it."

Albany looks away, then leans back in his chair and crosses a leg. Then he crosses his arms. A defensive posture. "If you already have her notes, then why are you asking me what you already know?"

"It's your call, Professor. You can tell us or lie to us, like you already have."

Albany loses the color in his face. He's been down the road of accusation with me before. He didn't like it so much last time.

"Then maybe—" Albany's throat closes, which betrays his attempt to stay cool. The smirk is long gone. "Maybe I should have a lawyer present?"

"I'm a lawyer," I say.

"Hey, Professor," Stoletti chimes in. "It's your office. You can kick us out. We'll come back later. Maybe in the middle of one of your classes. I'll bring my handcuffs."

"Listen to me," I say. "You've made false statements to a police officer. That's a felony. But if you come clean with us right now—and I mean right now—you have corrected your statement. No crime. Once we leave, that statement is complete. And false."

The professor gives a wide, bitter smile, coughs a brief laugh, before getting out of his seat and pacing behind his desk. "You blame me for what happened to those girls." He looks at me. "I know you do. Everyone does. I taught a class, teaching about the demeaning ways popular media depicts women, and suddenly I'm the *poster* boy for violence against women. The one person trying to *stop* it is now the one known throughout the country, throughout the academic community, for *sponsoring* it."

He waves his arms angrily. His eyes fill. "Now someone's doing it again and it's going to be my fault all over again."

Having been on the defense side for some time now, I can see his point in a way I never could, as a prosecutor. He's right. In some ways I *did* blame him. Everyone did. He fed this material to a monster who used it to kill six women.

"We're waiting," I say to him.

He takes a moment, a couple of heavy sighs, a wipe at his face, a long shake of the head. "I told that reporter that I didn't know what she was talking about," he says evenly. "Cassie was fighting a lot of demons. What, precisely, I didn't know. On the surface, she had everything. But she couldn't get past whatever was troubling her. She should have been the most popular girl on campus, but Ellie was her only friend. Yes, I knew her a little bit. Yes, I occasionally socialized with the students. But I didn't know *those* kinds of details."

Stoletti is smart enough to let this thing ride out, and we remain quiet until we're sure he's done. Done for the moment, at least. There's more, but I don't know what. I was bluffing before, of course. We don't have Evelyn Pendry's notes from her interview with Albany or with anyone else. We're completely in the dark. I just recognized something in his eyes and acted on it.

"Tell us the details," I try.

"I'm saying I *don't know* the details." He waves his hands, pleading. "I don't know if she was even pregnant, much less whether she got an abortion."

"Keep going," I say instinctively. In my job, you learn to control your reactions. I want to keep the focus on him so it's not on Stoletti or me. Stoletti has a notepad and she casually scribbles something.

Pregnancy? Abortion?

Cassie Bentley?

I feel a burn through my chest. All of this is news to me.

The professor, deflated now, shakes his head. He has nothing more to tell us. I believe him.

"Who told Evelyn about this?" I ask. "How did she know to ask these questions?"

"I have no idea. She's a reporter. She probably wouldn't have told me if I asked. And I didn't."

True enough. Christ, Evelyn said nothing about this to me. Then again, I didn't give her much of a chance.

"Did Cassie even have a boyfriend?" I ask, feeling something swimming in my stomach. That's a question to which I, of all people, should know the answer.

The rumor had been she was gay. And then none of the details of her personal life mattered, not for the case, once we dropped the charges on her murder.

"I have no idea," Albany says.

Stoletti looks at me and I shrug. She slips him her card and gives the standard line, *If you think of anything else, don't be a stranger.* I walk out first, through the hallway, down the stairs and out the door, not entirely sure where I am.

But having some idea where I need to go. I call Shelly on my cell phone.

"What are you doing this afternoon?" I ask her.

28

STOLETTI AND I drive back in silence. She was never exactly warm to me, but since learning that I'm Harland Bentley's lawyer the temperature has dropped still further. It feels odd, the silence, because both of us were floored upon hearing this talk of Cassie possibly having been pregnant and gotten an abortion. Such a blockbuster, and Stoletti treats me like a passenger in a taxicab. I sense that this supposed open-door policy has become decidedly one way.

When she drops me off at the station, I switch to my car. I dial information on my cell phone and ask for a number in Lake Coursey, where Harland thought his niece might still be living. "Gwendolyn Lake," I say.

The operator tells me there are two numbers. "A Gwendolyn Lake on Spring Harbor Road, and a Gwendolyn's Lake Diner on County Road 29."

Party girl–heiress Gwendolyn Lake runs a diner?

I tell him I want addresses as well as phone numbers, and I'll take them for both entries. Then I call my assistant, Betty, and tell her to get directions to both addresses off MapQuest.

I swing by the law school where Shelly works. She's waiting out front. She didn't have to be in court today and it's summer, so she's casual in a blouse and blue jeans. My disillusionment with Professor Albany's revelations notwithstanding, I feel an immediate lift.

She jumps into the car, and I take in her scent. I consider reaching over to kiss her, but then I think, *Slow.* I promised.

But I don't resist when she turns my face toward her and plants one on me.

"So this is how you entertain your dates?" she asks me. "A witness interview?"

I start driving. "It's up north," I explain. "Your kind of country."

Shelly grew up downstate, where her father was a prosecutor before running statewide for attorney general, and later governor. She's a city girl now, but she's complained more than once about not seeing the stars at night and how she misses the clean, crisp, unpolluted air.

"While we're up there," I add, "we can look for a second home. Some place on a lake with a boat."

She doesn't take the bait, so I keep going.

"But first things first: We have to get you pregnant. And then the wedding, of course, at the governor's mansion. I've got a preliminary invitation list. Is two thousand too many?"

I keep my face straight and my eyes forward.

"You mock me, Mr. Riley."

I take her hand, which she reluctantly yields, and kiss it.

"Ms. Trotter, you've never known *slow* like I'm going to show you."

"Don't forget, Paul, I've seen you on the jogging path."

Life is grand. I'm like a teenager after his first kiss.

"Tell me about last night," she requests.

I had to leave Shelly last night when I got the call about Evelyn Pendry. I give her the long version, and because we have almost a hundred miles to go I tell her about Professor Albany today, too.

When I'm finished, she says, "Whoever's doing this has an agenda."

The interstate is relatively clear midday. I push it past seventy as we head through the northern part of the state, mostly underdeveloped, rural flat land.

"The victims aren't random," she elaborates. "Evelyn called Fred Ciancio, and both of them are dead. And he lets you see the weapons, from the song. He writes 'I'm not the only one.' He's not hiding what he's doing. The question is, why?"

She's right about the victims. Ciancio can be linked back to the Burgos case because of the phone call he made to Carolyn Pendry. And then, recently, he called Carolyn's daughter, Evelyn. This is not random.

"The other question," she adds, "is where Cassie Bentley comes in. The thing about pregnancy and the abortion. You didn't know anything about that?"

I shake my head. "The word, back then, was that Cassie had been 'troubled.' That was the word we always heard. Intensely private, too. She had, like, two friends. And her closest friend was Ellie, one of the other victims, so we never learned too much about her."

"Troubled how?"

"Like locking herself in her room. Not going to class. Not socializing. Not even eating." I shrug. "Rich kid who can't be happy."

I feel Shelly's eyes on me.

"Don't be dismissive. It's not easy having a famous family."

Well, Shelly would know. She didn't exactly have a winning relationship with her folks as her father ascended to the highest office in the state.

"Apparently," I say, "it got worse around the time she died. She went into a cocoon."

Shelly doesn't respond, but I know the same words are on the tip of her tongue as mine. *Pregnancy. Abortion.* Enough to send an already troubled college girl into a nosedive.

"Did Terry Burgos know Cassie?"

"Not so far as we could tell. He certainly never said so."

"Do you think these things going on in Cassie's life have anything to do with why Burgos killed her?"

"No," I answer. "I think he killed Cassie because she was Ellie's friend. He needed another victim and she was it."

"What sin did Cassie commit? I mean, each victim had a specific sin, right?"

"Well, that's the thing. The last murder in the first verse was suicide. 'Now it's time to say good-bye to someone's family. Stick it right between those teeth and fire so happily.' He's talking about killing himself. Burgos knew, I think, that he was supposed to kill himself but he didn't want to. He came upon Cassie and killed her instead. Thus, she 'saved' him."

"How did he 'come upon' Cassie?"

We don't know. Burgos didn't testify, and when he talked to the shrinks all he talked about was God and sinners. He didn't get into specifics with any of the girls. I tell Shelly all of that.

"So you don't know how he abducted Cassie."

I feel like I'm on the witness stand. I've seen Shelly cross-examine witnesses and I wouldn't want to be on the receiving end.

"Does that bother you?" she asks me.

"No, it doesn't bother me."

"Then why are we going to Lake Coursey, Paul?"

"Gwendolyn Lake was Cassie's cousin." Other than Ellie Danzinger and a young guy whose name I can't recall, Cassie's cousin, Gwendolyn, is the only person I can think of. She wasn't around when Cassie was murdered, but she apparently flew into town now and then and spent time with Cassie.

"No," Shelly says. "I mean, why are *you* going?"

A smile creeps to my lips. Shelly can read me pretty well.

"You can't stand the thought that something happened on that case that you didn't know about."

Maybe I can't. But instead of responding, I punch the speed dial on my cell phone for Joel Lightner. I press the phone's SPEAKER button and place it between Shelly and me.

"Hey," he answers, having caller ID.

"Joel, I'm in the car with Shelly."

"With—oh, great. Shelly!"

"Hi, Joel."

I give him a brief rundown on what's happened. Lightner is the only person in the world who knows as much as I do about Terry Burgos.

"Cassie was pregnant?" he says. "I thought she was a dyke. I mean—a member of the gay and lesbian community, Shelly."

"You're a true Renaissance man, Joel," she calls back.

"Joel, I talked to Harland the other night. Evelyn Pendry had spoken with him, too. Asked him all kinds of questions about Cassie."

"These kinds of questions? Pregnancy and abortion?"

"He never specified, but my guess would be yes. And he was very concerned about these things getting out. You know, 'Cassie's already suffered enough,' that kind of thing. He wanted me to keep a lid on Evelyn."

"Pretty good lid on her now."

Yeah, that sure is true. I take my foot off the accelerator as I see what has the makings of a police car, hidden behind an overpass.

"Joel, what do you remember about Gwendolyn Lake?"

"Gwendolyn," he muses. "Cassie's cousin. The party queen? I remember nothing, that's what I remember. Mean and nasty, if memory serves—but she was in Europe during the murders so she didn't really matter."

"Right." I sigh. "What was the name of Cassie's friend? The guy who hung out with Cassie and Ellie?"

"Oh, the studly guy."

"Yeah, he was a good-looking guy—"

"Cried like a baby," Lightner says.

He did. He was an emotional guy. Held up pretty well while I prepped him for his testimony at the sentencing phase but broke down on the stand. Sobbed like a child.

"Handsome *and* sensitive," Shelly says. "Is he single?"

"Mitchum," Lightner recalls.

"Brandon Mitchum. Right, right. Joel, find him for me, okay?"

"Why?"

"Why? Because I pay you to do what I ask, not to ask what I do."

"Is this you acting tough in front of your girlfriend?"

I look over at Shelly, who blushes.

"I mean, you guys *are* boyfriend-girlfriend again, right?"

She laughs. I feel the color on my cheeks, too.

"Well, thank Christ," he says. "So—Brandon Mitchum? Seriously, Riley—why?"

Same thing Shelly asked. An itch I need to scratch, or something like that.

"Hey," he says. "Who are the cops you're working with?"

"Mike McDermott," I say. "And Ricki Stoletti."

"Don't know Stoletti."

"She transferred from the suburbs a couple years ago. Major Crimes."

"McDermott's a good man," Lightner says. "I know him a little. He's good. A cop's cop. Went through a tough thing there with his wife."

"How's that?"

"Few years back," he says, "his wife ate a gun."

Shelly recoils. McDermott's wife committed suicide? "Oh, Jesus."

"She was a—what was it?—manic-depressive, I guess. Bipolar in a bad way. He comes home one day, she's splayed out in the bathroom. Three-year-old daughter is curled up in the shower, sucking her thumb."

"Holy shit." I bring a hand to my face. "Three-year-old daughter?"

That explains McDermott's reaction, at the task force meeting, to the "whack job" comment. I can't even imagine what it must have been like for him.

"She didn't see it happen, at least. But, still. Walking in on that? Your mother, with the back of her head blown out? When you're five years old?"

I shake my head. "Okay, well, I'm going. Off to learn about Cassie Bentley."

Lightner doesn't answer immediately. Usually, he's quick with a line. "Suddenly, you have a personal interest in this thing?"

"Maybe I do," I say. "Find me Brandon Mitchum." I punch out the phone.

ANOTHER DAY, ANOTHER HOTEL. This one in the suburbs, a midlevel chain.

Leo laps the place in his car three times, peeking into the lobby, watching in the mirror for any new cars that might be entering the parking lot, because they'd keep their distance, they wouldn't be so obvious.

He is tentative, approaching the lobby, surveying the ambush points, the roof, any cars suddenly moving in the parking lot, but doing it without appearing to do it. He'll be ready when it comes, but they won't be ready for him.

The lobby is empty when he enters, but he steps just inside the main doors and hides in the recesses, waiting for anyone to pass, holding a magazine open, should anyone wonder what he's doing, reading a magazine, just reading, but his eyes are outside, still looking for them. He's pretty sure he wasn't followed, but he'll take no chances.

Five minutes, ten minutes, then he approaches the counter and gives false identification and pays in cash for one night, picks up a complimentary newspaper, takes the elevator up one level and steps out onto the mezzanine overlooking the lobby. Making sure he wasn't followed.

So he waits, casually opening a copy of the Watch. The front page is splattered with the news, murder, brutal murder, shocking murder, staff reporter, daughter of television anchor Carolyn Pendry, young reporter, crime-beat reporter, nothing in there about how quickly she could move, Leo knows, he has the pulled hamstring to prove it, bad pull, bad leg.

A strong will, he could see it in Evelyn's eyes, the defiance on her face, even as he exerted complete domination over her. Like Kat, a lot like Kat, the way she steeled her jaw as she stared at death, not like most of them—most of them, doesn't matter male or female, they freeze up, accept it at the end, the very end, accept it even if they can't believe it—

He takes the elevator and slides a key card into the door. The beds are a pair of twins. He spent so much of the night avoiding a tail, he needs some sleep. He'd prefer a bigger bed, but he's used to a whole lot worse than this. In Lefortovo, the metal rods supporting the thin cushion were spaced so far apart the cushion would fall through. He learned to take newspaper or magazines—whatever he was allowed to read—and stuff them between the rods to provide additional support. But he could never shake the feeling that he was sleeping on a set of monkey bars. They did that on purpose, he knew. They didn't want the inmates well rested. At least not inmates like him.

He falls on the bed and thinks of Kat. She had them all fooled. They saw her as a sweet girl who could never be part of something evil. He remembers tears—his own tears—falling on her face as she stared up at him. She almost made him believe, too.

Two years it took them—twenty-three months and seven days—because he kept count on the wall. Two years of staring into a black door, communicating with fellow inmates by talking into the toilet bowl, down the piping to another cell. Two years of conjuring up ways to get up the wall to the single lightbulb in the ceiling to light a cigarette stub. Two years before they discovered he was right, before the men in the blue piping came for him.

He closes his eyes, feels the exhaustion sweep over him, his eyes sinking beneath the shade of his eyelids.

But then the lightning strike in the stomach, the burning acid. He springs into a ball, the hamstring again, too, he can't relax, can't sleep, not until he's done, and he's not done, not after Evelyn, it has to be tonight, and he doesn't even know where Brandon Mitchum lives yet, lot of work to do, because it has to be tonight—

Leo gets off the bed and heads for the door.

ONCE WE'RE OFF THE INTERSTATE, Shelly reads me the written instructions from Betty. I follow a couple of county roads before I get to the point of intersection between Gwendolyn's house and the diner that bears her name. As it's nearing two-thirty, I call the diner. The woman who answers says Gwendolyn's not around, so I decide to go to her house.

"Fresh," Stoletti had said about interviewing witnesses. No notice. It makes sense. I'd just as soon pop in on Gwendolyn and see what I can find out.

The roads are wide and largely unmarked. I pass trees and various lakes, a blur of dark browns, greens, and blues. The sky is clouding up, but it's still bright, anyway. Living and working among high-rises, I don't get a lot of this. This is what Shelly, who grew up downstate, was talking about, how much brighter and cleaner it is away from the city. It's not like I've never left the city limits, but, despite the money I have, I've never owned a second home, or even vacationed much. The law is my job *and* my hobby. I suppose that says something about me.

Soon the roads are no longer paved and the signage becomes scarce. Following the turns, I find myself in what a city boy like me would describe as a subdivision, a cluster of log and wood cabins spaced well apart, little kids running around in swimsuits, dogs chasing after them.

Hoping I have the right place, I pull onto a gravel driveway and stop my Cadillac, the wheels sliding over crunched stone. The house is nothing special, a rustic pine cabin of modest size, heavily shaded with trees. The smell of freshly cut grass mixes with the airy, lake scent. I stretch my legs before we move toward the cabin. Shelly looks around with a serene expression. I look down the sloping backyard to the lake, and to a woman standing by a green canopy on a dock, her eyes shaded by her hand, staring back at me.

Natalia and Mia Lake's mother was a ballerina in Russia, a beautiful woman named Nikita Kiri-something-or-other. Nikita met Conrad Lake, the heir to the Lake mining fortune in West Virginia who had settled in the Midwest in the forties. The story went that Conrad saw Nikita, then eighteen years old, at the Russian ballet and immediately began to court her, eventually marrying her and bringing her back to the States, supposedly spreading plenty of money among the Soviet politburo to let him remove her from the country. Their daughters, Mia and Natalia, inherited all of their money and much of their mother's beauty; they, in turn, passed their exquisite features down to their daughters, Gwendolyn and Cassandra. I'm more confident of that assessment with regard to Cassie, having seen a number of photos of her over time; I'd seen one picture of Gwendolyn back then, when she would have been a teenager, which I struggle to recall now. She looked like a Lake, I remember that much, much like Cassie and Natalia and probably Mia, a brunette with a slim build and a hint of the Russian heritage in her long jaw and nose, overall glamorous features. I might have imagined her sixteen years later as something of a beauty, the pieces coming together in maturity and helped along with the finest hairdressers and accessories.

The woman who approaches from the dock fits a different bill. She has a more rounded, likable face, generous red hair that drapes lazily past her shoulders. She's dressed simply in a long shirt, cutoff denim shorts, and sandals. But even through her horn-rimmed glasses, I can see a glimpse of the beautiful party girl in her eyes, oval and piercing green, though any glamour is overcome by an extra twenty pounds and the granola look. More of a quiet, peaceful beauty about her now—the polar opposite of her former glitz. More my speed, actually.

I introduce Shelly and myself as attorneys from the city, and after an initial look of concern—"Is Nat okay?" she asks, referring to her aunt Natalia—her expression changes to one that tells me she has put the city well behind her, and is glad to have done so.

"How—exactly how did you find me?" she wonders.

Why? I want to ask. *You didn't want to be found?*

"If I had time to call you and set something up, I would have. I'm sorry. This is very important, and we won't take up much of your time."

She takes a moment for internal debate, and I pray this whole thing hasn't been a waste of time. Then again, if she shuts me out completely, that will tell me something, too.

"There's a thought," I say, "that someone is following the song lyrics again. Some people have been murdered."

That does the trick. Her eyes widen, the expression softening. She points back behind her, to the dock. "I was just about to take a boat ride," she says.

29

McDERMOTT only briefly glances at the glossies of the victim. He already knows the details—the wound to the right temple, then the massive beating she took to the top of her skull, multiple blows rained down on her. Whoever did this had no compunction about what he was doing, no hesitation whatsoever.

That's all he needs to see, and more than he wants to.

Stoletti scoops the photos off his desk and looks through them. She's been partnered with him long enough; she knows he has a problem with female murder victims. She's smart enough to know why, too, though the two of them have never discussed it.

It hasn't gotten easier. He figured he needed time after Joyce's death, after finding her lying dead in the bathroom, before he could look at another dead body without effect. But it's been four goddamn years, and, still, at least with women, he cringes every time. It's about a forty-sixty mix of female-to-male victims. That's a lot of crime scenes you don't want to handle, a lot of photographs you can't bear to study.

He can push out the images at night. He can push them out in the sunlight or in the heat of a busy day. Something about the crime scenes themselves, the smell and feel of death so prominent, that brings it back more vividly than his imagination otherwise permits: The vacant stare of her eyes, the awkward posturing of her body—her legs crossed in rigor mortis, her body toppled to the right like a statute knocked on its side—the pool of blood leading all the way to the bathtub, where little Gracie sat motionless, her eyes squeezed shut, her hands over her ears, her body gently rocking.

He sees these victims, like the one here in the glossies, and he imagines the reaction of the next of kin, something like his own response: Nothing, absolutely nothing, could be worse.

He alternates blame. There are times, yes, when he directs his anger at Joyce, when he attributes to his wife responsibility and self-awareness that he knows, in his heart, she simply no longer possessed.

Most of the time, he finds the right target. He should have seen the changes in her sooner. He should have been more demanding about her treatment.

And what happened the night before her death, and the next morning—there is simply no one else to blame.

Funny, that he never thought of leaving the job. He could make a pretty good argument for why he should. A homicide detective who doesn't like crime scenes is like an acrobat who doesn't like heights. But he's the son and grandson of cops. It's all he ever wanted. It's all he's ever known. He's done it right, too. He's sure of it. He's still a good cop.

Right, a good cop, a solid gut, keen intuition, who couldn't see that his own wife was slowly losing her mind.

"This whole thing," Stoletti says. "It just doesn't make sense."

McDermott snaps out of his trance. "What?"

"This doesn't work for me, Mike. It's weird."

He takes a breath, drops in a chair. Good. Case talk. Familiar terrain.

"How was he with the Albany interview?" McDermott asks her.

"Fine. Actually, pretty good," she concedes. "He got the professor to open up better than I did. He gets the credit for uncovering the stuff about abortions and pregnancies."

McDermott thinks about that. "I suppose, with this new information, you could look on that interview in a different light."

One of the other detectives, Koessl, walks into the conference room and flips open a notepad. "Mike, there are eight retailers that sell Trim-Meter chain saws. Two in the city, six outlying."

"Only eight?"

"Trim-Meter hasn't made a chain saw for almost ten years. A few places sell Trim-Meters used. But none of them has sold one in the last three months."

"Okay, Tom." McDermott blows out. "And they have instructions to call us if anyone tries to buy one?"

"You bet," he says.

When the detective leaves them, they are back where they started.

"Take your personal feelings out of this," he tells Stoletti.

She shoots him a look. She deserves better than that. However she may feel about Paul Riley, McDermott has found Stoletti to be a great cop. First time he ever partnered with a woman, and he wasn't thrilled with the assignment, but she's probably the best partner he's had. Something about the lack of testosterone, the smaller ego—she's always kept a clear head. He's come to find that he relies on her gut as much as his own.

"The question," she says, "is whether this new thing is isolated. A coincidence."

He nods. "It's hard to think this is a coincidence."

"But then that makes Paul Riley a murderer," she says.

Another detective, Bax, pops his head in. "Chief, we got something on Fred Ciancio. Come take a look."

Stoletti looks at McDermott. "To be continued," she says, as they both get up.

McDermott grabs her arm as she's walking out. "The lab should still have samples left over from Burgos, right?"

She says yes. The County Attorney Technical Unit has a massive archives building on the west side.

"We have something now they didn't have in 1989," he says.

She stares at him, then gives a slow nod of recognition. "You want to run DNA tests on Terry Burgos and the victims?"

"I do," he answers. "And we're not waiting two months, Ricki. You tell them what you need to tell them. Use the commander's name. This goes to the top of the list."

DOWN ON THE DOCK, Gwendolyn cranks a large wheel fastened to the boat. I offer to help but she defers, her face showing familiar strain. When the boat is down in the water, she looks back at me, like she's giving me a second chance. She can probably read the expression on my face. "You don't like water?"

Shelly eagerly turns to me as well, suppressing a smile, awaiting my response. She knows very well that I have a minor issue with swimming. The minor issue is, I can't swim. My arms and legs move like they're supposed to, but I sink, every time. Still, I'd be willing to hang glide over the Andes if it would loosen Gwendolyn's tongue.

She starts the engine while we step in. The boat is really one long, flat deck, surrounded on all sides by a white leather safety railing and leather-upholstered seating, with the steering and controls off to one side. The deck rests on what, to my eye, are glorified skis. This is like a giant, water-bound sled.

"A pontoon," she informs me, as she backs the boat out from under the canopy. "So you're the one who charged Burgos," she says. "And now you're Harland's lawyer," she says.

The way she puts it together like that makes me uncomfortable. Not altogether different from how Evelyn Pendry said it. "I am. He's doing well," I add, though she didn't ask.

"No doubt," she mumbles. She moves the pontoon forward, and I sit in relative comfort as the breeze cuts the heat from the overhead sun. We scoot out to the middle of the giant lake, and she idles the boat, which should make the choppiness of the water more apparent, but maybe added stability is one of the benefits of a pontoon. I see lake cabins on both sides of the water, kids jumping off docks and playing on large waterslides. The shouts of people water-skiing or tubing, the grinding hum of motorboats, echo around us.

Gwendolyn's reaction is consistent with Harland's opinion of her. When we were investigating the Burgos murders, Gwendolyn's name came up once or twice, only because there were so few people who knew Cassie. Gwendolyn, from what we'd heard, was the polar opposite of Cassie. Gwen was the spoiled, nasty party girl, Cassie, innocent and solitary. But I never laid eyes on her because she was out of the country the whole time.

Regardless, I have to say, I'm not seeing vile or spoiled in this woman. Time has worked its magic.

"You own a diner?" I ask.

She smiles gently. "The community is losing retail and restaurants. I like having a place where they can get together." She nods, thinking about that.

I decide to take this slow. Gwendolyn's expression turns placid as she lets the sun warm her face. This is her escape.

She offers me a drink from a cooler, but I decline. She takes a seat across from me. Shelly is next to me, keeping quiet. She rolls up her sleeves and the cuffs of her pants and closes her eyes to the sun. Shelly's playing it right. This is supposed to be a casual discussion, and two-on-one makes people uncomfortable. She's just going to listen.

The breeze carries Gwendolyn's coconut tanning lotion to me. She has a Russian's fair complexion and has obviously put the lotion to good use, her skin a dark pink.

Without the benefit of shade, the temperature is almost overbearing. I take off my suit coat, roll up my sleeves, and reconsider that drink offer.

"I like it here," she tells me. "People say what they mean and mean what they say."

I look at my briefcase and notice that I have no pen or pad of paper handy. I'm used to having someone else do the note taking, or a court reporter transcribing every word. But I'm sure as hell not going to pull out a notepad now. Notepads and tape recorders tie tongues. Instead, I rest my arms along the upholstery, put my head against the safety railing, and close my eyes to the sun. I could fall asleep out here. I could sleep for hours.

"Having money," she says, "you don't think about anything. There's nothing outside your grasp. So you keep reaching, hoping for some kind of limit. You don't find it, so you keep pushing until—until you're over your head."

"You were over your head," I say. The boat rocks with a wave.

"Of course I was. I was drinking and doing drugs and sleeping around."

I listen politely to the rich-kid-in-therapy story, the sad, wealthy socialite, dancing from party to party, jet-setting across Europe, when all she really wanted was to be loved.

"What about Cassie?" I ask, wondering if I should be interjecting here.

"Cassie." Gwendolyn deflates, stares at the can of soda in her hand. "Cassie had a big heart. A very generous soul. But she had absolutely no idea what she was doing. She couldn't decide if she wanted to be popular, or good, or what." Gwendolyn chews on her lip, her face coloring. "She was scared to death."

"I'm trying to get a feel for what was going on in her life back then, Gwendolyn. I need your help."

She shakes her head slowly. "I would think you would know better than anyone."

"As I'm sure you know, we didn't prosecute Cassie's murder, so we never got to the point that we were"—I note the look on Gwendolyn's face— "we never delved that deeply. You know that we didn't prosecute Cassie's murder, right?"

She shrugs her shoulders.

She didn't know that?

"Why didn't you prosecute Cassie's murder? I don't understand."

I explain it to her quickly, the notion of holding one murder back, in case Burgos got lucky, to give us a second chance at him. The legal niceties seem lost on her, and I'm still trying to understand how disconnected she was from this whole thing.

"Where were you when all this happened?" I ask. "We tried to get hold of you."

Another shrug of the shoulders. "I didn't know you were trying."

"Where were you?"

"I could have been anywhere. Back then? It didn't matter where I was. It was all the same place."

I sigh. This is like trying to grab hold of sunlight. I need to get this woman off the psychiatrist's couch and onto a witness stand. But I have no leverage here. She could flip me the bird. She could knock me off the boat and I'd drown.

"The Riviera, probably," she says. "Or the Caribbean."

"Then, how about this?" I try. "When was the last time you'd been in the city, before Cassie was killed?"

She poises a hand in the air. "It was probably a month or so before. If you told me it was three months, I'd believe you. If you told me it was three days, I'd believe you."

"Three *days*?" I can't hide the incredulous tone in my voice. "Don't you have some sense of how much time passed between the time you last saw Cassie and when you learned she was murdered?"

"Oh, that's a different question." She wipes a stray bang off her forehead, only to have the wind blow it right back between her eyes. "I found out long after. Months after. I don't think you really understand," she adds, noting my reaction. "My mother was dead. I never had a father. I'm sure my aunt

Natalia was trying to reach me, but she didn't know where I was. I didn't answer to anyone. It's not like there were cell phones, Mr. Riley. And I didn't exactly leave a forwarding address."

I try to see it from her perspective. Maybe my initial thoughts on her were a little harsh. Her mother had died in a DUI, and Gwendolyn apparently didn't know who her father was. I suppose all the money in the world wouldn't make that any easier.

"It sounds very lonely," Shelly says.

Gwendolyn smiles at her. Then she looks at me. "Ask me your questions, Mr. Riley."

"Was Cassie a lesbian?"

"Not to my knowledge." She smiles plaintively. "You go to an all-girls school and everyone thinks everyone's gay."

Okay, fair enough. Mansbury had only recently gone coed when the murders happened.

"Do you think you would know?"

She's amused by that. "Maybe. Maybe not."

"Was Cassie seeing anyone back then?"

"Not that I knew of," she says. "But that's not saying much. I don't recall Cassie dating much, period. She was painfully shy on that level. That was the weird thing. She could be very social sometimes—she would go out and party all night—but I don't think she had ever been with a man."

I think of the song lyrics, and of the passage from Deuteronomy, talking about stoning a promiscuous woman.

"You think she was a virgin?" I ask.

"Oh, I don't know."

"So I take it you don't know if she was pregnant?"

"Pregnant?" She draws back. "Why would you think *that*?"

I see no reason not to share what I know with her. Hell, I've come all this way. "One of the people who was murdered recently was a reporter. She had asked that question about Cassie."

She nods slowly yes, then shakes no. "I have no idea," she says. "I'm not sure I'm the one Cassie would have told, anyway."

Great. This whole trip is feeling like a waste of time.

"What can you tell me about Brandon Mitchum?" This was the

Mansbury freshman who hung out with Cassie and Ellie. Lightner had just reminded me.

Her face lights up. Recognition. "Brandon Mitchum," she says with reverence. "How *is* Brandon?"

"You knew him."

"Yes." She nods, a quiet smile on her lips. "Yes, I knew Brandon. God." She reflects on that memory a moment. "He was a nice guy. Oh"—she frowns—"oh, it must have been hard on him. Cassie *and* Ellie."

"Tell me about Ellie."

"Ellie." She makes a face. "Now, *Ellie,* she was more like me. A party girl. And she was afraid of him." She wags her finger. "She was very afraid of him."

"Afraid of Brandon?"

"No, not *Brandon.*"

I look at her, stone-faced.

"You mean Terry Burgos," Shelly says.

"She thought he would do something," Gwendolyn continues. "She always said a restraining order didn't mean anything to a psycho." She nods with conviction. "No, she was very afraid of him."

A mild breeze brings relief. This whole thing feels so weird. I'm questioning a witness on a boat. Home turf, I suppose, from Gwendolyn's point of view.

"Did you know Burgos?" I ask.

She frowns and shakes her head. "God, no. But Ellie would talk about him. He really spooked her."

"What else can you tell me about Brandon?"

"Well—like I said, he was a nice guy."

"Nice-*looking* guy, I recall," I say. "Anything going on between Ellie and him?"

She opens her hand. "I doubt it, but I don't know. I would spend time with them when I was in the city, Mr. Riley, but I wasn't in the city much. More likely, I'd be in Europe, or L.A., or—God, anywhere."

I take a moment, run through my mental list. "Cassie and Ellie socialized with one of their professors. The one whose class Terry Burgos was in. A guy named Professor Albany."

She nods uncertainly, then angles her head. "A professor, you said?"

"Yes," I say. "Does it ring a bell?"

She looks off in the distance. "I don't know—maybe."

Maybe. *Maybe* this whole trip was a boondoggle.

"What about drugs, Gwendolyn?" I ask. "Cassie. Or Ellie. Were they into it?"

Her eyes cast down. She nods meekly.

"Cocaine?" I ask. "Pot?"

"Coke." She frowns. "Oh, probably both. It was college."

"You ever see them do it? Ever witness them doing drugs?"

She tucks her lips in. "I think I did drugs *with* them."

"You think."

Her eyes fix on me in anger. She doesn't like the interrogation. "You ever try to block something out, Mr. Riley? You deny the memory for so long, until it's not there anymore? So it *won't* be there anymore? You stow it in some secret place in your brain and lock the door?"

I open my hands in compromise. "Gwendolyn—"

"Yes," she spits out. "I'm sure I did blow with them."

" 'Them' being—"

" 'Them' being Cassie and Ellie and—and sometimes Brandon, and sometimes Frank, and sometimes whoever the hell it was who had it at whatever party I was at. Okay?"

She stands up on the deck, the boat being heavy enough to support her without rocking once, and brings a hand to her red face.

"I had a rough childhood," Shelly says. "I know what you mean. You don't just turn the page. You close the book and throw it out."

Gwendolyn takes a moment, then nods. "Exactly."

"We didn't want to come up here and bother you," Shelly adds. "But we feel like we have no other choice. People are being killed."

"Well—" She raises a hand, like stop, as she looks over the lake. "I am truly sorry about that. I really am. But it has nothing to do with me." She gets behind the wheel and works some controls. "I'm going back to my restaurant now," she says. "I'm going back to my life."

Gwendolyn puts the pontoon into gear and moves us back toward the shore. She navigates under the canopy and kills the engine. She cranks that large wheel in the opposite direction to moor the pontoon.

She dutifully shakes both our hands and gives me a surprisingly gentle smile. The outburst was out of character for her, clearly, and she regrets it. But I've been treated a lot worse.

Shelly and I are quiet as we walk back to the car. I start the car and drive out of view before I ask for her opinion.

"She's scared," Shelly says.

That may be. At a minimum, she was dishonest. She went from not remembering Professor Albany to calling him "Frank."

"I think she's a good person," Shelly adds. "But she couldn't decide what to tell you."

"I suppose *that* tells me something right there. But what? She's protecting someone?"

"You'll find out soon enough." Shelly rolls down the window and faces into the wind. "She'll get in touch with you when she's ready."

"Yeah?"

"Trust a woman." She gives my hand a playful grab.

We drive in silence until I get back on the interstate. I put a lot of faith in Shelly's judgment of people and I think she was right on here. Gwendolyn is a sincere woman, someone not prone to evasion who was being evasive. I only wish I knew what she was holding back.

I sense Shelly watching me again and I look over at her.

"Something was going on with Cassie back then," she says. "You think so, too."

I don't argue. Instead, I search the roll call of numbers on my cell phone. When I was with the U.S. attorney, I worked a lot with a guy named Pete Storino with Alcohol, Tobacco and Firearms. He moved to Customs a few years later, and now he's the top guy at the city airport for the Bureau of Immigration and Customs Enforcement.

I get him on his cell and he spends ten minutes giving me grief. The small talk over, I get to the point.

"I need a favor, Pete," I tell him. "Passenger's name is Gwendolyn Lake."

30

H E'S NOT ANSWERING his cell phone," Stoletti says. "His secretary just said he's out of the office."

"Okay. We'll get him soon enough."

While he waits for what should be a very interesting conversation with Paul Riley, McDermott occupies himself with the reports thus far on Fred Ciancio and Evelyn Pendry. They have shit on Ciancio. The inventory looks meaningless. A complete lack of trace evidence. The only evidence they have, it seems, is the murder weapon and whatever they can discern from the body. He glances over the preliminary findings from the autopsy, which don't tell him much, other than the fact that Ciancio's body was ravaged with superficial wounds—

"What's this?" he says, taking a closer look. He reads it again but he doesn't recognize the term. "What the hell is a 'tarsal phalange'?"

Stoletti comes over. "Huh?"

McDermott points to a line in the report, listing the injuries to Fred Ciancio:

```
Postmortem incision at the base of the fourth
and fifth tarsal phalange.
```

"What's a 'tarsal phalange'?" Stoletti asks.

"I just asked *you* that." McDermott sighs. "Sounds like a tail. You think Fred Ciancio had grown a tail?"

"Maybe, Mike. Maybe he was a space alien."

McDermott looks up to see Tony Rezko, one of the CAT technicians. "Say, Tony, any idea what a 'tarsal phalange' is?"

Rezko pauses. "No."

"Then you got something on those notes for me?"

"Something on the second note," he says.

"Beautiful." McDermott drops the autopsy report on the pile of evidence. "Let's hear it."

I DROP OFF SHELLY and return to my office around four. I ignore the blinking light on my voice mail and go straight to the regular mail. I find myself looking for another letter and find none. But then I take a look at the manila envelope at the bottom of the pile. It has my name written on it in Magic Marker, no address. No return address. I open it carefully. Inside is a standard-sized white mailing envelope with the same handwriting, just my name. All indications are, this is another one of these letters. I open the smaller envelope just as carefully. The single page that falls out reads:

> *Others that hunted ensured respect. Sinners know not our wrath. Our ultimate response shall ensure consequences, reviling ethical traitors.*

"Am I even *supposed* to understand this?" I say to no one. "Betty!"

Betty pops in. "Oh, you're back. Detective McDermott was looking for you."

"This was delivered," I say, holding up the manila envelope. "Not mailed?"

"It came in a delivery."

"Timing," I say. "He controls when it gets here."

"What?"

"Nothing. Betty, get Detective McDermott on the phone. And find out who delivered this envelope."

Others that hunted. That's Burgos. *Sinners know not our wrath.* Apparently, it's time to show them?

Betty comes in through the intercom. "We have three messengers who dropped off envelopes this morning," she informs me. "We'll trace it back."

It's probably a dead end. This guy's been too careful. He wouldn't contract with a messenger service, leave a credit card or an address.

After a minute, Betty buzzes McDermott's call through. I tell him that I got another letter, and he should send over a uniform to pick it up.

"Got a better idea," McDermott tells me. "Why don't you stop by yourself?"

REZKO, THE CAT TECHNICIAN, is almost a caricature, a bald head and large, square glasses. If he had a squeaky voice, it would be a trifecta.

McDermott hangs up the phone with Paul Riley, a silent prayer drifting to his lips. "Tell me you found prints on the note, Tony."

"No, no—we had to examine it first. The ninhydrin screws up—"

"Impressions, then," he tries.

"Right. Well, indentations." Rezko is excited. This technical stuff is his life. "On the second note, he'd been writing something on top of it. He left indentations."

Rezko places the note on the desk.

I will inevitably lose life. Ultimately, sorrow echoes the heavens. Ever sensing. Ever calling out. Never does vindication ever really surrender easily. The immediate messenger endures the opposition, but understanding requires new and loving betrayal and new yearning.

"Right," McDermott says, prodding him.

"We didn't have time to go to the state lab for electrostatic imaging, so we photographed it in oblique light: You flatten it on glass, and use a light source positioned parallel to the document—"

These techies, they savor this stuff, it's like a tutorial every time you talk to them. McDermott has half a mind to grab Rezko by his skinny neck, but, hey, it's his profession, it's what he lives for, and he's good at it. He can give the kid thirty seconds.

"—a graphite powder to highlight the indentations, because they were vague—"

McDermott can't resist. "This is, like, when you turn over the paper and use the side of a pencil to shade a background, right? So you can read what's on the other side? Like what we did in second grade?"

Rezko draws back, smiling coolly. He's known Mike for years, he knows it's in good fun. From behind his back, he produces a photograph, showing a series of words written haphazardly, the indentations clear as day in white against the graphite background:

Vilification	*Verity*	*Verbosity*
Vow	*Vindication*	*Exude*
Elucidate	*Eliminate*	*Emanate*

McDermott looks up at the technician. "So these words were written on another piece of paper, on top of the note."

"Right. Exactly. He has a real thing with words beginning with *V* and *E*."

Looking over the note, McDermott finds one sentence that contains both. "Never does vindication ever really surrender easily."

Stoletti had commented on that sentence, too. He didn't need to say "ever," he'd already said "never." The word choice, though deliberate, was odd.

But, like she said: deliberate.

"Thanks, Tony," he says. "Great work."

But what the hell does it mean?

THE MAN WITH the long orange apron puts his hand on Leo and signals to another guy. "Guy needs your help," he says.

Don't touch. Leo slips his shoulder from the man's hand. *Don't touch me.*

"Sorry," the man says.

You touch me again, I'll shove my thumb through your brain.

Leo squats down, pretends to tie his shoe, does a one-eighty in the process, works on the shoelace while he scans—muscular guy in a tank top, pushing an orange shopping cart filled with small pieces of plywood, no, no, he was already here, check the entrance—

A woman walks in, pretty, dirty-blond hair, thin, pink satin shirt, tight black pants, heels, professional but stylish, she looks in his direction—not directly at him, but he knows it now, she's looking for him, he's not stupid, but he can't leave, can't run, not yet—

She turns away from Leo, down an aisle with lightbulbs and extension cords, where she stops.

I see you.

The hardware store is humongous. Most of the aisles are long, north–south aisles, like where Leo is standing, but the woman is down a shorter, east–west aisle.

With a perfect view of the checkout counter. That's her plan. Wait until Leo checks out and follow him.

"What do you need, sir?"

Leo looks up. Old guy, maybe fifty, balding, overweight, nearsighted, sagging flesh on the upper torso that used to be muscle, long orange apron.

He gets the words out: *Chain saw.*

"Sure thing. Right down here. Aisle Eleven."

Leo finishes with the shoe and scans his eyes around the store. Who else? Just one?

A pause. Leo looks up at the man again.

"Get me started," he says. "What do you need it for?"

Leo gets to his feet, pulling down on his baseball cap. The woman is still in that aisle. She glances to her left, toward Leo.

"To cut," he says.

The man gives him a look. A lot of people look at him like that. Like they feel sorry for him. Like they think he's not very smart. "You—you want I should meet you down there, mister?"

Leo nods. The man heads back down toward aisle eleven. Leo is standing near Aisle Four.

White woman, pink top, black pants, covering the exit. She reminds him of Cassie's cousin Gwendolyn.

GWENDOLYN. GWENDOLYN LAKE. He'd heard of her, yes. It was her house, but he'd never seen her. She was never there, but she was coming. She's nice, *Cassie said,* but she can be hard to get to know. Just—don't take it personally if she's a little—short with you. Okay?

Okay, he said. The way Cassie spoke to him, the kindness in her eyes, the warmth of her hand on his shoulder—and he didn't care about her cousin, Gwendolyn. He'd been through worse.

Cassie and Mrs. Bentley were there. He didn't think they were happy about it. Mrs. Bentley kept smoking and pacing outside the house. How long is she staying? *Mrs. Bentley asked.* How long?

Mother, for the last time, I don't know. It'll be fine.

The limousine pulled up within a few minutes. When the driver opened the door for Gwendolyn, she didn't seem happy, either. She was dressed like she was ready for a party. Tight pants with a bright red top. A cigarette in her mouth and a drink in her hand. Cassie ran to the car and hugged her. Mrs. Bentley stood at the doorway and embraced her, too, but with less enthusiasm.

Then Gwendolyn looked at Leo.

So this is the immigrant.

This is Leo, *Cassie said.* Be nice, Gwen.

Oh, right, right. *Gwendolyn twirled her index finger beside her head.* Well, hi there, Leo.

He put out his hand. Gwendolyn looked at it but didn't take it. She leaned into him.

Well, I can see why you and Cassie get along so well, *she said.*

Leo didn't answer. He went to the trunk of the limousine and brought her bags inside. Then he returned to his work, trimming the hedges.

THE WOMAN, pink top and black pants, turns to her left, toward Leo, but she's still far away, several aisles away, she looks up and acts surprised to see a man, a black guy, she greets him, gives him a quick hug.

Black guy with her now, they're good, like they're surprised to see each other, whatever they're saying to each other, he knows what they're really saying, *We've marked him, let's see what he does, you take the rear, I'll take the front.*

You don't fool me.

Leo starts toward them, but they separate, she touches him on the arm and says good-bye—looks like good-bye, anyway—and he walks out of Leo's view.

They separated, getting an angle on him. How many are there?

"Help you, sir?"

Leo jumps. Another man in a long orange apron. He shakes his head while keeping his eyes on the woman.

One thing at a time, no choice here, this is going to have to be fast, he has to do it now, he keeps his head down, walks to Aisle Eleven slowly, his head on a swivel, but he makes it look natural, you've marked me but you don't know that *I've* marked *you*, too, they're not going to make their move inside, they're just looking for information, they just have to report back on what I'm doing here—

He finds the old guy in Aisle Eleven, shelves and containers full of various chain saws.

"I was asking, professional or home use?" the man says. "What are you cutting?"

He needs a Trim-Meter chain saw. He doesn't see one.

"*Trim-Meter?*" The man shakes his head. "Sir, Trim-Meter hasn't made a chain saw for years."

Leo rocks on his toes, biting down into his lip.

The man taps Leo on the arm. "I know how you feel. You get loyal to a brand. That's the kind you've always used, am I right?"

Leo looks at him, sizes him up.

"Always had a Husky myself. That's what I'd recommend. Something lightweight, like a 137 here, will do you fine." He grabs a saw off a tackboard, a long security cord attached to the model.

Leo stares at the man, his hands at his side.

The man sighs. "Okay, well—place called Varten's? Over on Pickamee? Guy over there has lots of old, used saws. I mean, if you're dead set on Trim-Meter, he might have one."

The man gives Leo directions to Varten's, like he's dumb. Like he's a five-year-old.

I'm smarter than I look.

Leo walks back across the store. He lost the black guy. He lost them both. Wait.

The woman's in line. Okay, different now, she's not just a watcher, she's trying to get out of the store ahead of him, she's going to be waiting for him, or she's going to tell others—

They make eye contact, but her eyes dart away, she's in an express line, she's next up, she swipes her credit card and picks up two bags, lightbulbs, yeah, sure, lightbulbs, like he's an idiot.

Follow her out, see where she goes, keep close but not too close, not until it's time, sweep the eyes over the parking lot, lots of cars, but hardly any people, can't tell where the rest of her team is, or how many of them, how many members of her team, watch for an ambush, they could pop out from between any of these cars, head on a swivel—left-right, left-right—quick check behind, they could be anywhere but she was the one who followed, she was the one who stayed back—

She's the one who will report back, who will tell them about the Trim-Meter—

A receipt, carried into the wind, he picks it up, yes, a diversion, a diversion will work, slip out the knife, keep it in the right hand, against his side, close the gap with the woman—

She stops and turns, next to an SUV, nobody around her but hard to tell, other trucks parked on each side of her, smart of her, good cover, hard to see, hard to—

Hard to see her with trucks on each side.

He takes a breath and goes cold.

He steps left, gets an angle, and moves in. She has the back door open, throwing the bags of lightbulbs in the backseat.

Ten feet away. Five feet. Leo holds out the receipt. Shows it to her.

"Oh." Like she doesn't know him. She's well trained. She reaches out and takes the receipt. It happens in a snap. She begins a *Thank you*, looks up at him as his left hand grips her arm, shoving her into the backseat while he sweeps the knife across her throat with his right hand. Hardly has to move the knife, her neck moving across it, doing the work for him.

Not a sound. Her lifeless body falls to the floorboard, which immediately fills with her blood. He pushes her legs in the car and closes the door.

He looks around. All clear. He opens the door again, reaches in, gives the woman his signature touch.

Look around. All clear.

Pick up the keys on the ground, use them to open the back hatch, a blanket and a towel, good enough, take them and cover her. No one will notice unless they're looking hard.

When he's done, he wants a drink of water.

Punch the LOCK button on the remote, clenching sounds of the automatic locks responding, do it again, the car beeps twice, do it again, he likes the sound, *beep-beep*, no time, walk, casual walk, to the rental car.

Get in and wait. Nobody coming. They will soon. He will have to hurry.

Drive in a square, look for tails, look for them, any direction.

Then find that store that sells the chain saw.

I MAKE IT TO the police station before five. I give my name to the desk sergeant, who sends me up. The smells of burned coffee and cheap cologne over body odor, the sure signs of any cop house, greet me before Ricki Stoletti does. Behind her, the station house is buzzing. One cop is typing up a report on a computer, with a distressed woman giving him details. Another, in his office, a captain or lieutenant, is having a heated phone conversation. Other people are moving about, handing each other documents and poring over information. Faces I recognize from this morning. The task force at work.

Detective Stoletti greets me with her usual warmth and enthusiasm. I give her the paper bag that holds the letter I just received from the offender. She hands it off to a uniform and opens her arm to an interview room off the squad room. I follow her in and take a seat. She leaves me in there alone, which feels weird. Before my imagination has the chance to get too far down this road, McDermott walks in with Stoletti. They both make a point of sitting across from me. Stoletti plays with a folder resting in front of her.

"I confess," I say, trying to lighten the moment, but I get no takers.

McDermott stares at me with the poker face.

"You'll need to follow up on those messenger services with that last letter," I add. "See how he got the envelope into my building."

"We will," he says. He rubs his face. "Riley, I'm fucking tired. And I'm in a hurry, because our offender seems to be, too. So help me get my arms around a few things."

"Shoot."

"You don't have to—it's up to you to answer or not."

I stare at him, then at Stoletti. "You sound like a guy who's trying to read me my *Miranda* rights without reading them to me."

As I finish the sentence, I lose my smile. That matches the expression on the faces of the two cops across from me.

"You're here voluntarily," Stoletti says.

That's what you tell people to *avoid* a *Miranda* warning.

I adjust in my seat. "Why don't you tell me what the hell is going on?"

"Why's this guy picking you?" he asks me.

"Because I'm the poster boy. I'm the guy who put away Terry Burgos."

"So he sends you cryptic notes?"

I can't read this asshole's mind. I point that out to them.

"Ever heard of the Sherwood Executive Center?" he asks.

I shake my head. I have no idea what he's talking about.

"Fred Ciancio," he says. "He's working that shopping mall as a security guard, right?"

"Right," I say.

"Well, in June of 1989—about a week before the murders—he puts in for a temporary reassignment. He asks for a transfer."

"To the Sherwood Executive Center?" I gather.

"Give the man a prize." A joke without a smile.

"What's significant about that?"

McDermott makes a face but doesn't answer. He wants me to answer.

"I have no idea," I say.

"Cassie Bentley's doctors were at the Sherwood Executive Center," he tells me. "Sherwood Heights is right by Highland Woods, where she lived."

"Okay?" I don't know what conclusion I'm supposed to draw from that.

"Think it's a coincidence?" he asks me.

I don't answer. I wouldn't know how.

"Reason Fred Ciancio gave for the transfer," he continues. "He said that his mother was undergoing chemotherapy at the building. He wanted to be close to her. He asked for a three-week reassignment to that building, to cover the course of her treatment."

I think about that. Fred Ciancio got himself transferred by Bristol Security to one of their other buildings—a building that housed Cassie Bentley's doctors. I'm not a big fan of coincidences, but life can be strange, and, when it comes to coincidences, this is not exactly earth-shattering.

"The problem," McDermott adds, "is that Ciancio's mother had been dead for ten years. So I don't see where chemo was going to help her much." Now, that's a little closer to shaking the earth. I feel a flutter in my stomach.

"Ciancio used an excuse to work at that building, where Cassie's doctors were, right around when the murders occurred." This time it's Stoletti. A one-two punch. She would be the bad cop, but neither of them is showing me much collegiality. "And then, Ciancio calls Carolyn Pendry and says he wants to talk about the Burgos case. But he gets cold feet."

Why would a security guard make up a reason to be assigned to a building? I can only think of one reason.

"He helped someone break in," I assume. "Someone paid him off to get into one of the offices in that building."

McDermott's eyebrows rise. The notion, of course, has already occurred to him.

"And you think this is related to Cassie being pregnant," I add. "And/or having an abortion."

"What do *you* think?" she asks me.

I shrug. I find myself lacking a lot of answers right now. But it makes sense.

"You'd never heard about Cassie being pregnant, or having an abortion, back then?"

She already knows my answer. I gave it to her right after we talked to Professor Albany.

"You don't have to answer if you don't want to." Now she's provoking me, enjoying it.

"Do I need a lawyer?" I ask.

Stoletti looks at her partner. "He doesn't want to answer, Detective. That's his right."

"I had never heard anything about Cassie having an abortion or even being pregnant," I say, not hiding the anger. "You want to tell me what the hell is going on?"

McDermott speaks again. "Usually, when you're on a case, you work up the victim's background. How is it you didn't know Cassie was pregnant right before she was murdered?"

An icy smile creeps across my face. "First of all," I say, "we don't *know* she was pregnant or had an abortion. We just have a suspicion. You may have learned in cop school about the difference between facts and hunches.

And second of all, the reason we didn't delve deeply into Cassie's background is—"

I freeze on that. From the faces of the cops across from me, this is the next topic.

"Because you dropped the charges on Cassie's murder," Stoletti says. "At the request of Harland Bentley, I assume?" She slides the photograph across from me, the one of Harland and the reporters, with the ghoulish guy with the scar in the background. "The same Harland Bentley in this photo, which we found in Fred Ciancio's closet, hidden in a shoe box?"

"The same Harland Bentley," McDermott joins in, "who hired you and gave you all of his legal business, less than a year later?"

"You, a guy who'd practiced criminal law his whole life," Stoletti punches, "suddenly given responsibility for millions of dollars of civil litigation for BentleyCo."

I sit back in my chair and take a moment. My insides are on fire. I feel the sweat on my forehead, my heart pounding against my shirt.

In my law practice, I will often counsel people who are targets of a criminal investigation. I give them all the same advice. Don't talk about the case with anyone. You never know who's wearing a wire. And if the government calls, don't say a damn thing to them without me—or some lawyer—present.

The human impulse is to talk, to explain away something that appears to be incriminating. The instinct is also to lie, or if not lie, to massage the truth. Cops and prosecutors count on the vast majority of people succumbing to these basic principles. Federal prosecutors make a living on it. Even if they can't prove an underlying charge against you, if you abused the truth a little they will get you on that, and use that to flip you, or put you behind bars, for that reason alone.

Resist the impulse, I tell them. Let the government remain suspicious of you. It's better than being caught in a lie. You can always talk later.

Thing is, I have nothing to hide.

Stoletti is enjoying this. McDermott is trying to read me.

"This," I tell them, "is bullshit."

"Another name that's come up in the investigation," McDermott says, "Amalia Calderone. That name ring familiar to you?"

I shake my head no.

"You never made her acquaintance?" Stoletti asks.

"It doesn't ring a bell," I answer.

"Two nights ago," McDermott joins, "she was bludgeoned to death. Does *that* ring a bell?"

Bludgeoned. *Bludgeoned.* It doesn't fit with the second verse's lyrics. Next up is a straight razor, then a chain saw, then a machete.

"It doesn't ring a bell," I repeat. "Should it?"

Stoletti takes the folder from McDermott and produces three eight-by-ten glossies, in color, that she slides across the table.

I take one of the photos and a groan escapes my throat. It's a close-up of her face, turned to the right. A wound to the right temple, and then massive contusions on the top of the skull. A violent death. She was beaten severely. Whoever did this enjoyed doing it.

"Molly," I say. The woman who lured me outside of Sax's, when I got jumped and robbed. I look up at the cops. "You don't honestly think I killed her?"

"You tell me, Counselor," McDermott says. "Explain to me why your fingerprints were found on the murder weapon."

31

THE SIGN OVER the front of the store says VARTEN'S TOOLS AND CONSTRUC-
TION EQUIPMENT, a run-down shack attached to a large lumberyard. A
bell rings as Leo walks in. The store is empty, save for the clerk, an old guy
behind the counter on the phone. Leo walks up to the counter as he looks
over the chain saws attached to the wall.

Leo looks at the clerk, who holds up an index finger to him while he finishes his phone call. Leo drums his fingers as he looks around the store,
looking casually, just strolling through the neighborhood, thought you
might have a chain saw, yeah. Then his eyes move back to the clerk, and then
to the counter behind which the clerk is sitting.

He sees a scrap of paper taped down on the counter, a single word on it:
TRIM-METER.

He sucks in his breath. Trim-Meter. Pretend to cough, buy some time.

"Help you, sir?"

Leo nods to the wall. He says the words again: *Chain saw.* He isn't looking at the clerk when he says it, but he notes the pause, a couple beats too
long, long pause—

"Any, uh, any brand in particular?"

Shrug the shoulders, act casual. Like you don't care.

Look at the man, elderly guy, spotted forehead, tiny neck, seems relieved,
he likes the answer—

Leo says the brand the other guy mentioned: *Husky.*

"Sure, yeah, sure." That makes the man even happier, he taps the counter and comes around it, now much more animated, happy, shiny and happy. " 'Course, the Husky isn't gonna be the cheapest."

Follow him to the wall, good, he's away from the counter, follow up with him, he said *Husky isn't the cheapest*, ask him what is.

"Cheapest? Honestly, whatever's oldest." The man nods to the wall. "Got a Burly 380 that's good for shrubbery or small trees. Think it's about ten years old." He slaps another one. "This here's a Trim-Meter 220. Has a little wear and tear on it. Probably fifteen years old. These two are my oldest. What do you need it for?"

Same thing the other guy asked.

"Sir, what I mean is, what are you sawing? Shrubs, tree branches, that kind of thing?"

Nod your head yes.

"Give you either one for fifty," the man says.

Shrug your shoulders, ask him something, say something, say something—

What do you recommend? What do you recommend?

But he doesn't speak so well.

The man puts a hand on Leo's arm, like he's trying to help out someone stupid.

Leo recoils, a sharp pivot to the right.

The man withdraws his hand. His lips part and he breaks eye contact with Leo. He begins to slowly backpedal. "Okay, sir, well—well, I'll tell you what, I—I might have something in the back that's cheaper."

Leo shakes his head.

The man freezes, looks into Leo's eyes, then over toward the counter—

"Take whatever you want, sir," he says. "Please."

He feels a chill. He opens and closes his hands. Looks at the elderly man.

"I wish," Leo tries. "I wish it—wasn't me."

Do it fast, use your hands, no blood, *snap-snap*.

Scan the place for cameras. Anyone watching? No time. Drag him through a door that says EMPLOYEES ONLY and arrange some boxes in front of his body, in the corner. Go to the front door and reverse the OPEN sign to CLOSED, go back to the employees' room and finish up with the man.

Grab the Trim-Meter chain saw from the wall, open the door, the chime bids *Good-bye.* He makes it to the car before the pain in his stomach doubles him over.

MCDERMOTT LIFTS HIS HEAD off his hand after Paul Riley finishes his story. Stoletti, next to him, is writing down an occasional note, but McDermott likes to observe. When you're writing, you're not watching.

Stoletti is taking the lead among the two of them, though if anyone is in the lead here, it's probably Riley. Stoletti wanted to do the questioning. She has a real thing with Riley.

Way she explained it to McDermott earlier today, a few years back, Riley defended a guy accused of murder, up in the northern suburbs, which fell into the multijurisdictional Major Crimes Unit, where Stoletti worked at the time. Seems Riley took a pretty good piece out of the arresting officer, a guy named Cummings, during the trial. *Took him apart like a cheap model airplane,* was how Stoletti put it. Cummings took a Level One—a single-grade demotion—when Riley's client was acquitted and someone had to be blamed. Seems Cummings was a mentor to Stoletti, and Stoletti is none too friendly nowadays toward Mr. Paul Riley, Esquire.

McDermott thought Stoletti's hostility to Riley was amusing before, but now it could be a problem. Because now Paul Riley's fingerprints were found on the tire iron used to bash in the side of Amalia Calderone's head.

Riley, who is done with his story, looks at the two cops. Stoletti is writing a note. McDermott just wants to think this through a minute.

"You guys should take this show on the road," Riley says. "Raise your hand—anyone—if you think for one-tenth of one second that I killed this girl."

Say this for the guy, he doesn't back down. But McDermott's seen the bluster before. He's seen the look of defiance dissolve into a mask of terror in the blink of an eye.

"So Joel Lightner leaves," McDermott says. "He thinks you're about to get lucky and he wants to give you some room. You walk out of the bar with this woman. You think you're walking her home. You turn down an alley and you get one fresh on the back of the skull. You wake up, no 'Molly,' no cash."

Riley nods.

"You don't report it. You don't even tell your buddy Lightner because you're embarrassed about the whole thing."

"I felt like an asshole."

"And you're saying, this guy must have wrapped your hand around the murder weapon to frame you."

The police found the tire iron—an L-shaped metal rod with a very bloody lug wrench on the bent end, a prying tip on the other—in the trash, along with Amalia Calderone.

"Either that," Riley says, "or I'm a killer. What do you think?"

Putting the ball in their court. Riley's good.

"You admit being intoxicated," says Stoletti.

A fair point. People do dumb things when they're drunk.

"I could hardly stand," Riley answers. "And even if I could, I'm not a violent person. Your true personality comes out when you're drunk. Like you, Ricki. I'll bet you're even more of a raging bitch after a couple pops."

"Oh, keep *that* attitude up, Riley," she says.

McDermott suppresses a smile. He'll have a technician look over the bruise on Riley's head—the magnitude, the angle—to rule out self-infliction. "What about the hand?" he asks Riley, seeing the bandage near the knuckle.

Riley sighs. "I had to break into my house afterward. He took my keys. I cut my hand on the glass."

"You used your hand?"

"I would've used the tire iron," he answers, "but I left it at the crime scene."

Stoletti doesn't like the attitude, but McDermott is focusing more on what's ahead here. This doesn't work. They have the security tape from Sax's. Riley was almost stumbling drunk. He was wearing a tuxedo. He had nothing with him. He sure as hell wasn't walking around with a tire iron. Could be, it was a weapon of opportunity—it was lying in the alley maybe—but it's hard to imagine anyone in so intoxicated a state pulling it off. And this woman came up to him, not the other way around. Seemed clear from the tape that they were meeting for the first time.

"This woman was a pro, right?" Riley asks them.

Stoletti cocks her head. "Why do you ask?"

Amalia Calderone *was* a prostitute, the high-class, escort variety. She wouldn't be the first to be trolling the bar at Sax's, late night, which is how she bumped into Riley.

"She seemed like it, in hindsight," he explains.

"Where's your tux?" Stoletti asks.

"Dry cleaner's." Riley looks at them. "I was lying in a pile of trash, for Christ's sake. Ask my dry cleaner if there was any blood on it. Other than my own, at least."

"We will."

"Good, Ricki. Do that." Riley stands up. "And while you're at it, why don't you take the tire iron and shove it up your ass? I'd be happy to put a fresh pair of fingerprints on there and help you out."

McDermott raises a hand. "Sit down, Riley. You're talking pretty good smack for a guy with prints on a murder weapon who was the last person seen with the victim. You know damn well we could arrest you on suspicion right now. Sit," he repeats, pointing his finger down.

Riley takes a moment, then puts his hands on the table, leaning over toward the detectives. "Same guy," he says. "Had to be. This isn't a coincidence. That's the lead you should be following. Every second you waste trying to make me for this poor woman's killer is another second he walks around with a straight razor, or a chain saw, or wherever he is in that song."

McDermott exchanges a look with Stoletti. "Let's say you're right," he says to Riley. "You said it yourself. No razor. No chain saw. No machete. No kitchen knife." He shrugs. "If this is our offender, why does he deviate from the song?"

Riley shakes his head. He surely doesn't know, either. "All I can think," he says, "is this is payback. This guy is taking a personal interest in me. I mean, I'm the damn poster boy for the Terry Burgos prosecution."

"Yeah," says McDermott, "but you're *alive.*"

Riley doesn't have an answer for that. But that's the key problem here. If it's the same offender, why did he bypass the poster boy, Riley, and kill the woman with him? And then go to the trouble of wrapping his prints all over the murder weapon?

He thinks of Carolyn Pendry and her explanation of why the offender would go after her daughter: *There's no worse way to hurt me.* It made sense to McDermott. Hell, the worst way to hurt *him* would be to hurt Grace, his daughter. Maybe the offender took Amalia Calderone for Riley's girlfriend, tried to hurt Riley the same way he hurt Carolyn, by going after a loved one.

"He wants me involved," Riley says. "He's sending me notes. He kills someone walking next to me. He puts my prints on the weapon. He wants me to be a part of this."

But why? Why does the offender want Riley in on this?

McDermott nods at Riley. "Let a techie check out the wound on your head," he says. "The hand, too. We've got a CAT unit upstairs."

Riley straightens, smooths out his suit. "You wanna rule out self-infliction." He laughs. "Okay, sure. And then when the fun and games are over, maybe you guys could solve a crime or two."

McDERMOTT TAKES RILEY up to the CAT lab. When he walks back down, Stoletti is still in the interview room. "Something's not right here," she says.

McDermott eases into the chair. "You said Riley was helpful at your interview with the professor."

She agrees with that. "Albany was holding back on me. I didn't see it. Riley did. Why?" she asks, trailing his thought. "You think it was a song and dance for me?"

McDermott doesn't know, but it's a thought. "Riley asked to go along. Hell, he's the one who *gave* us the professor's name."

"And if he comes on strong with the professor, he looks like he's trying to get to the bottom of this." Stoletti seems to warm to the idea. "He's a smart guy, no doubt about that. But how does Amalia Calderone fit in?"

McDermott sighs. "Maybe it's more cover. It's an attack on him."

"Well, I'm no CAT techie," she says. "But that wound to his head didn't look self-inflicted to me."

"I'm not saying self-inflicted." McDermott shakes his head. "I'm not saying Paul Riley is killing these people. But he had a point. This guy wants him involved. He's going out of his way to make private citizen Paul Riley part of this thing. Why?"

Stoletti thinks on that. Neither of them knows.

"Maybe," McDermott tries, "he wants Riley's *help*."

Stoletti seems uneasy with that. She moves out of her chair and paces the interview room. McDermott's eyes move over her body. Her frame, courtesy of a German mother, she's said, is large but firm. Maybe her two teenage boys keep her hopping. Maybe being single again prompts her to watch her figure. They don't talk much about their personal lives. It's been a shield, he realizes, that he has kept raised for three years.

"I'm no fan of Riley," she says. "But still, Mike. Let's think about what we're saying here. We're thinking that someone else did Cassie Bentley and he *knew* it. He cut her murder from the case to cover it up. He got a nice big reward for doing so—all of the legal work Harland Bentley could throw at him. And now someone's opening a door that he wants closed."

"That case made him." McDermott gets up, too. "He jumped from Burgos to millions a year as Harland Bentley's lawyer. It's not a bad motive."

"Well, I'll say this much," she adds. "If he's a part of this, hopefully we've shut him down now."

"We keep him on the outside," McDermott decides. "We watch him, and we use him if we need him. I don't care what Carolyn Pendry wants."

The truth is, McDermott is less concerned with what happened during the Burgos case at the moment. The time will come for that. His first priority is stopping the flow of blood. If this does involve Professor Albany, or Riley, maybe they've put the fear of God in them. That leaves one person.

"Let's go see Harland Bentley," he says. "And get hold of Susan Dobbs at the M.E.'s lab. I want to know what the hell a tarsal phalange is."

WHEN I'M DONE BEING inspected by the county attorney technicians, I step out into the humid evening air and call Joel Lightner. Before I can say anything, he tells me, "I found Brandon Mitchum. He lives here in town."

"Great."

"Hand him off to the cops," he suggests.

I actually laugh, though I'm not feeling especially cheery. "They're off on wild-goose chases," I say. "I think I'm on my own here. Give me Mitchum's address."

———

McRae and Richmond. He parks at the corner, uses his binoculars, up to the third floor. Large canvas on an easel near the big window, violent swirls of purple and red splashed across it. Like splatters of blood.

He appears in the window, poising a paintbrush over the canvas, low evening sun spilling through the window, wearing a ratty shirt and gym shorts, long, stringy hair covering his handsome face.

You haven't changed a bit, Brandon.

32

CHECK THE REARVIEW MIRROR: Woman walking her dog on the sidewalk, another woman jogging, half past six and the sun is just now falling below the buildings. Nobody pays attention to Leo, no one ever does, but that's okay, it makes him better at what he does.

Okay, the street's clear now, the woman with the dog turns the corner, no more people, good time to do it. Look in the mirror one last time, get out, forget about the hamstring, check the road and work over the lines. Evelyn Pendry. Police. Evelyn Pendry. Police.

This isn't good, not the way to do it, no choice now.

He takes in the smell of curry from the Indian place down the street. He swallows hard, looks both ways, limps across the street. The short walk helps loosen the hamstring. He reaches the brick building and sees MITCHUM by the buzzer 3B. He hits that button, a shrill noise.

I'm smarter than him, he'll believe it, he will.

Police. Evelyn Pendry. Police. Evelyn Pendry.

A moment passes, then the violent sound of open air. A voice: "Hello?"

Evelyn Pendry. Police. Evelyn Pendry. Police, police, police.

All that comes out is *Police.*

A pause. Open air again: "What is this about?"

"Evelyn Pendry." He opens and closes his hands, rolls his head.

The intercom cackles again. "What about Evelyn?"

"Need to talk."

Good. Perfect. Need to talk.

"Okay—all right—I'm on three."

"Buzz me—"

"The door's broken. It just opens."

Leo breathes in deeply. He looks at the door, notices it's slightly ajar. He bites his lip. He could have walked right in. He could have snuck in.

No time. Take the first staircase, hit the landing, adjust the sport coat, check the wallet again for the fake badge, adjust the glasses, take a breath, you're a cop, you're a cop—

I'm a cop, Brandon.

Police, Mr. Mitchum. Need to talk.

Will you remember me, Brandon?

THEY WOKE HIM. *It wasn't hard. He didn't sleep well. A dream involving dark water creeping into his lungs, drowning him—*

But now he was awake. The voices. Gwendolyn, Gwendolyn Lake, was back home again, the second time since Leo had come to America to live here.

His room was behind the main house. He walked up to a window to check. He saw them, playing the stereo, drinking and smoking, Cassie and her friend, Ellie, and Gwendolyn and a boy. The window was open, and he could hear them laughing, the music blaring.

Oh, hey. *Cassie waved to him.* Did we wake you?

He shook his head and smiled.

This is my friend Brandon. *She pointed at the boy.* Leo *waved and walked away.*

But he heard them. Ellie's voice, he knew it well by now.

That's Leo, my boyfriend, *she said. They all laughed. Even Cassie.*

He went back to bed. But he didn't sleep. He opened his window and listened.

NO, BRANDON, you won't remember me. No one remembers me. Bend at the waist to stretch the hamstring, then keep going, hit the landing on the third floor.

The door to the right is ajar. A face is peeking through.

"What is this about, Officer?"

Officer. Good.

"What happened to Evelyn?"

Dead. A word he can say well.

Hold out the wallet, focus on the wallet—

Mitchum glances at the badge but looks longer at Leo.

Do you remember me, Brandon?

I remember you.

Mitchum opens the door but keeps the entrance blocked. "What happened?"

He can't turn back now. This isn't how he does this but here he is, he won't get another chance—

Murdered. Another word he knows well.

Mitchum looks over Leo hard, then down at his wallet, which is closed again. "What did you say your name was?"

I didn't, Brandon.

Leo hands him the wallet, just like with the woman in the parking lot, simple misdirection, Brandon, while you're opening the wallet to check the badge—remove the straight razor, flip it open while I step on your foot, so you can't move, then the blade under your chin, and if you move, if you move, Brandon—

Mitchum's eyes are frozen with terror. He gets it.

Grab his hair with the free hand for leverage, force him back, an awkward dance, until you're in, close the door, push it closed behind you, the smell, that smell, marijuana, yeah, like in Lefortovo, smuggled in, supposed to help the time pass but it always seemed to slow things down, slow, slow, like this last hour of your life, Brandon, so very slow.

I REMEMBER STOLETTI'S WORDS, about liking witnesses fresh, unprepared, unrehearsed. I decide to skip the buzzer to announce my presence, given that the security door is off its lock. As I take the final staircase, I hear voices in Brandon Mitchum's apartment. I knock on the door and hear a harsh whisper, then utter silence.

My breathing halts. My chest fills with heat.

"Brandon Mitchum?" I call out. I move to the side of the door, reach over and knock again, as I hear more noise above the pounding of my fist. A crashing sound, then violent footsteps across a hardwood floor.

I take a deep breath and brace my voice to keep it free from a mounting fear.

"Police!" I yell.

I turn the knob. The door's unlocked. I look into a loft, a twelve-foot ceiling, a couch, and a large window overlooking the street. A man lying on a rug near the couch, blood spraying from his face.

Someone is running toward the back door, his sport coat flapping. I give chase, without thinking. The man is shorter than me, a little wider, but he isn't moving well, a bad leg, and the adrenaline pours through me as I realize, in the space of a second or two, that I will catch him.

In the time he takes to open the back door, I lunge into him from behind with a bear hug, hoping to freeze him in place and keep his arms at his side. His body gyrates to the right, trying to shake me off. I try to hang on tight, but his right arm frees up and he jerks an elbow back into my face, an overwhelming force to my forehead. Stars flash through my eyelids, but my left arm comes up around his neck. He tries again with the right elbow, but I'm too far to his left now. I throw a punch into the base of his skull. I rear back again, but he spins before I know it, facing me now, putting a hand on my throat and throwing me backward—

I think of Shelly. I remember the first time I met her, in court, as opposing counsel, that crusading stride, that force of conviction. I loved her before I even knew her.

—My head slams against the wall. I fall into a heap on the floor. Through bleary eyes, I look up at the man, the same man in that photograph, behind Harland Bentley and the group of reporters. His eyes are lifeless, dead, but then he cocks his head and blinks his eyes.

"You," he says.

I try to gather myself into a defense, but he rushes out the door and down the fire escape. I struggle to stay conscious, try to focus, thinking of the phone, searching for it, from the kitchen floor, as I hear the man's footsteps barreling down the fire escape. I hear the screams from the other room, from Brandon Mitchum.

I don't try to stand, not sure that I could handle it. I crawl across the kitchen floor and reach up to the kitchen counter, sweeping my hand as I lose balance. I knock to the floor a pen, paper, and portable phone. The back of the phone breaks off, exposing the battery pack, which, luckily, is still intact. I lift the phone as I fall on my back. I dial the three numbers, and struggle for just those few seconds I need. The words come out, in no particular order—*intruder, attacker, someone's hurt, ambulance, police*—and then I go black.

LEO TURNS THE CORNER of the alley and stops, clutching his hamstring. He heads back toward McRae Street, running in front of Mitchum's building. They could be anywhere, he knows it, but he doesn't have a choice.

Traitor. Fucking traitor.

He keeps close to the building so anyone looking out, from Brandon's place, won't see him. But they already saw him, they already saw him.

I don't understand. I don't *understand.*

He starts up the car and drives off, keeping the speed under the limit.

Hands. Hands. He knows it. Prints. No time to clean up. He left his prints. Prints on the door. They'll know now. They'll know it's me.

All right, Paul Riley. You've made your choice.

I know how to hurt you.

"BRANDON," I say, fighting to wipe the darkness from my eyes. I struggle to my feet, staggering toward the cries in the front room of the condo. I find him in the fetal position, blood squirting between his fingers, which are covering his face.

"Tell me where he cut you," I say.

"My cheek," he shouts, his voice muffled with his hand. "Help me!"

"Ambulance is coming. Hang on, Brandon, you'll be okay." I manage my way back to the kitchen and find a damp rag, resting in the sink. I bring it to Brandon and press it against his face. He tries to sit up, pressing the rag against the wound, blood all over his shirt and the rug. I squat over him, examining him. Looks like it's just the cheek. Shouldn't be fatal, but the face has a lot of blood vessels and you bleed like hell. "Keep the pressure on it."

"Oh, my God," Brandon mumbles, gripping my sleeve with his free hand. "Oh, my God, thank—thank you."

"Do you know him?" I sit on the couch near him.

"A—cop," he manages, spitting the words out, unable to control his breathing.

I put a hand on his shoulder. "He's gone now, Brandon, okay? You're safe. This guy was a cop? Or he said he was?"

Brandon nods, his body shivering, both hands now on the rag against his cheek. This guy must have pretended to be a cop. I look back at the door, then around the place.

"He wasn't wearing gloves," I say.

"He knew about—he knew about the fa—the—"

From outside the opened front door, I hear footsteps pounding up the staircase.

"He knew about what, Brandon?" I ask, my face close to his. This doesn't look fatal, but this may be the last chance I get to talk to him. "Brandon, this is important. He knew about—"

"The father," he says, as two uniformed police officers burst through the door.

33

YOU DON'T BARGE into the offices of Harland Bentley unannounced," the commander says. "Not based on your *gut,* Detective."

McDermott grips the phone, looking at Stoletti and shaking his head. It was her call—a good one—to get clearance before bursting in on one of the wealthiest men in the world. If something went south, the governor would hear about it, the mayor would hear about, the commander would hear about it, and McDermott would hear about it.

"Sir, this is about his daughter—"

"I understand what this is about. You can interview him, and you can do it fast. But you set it up. You don't barge in. You tell him it's urgent, but you show him every courtesy."

McDermott stays quiet. He's afraid of what might come out of his mouth.

"Listen, Mike—you tell me he's a prime suspect, I give you a different answer. You may be onto something with what you're telling me. But you might be dead wrong. This might be some psychopath who wants to bring back Terry Burgos's crusade."

"Yes, sir."

"Set it up, Detective. Handle it right."

The line goes dead.

"Shit." McDermott hangs up the phone. "Christ on a bike, he wants me to stop a serial killer, but only if I mind my manners. Set it up," he says to Stoletti. "We have to set it up."

He checks the message on his cell phone. A call from the morgue. Susan Dobbs returning his call.

"Working late, Susan?" he says when she answers the phone.

"I'm eating dinner, Mike. You called my cell phone. Don't tell me it was an accident."

"Okay, I won't."

"I don't know why I ever gave you that number."

"Because you're a dedicated public servant."

"You were calling about the Ciancio autopsy?"

"Yeah, it says there was an incision between the—hang on." He grabs the autopsy report. "A postmortem incision at the base of the fourth and fifth tarsal phalange."

"Right. The fourth and fifth toes. There's a web of skin between the fourth and fifth toes. He sliced it. After the guy was dead."

"Why you think he did that?"

"You're the cop. But it was deliberate, I'll say that. You'd have to go out of your way to separate the two toes and make the incision. You don't do that accidentally."

She's right about that. Ciancio was wearing socks when he was found, tortured and murdered. The offender went to the trouble of making that incision after everything else he did to Ciancio and then putting the sock back on.

Deliberate, like Susan Dobbs said. This offender isn't doing anything by accident. He's doing everything he wants to do. And he's doing it well.

PART OF THE JOB. It never goes as planned. You improvise. It's what makes you good.

The adult video store is boarded up, seemingly abandoned, but Leo knows that it's open. He pushes through the door, walks past two aisles of magazines and videos, and heads directly to the counter.

The man sitting behind the counter is thick through the neck and shoulders, reading a newspaper and mumbling under his breath.

"*Menja zovut Leonid,*" Leo says, introducing himself.

The man peeks over his paper with disinterested eyes. "*Leonid?*"

"*Da.*"

The man speaks through the newspaper, still poised over much of his face. "*Kogda?*"

"*Sejchas,*" Leo answers. *Now.*

The man directs him down the street, but Leo already knows. The warehouse has no sign, just a single unmarked door along the alley. Leo knocks on it. After several locks are opened, another oversized man, with a belly fighting to get out of a dirty white shirt, opens the door, turns his deeply set eyes past Leo, and lets him in.

He smells bad. Like grease and booze. Booze and grease.

Inside, stolen cars are being stripped for parts. The sounds of the equipment at work echo off the high ceiling. Even with the wide-open space, the smells of body odor and tobacco fill the air. Another reminder of Lefortovo. Men smoked continuously to pass the time. Time was meaningless, but it was all they had.

The man takes him into a small room with a round table.

"*Skol'ko?*" Leo asks.

"*Dvesti.*"

Leo nods, turns his back on the man, peels two hundred dollars from his roll, and sets it on the table. The man picks up the money and leads him through the warehouse. Leo doesn't look at the men working on the cars. He listens to the drumming of his heart. He listens to the blood coursing through his head.

The man opens a large door with a key. Inside, over a dozen women are springing to attention, seated on beat-up couches and chairs. The room is warm. The women—girls, some of them—are scantily dressed, halter tops and hot pants or tiny shorts. Cheap perfume and cigarette smoke fill the air. Some pop music is playing on a small portable stereo.

He surveys them. Some of these girls are teenagers. Most of them have damaged skin, bruises, in one case. Their eyes are dispassionate. Most of them are skinny, though not toned. He finds the one he wants and nods to her.

"*Skol'ko vam let?*" Not that he expects her to reveal her true age.

"Dvadcat' odin," she says. Twenty-one. That's a lie, closer to thirty, liar. He asks her for her name, so she can lie again, that's all they know, lying—

"Dodya," she answers. He points to her. She'll be fine.

The room upstairs is small, dim, and dirty. It takes him back yet again. Lefortovo held eight to a cell, and the ceiling was much higher, but the confined feeling is the same.

He thinks of Kat, even pictures her face. He closes his eyes as if that will erase her. When he opens them, this one, "Dodya"—

—He knew a *Dodya* in Leningrad, a chubby, sad girl, with orange-blond hair, who they teased, made Leo feel sad because he knew what it was like, but he didn't do anything, let them tease her and make her cry—

Dodya wiggles out of her shorts and removes her top. Her body seems undeveloped; her breasts are flat and her ribs are prominent. She looks at him for direction, but he says nothing, does nothing. She approaches him and reaches for the buckle on his pants.

"Net," he says. Shakes his head slowly.

She steps back. *"Ja ne ponimaju."*

But she understands just fine. He uses the back of his hand, to avoid any significant bruising. She falls to the hard floor. Touches her cheek. Looks back up at him for direction.

He unzips his own pants. She watches him, unsure at first if she's supposed to watch or look away. Soon she understands: She is supposed to watch.

When he's satisfied, he zips up his pants and draws near to her. He notices that she winces as he approaches her. Also notices that she doesn't try to move away.

On his way out, he stops at the same room where he first negotiated the deal. The fat guy has his feet up, reading a magazine about automobiles.

"Ja hotel by kupit Dodya," he says.

The man stares at him a moment, his thick eyebrows meeting in confusion. Then he bursts into laughter. He enjoys the moment, then looks at Leo, a man, he seems to understand, whom he should not regard lightly.

"Skol'ko?" Leo says. *"Odna tysjacha?"*

The man grows serious. He thinks about it a moment.

They settle on eight thousand.

I WANDER AROUND THE hospital, holding an ice pack to the back of my head. They say it's going to be some time while they work on Brandon Mitchum. A plastic surgeon is being called in to sew up the side of his face. Turns out he had a number of other superficial wounds, too, on his torso, but nothing life-threatening.

The cops told me to stick around. I gave them McDermott's name, and he's presumably on the way. But they're letting me wander. Mitchum couldn't say much by the time the cavalry arrived—he may have been going into shock—but he managed to describe me as the hero, not the villain, in the story.

So I walk outside, enjoying some fresh air and the chance to use my cell phone. First call is to Shelly. We were going to see each other tonight. I assure her I'm no worse for the wear, and, no, there's no point in her coming to the hospital, I'm just going to be tied up with a bunch of cops who—this part I leave out—aren't viewing me in the most favorable light right now.

"Lock your doors, baby," I tell her. "No kidding."

"What about *you*?" she says to me.

A natural response, but it gets me to thinking. This guy had his way with me. No doubt, he could have taken me out. But he let me go. Throw in Amalia Calderone in the alley on Monday night, and that's twice he's let me live.

You, he said to me, like of all the people in the world, he never expected to see me.

Those letters he's sent me. I need to see those letters again.

"I love you, Shelly," I tell her. My heart does a flip, circumstances notwithstanding.

Second call is to Harland Bentley's cell. He's out at some restaurant, probably with a new cover girl. I impress upon him the importance of the call, and he says he'll call me right back.

He does, and I can tell from the traffic sounds that he's outside now. I give it to him quickly, everything that's happened. He lets me finish, and then says, "The police want to interview me tomorrow."

"Harland, did you hear everything I just said?"

Silence. Someone is laying on a horn in a big way in the background. The sound effect feels appropriate.

"I heard," he says.

"Brandon mentioned 'the father.' The guy from the photograph almost just killed me. Again. You want to help me out with any of this?" A near-death experience brings out a lot of things, but one of them is not diplomacy, not even for your multimillion-dollar client. Plus, I'm beginning to feel like I was left out on a story back then on one of the murder victims.

"Not over the phone," he says. "Call me when you're done there."

"It could be a while."

"When you're done," he says firmly, "call me."

McDERMOTT AND STOLETTI show up about five minutes later. The responding officers are there, a man named Wilson and a woman named Esteban. Riley is sitting in a chair down the hallway, holding an ice pack against his head.

Esteban gives them the rundown, the call from dispatch, the response to the building, Riley holding Brandon Mitchum in his arms when they burst in, the things they learned afterward.

"Looks like Riley saved Mitchum's life," says Esteban, nodding in his direction.

McDermott looks over at Riley, who sees them but stays where he is. "You believe that?"

"Yeah, I do. The vic, Mr. Mitchum, he was clutching Riley, thanking him."

"Riley says the offender was 'the guy from the photo,'" says the other cop, Wilson. "He said he had a scar. That mean anything to you?"

"Yeah." McDermott feels a chill course through him. The guy in the photograph, behind Harland Bentley and the bank of reporters.

"We've got the CATs there," Esteban says. "This guy Riley kept telling us to look for prints."

That makes sense. If the offender was posing as a cop, he couldn't very well be wearing gloves. And he wouldn't have had time to clean up. This might be a break.

Stoletti says, "That's very helpful of Riley."

Wilson and Esteban don't get it, of course. McDermott does. He makes his way over to Riley, who gets up.

"You okay?" he asks Riley.

"I'll live."

Yes, you will, he thinks to himself. *That's twice now.* "What were you doing there?"

"Brandon Mitchum was Cassie's and Ellie's friend at Mansbury. The three of them were tight. I thought if anyone might know something about Cassie being pregnant, he would."

"And you didn't think to tell us?" Stoletti says. "You're playing cop now?"

"I thought someone should."

"All right, pal." McDermott steps closer to Riley. He's no fan of lawyers but he doesn't have a real problem with Riley, not on a personal level. Still, things are starting to get real coincidental. "Tell me what you can about this. Leave out the damn commentary."

Riley gives them a story that sounds a lot like what they just heard from the responding uniforms. It gets interesting when he reaches the part about confronting the offender.

"*You,*" McDermott repeats. "Like he knows you. He's surprised to see you."

"Or, like he couldn't understand why you were stopping him," Stoletti adds. "Why would he do that? Why would he think of you as an ally?"

Riley doesn't know. "I'll say this much. I had some height on this guy, but he handled me like I was nothing."

"He was strong."

"Yeah, I suppose he was strong, but that's not what I mean. He knew what he was doing. I tried to get this guy in a headlock from behind, and, in about two seconds, he'd slipped out, spun around, and pushed me against the wall. Seemed like he had some training."

McDermott deflates.

"He had an accent," Riley adds. "Eastern European, seemed like. Let's talk to Brandon, he might know more when he's sedated."

McDermott puts out a hand.

"Oh," Riley says. "I'm not invited?"

"You're not invited. You're lucky I don't take you into custody."

Riley eyes them a long moment, then puts out his hands for the hand-cuffs.

"Oh, cut the fucking drama."

Riley drops his hands. "By the way, you're welcome. I'm leaving."

Riley brushes past him. McDermott looks at Stoletti. Neither of them is entirely sure what to do with Riley. Under certain circumstances, the play might be to lock him up. Clearly, they could claim his prints on the tire iron for justification. But Paul Riley's not someone you lock up unless you have a good reason.

"He was sloppy tonight."

They turn to Riley, who hasn't gone far.

"His first two kills," Riley explains. "Perfect planning. In and out without a trace. Clean kills. He messed this one up."

"How so?" Stoletti asks.

"The front door to the building," he says. "Security door. It's busted. I walked right in. But this guy didn't. Brandon buzzed him up."

McDermott thinks about that. "If this were well planned, he would have known the security door was busted."

"And he would have ambushed Brandon. Like he did with Ciancio, and probably with Evelyn, too."

"So why is this different?" Stoletti asks.

"I don't know. You're the cops. Figure it the hell out." Now he walks away.

McDermott calls out to him. "Stick around town, in case we need you."

"Yeah, right."

This guy. The problem with lawyers, they know their rights. McDermott can't stop Riley from doing anything, not unless he arrests him, and Riley knows that better than anyone.

But he made a good point, about the attack on Mitchum. Why was it different this time? The well-planned, cold-blooded executioner is suddenly improvising.

"Let's talk to Mitchum," he says.

34

THE SIXTY-THIRD FLOOR of BentleyCo Tower is reserved exclusively for its CEO, Harland Bentley. Taking up the entire south side of the floor is Harland's personal office, a palatial job with an interior conference room and a private bathroom and spa. There are large and small conference rooms on the north, east, and west sides, and then the gratuitous luxuries that Harland affords himself, including an entertainment room with embedded stereo and speakers, a sixty-inch plasma television and leather chairs; an exercise room with a stair-climber, treadmill, stationary bike, and assorted weight-lifting equipment; and sleeping quarters on the north side, too, though I haven't seen them, and I doubt there is much "sleeping" going on in there.

But tonight, I am led into what Harland calls the "Green Room," where my client stands over a golf ball and knocks it wide of the hole on the putting green. Instead of cussing, he simply uses his putter to tap another orange ball in front of him, and says, "You're late."

That's Harland. We're meeting, as agreed, after I left the police at the hospital, but still he's putting me on the defensive up front. The assistant who escorted me into the room—a private security guard with an earpiece and wraparound mike who speaks in a deep British accent—leaves us alone in the room.

Harland taps the next one wide left, too, banging the orange ball off the wooden backdrop, and this time he spits out a cuss. "Hate making the same mistake twice, Paul. Know what I mean?"

No, I don't, and I'm in no mood for games. I almost got killed for the second time this week by a guy who tried to frame me for murder, and I have cops breathing down my neck for my trouble.

"You had something to tell me," I say.

Harland, in the midst of measuring up another putt, freezes in place. This is his way of showing offense. He decides what, and when, to discuss topics. He returns his focus to the ball and taps it straight into the hole, which proceeds to spit it back out and off to the right. "There," he says. "I'm not keeping my wrist straight." He takes a break from the putting and looks at me for the first time, as if finally attending to an annoying child.

He is wearing a bright blue shirt, open at the collar, with immaculate slacks, and caramel loafers polished to a shine. His sport coat, matching his shoes, is hanging on the door.

"While you kept me waiting," he says, "I had the chance to review some recent invoices. I see for the month of April, I paid your firm over 1.2 million dollars in fees."

That sounds about right.

"I take it," he says, "you enjoy being my lawyer."

I don't respond.

"I take it you'd like to continue being my lawyer."

I open my hands. "Harland."

"I just want to know who I'm speaking to, Counselor." He places the putter in the small stand and puts on his sport coat. "Am I talking to someone working for the police or am I talking to my lawyer?"

I take a moment with that. A guy with his kind of money, it's always an implied threat. But he's never said it before.

"I didn't realize I'd have to choose," I say.

"And if you did?"

"I'm a lawyer, not a cop." I'm too stubborn to entirely capitulate, but I gave him what he wanted.

The smug expression returns. Harland always gets his way.

"Good," he says. "Then we can talk." He moves past me. I follow him down the hall to his office.

A DOCTOR EMERGES FROM Brandon Mitchum's room and tells McDermott and Stoletti that the patient is ready for a short interview. McDermott is on his cell phone, a call he just got from the CAT unit.

"Looks like we got some latents off the door, Mike," the lab tells him.

McDermott's heart does a leap. A break—maybe. Best thing they've had yet.

And just like Riley predicted.

"Okay, no one goes home until we've run them." McDermott punches out his cell phone before he can hear the groan on the other end. He gives Stoletti the good news. "Finally, we catch some damn luck."

Brandon Mitchum is in a hospital bed, awake but sedated. His face is heavily wrapped, but his cloudy eyes, peeking over the bandage, stare at the photograph of the man standing in the background behind Harland Bentley.

It only takes a beat, looking at the photo, before Mitchum inhales sharply. That's as good as an identification.

"He said he was a cop," Brandon says, handing back the photograph. "He had a badge. Said—said he wanted to talk about Evelyn . . ."

The sedatives are doing their work. Good, for his sake, but bad for McDermott. He reaches for Brandon and touches his shoulder. He needs this kid tonight, not tomorrow.

"I didn't want to let him in," Mitchum continues. "He sort of forced his way in."

Right. Put his hand on the door. Thus, the fingerprints.

Brandon asks, "Evelyn's dead? Was that part true?"

Stoletti answers. "She was murdered, yes."

"Ohhh . . ." Mitchum's eyes close. "And it was this guy?"

"We think so, yeah."

His eyes still closed, Mitchum swallows hard, nods his head. "I was next. I could tell."

"We need to know what happened, Brandon. Hard as that may be."

"I know." His eyes open, turn toward the window. "Guy was a freak."

"Start at the beginning," McDermott says. "He says he's a cop. Comes up. You let him in—"

"Before I knew it, he put that blade against my throat and pushed himself in. He got me"—his voice halts—"on the floor. He—God, the guy was, like, crazy. He started talking, like, almost gibberish. He said my name over and over. 'Brandon, Brandon, Brandon.' Then it's, 'Tell me what you told her, tell me what you told her.' He knew I'd talked to Evelyn."

Brandon shakes his head absently. McDermott is suddenly glad for the sedative. "You're doing great," he tries.

"He started with the blade." His hand reaches to a spot on his hospital gown around the rib cage. "He stuck it in pretty good. Y'know, it wasn't gonna kill me. It just hurt."

"Right. Sure."

"I told the guy, Evelyn just wanted to know about Cassie and Ellie and Gwendolyn."

Gwendolyn. "Gwendolyn—Lake? Cassie's cousin?"

Brandon doesn't respond, lost in the nightmare. "So he goes, 'Gwendolyn, Gwendolyn, Gwendolyn.' He gets all excited. 'What about Gwendolyn? What about Gwendolyn?' Then he goes again with the blade." Brandon slashes his fingers diagonally across his chest. "I yelled out but his hand was over my mouth. He'd do that. He had one hand on my throat, but before he'd cut me he'd cover my mouth."

McDermott thinks about what Riley said when he struggled with the offender—the guy knew what he was doing. He'd done it before, too. He managed to torture both Fred Ciancio and Evelyn Pendry in what appears to have been relative quiet. That's not easy to do.

"So, then I told him what I told Evelyn about Gwen. I told him about the fight."

"The fight."

"Yeah, back during finals that year—y'know, late May, early June of that year—a couple of weeks before the murders. Gwendolyn came into town. Y'know, she'd do that. She'd pop in from Europe, or the Caribbean, or wherever, and she'd party with Cassie and Ellie. Anyway, Cassie and Gwen, they didn't exactly get along. They were so different. Gwen was, like— aggressive, I guess. Kind of harsh, y'know? But, okay, so Cassie and Gwen had some monster fight, like, a few days before exams started. It was one of those things, we were—well, we'd been—we weren't necessarily sober, I guess—"

"I don't care about that, Brandon. You guys were, what, stoned? Wired?"

He nods. "We'd been doing some blow. So, we're at the house, and it's me, Cassie, Ellie, and Gwen. It's, like, three in the morning, we've been out, and now we're back at the house—"

"House. What house?"

"Oh. Gwendolyn's house. Her mother's house, which was now all hers. Y'know, her mom died in a car crash a few years earlier. I think Mrs. Bentley moved in there, after the divorce. But this was before that."

"Go on, Brandon."

"So, anyway, Ellie and I had basically passed out on a couch downstairs, and, suddenly, upstairs, Cassie and Gwen are having some knock-down, drag-out fight. I mean, everyone was pretty fucked up. I'm not sure Ellie even woke up. But, anyway, yeah, there was this big fight, and, by the time I'm on my feet, realizing what's going on, Cassie's running down the stairs and out of the house. She jumps in her car and drives away."

"Why were they fighting?" Stoletti asks.

He shrugs. "I never knew. She wouldn't talk about it. And, honestly, the next day, for me, it was back to studying. I needed to do well. Ellie and Cassie, they didn't need grades. They had all this money. But not me. I had to cram for finals."

"Point being," McDermott says, trying to move it along, "you never really got the scoop."

"Right. I have to say, the rest of that week, Cassie was even moodier than usual. Normally, I'd hang with her more, get her to open up to me. But not that week. I was afraid I might flunk Sociology."

"And you told this to the intruder."

"Yeah." He clears his throat painfully, his face in a grimace. "Yeah, it wasn't quite as calm as now, but, yeah—I told him they had a fight, I didn't know why. Then he was like, 'What else about Gwendolyn, what else about Gwendolyn, tell me, tell me, tell me'—I mean, this guy was whacked-out. Meanwhile, he's cutting my skin, muffling my shouts. I mean, this guy was, like, totally out of control, but, y'know, totally *in* control, too. In control of me, at least."

McDermott rolls his hand to keep Mitchum on story.

"Well, then, I'm telling the guy, I never saw Gwendolyn again after that— I mean, like, couple weeks later there was the murders, and then, y'know, there'd be no reason I'd ever see her again, I guess. She was Cassie's cousin, and Ellie's friend. I wouldn't have expected her to look me up again."

"All right—"

"So then it's on to Cassie, and he's doing the same shit. 'Tell me, tell me, tell me.' Man, I didn't even know how to answer that. But then he says to me, 'Fucking father, fucking father, fucking father,' and then I know what he's talking about."

McDermott rocks on his toes.

"He goes into this ramble. First he says 'Fucking father,' like, eight times, then he says 'Evelyn, Evelyn, Evelyn, Evelyn,' then 'What did she say, what did you say'—I mean, this guy. I thought he was going to do it right there, just stick that blade in my eye or slit my throat or something. He cut me again on the chest."

"So what did you tell him about the 'fucking father' thing?"

"The truth. See, that week, that week of the fight, Cassie was all upset, like I said. Worse than usual, and she was always a troubled girl. Sweet as candy but really unhappy. So, anyway, I heard her on the phone, in her dorm room. I'm walking by, and she's yelling into the phone. At least, the last part she's yelling. She says, 'You're the fucking father!' And I walk in, and I'm, like, 'What's wrong?' But she wouldn't talk about it."

You're the fucking father. "And the intruder knew about that, Brandon?"

"Yeah, he knew about that. He must have gotten it from Evelyn. Because *I* told *her.*"

Makes sense. Brandon told Evelyn, and Evelyn must have told the offender, probably under compulsion. So now the offender wanted to get the full story from Brandon.

"Okay," Stoletti chimes in. "You told the intruder about the 'fucking father' story. Then what?"

"This guys says to me 'Who's the father, who's the father,' going on like that. But then he freezes, he covers my mouth and looks at the door. I could hear it, too. Footsteps. Then Mr. Riley is banging on the door, and I think he yelled out 'Police,' which was pretty smart of him."

"And then what?"

"Well, I saw it as my chance. He took one swipe at me with the blade, and I think he was trying to kill me, but I moved, y'know? He caught my face.

Then he was off and running, and Mr. Riley came in, and Mr. Riley went running after him, and then—well, that was it."

McDermott nods. "What took place between Riley and the intruder?"

Brandon shakes his head. "I was so freaked-out, I couldn't tell you. I thought I was gonna pass out, and Mr. Riley ran in and called 911, and put a towel on my face and talked to me." He blows out a nervous sigh. "Thank God for that guy. He saved my life."

The door pops open. A doctor walks in. He wants a moment to check on the patient. McDermott nods to Stoletti. They're not done, but it's not a bad time for a break.

Out in the hallway, Stoletti walks in a small circle, a habit when she's lost in thought. Usually, she does two or three laps, then comes up with something good.

"Maybe this idea of Cassie being pregnant isn't such a bad one," McDermott says. "Sounds like Cassie had an angry phone call with the father of her child."

Stoletti stops and says, "The offender was doing the same thing to Mitchum that he did to Ciancio and to Evelyn Pendry. The superficial wounds. But now we have a different context for it."

McDermott agrees. "We thought he was torturing them for fun. We were wrong."

She nods. "He was interrogating them. He wanted to know what *they* knew."

"This isn't a copycat, Ricki." McDermott looks up at the ceiling. "This is a cover-up."

35

WITH TREMBLING HANDS, Leo tapes the photograph on the bathroom mirror in the hotel room. He calms himself, uses a breathing exercise Dr. Pollard taught him, straightens himself, and tries to smile at the photograph. She needs him to be calm.

It's a double from a high school yearbook photo. Her head is tilted in a slightly unnatural way, her focus just off center. She is wearing a simple, pink V-neck sweater with a charm necklace. Her hair is freshly cut, above her shoulder, her smile simply angelic.

You look pretty.

In his mind, the conversation is fluid:

No, I don't.

Yes, you do. I promise, you look pretty. And I don't want you to worry. I'm going to take care of everything. They're going to say things about you, but I will stop them. I won't let anyone find out.

But Brandon's alive.

I know he is, my love, my beautiful, but I have a plan now.

He traces his finger over the outline of her face. Very pretty, so very pretty.

I love you, Leo.

And I love you, Cassandra.

If you love me, then tell me your plan.

Shhhh . . . please don't worry.

Leo puts his face close to the photo, brushes his lips against her forehead. I have to go now, but I'll be back soon.

ROUND TWO WITH BRANDON MITCHUM. He looks calmer now, as the sedatives do their work. He chews on his lip as Stoletti and McDermott resume their places.

McDermott realizes that Riley is right. The offender was sloppy this time. He's off plan now. He must have Evelyn Pendry's computer, which is why they can't find it. He's reading what she had written about her investigation. He found Brandon Mitchum's name and paid him a visit, but he worked quickly—just one day after killing Evelyn—and didn't have time to scout out the place. He didn't know that the security door on Brandon's building was busted. Didn't think he had time to break into the apartment and ambush him, like with the others.

And he's good. He's skilled at controlling people, and he knows how to pick locks.

Evelyn was on the right track, and now the offender is following the same trail she was, trying to clean it up. Evelyn talked to Ciancio and he's dead. Evelyn talked to Brandon and he was next. They know Evelyn talked to Professor Albany, too, which is why McDermott just put in a call and sent a patrol car to Albany's house.

Stoletti begins. "Did Evelyn Pendry tell you what she was up to?"

"Writing about Terry Burgos, I assumed." Brandon's voice is scratchy and flat now. He's wearing down. "Doing some exposé or something."

"An exposé," McDermott says, joining in again. "Something beyond background."

Brandon brings a hand to the bandage on his face. "Evelyn—y'know, she's a reporter, so—she was pretty coy about the whole thing. Protective, y'know, about her story. But she seemed concerned. I got the feeling that she thought there was more to the Burgos murders than everyone thought. She was all interested in Cassie and Ellie and Gwen, like I said. Seemed like, as much as anything, she was just trying to get down their personalities."

"So give them to us."

Brandon's eyes move to the ceiling. "Mansbury, y'know, it fancies itself one of the elite liberal arts colleges, right? And it is, I guess. But you get an elite school, you get a lot of money. Lots of trust fund babies, y'know? Me, I came from downstate, but Cassie and Ellie? They had money. Cassie, obviously—but Ellie's family owned some big steel manufacturer, I think, in South Africa."

"Anyway?" McDermott prompts.

"Yeah, anyway. Ellie? She was one of these rich girl partiers. Nice enough girl, don't get me wrong, but she didn't have a whole lot of—I don't know, what's the word?—substance, maybe? Yeah." He chuckles. "Not a lot of substance. Trendy clothes, expensive hairstyle, all the right connections. Oh, she was okay, I guess. But the only reason she ever gave me the time of day was Cassie.

"Now, Cassie," he says, realizing that the detectives are listening closely, "was a real sweetheart. I mean, that girl had soul. Know what I mean? She had more money than God, but she was such a generous spirit. She did volunteer work, she studied hard, she was always there if you needed her. But here's the thing—"

McDermott rocks on his toes.

"Cassie was *so* fucking messed up. I mean, look, she's got all this money and everything, so I'm not saying we should play the violins for her. And she wouldn't have wanted that, either. It's more like, she just wasn't really sure who she was." He sighs. "She could never make herself happy. I had no idea why. She was kind, she was intelligent, she was beautiful, but she was a train wreck inside. And then, after that fight with Gwendolyn—I mean, there was no talking to her. She was a basket case. Here, everyone's cramming for finals, so we're all a little off-kilter, right? But Cassie? I mean, she wouldn't eat. She wouldn't talk. And as far as anyone could tell, she wasn't even studying. After finals that year, we're all heading out for one last hurrah before summer break, and Cassie sat in her dorm room with the door locked. I mean, she even gave Ellie the cold shoulder, and Ellie lived with her."

McDermott sneaks a peek at Stoletti. He knows what she's thinking. This sounds a lot like a girl who had just found out she had an unwanted pregnancy.

"And I was thinking to myself," Brandon adds, "I didn't know who Cassie was talking to about whatever was bothering her. She hated her father—"

That's interesting.

"—And her mother? Nat? I mean, I never met her, but—well, that lady was 'overmedicated.' That's the PC way of saying it. She was a pill popper. And that was her family. Well, there was Gwen, the cousin, when she was around, but even when she *was* she was no help. I mean, *that* girl was a freak. She partied harder than Ellie. Those two were peas in a pod. Cassie wasn't like them." Brandon comes out of his memories and looks at McDermott.

McDermott watches him a moment, a common tactic—stare at someone and he'll keep talking. But Brandon seems finished, and, if anything, his eyes are beginning to cloud as exhaustion and sedation do a one-two on him.

"All of this, you told Evelyn," he gathers.

Brandon nods.

"And what did she say back to you?"

"Well, she asked me the same thing you're gonna ask me—if Cassie was pregnant, and, if so, who would have been the 'fucking father'?"

McDermott smiles tightly.

"I don't know if she was pregnant," he continues. "I understand the suspicion. Hell, most people thought she was gay. I admit, I was curious about that myself. So now we're taking a big jump to not being gay, and being pregnant to boot."

"So," McDermott says, "let's jump."

"Look, I don't know."

There's an obvious name here, but McDermott doesn't want to be the first to say it. It would make sense, too. It wouldn't be the first time a college professor slept with a beautiful coed. And said professor would be none too pleased about that coed turning up pregnant. He could see how Professor Albany might play the risks: If Cassie turned around and accused him, he could always deny it. It would be a he-said, she-said. But if she were *pregnant*, it would be an entirely different story. Paternity tests. Tangible proof. End of promising career.

"Cassie didn't have a lot of friends—certainly not male friends," Brandon says. "I was pretty much the only guy."

Another obvious thought, but McDermott has already discounted it. He trusts his gut, and this kid isn't pulling any chains—especially now, after he stared death in the face and has a strong sedative calming him. Mitchum isn't lying. He wasn't the father.

Come on, Brandon.

"Well, okay—here—this was something Evelyn and I talked about, too. There *was* one guy, a C.S. prof. A—a professor in cultural studies. Oh, right, of course." He snaps his fingers. "The guy who taught the class that Terry Burgos sat in on. Professor Albany was his name. Frank Albany."

Stoletti says, "Why does his name come up?"

"Oh, he was—" Brandon makes a face. "He was one of those—you know, these professors who socializes with the students? I always thought the guy was kind of creepy, personally, but Cassie really thought he was the shit."

"The shit."

"Cool, I mean. She really looked up to him." He thinks for a moment.

"You discussed that with Evelyn."

"Yeah, she was all interested in how much time Cassie spent with Albany."

"Did she say why?"

"Well, I mean, she's asking about Cassie being pregnant—so, I'm not stupid."

"No, I know that," McDermott assures him. "But did she put it in a bigger context?"

He shakes his head. "I asked her, but she wouldn't tell me."

They press Brandon more on the details, any names or events or places Evelyn might have mentioned. Seems that it had been a typical conversation with a reporter, where the subject does all the talking. Evelyn Pendry was playing her cards close to the vest.

"What about this Gwendolyn Lake?" Stoletti asks. "Know where we can find her?"

He doesn't. "At the rate she was going, I'd be surprised if she was still alive."

"You never saw her again, after the night just before finals—that fight?" McDermott tries. "Never? Like, what about Cassie's funeral?"

Brandon's eyes trail up. "No, no. She wasn't there."

That's odd. Gwendolyn skipped out on her cousin's funeral? He looks at his partner. She shrugs at him.

Stoletti asks, "Did you tell the police about all of this back then? The fight with Gwendolyn? The 'fucking father' comment?"

"No," he answers. "Mostly, because it didn't matter. They, like, caught Burgos right away, and he confessed. So, I figured, it was nobody's business.

I thought I owed it to Cassie to keep her confidence. But also, they dropped the part of the case about Cassie, right? So they weren't concerned with her. The only time I testified was after the conviction, during sentencing—and I didn't testify about Cassie. I testified about Ellie." He looks at each of the detectives. "Really, I saw no reason to smear the name of such a great person when there was no reason to do so."

Mitchum sounds a little defensive here. He's probably worked through this rationalization before. But he makes sense. And McDermott knows a little something about keeping secrets for the greater good. But he's thinking more about the dropping of Cassie's murder from the case. Once again, it has proved to be a reason that a lot of hard questions didn't get asked.

McDermott goes with the wrap-up. "Is there anything else, Brandon? Anything about this intruder, or Evelyn, or what happened back then—anything we haven't covered?"

Happens all the time, in the heat of Q and A, witnesses get so caught up responding to specific questions that something important gets lost. He's had countless re-interviews where he learns new information, and the witnesses politely inform him, *You didn't ask me that before.*

Brandon Mitchum makes a small *o* with his mouth, blinking his eyes quickly. Doesn't feel like he's reaching into his memory. He's debating.

"Anything," McDermott says. "This guy isn't going to stop until we catch him."

"I'm not sure there's anything else," he says.

"I'm not sure about that baggie of dope we found in your apartment," McDermott replies. "Here, we were getting along so well, I was just gonna let you off with a lecture."

Brandon raises a hand. "Okay, okay. I just—didn't think it was important. And I don't know if it's even true." He shakes his head. "Okay, I'll tell you. But you didn't hear this from me."

36

WE WALK into Harland's office, which looks out over the southern view of the city, and then well beyond, a good shot of the river and the new theater being built. He owns some of the property to the south, off the expressway, and has plans for significant big-box retail down there.

I look down at the red oak flooring and the Persian area rug Harland got while in the Middle East, poking through whatever trade barriers may have existed.

Harland stands at the window, rubbing his eyes carefully, like everything else he does, the index finger and thumb massaging his eyelids. "Do you know why I hired you, Paul?"

I think I do, but I don't like the question. I don't say anything.

"It wasn't a thank-you. It might have been perceived as that. But it wasn't. If I wanted to thank you for putting away my daughter's killer, I wouldn't have rewarded you with money. Because that would be cheapening what you did. That would be putting a price on it."

"I agree."

"I hired you because I thought you were the best lawyer in the city. And I wanted a lawyer in this city. Here, close to me."

I don't know what he expects me to say. Hell yes, he's a primo client, but he's gotten plenty in return. I've given him my best.

"Harland, the Sherwood Executive Center. Is that where Cassie's doctors were?"

He doesn't answer immediately. I think of my own daughter, Elizabeth, realizing that I wouldn't be able to recall where her doctors practiced when she was growing up. I never took her to a physician; Georgia, my ex-wife, would have handled that chore. And I wouldn't exactly expect the Bentleys to be a nuclear family, either. I couldn't imagine Harland or Natalia packing the kid in the station wagon for a physical. It was more likely a chauffeured limousine.

"I remember the building," he finally says, to my surprise. "When she was, oh, eight or so. She had to have her teeth cleaned. She was so scared she had a cavity. She"—he takes in a breath—"she begged me to go with her. She was so sensitive—so sensitive to—pain."

I look away, not wanting to gawk at someone reliving a painful memory.

"I made them bring in a chair, and I sat next to Cassie while they cleaned her teeth. She never let go of my hand. She squeezed it so hard. So hard, for such a little girl."

I clear my throat. I think it might be best, for everyone's sake, that he move on.

"I think all of her—I think all the health care group was in that building, too," he adds. "I think it was all one wrap-up group."

"Like her general practitioner, her ob-gyn, that kind of thing?"

He waves a hand. He thinks so, but he doesn't know.

"Was she pregnant, Harland?" I ask in a gentler tone.

He takes a moment, then makes a noise, something between clearing his throat and chuckling. "As if she would have told me," he says quietly. "That little girl who held my hand at the dentist? By the time she was in college, that girl was long gone. No, I had managed to alienate all of the women in my family."

He runs his hand over the walnut desk, like he's checking it for dust. Another way of looking at it might be that he's avoiding my eye contact, which is not like him.

"Why am I here, Harland?"

He considers his fingernails. "You're probably aware that I have a certain reputation with women."

"I'm aware that you have excellent taste," I answer. "If a little fickle."

He likes that. "A little fickle. Yes." He looks at me. "A little fickle. And I imagine you've heard rumors that I began earning that reputation before the end of my marriage?"

"I don't listen to rumors," I say, which is the same thing as answering yes. The word was that Harland was playing around for years on his wife, Natalia. My heartbeat strikes up again.

Harland turns toward the window. He's turned on overhead lighting that illuminates my space, by the door, but leaves him in semidarkness, also allowing for a picturesque view through the window, lights sprinkled about the evening cityscape like a pinball machine.

"It's a weakness, really," he continues. "Younger women. Not *that* young, of course. I don't mean teenagers."

"Harland," I say.

"Okay, all right." He takes a moment, looking in my direction, then back at the window, before he spits it out.

"That weakness," he says, "extended to Ellie Danzinger."

BRANDON MITCHUM squirms in his bed, uncomfortable with the revelation he's just laid on the detectives.

McDermott stares at the wall over Mitchum's head, trying to see where this all fits in. "You're telling me," he says, "that Cassie thought her father was sleeping with Ellie Danzinger?"

Mitchum doesn't answer, but there's no doubt McDermott heard it right.

"When did Cassie tell you this?" Stoletti wants to know.

"Oh, right about the same time. Just a little before finals, maybe. May, June of that year. I know," he adds, laughing nervously, "it's pretty intense."

Intense, is one way of putting it. But it matches Harland Bentley's reputation, the wealthy playboy. And it seems that Cassie Bentley was having a rough semester. She thought her best friend was screwing her father, and she was pregnant.

"This was a suspicion," Stoletti says to him. "Not a confirmed fact."

"Right. Cassie thought it was true, but she never knew for sure. She said she was going to find out."

"How do you know she didn't?" McDermott asks. "How can you be sure she never confirmed it?"

Mitchum shakes his head slowly, causing himself some pain in the process. He touches the bandage on his face. "She would have told me," he says confidently. "She would've *had* to tell me. I made her promise."

"You made her promise?"

"Yeah." Mitchum's tongue runs over his dry lips. "I was afraid of what she might do. I wanted to be close to her, so she wouldn't—so she—" His eyes narrow, frozen in a sixteen-year-old memory.

McDermott says, "So she wouldn't take her own life?"

"It—yeah, it had crossed my mind. Who knew *what* she might've done?"

Mitchum's head falls back against the pillow. McDermott looks over at Stoletti, wondering if she's thinking about what, exactly, Cassie Bentley might have done.

Like confront her father, maybe.

A LONG SILENCE HANGS between Harland and me. I finally repeat the words, to be sure I actually heard them.

"You and Ellie were having an affair?"

"Oh, an 'affair,' I don't know. But, from time to time, yes. She was so—so . . ."

He doesn't move from the comfort of the darkness on his side of the room. His head angles up. He sighs whimsically. Jesus, this guy really couldn't keep his dick in his pants. He couldn't keep his paws off Cassie's best friend?

"She was so what, Harland? Young? Sexy? Forbidden?"

"Vibrant."

"Oh, she was vibrant. Oh, that explains it, then."

"If there is one thing I *don't* come to my attorney for," he says evenly, "it's the passing of judgment. I come to my attorney for protection. I don't want this to come out, Paul. It's nobody's business."

He's right, to a point, but that doesn't stop my stomach from churning. I don't like being left out of the loop, not when I'm prosecuting a case. He could have told me back then. We would have seen it for what it was—a nonstarter, an irrelevant detour. We caught Burgos red-handed, and it took only hours before he was admitting to killing all of the women. Ellie Danzinger's extracurricular activities would have had nothing to do with Burgos's guilt.

"Who knew about this?"

He clears his throat. "Ellie," he says, "and me."

"Are you sure?"

"Discretion is one thing we both understood."

"I can't believe this," I mumble.

"I'm not concerned with what you can believe." Harland emerges from the darkness of the corner. "You've defended murderers. You've defended executives who steal from their shareholders. You defended us, with that pollution problem in Florida. I'm guilty here of far less. So defend me, Paul. Keep all of this quiet." He stands face-to-face with me now. "Or I'll find someone who will."

I stare at him. Again, he's holding his money over me. He knows there are dozens of lawyers at my firm who would be on the street without his business.

"Find someone who will," I say.

I see that I've surprised him, as much as Harland ever shows surprise. His eyes search my face for a break in my reaction.

"You're afraid." He nods his head once, slowly. "I've never seen that from you."

He's not talking about our relationship. He's not talking about the millions of dollars of business he sends my way every year.

And he's right.

"Who killed my daughter?" he asks me.

I say it quickly, "Terry Burgos," but the answer surprises both of us, the speed of my response, the fact that the question is even remotely credible. Three days ago, it wasn't.

His expression lightens a bit, amusement, he wants me to think. Like he's not afraid of anyone.

"I'm going to find out what's going on," I tell him.

"Even if it proves you wrong."

"Even if."

I turn for the door. I navigate the hallway, my legs shaky. The British guard eyes me suspiciously as I push open the front door and head to the elevator.

"IT DIDN'T MATTER," Brandon says. "What's the point of ripping apart these people's lives when it served no purpose?"

"I'm not asking why you didn't tell the police back then," McDermott says. "I want to know why you didn't want to tell *us* tonight. And why we 'didn't hear this from you.' You afraid of someone, Brandon?"

Brandon waves off the notion, trying to give the impression that McDermott's off base. But he's not. He can read it all over Mitchum.

"Harland Bentley," he guesses.

Brandon's eyes shoot to McDermott, then retreat. He might as well have said yes.

"Tell me about you and Harland Bentley, Brandon."

"Look, it's not just me." He says it like it's wrong, whatever it is. "Mr. Bentley is one of the biggest benefactors to the arts in this city. He gives money to a lot of artists."

Oh. Right. Mitchum is an artist.

"He endowed a grant through the City Arts Foundation for me," he concedes. "Okay?"

McDermott drops his head and peeks over at Stoletti.

"When did this happen?" Stoletti asks.

"When I graduated Mansbury. That was 'ninety-two."

"He gave you a grant in 1992?"

"Yeah. Well—it's a continuing grant. He refreshes it every year."

"How much does he 'refresh' it?" McDermott asks.

"Oh." Brandon waves a hand. "Started out at twenty-five thousand. Now it's seventy-five thousand a year."

"Seventy-five *thousand*?" McDermott makes a face. "And what do you do for this refresher, Brandon? Why you?"

The coloring on the face of the young artist has changed to a light crimson. This is not a topic he enjoys. "He told me that Cassie would have wanted him to help. He said he appreciated that I was there for Cassie."

A doctor comes into the room and wants to know if they're done. McDermott says he needs five more minutes. Mitchum, it seems, was hoping for a reprieve. The doctor stands next to McDermott to let him know the clock is ticking.

"There's nothing wrong with accepting a grant," Mitchum says.

McDermott nods at him. "You and Mr. Bentley ever discuss what we've just discussed?"

He shakes his head. "Never."

Stoletti asks, "You think he knew that *you* knew about Ellie and him?"

"No," he insists. "I don't know if there's even anything *to* know. It was just a thought that Cassie had. See, I knew you'd try to make this look bad. He gives millions a year to the arts. I'm one of many. I haven't done anything wrong."

The doctor moves between the detective and the patient. "That's enough for tonight, guys. Really."

"We'll have a guard at your door," McDermott tells Brandon. "You think of anything, I want you to call me."

They step out into the hallway. Stoletti digests the conversation while McDermott checks for messages on his cell phone. None.

So Cassie is pregnant and having unpleasant conversations with whoever the father is, who seems to want to deny it. Then Cassie is murdered. Then someone gets Fred Ciancio to help break into the building where Cassie's medical records are located. None of this, save Cassie's murder, is confirmed. But it makes sense.

Nor can it be confirmed that Cassie's father was playing around with Ellie's best friend. But if he was, then Cassie was having a pretty rough time right before she was murdered.

"You think Cassie confronted her daddy?" Stoletti asks. "He marries into a billion dollars, and he's afraid of his wife finding out that he was screwing their daughter's best friend?"

"And," McDermott adds, "we have another someone who doesn't want Cassie's pregnancy to come out. Professor Albany sure looks good for the 'fucking father.'"

"And just about this time," she replies, "Ellie and Cassie conveniently turn up dead."

Right. But they don't have proof that Cassie was pregnant, and they don't have proof Harland Bentley was stepping out with Ellie Danzinger.

Only one way to find out. He's supposed to see Natalia Lake Bentley, who is returning from vacation tomorrow morning early. And they have Harland Bentley at ten.

"We'll need to add the professor to our social calendar tomorrow," he says.

37

McDermott makes it back to the station after leaving the hospital. Grace is already asleep when he calls. His mother says she had a good night. It's only the third night since Joyce died that McDermott hasn't put her to bed and read to her. He misses it. It's part of his pact with her.

What would he do without his mother, Grace's gramma? A nanny on a cop's salary would almost break him. His mother, seventy-four next month, is the one now holding this together. She's healthy as a horse, but he can see she's slowing down. He thinks about it every day. What would happen to Grace without her?

He shakes away the thought. He pushes out the memory of Joyce lying dead on the floor, the bathroom floor and rug soaked with her blood. He turns from the sight of Grace, huddled in the bathtub, her eyes shut, hands over her ears.

He pretends he didn't say those things to Joyce, the night before her death.

Joyce was sick, and it had become too much for a husband who worked ten-hour days. Worse yet, there was Grace. If something had happened to her under Joyce's watch, he'd never forgive himself. Joyce loved Grace more than life, but that wasn't the point. Sickness was sickness. You can love your daughter with all your heart, but what good does that do if you've locked yourself upstairs while your three-year-old daughter is downstairs, wailing for her mommy?

That's when he'd made the decision, after arriving home late from a double homicide, after gathering his hungry, soiled daughter in his arms as he searched the house for his wife, his heart rattling against his chest in anger and terror with such fury that he could hardly push the calls to his wife out of his lungs. He found her in the spare bedroom, in the corner, wrapped in a ball, weeping quietly. She'd lost track of time, hadn't any sense of whether Grace had eaten dinner or whether she'd had a nap. She was losing control.

It was time—past time—to institutionalize her. *To get some rest,* as he put it to her later that night.

He'd consulted an attorney the week earlier. Involuntary commitment was an option. But he wanted so badly for Joyce to agree with him. He wanted her to feel like part of a solution, not a prisoner being locked up. *Just give it a try,* he pleaded. *It's nothing permanent.* The point, he emphasized, was to get her full-time attention and get her on the road to recovery.

We'll make it through this, he promised.

That was a Thursday night. They talked about the weekend. She had reluctantly agreed. They would do it that weekend.

Why had he given her advance warning?

Why had he left for work on Friday?

He had rationalizations for that one, too: The double homicide he was working. The fact that Joyce looked great—fresh, alert, positive—that Friday morning, seemed to be having one of her *good days.* Because they weren't all bad; it wasn't every day. She was up and down. That morning, he was *sure* of it, she was up.

He was *sure.*

I'm fine, she'd said, placing a hand gently on his chest. *Like you said— think about the future. This is the right move for us.*

Go, she'd said. *You can help me pack when you get home.*

Eight, ten hours, and he'd be back home, helping Joyce pack a bag for what, hopefully, would be a short stay at the Pearlwood Center. It was really only seven. He'd left work early.

Seven hours, when it all came apart.

"We'll catch a break tonight," Stoletti tells him as she plays on her computer.

"What? Oh." McDermott sighs. She's referring to the fingerprints that were found on the door to Brandon Mitchum's apartment. Until they hear back from the lab, there's not much to do, and it's no time to rehash the past, so he busies himself with the reports from the Burgos file.

Burgos is not his case, of course, and it's been solved. His job is to catch the current offender. But there's no denying a connection. Something was missed. He knows it. And he has to figure it out fast, because *fast* is a good description of how the offender is moving. Sunday was Ciancio. Monday was Amalia Calderone. Tuesday was Evelyn Pendry. Today, he took his shot at Brandon Mitchum.

McDermott rubs his eyes, finishes off his second cup of coffee and goes for another, his eyes heavy but his body motoring on the caffeine. God, the energy he used to have, as a young cop, working an overnight shift, the thrill he felt when he cruised some of the scariest of neighborhoods. It felt clearer to him then, more tangible, the front lines. Now he's playing catch-up, solving crimes already committed instead of preventing them. He likes the puzzle, no doubt. But the truth is, most crimes aren't that hard to solve. Motives usually show themselves almost immediately. Canvass the neighborhood, check the vic's background, work the forensics, and nine times out of ten, you're done. And in the end, you don't bring the vic back, you just put away the offender.

Maybe that's why, whatever the pressure he may feel, he's enjoying this case. A chance to prevent, to stop this offender from killing again.

He feels sure that this is an offender covering his tracks. And what, precisely, he's covering is contained somewhere in these files.

He looks back over the notes he's made on Burgos. He noted details on times, places, and came up with a clear pattern. There were the hookers, there was Ellie, and there was Cassie. The hookers lined up nice and neat. They had a little bit of information on Ellie and basically nothing on Cassie.

One: The hookers' disappearances could be pinpointed to particular nights and times, and at least general locations. Two of the hookers were seen getting into a blue Chevy Suburban, and the other two left fingerprints in that same vehicle, belonging to Terry Burgos. Ellie Danzinger's house was forcibly entered, and the action took place in her bedroom, literally on her bed. Her murder can be pinpointed, circumstantially, to the first night of the murders, a Sunday.

Not so with Cassie. They didn't know when, or where, Cassie disappeared. They only know she was the last one murdered. And they know there was a two-day break between the last hooker's death and Cassie's death.

Two: The hookers were raped before Burgos killed them. Ellie and Cassie were raped postmortem.

Three: Professor Frankfort Albany knew both of the girls. He didn't know the prostitutes.

Two—the sex thing—was probably not a big deal. Hookers let you have sex with them, that's the whole point. Nice college girls like Cassie and Ellie—they probably wouldn't look twice at a guy like Burgos. He'd have to kill them first.

He sits back in his chair and lets it work out in his mind. Let it all out, see what comes back. Usually works for him.

Burgos left bread crumbs all the way to his door, Riley said. They found him before they even began to investigate. Sure, that happens all the time. First place you look, you find your offender. Who wants to make work for themselves? The guy's right there. He confesses. His basement looks like he was conducting a seminar on torture murders. Don't make it more complicated.

He remembers what he read about Ellie Danzinger. She'd been bludgeoned in her bed, but then she was left there, her head hanging over the side. The M.E. figured, based on the volume of blood that dripped to the carpet, that it had been at least sixty minutes that Ellie lay there before she was moved to Burgos's garage, where he removed her dead heart from her corpse.

What happened during those sixty minutes?

He looks back at his notes. You always ask the question, *Who gained?* If you believe rumors, the father of Cassie's child and Harland Bentley both gained from the deaths of Ellie and Cassie.

But Burgos confessed. McDermott had read the transcript of the interrogation. There was no coercion at all. Burgos knew damn well that Ellie was his first victim, before anyone mentioned her name or showed him her photograph. Hell, he was pissed off that Detective Lightner *hadn't* included her picture in the photo array. And there's no way that evidence of six dead women just found their way into his basement.

Is there?

But what if Professor Albany had been the father of Cassie's child?

There's little doubt he'd lose his job if it came out. And he knew Burgos—he *employed* him, for God's sake, and he took him under his wing.

Could a college professor come up with keys to the Bramhall Auditorium basement?

So many things unconfirmed. But if Harland Bentley really was slipping it to Ellie Danzinger, he was looking at the loss of a fortune if it came out. He and Albany both had plenty to lose.

So which one is it? Bentley or Albany?

"Hey, Mike."

McDermott looks over at Stoletti, who is banging away on the computer.

"We've been sitting here thinking, Who looks worse right now? Harland Bentley or Professor Albany?"

"Right." When he walks over, she points at the computer, a results screen from a Google search. "We're looking at Albany, we're looking at Harland Bentley," she says. "I thought, why not search both their names together?"

"They were both players in a heater case, Ricki. It's not that surprising they'd appear in articles together."

"Yeah?" She clinks on a link. "Well, is *this* surprising?"

The link is a biography page for Mansbury College. At the top corner of the page is a photo of Professor Albany in a thoughtful pose.

Then McDermott starts to read the one-paragraph biography:

Professor Frankfort J. Albany is the Harland Bentley Professor of Cultural Studies at Mansbury College. Endowed in 1990, the chair recognizes Professor Albany for his outstanding contributions . . .

"The Harland Bentley *what*?"

Harland Bentley endowed a chair at Mansbury College in Albany's name?

"Maybe we don't have to pick between Harland Bentley or Professor Albany," he says. "Maybe it's both."

Stoletti says, "Well, that explains how Albany got tenure after teaching a class that got six women killed. A billionaire having your back doesn't hurt."

"He hires Riley right after the Burgos case is done and makes him a millionaire ten times over," McDermott says. "He gives Brandon Mitchum a yearly stipend after the case is over, maybe as a thank-you for keeping quiet about his supposed affair with Ellie Danzinger. He endows a chair for Albany right after the case and gives him permanent job security."

"Harland Bentley was buying *something*," she agrees.

His cell phone rings. His caller ID doesn't recognize the number.

"Mike, it's Susan Dobbs."

"Susan." He checks his watch. What's an assistant county medical examiner doing this time of night at the morgue?

"You piqued my curiosity," she says. "And I know this is important."

"I appreciate—"

"I just checked all three of the victims: Ciancio, Evelyn Pendry, and Amalia Calderone."

"And?"

"Every one of them has a postmortem incision at the base of the fourth and fifth tarsal phalange."

McDermott releases a breath.

"This guy's clever," she says. "Or stupid, depending on how you look at it."

Right. He's branding them. He's leaving a signature.

"So Susan, how come none of the other autopsy reports show this? Other than Ciancio's?"

She sighs. "Mike, you bring in a body that's overwhelmed with physical trauma—contusions, stabbing wounds, whatever—you're not looking there. It's not like there was evidence of poison, so you're not looking for injection points. Who's going to think to open up the space between the fourth and fifth toes?"

"Well, *you* found it on Ciancio," he says. "I owe you one."

"You owe me more than one."

He closes the cell phone. "All three victims," he says to Stoletti.

"That was the M.E.?" Stoletti looks up. "So we know they're all connected. If we had any doubt. Why does he go to the trouble, after mutilating these people, to find the space between their fourth and fifth toes and make a little incision?"

McDermott rolls his neck. "He wants us to know."

"Put it on their face, you want us to know. This is the most hidden signature I've ever heard of." She nods at him. "You didn't see that incision in any of the autopsies from Mansbury?"

"No." McDermott had run through every autopsy from the Burgos prosecution. "But they might have missed it, just like they missed it with two of our three victims, until I had her check."

Stoletti doesn't like it. McDermott can't disagree. She's right. This guy is leaving a brand, a small incision in the taut skin between the fourth and pinkie toes, but one that would be incredibly easy to overlook, especially when the bodies are beaten and tortured.

Why leave a signature that nobody might find?

"He's doing this for someone," McDermott says. But who?

ACROSS FROM ME at the all-night diner, Shelly chews an ice cube from a glass of lemonade. I nurse a cup of coffee and a number of nagging wounds. I lay it all out for her, the recent developments since she accompanied me to visit Gwendolyn Lake earlier today.

I've flown solo long enough that I'm unaccustomed to seeking out solace. A bachelor's life is uncomplicated, particularly when money is not an issue, which it certainly is not. Work is not difficult at this stage of my career. Litigation consists primarily of putting up a sufficient fight to force the other side into compromise, and, if it gets as far as trial, most of it is theater, anyway. My personal life? The biggest decision I have to make is whether to watch ESPN Classic or old movies on A&E. It becomes comfortable and that, in turn, becomes enough.

I turned that all upside down with Shelly. I met her initially like I meet most people in my life—in a courtroom. I got the verdict and heard nothing from her again until years later, when she asked me to represent a client on a murder charge. Away from the heat of the adversarial duel, I felt something immediately with her, her spirit, her conviction.

And when she broke things off, I couldn't go back. I couldn't find the comfort. My assistant Betty was right. I've always enjoyed a drink, but I turned it into an Olympic sport, starting that night. I've been a wreck the last few months. I've been on autopilot at work and feeling sorry for myself.

Now she's back, with the proviso that I hold off the pressure, and I'm dumping these problems into her lap immediately. I didn't want to call her to meet me here, scolded myself as I dialed the cell phone. But I need her, whether I like it or not.

So far, she hasn't said a word. She's good like that, a great listener. When I'm done, she says, "Tell me what's bothering you about this."

I laugh. After everything we've discussed, I wouldn't know where to start.

"It's not Harland," she says.

I push my cup to the waitress, who freshens it. "Fuck Harland."

Shelly is briefly amused. She probably never expected to hear those words from me. She's never been much for the corporate legal world, anyway. I once tried to woo her to my law firm, with a full partnership offer, but I couldn't drag her away from her children's advocacy work. For her, it's about the work, not the compensation.

That used to be me, too.

"You think you missed something back then."

I cringe at the words. "What I can't figure out is why it would matter. If Cassie was pregnant, that was a problem for someone, maybe, sixteen years ago. But not today. Harland was sleeping with Ellie Danzinger? Sure, it's scandalous, sixteen years ago. Not today. I—I can't see how any of this is relevant."

She reaches across the table and takes my hand. "But you can't see how it's *not*."

People are dying for a reason, she means. These aren't random victims of a psychopath. There's a connection.

The waitress brings a bagel with cream cheese for me and a salad for Shelly. I missed dinner altogether and I have to eat something, however turbulent my stomach. We play with our food awhile in silence.

"He confessed, Shelly. I watched Burgos confess."

She considers her salad, rearranging the cucumbers and tomatoes with her fork. She thinks twice before she asks, "You're sure it was Burgos who killed these girls?"

"A hundred percent." I rip off a piece of the bagel and stare at it.

A group of college kids walk into the diner, smelling of liquor and cigarettes and talking too loudly. Those were the days. They are blissfully ignorant. They haven't blazed their trails yet. They haven't made irrevocable decisions. They have no idea about regret. They think life is one gigantic music video.

I watch them move to a corner booth, their animated conversation fading, then I turn to Shelly, who is watching me.

"Ninety-five percent," I say. "No. A hundred percent." I put a fist down on the table. "Goddammit—a hundred percent. He knew all of the victims by name. He knew the order they'd been placed in the basement. He'd been stalking Ellie, for God's sake. He killed them in his own damn house. People saw the prostitutes get into his truck."

She takes a moment with that, letting me cool. Her expression shows concern, which for some reason pisses me off.

"Don't look at me like that," I say. "This—y'know what? This isn't my problem. If there was some side issue, some secret that someone doesn't want to come out, that's not my problem. I haven't been a prosecutor for fifteen years. I solved my crime. They can solve theirs."

Shelly tucks her lips into her mouth, her eyes dancing.

"Say something, for Christ's sake, Shelly."

She sets down her fork, places her hands in her lap. "If it's not your problem, then let it go."

"Let it go." I throw up a hand. "*That's* your advice."

"You said your—"

"I know what I said. Forget what I said." I turn in the booth toward the window, taking a couple of deep breaths and staring at my reflection, at a lawyer who, at the moment, is acting like a supreme asshole. In my peripheral vision, I see Shelly gesture to the waitress. I'd do the same, if I were her. Check, please, and step on it.

"You don't need my advice," she says. "You know what to do."

The check slaps down on the table. Shelly slips some money out of her wallet.

"It's gonna hurt," I say.

"Of course it will. If you go against Harland, attorneys at your firm will suffer. Maybe your firm will fold. If you discover that you missed something in the case, it will be embarrassing to you, personally. And maybe professionally. And yes, for that five percent chance that you convicted the wrong man—you'll have to live with that."

I rub my face. She's right. There's no doubt about this. I just needed to hear it.

"You could walk away from this," she adds. "You're right about that. You're not a prosecutor anymore. Anyone would understand that."

I don't let her see my smile. She understands me better than I care to admit. She's giving me an out so I can feel good about not taking it.

She hooks her arm into mine as I walk her to her car. The gesture is innocuous but meaningful to me. I want more of it. I want to hold her in my arms tonight, smell her hair, run a finger along her smooth stomach.

Instead, she kisses me softly and her hand flickers away from mine. I close the car door behind her. She waves good-bye, while I appreciate the fact that, this time, it's not *Good-bye* but *See you soon.*

DON REGIS, from the County Attorney Technical Unit, rushes into the squad room. McDermott and Stoletti are eagerly awaiting him, after his call ten minutes ago.

A latent on the door of Brandon Mitchum's apartment found a hit in the database.

"The prints belong to one Leonid Koslenko. A Russian immigrant." Don Regis drops the file on McDermott's desk. "Prior arrests for battery and suspicion of murder. Charges nollied both times."

McDermott opens the arrest reports, first going right to the mug shots from Koslenko's booking, the black and white of the square-faced man with the half-moon scar under his eye. His hand curls into a fist. A wave of both relief and adrenaline floods his chest. This is the same person from the photograph found in Fred Ciancio's apartment. The same person who was in Brandon Mitchum's apartment tonight.

He scans the officer's summaries of each arrest. Five years ago, Leonid Koslenko was arrested for battery of a woman on the west side. Two years ago, he was picked up on suspicion of murder of a woman, three blocks away from the first charge.

In each case, the charges were dropped—*nolle prosequi,* a term for declining to prosecute.

In each case, the victims were prostitutes.

The first arrest report is thick. He looks under the initial summaries. "A psych workup," he says. Koslenko was ordered by the court to undergo psychiatric evaluation for competency.

"They never got to the competency hearing," says Regis, who has already read the reports. "The Vicky dropped the charges."

Okay, fine, but McDermott is more concerned with what the shrinks said:

```
Patient displays inappropriate affect, inat-
tention and disordered thoughts. Delusional
persecutions and auditory hallucinations are
manifest.
```

"Auditory hallucinations," McDermott mumbles. He hears voices?

```
Patient suffers from DSM-IV paranoid
schizophrenia.
```

McDermott checks his watch. It's only a few minutes before midnight. He picks up the phone for the overnight desk sergeant. "I need the RAID squad, Dennis. Right now."

He hangs up and looks at Stoletti. "Whoever's on call," says McDermott, "call them. We're moving on his house tonight."

LEO SITS IN THE rental car. The neighborhood is peaceful, as it approaches midnight. He's been here before, looked over the brownstone, three condos stacked on top of each other, a security door in front that won't be a problem.

The lights on the third floor are out.

He needs this tonight. It has to be tonight.

They know who I am now, my mistake, doesn't matter, I'm too smart for them, even if they know who I am, they won't know where I am, and they won't know why, that's the difference between Terry and me, Terry was brave, but he wasn't smart.

From his angle, he can see the brownstone, and, behind it, the small parking lot. He can wait. He doesn't mind waiting. That's not the problem.

It's been over an hour now. Almost midnight. He'll need to improvise *again.*

He jumps at the headlights in the parking lot, coming from down the alley. He can't see who gets out, not in the dark.

But it's only one person.

He looks up at the third floor, as his hands drum the steering wheel. Yes. It happens. The lights go on. The third-floor apartment.

He waits. Five minutes. Ten. Fifteen.

Twenty minutes later, the lights go out.

Shelly Trotter has come home and gone to bed.

People v. Terrance Demetrius Burgos

Case No. 89-CR-31003

September 1989

It was only Riley's third trip ever to a morgue. He didn't spend much time with dead bodies as a federal prosecutor, and, when he did, cause of death was rarely an issue. The bodies had usually been riddled with machine-gun fire from rival drug dealers.

He wasn't sure why he was here. He wasn't even sure why he was still reading about Cassie Bentley, when her murder had been dropped from the case.

He found Mitra Agarwal, an assistant county medical examiner. Mitra was a slight woman with a playful side who spoke with a soft Indian accent. She'd been one of the coroners on duty when the bodies came in. She'd been the one who showed Natalia Lake Bentley her daughter's corpse.

Doctor Agarwal showed Riley into a large, sanitized room. On the beds rested the bodies of four women murdered by Terry Burgos.

Riley opened the autopsy report for Cassie Bentley.

"So," he said to her, reading from the report. " 'A postmortem incision at the base of the fourth and fifth tarsal phalange.' That means her toes?"

"Basically."

"Why don't you just say *toes*?"

"Why don't you just say 'the charges are dropped' instead of *nolle prosequi?*"

Riley smiled. "Touché, Doctor."

"None of the prostitutes have been claimed," she said, opening herself to the three bodies. "You're lucky anyone's still here."

Families had one hundred twenty days to claim the bodies of their loved ones, so technically there was still time. But these girls had probably become prostitutes, in large part, because they didn't have much for families to begin with. These women, he knew, were destined for unmarked graves in the county cemetery.

"Don't keep me in suspense, Mitra."

She led him to Angie Mornakowski's cold, white corpse. She separated the fourth and pinkie toes on her left foot. Riley saw a bloodless incision, a precise cut slicing the small webbing of skin.

"They all have them," she said. "All four that we have here. And Cassie."

"Wow." Riley sighed. "And nothing in the autopsies."

She shook her head. "Other than Cassie's. Frankly, I'm surprised they caught it with her. That's something that could easily slip through the cracks. When you're dealing with traumatic injuries to the head and body, it's not at all surprising you wouldn't notice an obscure slice between the pinkie toe and fourth toe. It's not like this was a drug or poison case. You're not looking for injection—"

"No, I know. I'm not criticizing." He took a deep breath. "This is post-mortem," he said. "This is an afterthought."

"This is a signature," she said.

Riley agreed with that assessment. "He's leaving his mark."

"Well, look at it this way," the doctor said. "If you had any doubt that the same person killed all of these girls, you don't anymore."

Riley smiled at her. "I didn't have any doubt."

"Okay," she said. "Well, what do you want me to do? Want me to exhume the other bodies? Amend the autopsies?"

It was hard to see how this mattered. Burgos had admitted to the killings, both to Joel Lightner and to the psychiatrists. This wasn't exculpatory evidence—evidence that favored the defense, which Riley would be required to turn over. If anything, it hurt Burgos. It proved even more clearly that the same person killed all of these women.

And it could backfire. The defense could play it up, make the medical examiner's office look incompetent. Make the coroners the issue, a distraction. Jeremy Larrabee would be more than happy to talk about anything that took the focus off his client.

To say nothing of the fact that Riley would have to ask Ellie Danzinger's family for permission to exhume their daughter's body, only a few months after they buried her. And for what? To prove something they already knew?

Cassie Bentley's autopsy wasn't public record. It wasn't part of the case, and it was no longer anyone's business.

"Let's drop it," Riley said to her. "Thanks for satisfying my curiosity."

"Oohh." Mitra Agarwal nudged him with her elbow. "How exciting. A secret. You and I are the only living, breathing people who know about the tarsal phalange incisions."

"You, me, and Terry Burgos." Riley thanked her and headed back to his office.

Thursday
June 23, 2005

38

LEONID KOSLENKO lives in a small bungalow on the northwest side of the city, fourth home in from the south. Detective Michael McDermott takes one last look through his binoculars at the home from his position across the street. He checks his watch. It is precisely two-thirty in the morning, Thursday.

McDermott raises the radio to his mouth and says, "The code is Yellow, Team Leaders. That's Yellow."

From the north and south of the two-story house, members of the Rapid and Immediate Deployment Unit creep forward, keeping low and close to the neighboring homes, concealing themselves from any sight line from Koslenko's house and avoiding the illumination of the streetlights. Two eight-man teams, dressed in dark blue flame-resistant uniforms, Kevlar ballistic helmets, Tac vests, and night-vision goggles, armed with bolt-action rifles or shotguns, slowly converge on the house.

Half of each team breaks to the rear of the house. The other half gets within feet of the front door on each side, staying below the view from the windows.

McDermott hears the voice cackle through his radio, from the built-in mikes in their Tac vests.

"Team A in position."

"Team B in position."

McDermott takes a breath, then says into the radio, "The code is Green. That's Green."

The teams meet at the front door, where they use a battering ram to enter the house. Tactical vans race down the street from each side, squealing to a halt in front of Koslenko's, turning toward the house and shining bright lights over the entire property. Police officers pour out of the vans and circle the perimeter of the property.

McDermott hops out of the brush and draws his weapon. The interior lights in the house pop on one after the other. McDermott stops at the sidewalk, his handgun in one hand, the radio in the other. He puts out a hand to block Stoletti, who stands next to him, weapon drawn as well.

"First bedroom—clear."

"First bathroom—clear."

"Kitchen is clear."

"Living room—clear."

McDermott holds his breath, steeling himself for the sound of gunfire.

"Second bedroom—clear."

"Second bathroom—clear."

"Third bedroom—clear."

It feels like he holds his breath forever, his pulse pounding.

"Basement is clear."

"That's all clear. We are all clear."

McDermott jogs up the driveway and into the house. A foul smell fills the ground floor, like a combination of body odor and dirty socks. The place is in deteriorating condition. The paint is peeling on the walls. The kitchen looks like it was last upgraded in the seventies. There is little furniture in the living room, unless you count pizza cartons and oil-stained food bags thrown about, plates with crusted ketchup and remnants of food, now being feasted on by flies and other bugs.

"Well, shit," he says, as Stoletti walks up to him. "He's gone, and he's *been* gone."

His radio cackles. *"Detective McDermott, the basement."*

McDermott takes the stairs down. The space is unfinished and unfurnished, save for a workout bench, some weights, and some taped-up boxes.

The walls are a different story. Corkboard has been attached from floor to ceiling, all the way around three of the four walls. Various documents and photographs are tacked up everywhere.

When Stoletti hits the bottom step, she says, "What the hell is this?"

McDermott walks up and gets a closer look at the items on the wall. A newspaper article from the *Watch,* a story about the divorce of Harland and Natalia Bentley. A notice from the IRS for underpayment of tax. A newspaper story on Paul Riley leaving the county attorney's office to start a new law firm. A page downloaded from a Web site called "Russian Serial Killers," detailing the exploits of Nikolai Kruschenko, who murdered over two dozen prostitutes before being captured in 1988 in Leningrad. A magazine article on Paul Riley's purchase earlier this year of the home formerly owned by Senator Roche. Page after page, downloaded from Web sites, about Terry Burgos, detailing the murders and his victims. A black-and-white photograph of a young girl standing by a tree.

It goes on and on. There are hundreds of documents.

"This," McDermott says, "is his office."

39

T RY THE DOOR.

A lesson learned from the Brandon Mitchum debacle. But the front security door is locked, as expected, so he pulls out the tension wrench and short hook and picks the lock, opens it slowly and closes it carefully behind him. He opens the door and closes it delicately behind him. Now inside the main security door, he removes his shoes and walks up the stairs.

One apartment per floor, as he walks up slowly in his stocking feet, gets to the top floor and looks over the door—standard lock, maybe, probably a dead bolt, too—then heads back down the stairwell to the landing, halfway between the second and third floors, so that he'd be out of view if Shelly Trotter were inclined to look through her peephole, *Peekaboo, you don't see me.*

He checks his watch, just past four in the morning, she's sleeping, she'll be sleeping another two, three hours, probably, so he sits on the landing and waits.

He can wait. He's good at waiting. He's been waiting for sixteen years.

I PUSH MYSELF OUT of bed at six, not having slept at all. By seven, I'm in my car. Traffic is already thick. I'm thinking up a creative cussword to describe how I feel about the woman driving in front of me when my cell phone rings. My caller ID says it's Pete Storino, from Immigration and Customs Enforcement, getting back to me about that favor.

"Pete, you're up early for a G-man."

"Don't say I never did anything for you, Riley."

"I would never say that, Pete. Never."

He snickers. "And you didn't hear this from me."

"Right. Never heard it."

"Okay. Gwendolyn Lake, right? You want to know when she left the States?"

"Right."

"Gwendolyn Lake flew out of the country on Wednesday, June 21, 1989."

June twenty-first. That was the week of the murders. Wednesday. Three dead by that time. Cassie was killed the following Sunday.

Could have been three months, could have been three days, Gwendolyn had told me, when I asked her how long she'd been gone before Cassie was murdered.

"Where'd she go?" I ask.

"Flew into De Gaulle," he tells me.

Paris. That makes sense. When I asked Gwendolyn where she might have been around that time, her first guess had been the Riviera. Rich girl like that, she probably has a place there.

"Do you know how long she was there?" I ask, for no apparent reason.

"Can't help you on that, my friend. The domestic stuff, I can ask for a favor here or there. I have to involve too many people if I call the French."

"No, no. That's fine."

"I assume she was probably staying with family over there," he adds.

"Family? In France?"

"Gwendolyn Lake is a French national," he says. "You didn't know that?"

No, actually, I didn't. Gwendolyn Lake was born in France? I guess that's not too surprising. These rich people, jetting about the globe, probably have villas on every continent and can afford elite medical care wherever they are.

Storino continues, "Says here, born in—I'm going to mispronounce this—Saint-Jean-Cap-Ferrat. September 8, 1969. Anyway, that probably explains the length of her visit."

"How's that?" I ask. "When did she return to the States?"

"Let's see—August twenty of 'ninety-two."

"'Ninety-*two*? She was gone for *three years*?"

"From the States, *oui, oui*."

I thank Pete and punch out the cell phone, digesting that information, while waving off a guy at an intersection who wants to sell me a newspaper.

Gwendolyn Lake left the country the same week that Cassie and Ellie were murdered and didn't return for *three years*?

Have we been looking at the wrong troubled young heiress?

MCDERMOTT CALLS HOME, talks to his mother and to Grace, explaining his situation. When he's done, he stretches his arms, shakes the cobwebs from his weary head. Members of the County Attorney Technical Unit are photographing the walls in the basement.

"Dammit," he says to himself, not for the first time this morning. They found their guy, but they didn't *find* him. And it's not like he just happened to be out running an errand. They raided his place in the middle of the night.

He's in the wind.

The dust in the basement brings out the worst in McDermott's allergies. He wipes at his nose and scratches the roof of his mouth with his tongue. By now, he has taken at least a cursory look at every document pinned up to the corkboard on Koslenko's basement walls. The information is neatly divided into certain categories. Much of the documentation is devoted to the Terry Burgos case, or one of the players involved in it. Harland Bentley. His ex-wife Natalia. Their daughter Cassie Bentley. Terry Burgos. Paul Riley. Even a pair of photographs from a gossip column of Riley and his girlfriend Shelly Trotter, the governor's daughter.

Another section of the wall contains photographs of women on the street, virtually all of whom look like prostitutes in their on-the-job outfits. Below many of the photos, Koslenko has handwritten their names—at least their street names. *Roxy. Honey. Candi. Delilah.*

"Jesus, there must be a hundred photos," he mumbles.

"Close. Ninety-eight," says Stoletti. "This guy has a real hard-on for hookers."

"Mike." Powers, one of the other detectives who has arrived, comes bounding down the stairs. His hand, in a latex glove, holds up a piece of paper. "Found this in his bedroom."

McDermott, also wearing a latex glove, takes the paper. It's a Xerox copy of a smaller, typewritten note:

> *I know that you know about my relationship with Ellie. And I know*
> *about your relationship with my daughter. If you tell, so will I. But if you*
> *keep quiet, I will endow a chair in your name at Mansbury College.*
> *I need your answer right now.*

McDermott rereads the note, then takes a breath. He feels a number of scraggly lines in his brain, now forming into circles.

"Bentley *did* buy off Albany," Stoletti says. "Bentley *was* sleeping with Ellie."

"And Albany *was* sleeping with Cassie," he adds. "Christ Almighty."

"Koslenko was Bentley's bagman." Stoletti takes a breath. "He does Bentley's dirty work."

McDermott works that over. Something about it doesn't seem quite right. His cell phone on his hip buzzes. The call is coming from the station house. "McDermott," he says, but the reception is weak, the voice of one of his fellow detectives mired in static. "Call you back," he yells. He takes the stairs and heads outside.

HE DIDN'T SPEAK WELL. *But he listened well. Gwendolyn and Mrs. Bentley, in the kitchen.*

This is my fucking house, *Gwendolyn said.*

No, it's my house. All of this is mine until I decide to give it to you. Would you like to take a look at the trust documents?

It's not fair. *Gwendolyn pounded on the kitchen table.* I'm not a minor. Give it to me.

Mrs. Bentley said, You'll have it when you show me you can handle it.

You fucking Bentleys. You think you're so much better than me. Well, Auntie Nat, do you know where your darling husband is right now? Any idea? And that daughter of yours? Precious little Cassie, the freak show? *Gwendolyn broke into hideous laughter.*

They came into his view now, Mrs. Bentley grabbing Gwendolyn by the arm.
Gwendolyn tried to wrestle away, but Mrs. Bentley took her other arm, too.

Don't you *ever* talk about my family. *Then she turned and saw him stand-*
ing there. She broke away from Gwendolyn and approached. She said nothing
for a long moment. Leo didn't know what to do—

Do you like it here, Leo?

He nodded yes.

Do you want to be deported? Do you want to go back to the Soviet
Union? Back to that institution?

Back to—was she asking him or telling him? What did she—

Then mind your own business. And get back to your chores.

Leo's eyes dropped. He'd disappointed Mrs. Bentley. He turned and headed
out to the yard, the shame burning in his chest.

Leo jumps at the sound of footsteps in the apartment on the third floor.
It's now half past seven. The timing is about right. He stands up, stretches,
still on the landing halfway between the second and third floors.

From inside the apartment come four quick beeps, as the intruder alarm
is disarmed. Okay. There's probably a motion sensor that cuts through the
middle of the small apartment, and you can't walk around for a cup of coffee or juice unless you disarm it. Why leave it on in the morning? You got
through the night.

That's how all of you think. Once the sun comes up, you feel safe.

Leo climbs the stairs slowly, still in his socks. He puts his ear against
Shelly Trotter's apartment door and listens. He hears the pressure release,
then the gentle cascade of water.

She is taking a shower.

First, he puts on his shoes. Then he removes the tension wrench from his
bag and gets to work. She has a dead bolt on the door, too, one that uses a
cylinder lock. He surprises himself at how efficiently he uses the hooking
pick to line up the pins and get the door open.

The water is still falling. She's still in the shower. Now is the time, while
she's naked and on wet footing, utterly unable to defend herself. He places
the bag, heavy from the chain saw, near the couch but out of view from
other parts of the house. Just in case.

He knows how to do it. Move swiftly toward the bathroom, toward the
sound of falling water, get to the door and listen, distinguish the sounds—

The water is slapping against something that produces a hollow sound, something plastic, a shower liner, a curtain, not a glass door.

Duck your head for a quick peek, once, confirm it, a red curtain, can't see through it, you can't see me, here I come, Shelly, here I come—

Pivot quickly into the bathroom, go right to the curtain, yank it open, her hands are buried in her soapy hair, she tries to react but loses her footing.

She never makes a sound.

40

I HANG MY COAT on my door and take a quick look at my calendar. Betty puts everything I do on my desktop calendar, which is better for me than a handheld weekly planner because I can't lose a computer. I don't have court today and there are two meetings that I will tell Betty to cancel. Most of what I'm doing these days is overseeing a cadre of other lawyers, anyway.

Gwendolyn Lake left the country the same week as the murders, went to her home in France, and didn't return to the U.S. for three years. That's not inconsistent with the impression she gave me of herself—the directionless, globe-trotting party animal. With that kind of money, she could find comfort and fast friends on any continent. But that's judging from the impression she gave me.

I start toward my files on the Bentley case, which Betty has allowed to remain on the floor of my office but tucked neatly off to the side. But I stop. There is virtually nothing in those files about Gwendolyn Lake. She wasn't around back then. We didn't look at her because we couldn't. Because we had no reason to. We had no *reason* to.

"Dammit." I swipe at some papers on my desk.

Was Gwendolyn Lake the one who was pregnant? The one who had the abortion? She was an orphan who lived, at least in part, under the watch of Harland and Natalia. She'd have the same health care provider, right? At the same Sherwood Executive Center?

I don't know. All I know is that I didn't get the answers I wanted from

Gwendolyn Lake. Harland has all but shut me out—or maybe it's I who shut him out.

The notes. I still have copies. It's all I have right now. I spread them out on my desk, focusing on the second one, the one Stoletti commented on.

I will inevitably lose life. Ultimately, sorrow echoes the heavens. Ever sensing. Ever calling out. Never does vindication ever really surrender easily. The immediate messenger endures the opposition, but understanding requires new and loving betrayal and new yearning.

What had Stoletti said? The word choices looked forced. The handwriting is immaculate, like she said. He wasn't rushed. He was deliberate. Yet the words he used—

Never does vindication ever really surrender easily. No need for the word *ever* when you already had *never*. It's redundant, bad grammar. *But understanding requires new and loving betrayal and new yearning.* Same problem. He used "new" twice.

Is it just bad grammar? Am I taking the ramblings of a nut job and inferring too much?

"Shit." Something about this is wrong.

My phone rings, an internal call, but not from anyone in the office—their caller ID would show up. It's not from Betty because she's not here. It's a call from outside, being routed through the directory to me.

"Paul Riley," I say.

"Mr. Riley, this is Gwendolyn Lake."

Speak of the devil. I don't say anything. If she has something to tell me, she has to want to do it.

The phone line goes quiet. There is background noise, someone shouting an order, people talking. She's at her diner, presumably.

"I wasn't honest with you yesterday," she says.

"I—" I decide not to comment.

"You figured as much."

"I had my suspicions."

"I said I didn't want to help. But I do. I want to talk to you."

"I'm free now." I sit back in my chair.

"Good," she says. "I'm across the street."

MCDERMOTT STEPS OUT INTO the fresh air for only the second time in six hours. He savors it, despite the thick humidity. The neighbors and press have gathered around the police tape surrounding the perimeter of the property. An officer, taking statements, walks over.

"This guy's a friggin' ghost, Mike. Neighbors say he stayed in his house practically all the time. He'd leave at night sometimes, at most. Hardly ever saw him. Said he orders pizza or Chinese food every night, and him answering the door was about the only time anyone laid eyes on him. He even paid someone to mow his lawn. Neighbors said they kept their kids away from his property. Looks like he creeped everyone out."

"Keep talking to 'em," McDermott says. He turns to Powers, one of the detectives. "I want Professor Albany at the station," he says. "I don't care what he's doing. Grab the ACA"—the assistant county attorney assigned to the station house—"and start with affidavits for warrants. We're moving this morning."

"Got it, Mike."

He grabs his arm. "And do the same thing for Harland Bentley."

He uses his cell phone to call Sloan, one of the detectives on the case, the same one who called him earlier.

"Hang on, Mike." Sloan takes a minute, giving instructions to someone. "Okay. So here's what we have so far. The Vicky is one Brenda Stoller. Grad student and part-time model. Found in her SUV, backseat, in the parking lot of E-Z Days Hardware. Her throat was slashed."

"And?"

"And yeah, a guy came in yesterday asking for a Trim-Meter chain saw. We got the store vids and an ID from the salesman. It's our offender. Why this lady, Mike? She walks in and buys some lightbulbs and this happens?"

"Hell if I know. She got in the way somehow." He thinks about that a moment. "Describe her to me, Jimmy."

"Young, pretty, dressed to the nines."

"Describe her outfit."

"Oh, hot pink shirt, black pants, heels. Nice body. I mean, this was a very pretty lady."

"Any chance she could be confused for a pro?"

"A *pro*? Well, shit—I *guess* so. Pretty sexy outfit, but not *that*—oh, yeah, I suppose. Why you asking?"

"I'm not sure." He wipes the sweat off his forehead. The basement turned into a sauna, once everyone was down there working on it. "Something about this guy and prostitutes. Run a sheet, just for the hell of it. Anything from the vids in the parking lot?"

"Not yet, but we're working on it."

"Get me the car he was driving, Jimmy. His own car is in the garage. He's using a rental. Get me plates. He's on the run."

"Got it."

McDermott sighs. They were so close to getting this guy. "Tell me about the other one."

"The male vic is one Ray Barnacke, the owner of Varten's Tools and Construction. His neck was broken. And you were right, Varten's was one of the distributors of Trim-Meter chain saws. One of the employees says there's a Trim-Meter missing from the wall."

"Shit." McDermott shakes his head. "He was supposed to call us."

"No vids, either. Place had no cameras."

"Great. And it was a broken neck? That's it?"

"That's it. No signs of torture. No signs of any of the other weapons from the song. But obviously, now he's got the saw."

"Yeah. Jesus Christ. Listen, Jimmy—have them check the victim's left foot, between the pinkie toe and the fourth toe, for an incision."

"Huh?"

"Just have them check, Jim."

"Okay. Left foot. Okay. So you have a motive for this guy yet? You find anything good?"

McDermott squints into the sunlight. "I'm beginning to wonder if there *is* a motive. That assumes we can apply rational thought to this guy."

"Okay. I'll get back to you, soon as I have anything. What are you doing now?"

"I'm going to brief the commander," McDermott says. "And then I'm going to see Harland Bentley's ex-wife."

I MEET GWENDOLYN LAKE at the diner across the street from my office. She is sitting in a booth with her hands around a cup of coffee.

"I don't like being here," she says, shaking her head slowly. "I don't want to be here."

Like an alcoholic returning to a bar, I suppose she means. This is where she lived when she started self-destructing. She even looks like she doesn't belong, at least in the commercial district, wearing a soft blue T-shirt, shorts, and sandals. Her hair is hanging, as before, straight past her shoulders. Her bright green eyes peer sadly through her glasses at me.

"It took me so long to wipe the grime off. Y'know?"

I tell the waitress I'll have some coffee, because I could use the boost. "I'm not your psychiatrist, Gwendolyn."

She smiles, her face blushing. She takes a deep breath and says, "I pretended I didn't know who Frank Albany was. That wasn't true. I do."

That much, I'd already suspected, when she slipped up and referred to "Frank" during our conversation after claiming not to know him. Okay, so score one for her.

"What a creep." Her lips curl inside her mouth. A hand comes off the counter. "Hanging out with college girls. Girls in his *class.*"

"Tell me," I say.

"I can't say for absolutely certain. But I thought that—I thought that the two of them—"

I take a sip of the coffee put in front of me, burning my tongue.

"Professor Albany and Cassie were having an affair. Is that what you're telling me?"

"I thought so." She looks up at me. "Ellie thought so, too." She gauges my reaction before continuing. "I'd have thought you, of all people, would know this."

"And how in the hell would *I* have known that?" I ask, defensively. "Ellie was dead, you were gone, and Professor Albany wasn't going to publish that information."

Gwendolyn moves her hands around the coffee cup, as if she were molding pottery.

"Okay." I cool down. No point in going backward. "What else, Gwendolyn?"

She continues with her nervous, fidgety hands. "Ellie told me that Cassie was pregnant."

I close my eyes. A suspicion confirmed. The lawyer in me is thinking through admissibility problems, the hearsay rule. *Cassie told Ellie told Gwendolyn.* "When?" I ask.

She shrugs, still staring at the countertop. "Sometime during the school year, is the best I can tell you. When it was warm. May or June."

"The murders happened in mid-June," I remind her. "Can you relate it to then?"

"No." She looks up at me. "I don't even remember when I left."

"Try."

I think back to what Pete Storino told me an hour ago. Gwendolyn left the States on Wednesday, June 21, 1989. Only days before Cassie was murdered.

"Mr. Riley." She frames her hands on the table. "People measure time by days of the week if they work. They measure them by semesters or trimesters if they're in school. I didn't measure time any of those ways. I didn't work and I didn't go to school. Every day was a vacation to me, because—"

"Gwendolyn, can you help me or not?"

"June, I think," she says, surprising me. "I've been thinking about it since you asked yesterday. Probably sometime in June, I flew back to Europe."

Okay, so that's pretty close. I decide to test her some more.

"Do you remember where you went when you left the States?"

She shakes her head. "I would assume the Riviera. I have a place on Cap-Ferrat."

Okay. Storino had said she was born in Saint-Jean-Cap-Ferrat.

So maybe she's straight after all.

"So sometime in May or June," I say, "Ellie told you that Cassie was pregnant."

She nods her head. "Cassie told her one night and was very upset."

"What else?"

"There's no 'What else?' That's it."

"Did you ask Cassie yourself?"

She shakes her head, smiling. "Cassie and I weren't—she didn't approve of how I lived my life. I was closer with Ellie."

"So you suspected that Cassie was having an affair with Professor Albany, and you understood she was pregnant. But you can't confirm any of that."

She looks in my eyes. "You think I'm lying?"

"So I take it, you don't know for sure if Albany was the child's father."

She thinks about that a minute. "Well, no, I don't."

"Do any other possibilities come to mind?"

She drinks her coffee, makes a face, and shakes her head slowly.

"What about Brandon Mitchum?" I ask.

"Oh, no. Not Brandon."

"Then who, Gwendolyn? Give me a guess."

She draws circles with her finger on the table. She has a name. I know she does.

"There was this guy," she starts. "He was a nice enough guy, I guess. He worked at the houses some, back then. Y'know, Nat had her house, and my mother had ours, across town. Some of the staff sort of jumped around from one house to the other." She sighs. "He did yard work and errands, and I think he was a driver, too. I always thought he had a thing for Cassie. You should have seen the way he looked at her. I used to tease her about it. Mostly, he was harmless. But sometimes I thought he—he could be a little scary."

I try to maintain calm, as much as I want to shake her. But I let her go, seeing the animation across her face, and something beyond excitement.

Fear.

"Leo," she says. "His name was Leo."

From my jacket pocket, I remove the Xerox of the infamous photograph of Harland Bentley with reporters and the man in the background with the scar beneath his eye. The man who attacked Brandon Mitchum. The man who probably killed Fred Ciancio, Amalia Calderone, and Evelyn Pendry.

"God." Gwendolyn takes the photograph, then looks at me. "That's him."

LEO LOOKS OUT THROUGH the sliding glass door in Shelly Trotter's apartment, onto the parking pad below. It's nearing nine o'clock, work time. He hears footsteps on the floor below him, the shuffling of shoes as the occupant on the second floor leaves through her sliding glass door, bounding down the stairs. A moment later, she drives off, leaving only Shelly Trotter's car out there.

Leo unlocks the sliding glass door but doesn't open it. He takes a quick look into the bathroom at Shelly Trotter's body, then heads out the front door of the apartment, down the internal stairs. He finds his car on the street and drives it through the alley to the parking pad behind the brownstone.

Let's see whose side you're on now, Mr. Riley.

41

"HELL, YES, I want an APB. And get his name and photo all over the fucking media. Print, television, radio, Internet." McDermott punches out his cell phone and looks through the passenger window at the addresses of the gargantuan homes. When he finds the one he wants, he pulls up to a steel gate. McDermott shows his shield to the man in a booth. "Mrs. Bentley is expecting me," he says.

"Mrs. *Lake.*" The man picks up the phone and makes a call. "Detective, follow this road around the curve, please."

The home, like many homes of the megarich, is set back on the grounds. McDermott cruises past a fountain and an elaborate garden until the road curves around to the front door of the mansion.

No one deserves this much money. This place has three front doors.

A woman dressed all in white, her hands clasped behind her, stands under the awning between two ornate pillars. She greets him warmly, and seems unsure what to make of the files he's carrying in his hands. "I'll hang on to these, thanks," he tells her.

The foyer is not surprising, a long, angled staircase, chandelier, antique furniture. His escort takes him into a parlor with more of the antique thing going on. McDermott's wife was the decorator in the family. All he'd requested was a comfortable couch.

He declines a beverage, and the woman leaves him sitting on something uncomfortable, staring at a baby grand piano. They wanted Grace to be musical. Talked about piano lessons. He's going to have to follow up on that. He'll have to find a used upright piano somewhere.

He'll have to find some money, too, to afford it.

"Detective."

McDermott gets to his feet. Natalia Lake is tall and fit, dressed in a sleeveless turtleneck. Her gray hair is pulled back slick against her skull. Her skin is tanned and artificially tight. Her eyelids, though, are a darker shade.

"Forgive me if I'm a little out of sorts," she says. "I do not sleep well on overnight flights and we just landed two hours ago. I've barely had time for a bath."

"Sure," he says. "How was your flight?"

"Turbulent."

"What airline?"

She blinks her eyes. "Airline?"

"Oh." Right. She has her own jet.

"I'm so sorry I've been unavailable," she says. "I did cut my stay short."

McDermott scratches his nose. "Yeah, I appreciate that. Italy, right?"

She takes a seat on the couch opposite McDermott. "I have friends in Tuscany who absolutely insist that I take a few weeks every summer."

"Oh, absolutely." McDermott reaches into a file and pulls out the photo of Harland Bentley and the man standing behind him whose name he now knows.

"Mrs. Lake, can you identify that man in the background?"

"Please, it's Nat. Oh." She recoils, probably upon seeing her ex-husband. "In the back?" She puts on her eyeglasses and looks again. "Oh. Is that Leo? This is an old photograph." She looks at McDermott. "Leo—Leo Koslenko," she says.

"Do you know where he is now, Mrs. Lake?"

"No, I don't." She shakes her head. "I haven't seen Leo for years. I don't think I've seen him since—since Cassie died."

"You haven't spoken to him, either?"

She stares at him. "Oh, no," she whispers. "Leo's done something?"

McDermott deflates, waves a hand. "Let's back up," says McDermott. "Who is Leo Koslenko?"

She sighs, raises her chin. "Leo's family in the Soviet Union was close with mine. Leo had some trouble, and his family felt he would be better off here, in the States."

"What kind of trouble?"

She shakes her head dismissively. "Disciplinary, I assume. I don't know. His family asked if I would take him and I did."

"And when was this?"

Koslenko's sheet showed that he immigrated to America in 1986. He wants to hear Mrs. Lake's answer.

"Mid-eighties," she answers. "During the Reagan administration."

He nods. "And he came to live with you?"

"Yes." She crosses her leg. "He worked for us. His quarters were here, in fact." She gestures with her hand. "This was my sister Mia's home, originally. I lived on the other side of town."

"Where Mr. Bentley still lives."

She smiles weakly. "We're both too stubborn to move."

"Leo, you called him—Leo lived here?"

"Yes. There is a coach house." Her eyes run over him. He imagines she has made many judgments of many people with those eyes, most of them unfavorable. "Am I to assume that Leo is under suspicion? They mentioned a homicide over the phone."

"More than one homicide."

"More than— Oh, dear God." She touches her face, her hand trembling. "Leo was a sweet boy, but—well, he'd been in therapy. I thought he'd come along quite well."

"When was the last time you spoke to him or saw him?"

"Oh, quite some time ago." Her eyes cast off. "Well. Cassie died in June of 1989. I left Harland almost immediately afterward. It was—oh, it was—it was rather chaotic, to say the least." She picks absently at a fingernail, shaking her head slowly.

McDermott watches her but keeps silent. In his experience, the best Q and A's are long on the A's.

She clears her throat with some difficulty and continues. "When I left," she says delicately, "I never went back. I moved in with my niece Gwendolyn, and I no longer wanted our staff to intermingle. I wanted Harland's staff to be Harland's and ours to be ours. I wanted the separation to be complete."

He nods. "And Leo?"

"Leo probably should have stayed with us, with me," she says. "But he didn't."

"Did Leo stay at Harland's place?"

Natalia closes her eyes. She brings a hand to her forehead, pushing back hair that is already pushed back. "You would think I would know that answer," she says. "You would think someone who took responsibility for Leo would see to it that he was doing all right."

"But you didn't."

She offers the tepid smile again. "After my daughter's death, I was hardly functional for a good year. I've had some abuse problems of my own, if you didn't know."

He shakes his head no.

"Yes, well—my daughter had been the best antidote." She sighs, and continues in a flat tone. "I was not sober for at least twelve months after they found Cassie. So no, Detective, I did not know what became of Leo."

McDermott scribbles some notes on his pad.

"Could *you* tell me what's become of him?" she asks.

"I wish I could. Can I ask—the reason for your divorce? So soon after Cassie's death?"

"You can ask." She removes a gold case and produces a cigarette. "I hope you don't mind. It's the only vice I'm allowed." She lights the cigarette and holds it close to her face, her elbow held high.

McDermott opens his hands.

"Is that really important to your investigation?"

"It might be," he says.

"I can't imagine how."

"Mrs. Lake, in my job sometimes you don't know what's important until you discover it."

The smoke billowing around her face, Natalia picks at her lip with a long fingernail. "That's rather evasive of you."

"I'd like the answer, please. I'm in a hurry."

She smokes her cigarette a moment, as if she's deciding whether to answer. McDermott thinks she's deciding *how* to answer.

"My husband," she says, "had an ongoing struggle with fidelity."

Now we're getting somewhere. He thinks of the note found in Koslenko's house, the reference to Harland's relationship with Ellie Danzinger.

"Anyone in particular?" he tries.

She taps her cigarette with earnest in a fancy ashtray. "I suppose the point is that it's *no one* in particular."

McDermott stares at his notepad. At the top of the small page, he has scribbled a few bullet points, a cheat sheet. This line of questioning seems to be hitting a dead end.

"Mrs. Lake, how well did you know Cassie's friend, Ellie Danzinger?"

"Oh, for goodness' sake." She shields her eyes, as if she's avoiding sunlight. "Mr. McDermott, if you already knew, you could have simply told me and spared me the embarrassment."

"You're talking about Ellie."

Her hands fly open, her face ashen. "Well, isn't that the point of this—this dancing around? Yes, Detective, yes—Harland was sleeping with Cassie's best friend. She was just another beautiful young woman he couldn't resist. Forgive me," she adds, her tone softening.

McDermott stays quiet a moment. He's not good with emotions, especially from women. But this is too important to back off.

"I'm sorry to ask these questions, Mrs. Lake. I'm trying to solve a series of murders. Murders that haven't stopped. This—affair—was something you discussed with Harland?"

"Oh, *God* no. Of course not." Her body is now entirely turned away from McDermott. "Harland would never have wanted *me* to know about his extracurricular activities."

McDermott waits her out, but when she doesn't elaborate he starts, "Then how—"

"Well, Cassie of course."

He jots another note. This is getting interesting. Cassie knew that Harland was carrying on with Ellie.

"I need some kind of time frame, Mrs. Lake. When did Cassie tell you about Mr. Bentley and Ellie? When was this happening?"

Natalia stands by a window, a hand cupped under her elbow, the cigarette burning near her nose. "You mean," she asks, "was it near the time Cassie died?"

"That's what I want to know."

"Yes. It was that school year. It was within a month of—of when she died." She turns and looks at McDermott, speaking in a controlled, angry tone through clenched teeth. "One of the last things my daughter learned was that her father was—was *intimate* with her best friend. You understand why, after her death, I could not be with him." Her eyes are fiery, her mouth bent in anger.

McDermott takes some notes. A painful sound comes from Natalia's throat. Her head drops in despair.

"Let me ask about Cassie, if I could," he says.

Natalia weeps softly. McDermott thinks of his daughter Grace and how a child's pain hurts the parent even worse.

"One of the recent victims was asking questions about Cassie. We think maybe those questions got her killed. That's why I'm asking."

Still unable to speak, she gestures for him to continue.

"Were Cassie's doctors at the Sherwood Executive Center? It's a building in Sherwood Heights. It's on—"

"Yes," she says with a hoarse voice, taking heavy breaths. "Yes, that's where her doctors were. Why?"

One of the hard parts of these conversations is that they aren't really conversations. It's not his job to answer questions. "Ma'am, was Cassie pregnant?"

The meager restraint Natalia has mustered fails her now. She buries her face in her hands and weeps openly. McDermott looks away, feeling like an intruder, but his adrenaline is surging.

"Ma'am?" It's the woman in white, standing at the threshold of the room, bouncing on her toes. Natalia holds out a hand, shakes her head as she composes herself. "I'm fine, Marta, thank you." The woman disappears.

"I'm terribly sorry," Natalia says.

"No need, ma'am. I'm a parent, too. I wouldn't want my daughter's privacy violated, either. But, Mrs. Lake—something strange was happening back then. It looks like someone orchestrated some kind of break-in into that building. The man who orchestrated it is now dead. The woman who was asking *questions* about it is now dead. And, ma'am, it's our understanding that Cassie wasn't pregnant when she—when she died."

The room goes quiet. He hears sounds from what he assumes is the kitchen, plates and pots clinking together, a faucet running. Better not to push here, he decides. She'll come around.

Natalia takes a deep breath. "All right, Detective." She nods her head. "All right. But I want your promise that this information will stay confidential unless you absolutely have to use it." She looks at him. "Do I have that promise?"

"Of course you do. As a cop and as a parent, Mrs. Lake."

He hates making a promise he won't keep.

"Very well." She struggles again momentarily, as if having second thoughts. But she's already given McDermott the answer.

"Yes," she says. "Cassie was pregnant that year. And you are correct that she was not pregnant at the time she died. She had that procedure," she adds tersely, preempting a follow-up, "but I didn't know about it until it was over. Cassie only came to me after it was done. Because she knows I would have talked her out of it."

"And who—"

"I do not know who the father was. It would be an understatement to say that I tried to find out from her. In fact, I probably focused too much on that issue and too little on how the entire thing was affecting my daughter. That is something I have to live with every day."

He thinks again of the note found in Koslenko's house, the reference to Professor Albany and Cassie. This time, he won't front the name, like he did with Ellie. "Can you give me any possible names? Boyfriends or anything?"

"She wouldn't tell me. She absolutely refused. She was very protective of this person."

McDermott watches the expression on her face. "But."

She makes eye contact with him, the anger rising in her again. "Of course I had certain suspicions. She seemed to have a rather unique relationship with one of her professors."

McDermott starts. His reaction is not lost on Natalia.

"You know, don't you?" she asks, emitting a bitter laugh. "This is another time you are asking me something you already know. This is what you do. You tell people—"

"Mrs. Lake, listen." He raises his hand. "It's very important that I hear the information from you and not the other way around. You can understand that. Please, just give me a name."

"The one who testified at the trial," she says. "Mr. Albany."

WHEN GWENDOLYN LAKE excuses herself for the ladies' room, I use my cell phone to call Mike McDermott. I get his voice mail and leave him a vague message that I need to speak with him right away.

Now we have an ID, the mysterious "Leo." Connected to the Bentley family, pictured in the background of that photograph of Harland and the reporters.

Gwendolyn returns from the restroom and drops in the seat opposite me.

"Is he committing these crimes?" she asks me. "Just tell me."

"Leo? I think so," I concede.

She moans. "I think he was—not all there. Mentally, I mean." She looks at the table. "I didn't exactly hang out with the staff. But he seemed—a little off. Y'know, like he'd hold his stare on you or he'd be mumbling to himself. My mother once said he'd had some problems in Russia."

"Russia?"

"Oh, yeah. He was an immigrant. I think his family knew my mother's family there. My grandmother was a dancer in Russia—"

"Right, I know."

"—Okay. And I think his family asked if he could stay with us. Like, as a favor."

"What kind of problems did 'Leo' have in Russia?"

She shakes her head. "Beats me. I don't think I said two words to him. But Cassie, she was different. The staff loved her."

My mind races through my talking points. Last time I talked to Gwendolyn, I didn't do such a good job of interviewing her. I've been given a reprieve, and I want to cover everything.

A waitress passes us with a cholesterol special, hash browns and dripping eggs and bacon. The smell of fried food turns my stomach in knots.

"Gwendolyn," I say, "where were Cassie's doctors located?"

"Her doctors? I have no—well, wait," she says, stopping on that. "Probably the same as mine, actually. I had a doctor named Sor—I think it was Sorenson? Yeah, Dr. Sorenson." She nods. "Yeah. Dr. Sorenson was my general practitioner. When I'd come to the States, I'd usually get a checkup."

"Where was Dr. Sorenson located?"

"Oh." She sighs. "It was in some building in the next town over."

"The Sherwood Executive Center?"

She shrugs. "The name of the building? I have no idea."

"On Lindsey Avenue in Sherwood Heights? A brick building?"

"Yeah." Her eyes trail off. "Right, Lindsey. It was the Mercy Group, or something like that. Yeah, it was, like, maybe ten or twelve stories, something like that." She looks at me again. "Why?"

"They might want to talk to Cassie's doctors."

The waitress refills her coffee. Gwendolyn smiles at her. I have hardly touched mine because it's weak, like the stuff at work.

I sit back in my chair and try to digest this. Looks like Cassie and Professor Albany had something going on. Cassie was pregnant. She must have had an abortion. Her doctors were located in that building in Sherwood Heights where Fred Ciancio transferred the week of the murders.

"You need to talk to the police," I say.

She nods, though she's not exactly jumping at the prospect.

"Are you staying here with Nat?"

She seems surprised by that. "I just got into town. I was planning to go back."

"Talk to Detective McDermott." I take a business card and write his cell number on the back, as well as my own. "Don't go far, Gwendolyn," I tell her.

WITH A TREMBLING HAND, Natalia Lake signs the consent form and hands it back to McDermott.

"Thank you, Mrs. Lake."

"You will let me know what comes of this, I trust." Her eyes search his face for something. McDermott has seen that look too many times. Family members of victims, looking for the cop to tell them it will be okay, that if they close their eyes and pray their loved one will come back.

"Of course I will." He takes her cold hand and holds it an extra beat.

When he turns for the door, she grabs his arm. He looks back at her. She looks as if she has aged during their conversation, the composed, well-groomed woman replaced with a grieving mother with memories that have returned with a vengeance.

"You think that what is happening now is because of this? Because of Cassie's abortion? Someone is covering this up?"

McDermott offers what he can, a compromising expression and generic words of comfort. He does not know the answer. And in many ways, he doesn't care. He is not here to solve a sixteen-year-old case.

He is here to find Leo Koslenko.

ONCE BACK INSIDE Shelly Trotter's apartment, Leo slides the glass door closed again and wipes the sweat off his forehead. He takes a moment to catch his breath. What to do first?

He looks back into the living room, where the chain saw rests in his gym bag. Then he checks his watch.

Soon. Very soon.

42

McDERMOTT WALKS into the station at a barely controlled pace. Powers comes up to him and tells him, "The affidavits are on your desk. Albany will be here any minute."

McDermott checks his cell phone, hears a message from Riley.

"We're looking for Harland Bentley, too. There's a G-lady here for you?" He gestures to McDermott's desk. "Got a real mouth on her, that one."

McDermott allows himself a smile. That much is true.

"Hey, Mickey." Special Agent Jane McCoy gets out of her chair and winks at him.

" 'Mickey'?"

"Yeah, it's my new nickname for you."

"You got tired of 'Shithead,' did you? How's business in CT?"

"Business is booming. Can we talk somewhere?"

The cops and the FBI are generally none too friendly with one another. But years ago, when McDermott was a new detective and McCoy was in Narcotics, they worked together on a large-scale bust of a west-side street gang.

Nowadays, McCoy is in counterterrorism. Since she's the only fibbie he knows, and it's close enough to immigration, he called her in on this.

They sit in the same conference room that McDermott has taken over as his own, filled with information on Terry Burgos. McCoy, never one to miss much, manages to take it all in without comment.

She throws a file on the desk. "This is the A-file on Leonid Koslenko. You're not supposed to have this. Copy what you want. Give it all back."

McDermott takes the manila folder and nods. "Thanks, Jane."

"The guy at ICE who ran Koslenko retired ten years ago. He was kept in a general assignment pool after that."

McDermott shakes his head. He doesn't get the meaning.

"Meaning," McCoy says, "since he'd been in the country for ten years without incident, there was no one in particular assigned to look at him. Sounds like maybe there's a reason to look at him now?"

"That's a fair statement." He smiles at her.

"You're talking like a fed now, Mickey. You're scaring me." She tucks her curly hair behind her ear and holds her stare on him a moment too long. Then she blinks it off, turning serious. "Leonid Koslenko was born in 1967 to a wealthy family in Leningrad. When he was fifteen—1982—he was sent to an institution in Lefortovo. He was released almost exactly two years later."

"An institution? You mean an insane asylum?"

She shrugs her shoulders. "Asylum, prison—sometimes hard to tell the difference in the Soviet Union. But the records showed it was a mental illness, yes."

"Okay. But he was released after two years?" McDermott recoils. "What, he was cured?"

McCoy is with him on that, one side of her mouth curling up. "He was diagnosed with 'creeping paranoid schizophrenia.'"

"Which means?"

"Which means, from what I understand, absolutely nothing. Understand, back then, the Soviets locked up political dissidents, Christians, all sorts of people they didn't want in the general populace. But they didn't lock them up in prisons. They looked them up in loony bins."

He winces. He used to use phrases like that, too.

"They used bullshit diagnoses like 'creeping schizophrenia.' They would keep them for years that way."

That makes sense. But the difference here is that American doctors have also diagnosed Koslenko with paranoid schizophrenia. He tells McCoy so.

She shrugs. "So maybe he really did belong there. Regardless, he escaped from the Soviet Union in 1986 and applied to the United States. His parents helped him. And that was the excuse he used. He said he'd been persecuted for religious and political beliefs, and that was why he did time in Lefortovo. And, apparently, the fancy lawyers who helped him out convinced our government that he was telling the truth. Here's the kicker: You're going to love who helped him in the States."

He doesn't have to guess. But why burst her bubble?

"Harland Bentley," she announces. "*The* Harland Bentley. And his wife Natalia."

He nods.

"I'm not surprising you," she gathers.

"Not with that part, no. Jane, he went into that asylum in 1982. He got out in 1984. He got over the Soviet border in 1986 and came to America."

She doesn't say anything.

"What happened in those two years? 'Eighty-four to 'eighty-six."

She smiles, but only for a moment. "That's why they pay you the big bucks, Mickey." She leans forward, touches the file she has given him. "And *that's* why you're not supposed to have this file."

I RETURN TO MY OFFICE after talking to Gwendolyn. I still haven't heard back from McDermott. I return to the notes that were delivered to me, spread out on my desk. I've been over these notes a dozen times over the past few days, but I'm certain that I'm still missing something.

The first one:

If new evil emerges, do heathens ever link past actions? God's answer is near.

Second:

I will inevitably lose life. Ultimately, sorrow echoes the heavens. Ever sensing. Ever calling out. Never does vindication ever really surrender easily. The immediate messenger endures the opposition, but understanding requires new and loving betrayal and new yearning.

Third:

Others that hunted ensured respect. Sinners know not our wrath.
Our ultimate response shall ensure consequences, reviling ethical
traitors.

The first note makes sense, at least. He's talking about a link between his crimes and Terry Burgos's murders. The third one makes some sense, too, I guess. *Our ultimate response shall ensure consequences, reviling ethical traitors.* Reviling ethical traitors? It seems awkward, forced.

The more I think about it, the more I agree with Stoletti about the second note. The word choices are odd. Some of it is nonsensical.

Never does vindication ever really surrender easily.

But understanding requires new and loving betrayal and new yearning.

Why did he insert *ever* in a sentence that didn't need it? Why use *new* twice?

Maybe—maybe these notes aren't meant to be taken literally. We're expecting someone following Burgos's crusade to be mentally ill, like him, mixed in with some pathological religious fervor. These notes bear the markings of all of that.

But maybe there's more to these notes. Maybe these are in some kind of code.

I get out a separate piece of paper and play with the words, looking for anything. I read it with every other word. Every third word. I don't discern a pattern. I try to focus on the extra words, what they might mean. I come up empty. But I can't shake the feeling that some of these words look like they don't belong—not just *ever* and *now* but words like *reviling,* sentences like *Never own worry.*

Forced.

Why did he need these words, in particular? What role did they play in this code?

Wait a second. *Wait a second.*

I start scribbling, playing out my theory. My heart starts to pound as it crystallizes. He chose those words because he needed a word that started with that particular letter. He chose *ever* because he needed an *e.*

I write the first letter from each word in the first note.

I-N-E-E-D-H-E-L-P-A-G-A-I-N.

Jesus Christ.

I need help again.

The second note:

I-W-I-L-L-U-S-E T-H-E S-E-C-O-N-D V-E-R-S-E T-I-M-E T-O B-U-R-N A-L-B-A-N-Y.

I will use the second verse. Time to burn Albany.

The third note:

O-T-H-E-R-S K-N-O-W-O-U-R S-E-C-R-E-T.

Others know our secret.

He wrote these notes to me. He needs my help again. Now he will burn Albany. Others know our secret.

Our secret? He needs *my* help? *Again?*

What the hell does this mean?

IT'S TIME. TIME NOW.

Leo walks over to the window overlooking the street: A woman is show-ing a piece of real estate to a couple of men on the other side of the street and down about eight houses; a FedEx truck is parked up the street a ways; two Latino women and their small children walk on the sidewalk, eating fresh corn dipped in butter and salt.

Leo puts on the plastic smock and fastens the ties behind his neck and back. Then he walks over to the stereo in the apartment. On top of the receiver is a framed photograph of Shelly Trotter and Paul Riley in a park, waving to the camera. He waves back.

Hello, Paul. You see what I'm about to do?

The CD already in the player is classical piano music. He pauses a moment, closes his eyes, listens to the graceful, spirited hands of Horowitz. Katrina had played, though not this beautifully of course, her young, inex-pert hands clanking clumsily over the keys. Mother taught her. She'd wanted to teach Leo, too, but Father wouldn't allow it. Men of the world had no time for such trivialities, he'd said, but Leo had been envious of Kat, and was sure that she'd continued her play over the years as one of many ways to taunt her younger brother, to display her dominance over him. Oh, they hadn't seen it in Kat, even afterward, the many ways she'd seduced and manipulated the entire family, her treachery, the evil in her soul, until his moment finally came on the ice when she'd slipped and was finally at last vulnerable, unable to gain traction with her skates, as he fell on top of her, pressed his thumbs into her throat, and, yes, he cried, though she'd given him no choice, only *he* had the courage to do it, and he knows that Mother and Father knew, in the recesses of their minds, even as they sent him off to Lefortovo, that he'd been brave and wise and just—

He opens his eyes, adjusts the volume control on the stereo so that Horowitz's piano is very loud but not deafening. Then he walks into the bathroom.

Her naked body is in a ball, stuffed horizontally into the tub. He debates it for a second, then takes her ankles and moves her legs over the side of the tub. Now she is on her back, looking up with vacant eyes at the ceiling. Her nose is broken. So is her neck. Otherwise, she is beautiful.

Leo tugs on the chain saw, the violent buzz drowning out the music.

McCoy PREFACES HER COMMENTS. No one is sure about this. The government had its suspicions but never confirmed them.

"After the Soviet Union collapsed," she explains, "we learned a lot of things about them. Some of it was ancient history. Some of it not so ancient. Koslenko's name came up once during a debriefing. That's all."

McDermott nods along, impatient. "What did Leo Koslenko do from 1984 to 1986, Jane?"

McCoy clears her throat. "This isn't my specialty, Mike. But you needed this on short notice, so I'll try." She takes a moment. "There is something known as the 'Thirteenth Department.' It was the part of the Soviet State Security Service—the KGB—devoted to what they called 'executive action.' We learned in 1993, from a former spy, that Leonid Koslenko may have been recruited from Lefortovo to be a part of the Thirteenth."

McDermott stares at her for a long time without speaking.

"There is some suspicion," she continues, "that this is why he only served two years in Lefortovo. It was not unheard of for the Soviets to recruit people from their asylums, or their prisons, for this executive action work."

McDermott raises his eyebrows. "And executive action is?"

"Wet work. Abductions, beatings, torture," McCoy says. "Maybe murder. Strong-arm stuff. Domestic, mostly. It wouldn't be uncommon for them to use someone from an asylum with the requisite talents, then throw them back inside. If they try to talk about it, the simple explanation is that these people are 'crazy.' They'd be easily discredited. Who's going to believe a loony tune?"

McDermott looks away, again trying to ignore the remark.

"Oh, shit." McCoy covers her face. "Mike, I'm so sorry. I didn't—"

"Forget it." He pushes himself out of his chair, shows McCoy his back.

"I'm such an idiot, Mike. How—how is Grace doing?"

He doesn't answer. It's not the time to think about his daughter. McCoy cusses herself out again, tries again for the apology, while McDermott works on the information. He thinks about what he found in Koslenko's basement. The massive documentation about the Bentleys and Paul Riley and Terry Burgos, the photos of the prostitutes.

"You're telling me," he says slowly, "that Leo Koslenko was a Soviet operative?"

"I'm using past tense, Mike. There is no 'Soviet' anymore. And I'm saying maybe. Look"—she frames her hands—"we're not talking about a guy who could assassinate a target from a hundred yards away. We're not talking about a guy who could be trusted with state secrets. But a lot of what the KGB did wasn't sophisticated at all. It was simply keeping the dissidents in line. Bring them in for some friendly, government-style torture. Shake them awake in the middle of the night and remind them that you know where they live."

McDermott drops his head. "I'm talking about a guy who can get past a locked door. Who can come in and out without a trace. A guy who knows how to torture for information."

She nods. "He'd be the perfect candidate. He had mental problems, so deniability would be easy. They'd just put an idea in his head, wind him up, and turn him loose."

Put an idea in his head, wind him up, and turn him loose.

"This conversation never happened," she reminds him. "No foolin'."

Right. The government doesn't want to admit it let a psychotic into the country. There can be no blowback, she's saying. That's why McCoy came herself to tell him, and why she needs the A-file back. Because no one was supposed to tell him any of this. It could mean her job, if it came out.

"So the Soviets taught this guy how to torture and kill and sent him here."

"What I'm hearing," she replies, "is that the Koslenko family had serious sway in the government. They got wind of what he was doing and got him out. They played it like he was a political dissident unfairly accused of a mental disorder to silence him. And like you already know, he had help on this side."

"Great. That's a real consolation."

"Mike, none of this came out until the nineties, and, even then, it wasn't something we could prove. And, look, from what we knew, this guy had been a good citizen while he was here."

A good citizen. A good citizen, that is, until someone put an idea in his head, wound him up, and turned him loose.

43

McDERMOTT STANDS in the conference room, his head against the wall. "I'm thinking, that's what I'm doing," he says before Stoletti can ask.

"Professor Albany's here, Mike. What did the fed tell you?"

McDermott gives Stoletti the *Reader's Digest*. She takes a seat as she listens. He ends with the reminder, nobody can know about this. "McCoy put her ass on the line to tell me."

"A KGB henchman," she says. "Holy Christ."

McDermott pushes himself off the wall. "It explains his proficiency. We're looking at a professionally trained paranoid schizophrenic."

One of the detectives, Williams, pokes his head in. "Mike, Paul Riley's on the phone."

"Okay, tell him—"

"He says it's urgent, Mike," says Williams. "You should probably take it."

"THE GUY IN THIS PHOTO is named Leo Koslenko." Riley shows them the photo, points at the tough guy in the background. "He was an immigrant laborer for the Bentleys."

McDermott isn't sure how to play this. He's off guard here, in every way. He didn't sleep a wink last night and feels the effects, the fuzzy brain, dirty clothes, heavy eyes. Maybe he should feign surprise, but neither he nor Stoletti has the spirit for it.

Riley's no dummy, anyway, reading their expressions. "You know this," he says.

"Just found out. We raided his house a few hours ago." He nods in acknowledgment at Riley. "He left his prints on Brandon's door, like you said."

"He has a sheet," Riley says. Otherwise, prints would be useless. He waits for the details but the detectives keep mum.

Stoletti says, "Tell us about this Gwendolyn Lake."

Brandon Mitchum had mentioned her last night, too.

Riley says what he knows. Cassie's cousin, orphaned wild child, flying around the globe, mingling with the rich and famous. Yesterday, Riley says, he visited her up north, had a follow-up with her this morning. She told him about Koslenko, who supposedly had a crush on Cassie and may have been mentally unstable. Gwendolyn told him that Cassie was having an affair with Professor Albany. And she told him that Cassie was pregnant near the time she was murdered.

"Someone broke into that medical center to steal the records of the pregnancy," Riley concludes. "Or the records of the abortion. Or both. It must be Albany, right?"

McDermott still plays it coy, giving nothing. He knows all of this now, and more. He knows that Leo Koslenko has a thing for killing prostitutes—or girls who look like prostitutes, in the case of the woman at the hardware store. He knows that Koslenko had a note in his bedroom drawer that was obviously written for Professor Albany, probably back during the time of the murders, threatening him to keep quiet about Ellie Danzinger's affair with Harland Bentley.

Does Riley know that Harland Bentley was sleeping with Ellie Danzinger?

When Riley's finished, McDermott glances at Stoletti. Both of them are wondering about Riley, whether to share with him, whether Riley is on their side.

No way that Riley killed these people. Koslenko looks like the guy, every way you view it. But someone wound him up and turned him loose, to use McCoy's phrase, and the identity of that person is of particular interest. Harland Bentley's not a bad bet, but Riley works for Bentley.

It looks like Riley saved Brandon Mitchum's life, but, then, maybe he knew Koslenko was headed there.

He thinks about that. Maybe Riley knows what's happening but he can't say so, because of attorney-client privilege or something. Maybe he's trying to stop the murders without breaking any confidences.

"You figure Albany's dirty here?" he asks Riley. "You think he's killing a bunch of people now because he doesn't want anyone to know he knocked up Cassie Bentley?"

Riley shrugs, exasperated. "I don't know what else it could be."

McDermott bursts out a small laugh. "You can't think of *any* other reason?"

"Give me a better one," Riley challenges.

McDermott smiles at him. Nothing doing. Not yet, anyway. "So tell me about these notes. This code."

Silently, McDermott cusses himself out. These notes contained a code? He wasn't even looking for one. He thought the ramblings of a madman were nothing more than that.

"He uses the first letter of every word." Riley lays out his copies of the notes he received on the conference-room table. "That's why the notes seem nonsensical. They are. He needs words that start with certain letters, like Stoletti said."

"Ah, shit." McDermott claps his hands. "There were indentations on the second note. He'd been trying to come up with words that start with *V* and *E*. The first letter mattered. Jesus." He looks down at Riley's work:

I NEED HELP AGAIN.
I WILL USE THE SECOND VERSE. TIME TO BURN ALBANY.
OTHERS KNOW OUR SECRET.

"I'll be damned." McDermott shakes his head furiously, trying to clear his thoughts. He's a little old to be pulling all-nighters. "This is a very easy code—once you realize you're *looking* for a code."

Riley agrees with that. "Took me ten minutes, once I started looking. I guess that's the point. I had to be able to decipher it."

"He needs help *again*," Stoletti says. "He's talking to you, Riley."

"I know." Riley shakes his head. "I don't get it."

"Others know *our* secret." McDermott looks at Riley. "You and this guy have a secret."

"He's telling you what he's going to do," says Stoletti. "He says he needs your help, the secret is out. He tells you he's going to use the 'second verse' and it's time to burn Albany."

McDermott tries to size up the situation. These notes, if anything, implicate Riley. Why would he bring these notes to their attention?

" 'Time to burn Albany.' He's telling you to implicate the professor," Stoletti says. "He's saying, keep our secret by pointing the finger at Albany."

"Maybe," Riley agrees. "Or maybe we have the punctuation wrong. Maybe there's a period after 'burn.' "

" 'Time to burn. Albany.' Like he's signing his name, in case you don't get it." Yeah, McDermott thinks, that might make sense.

A knock on the conference-room door. Detective Sloan, the one who was investigating the murders at the two hardware stores, waves a hand to McDermott.

"Have a seat," McDermott tells Riley. "Give us a second."

McDERMOTT AND STOLETTI leave Riley in the conference room and huddle with Detective Sloan.

"We got a vehicle and a plate," Sloan says proudly. "Chrysler LeBaron, plates J41258. He rented it from a Car-N-Go downtown with a phony license. Paid in cash for two weeks."

"Good job, Jimmy. Get that on the wire. Right now." He looks over at Williams, who is walking back into the station.

"Albany's here," Williams says. "He's crying for a lawyer already."

"What about Harland Bentley?"

"Still looking for him. The office doesn't seem to know where he is."

"Find him, Barney. Go."

McDermott turns to Stoletti, who raises her eyebrows.

"What the hell do we do?" she asks.

"The question," he answers, "is what we do *first*."

44

I WANT MY LAWYER."

Professor Frank Albany, wearing a light purple shirt, matching tie, and dark sport coat, folds his arms as McDermott and Stoletti enter the interview room.

"This is pure harassment."

Police officers picked up Albany at his office, scooped him up and threatened handcuffs. Not a fun way to come down to the station. The best way to rattle a witness.

"Tell me where Leo Koslenko is," McDermott says. "And I'll let you go."

"Who?" Albany cocks his head. His lips part but he doesn't elaborate.

"Don't bullshit me, Professor."

Albany gets out of his chair, directing a finger at McDermott. "You have no right—"

McDermott grabs his arm at the wrist, cuffs him, and attaches the second cuff to the ring in the center of the table. As Albany whines and protests, McDermott holds out his hand to Stoletti, who hands him a mug shot of Leo Koslenko from one of his arrests.

McDermott slaps the mug shot down on the table and stands back. He sees the recognition in Albany's eyes immediately. His eyes move from the photo to McDermott. He doesn't even try to deny it.

"Leo Koslenko," McDermott repeats.

"I want a lawyer."

McDermott reaches into the file and places a copy of the note found in Leo Koslenko's bedroom on the table.

I know that you know about my relationship with Ellie. And I know about your relationship with my daughter. If you tell, so will I. But if you keep quiet, I will endow a chair in your name at Mansbury College. I need your answer right now.

Albany begins to read it, then looks away, his face crimson. He closes his eyes and turns his head so he cannot see the note.

That's as good as a confession. He couldn't have read more than a line of it. Had he no idea of its contents, he would have read the whole thing.

McDermott takes a seat across from Albany. Stoletti does the same.

"We already know what your 'answer' was," he tells Albany. "It was yes. You kept quiet about his affair and he kept quiet about yours, plus he threw in the endowed chair."

The professor deteriorates slowly, his face melting in fear, his skin glistening with hot sweat. His position is awkward, his body turned away from the table but his right arm cuffed to the center of the table.

McDermott can smell him now, that acidic scent of pure terror. Some are easier to break than others. This college professor is a cupcake.

"Harland Bentley already gave you up," he adds. McDermott is largely in the dark here; deception is one of the few cards he holds, so he goes with the standard interrogation in a multiple-defendant case—claim that one turned on the other. Last one to confess loses.

"I want a lawyer." It comes out as a trembling whisper.

"The only question I have now," McDermott continues, "is which one of you killed the girls."

Albany's head whips around, his wet, bloodshot eyes moving over the detectives.

"He says it was your idea." McDermott falls back in his chair, calm with the upper hand. "Want a chance to give your side?"

"I want a lawyer—"

"See, here's why that's a bad idea, Professor. This is like a race now. The first one to cut a deal wins. Me, I figure each of you is guilty of something. One of you's getting the needle. I don't really care which. But, see, Bentley, he has those fancy lawyers, he'll cop to something probably that doesn't involve much jail time. You feel like taking on Harland Bentley, one on one? Who do you think's gonna win?"

"That's"—the professor, having lost all composure, sprays the room as he shouts—"That's—all a lie! How could anything have been *my* idea? *He* gave *me* that note!"

McDermott doesn't answer, but he's already gotten something here. Albany has admitted to receiving the note from Harland Bentley.

"Which one of you killed Cassie?" he asks.

Albany's arm flies away from his body. "What the hell are you *talking* about?"

"Which one of you killed Ellie?"

"*What?*"

"See, Bentley says it was you, Professor. You were the one who gained from Cassie dying. You would've lost your job if it came out that you were banging a student. And it wasn't just a he-said, she-said, was it?"

Albany shakes his head furiously.

"No," McDermott continues, "it wasn't. Because she was pregnant. That's pretty solid proof, right, Professor? You were the 'fucking father.' Even back then, before DNA, you could identify paternity. You knew you wouldn't be able to deny it. You knew the paternity test would point to you."

"You've got this wrong," he insists. "You've got this all wrong."

"You figured, with Ellie out of the way, there'd be no one to talk about pregnancy and paternity tests and abortions."

"No—"

"You didn't figure on her telling other people about it, too."

"No!" Albany slams a fist on the table, floundering in his chair while his arm remains cuffed to the table.

"A deal is made," McDermott says. "Two girls dead, two secrets covered up."

"No. No. This isn't *right*. And what—what about Terry?"

"Oh, framing Terry Burgos was the easy part, Professor. You were, like, his mentor, right? You'd already fucked with his head, showing him all those lyrics about mutilating women, and how the Bible liked that crap. You knew he had a thing for Ellie Danzinger."

Albany's eyes, moving about chaotically, now rise to meet McDermott's.

"He drove that Suburban of his to your printing plant every night, Professor. What, you somehow got hold of his keys? Helped yourself to his truck, and maybe to his basement, too. What I want to know is, how'd you manage to fuck with his mind so he thought *he* killed those girls?"

"Oh, Jesus. Oh, Jesus God." Albany shields his eyes. "Get me a lawyer. Get me a fucking lawyer!"

"Bentley's gotten a big head start on you," Stoletti says. "If you have something to tell us, it better be now."

"We walk out of here," McDermott adds, "it's over for you. We'll get you that lawyer, but it'll be too late." After a moment of silence, he nods to Stoletti. "Let's go, Detective. Let's get that written statement from Harland Bentley."

A gasp of air, a bitter snicker, and Albany is shaking his head. McDermott and Stoletti, half out of their seats, sink back down. Albany's no dummy; he might see through the ruse. Hell, he's already asked for counsel several times. But he's been broadsided here, with information he never expected would see the light of day. McDermott's seen it happen to far better people.

"Harland-fucking-Bentley," he mumbles. "I should've known."

"Give us your side," McDermott says.

He looks up at the detectives, a rotted fruit of a face, a pathetic semblance of the defiant man who first sat in the room. "Do you know what's worse than fucking your daughter's best friend?" he asks.

McDermott doesn't answer.

Albany takes a deep breath. His mouth curls into a snarl. "Then you don't know everything."

WHILE I WAIT FOR the detectives to return, I spend my time on the notes.

I NEED HELP AGAIN.
I WILL USE THE SECOND VERSE. TIME TO BURN ALBANY.
OTHERS KNOW OUR SECRET.

What secret did he think I knew? What "help" did I give him?

I prosecuted the damn case. I built a case against Burgos and beat him at trial. What favor could I have performed?

I sit back in the chair, close my eyes, play out the history of the case. That first day, finding the bodies, then Burgos, then getting the confession. Defending the confession in court. Burgos pleaded insanity. Everything turned toward proving his rational thought, his consciousness of guilt.

Did Koslenko ever show himself to me? Was there anything he did? Did he send me one of these notes back—

My eyes open, the adrenaline flooding through me. I pick up the cell phone and dial my law firm.

"Betty," I say, "remember during the Burgos trial? Remember all that mail we received?"

"Sure," she says.

"We still have the letters?"

"Sure. For the book you never wrote."

"Have them ready," I say. "I'm coming back now."

45

LEO WAITS across the street from Paul Riley's building. No sign of any of those messengers, with their fluorescent jackets and bike helmets. He thinks of his LeBaron, parked in a lot half a block away. He needs to get back to it. He doesn't have long.

He adjusts his glasses—fake ones with clear lenses—and tugs down on his baseball cap. Disguises aren't that important here, the key is simply that he can't be identified.

If I go into the building, they'll catch me on camera. But I don't have time.

Leo drops his head, his heartbeat ricocheting. He crosses the street with pedestrians and walks into the building. He looks at the escalator, and the security up on the mezzanine.

They're looking for me.

At that moment, Leo sees one of the messengers taking the escalator down, toward him. He breathes in relief. The man is young, an empty bag over his shoulder.

Leo waves to him, holding the envelope in one hand, a fifty-dollar bill in the other.

MCDERMOTT WATCHES PROFESSOR ALBANY slowly recover his bearings. He's taking the whole thing in, McDermott realizes. He's thinking through his options and seeing no reason why he shouldn't spill whatever it is he has to say.

"What's worse than fucking your daughter's best friend?" McDermott asks.

The professor pops a cigarette in his mouth and lights it. He blows out smoke and looks up at the ceiling.

"Fucking your wife's sister," he says, exhaling.

Your wife's—what?

"You're talking about Natalia's sister?"

A hint of a smile creeps onto his face. "Mia Lake," he says. "Gwendolyn's mother."

"Harland was sleeping with Mia Lake?"

Albany nods. "Cassie was talking about paternity? I'll bet she was talking about Gwendolyn."

McDermott falls back in his chair. "Harland is Gwendolyn's father?"

Albany seems satisfied with the revelation. "Apparently, while Natalia was expecting, and presumably not open to sexual advances, he turned to her sister." He shrugs. "You don't believe me, just ask Gwendolyn. Hell, *test* her."

McDermott looks at Stoletti.

"You can imagine," Albany continues, "how a man who married an heiress—with an ironclad prenup, by the way—would feel about that information coming out. Cassie sure didn't think her father would want it public."

This, McDermott realizes, is the knock-down, drag-out fight that Brandon Mitchum described, just before finals at Gwendolyn's house. This was what sent Cassie running out of the house.

"Wait a second." McDermott places his palm on the table. "Cassie told you this."

"Sure, she did. How else would *I* know? Gwendolyn told Cassie, Cassie told me. Oh, that Gwendolyn was a piece of work. She hated Cassie. She wanted to spite her."

"And who else knew? Cassie told you. Who else knew?"

"You mean, did *Ellie* know?" Albany savors his cigarette a moment. "It would stand to reason, but I couldn't tell you."

No, McDermott's not thinking of Ellie. He's thinking of Harland Bentley. Maybe a phone call Cassie made to Harland:

You're the fucking father.

Maybe Cassie wasn't talking about her own pregnancy on that phone call that Brandon Mitchum overheard. She was talking to her father about Gwendolyn.

You're the fucking father.

That's why she was so distraught. A trifecta—her father had sired another daughter, whom Cassie had always taken as her cousin; her suspicion that her father was at it again, this time with her best friend, Ellie Danzinger; and her own pregnancy.

Enough to send anyone over the edge. And most of her torment attributable to one person. Harland Bentley.

Which would mean the reason for breaking into Cassie's doctor's office had nothing to do with Cassie. It was Gwendolyn. Sure. She probably had the same doctors as Cassie. Why wouldn't she? Maybe she submitted to a blood test, the first step of a paternity test.

"Cassie would tell you things she wouldn't tell Ellie," Stoletti follows up. "You two were especially close."

Albany smiles with bitterness. "You're very crafty with your questions, Detective Stoletti. You're trying to trick me into admitting I had a relationship with Cassie? Well, you don't have to. She was nineteen, you know. It's not like I was breaking any laws. She was bright, full of energy—she was a wonderful girl whom I miss very much, to this day. But if she was pregnant, she certainly never told me so."

McDermott nods at the note on the table. "When did you receive that note?"

Albany, with his free hand holding the cigarette, points to the note, too. "That note was delivered to me by the man in that photo. That is the first, and last, time I've seen him."

"Leo Koslenko."

"I don't know his name," he says. "I never did. He didn't even let me hold the note. He came to my office and held it up for me to read. I had to give him an answer, right then."

"And when was 'right then'? When was this note delivered to you?" McDermott asks.

"I—I don't know the precise day of the week, but it was a weekday. It was a few days after the bodies were discovered." He gestures with his free hand.

"This man just waltzed into my office, held this up for me to read, and told me he wanted an answer. I told him yes."

"And you never felt the need to bring this up to the police?" McDermott asks, his tone less than gentle.

"Not when it was obvious to everyone that Terry Burgos killed those poor girls—no, I didn't." He taps his cigarette into the black ashtray. "Self-preservation was certainly a motive, I will admit to that. But if I thought it had *anything* to do with the murders, I would have said something. Terry immediately confessed to all of the murders. Why on earth would I reveal painful secrets about myself and others when it was utterly irrelevant?"

McDermott opens his hands.

"I had nothing to do with Cassie or Ellie being murdered." He drills his finger into the table. "Cassie, in particular, was very dear to me. The notion that I could hurt her—that's about the worst thing you could say to me."

"We might come up with worse, Professor." McDermott pushes himself out of his chair. "You're gonna need to sit tight awhile."

By the time I've returned to my office, Betty has retrieved the book of mail that we received at the county attorney's office during the Burgos case. Each piece of mail, at the time, had been date-stamped and filed away. It was a mere precaution. Nothing came of it. And when the case was officially over—when Burgos was executed—and people were scrambling for mementoes, I scooped up the mail. I'd had an idea in the back of my mind that I would write a book, and some of this mail was precious.

But I remember now, one particular piece of mail that stood out. It wasn't fire-and-brimstone stuff about the Old Testament. It talked about morality, not so much in biblical terms but in—well, nonsensical terms. More than anything, it was just weird. Like the notes that have been sent to me now.

I flip through the pages of the three-ring binder, a full page dedicated to each letter, enveloped in plastic. "Any idea of when that letter came?" I ask Betty.

But she doesn't even know what I'm talking about. I keep flipping, then suddenly stop. There it is.

As justice or belief will eternally live, likewise do others need evil. I must ask your new, educated elite: Does opportunity now evade morality or respect ethics and love? Behold a new year.

I immediately go to work on it:

A-J-O-B-W-E-L-L-D-O-N-E-I-M-A-Y-N-E-E-D-O-N-E-M-O-R-E-A-L-B-A-N-Y.
A JOB WELL DONE. I MAY NEED ONE MORE. ALBANY.

I check the date stamp on the letter. The letter was received on Tuesday, August 15, 1989.

I open the rings on the binder and remove this page, leaving the letter enclosed in plastic. I place the letter on my desk and stare at it.

Again, "Albany" at the end of the message. But this time, there's no doubt about the punctuation. The word *Albany* stands alone. Maybe it's a colon. "I may need one more: Albany." Or maybe it's a sign-off. Maybe he's telling me it's him—Albany.

"A job well done?" In August of 1989? The case was barely off and running by then. There was nothing to congratulate.

"Betty," I say into the intercom. "Where is the pleadings file for Burgos?"

"It should already be in your office."

I find it, tucked in the corner with several accordion files from the case. The pleadings file, which contains most of the documents filed in the Burgos case, is seven volumes, with the documents filed in chronological order, with numbered tabs, and bound at the top. I flip through the first volume, thinking about the date stamp on the letter. If the letter was received on August 15, 1989, then "a job well done" must relate to something that happened before that date.

I flip through June and July. The search warrant, the complaint by which we indicted Burgos, motions concerning bail, the written arguments over Burgos's attempt to suppress the confession, Burgos's official plea of insanity. Could this note have been referring to our victory when Burgos tried to have his confession kicked? It's possible, I guess.

When I get to August—especially before August 15—it is relatively bare. On the first day of the month, a motion was filed by Burgos's lawyer requesting additional money for psychiatrists. And then there's a motion filed by the prosecution on August second.

That motion was heard on August 11, 2005—the Friday before this note was received.

"Oh, Christ."

On August 11, 2005, we asked, and received, permission to drop Cassie Bentley's murder from the case.

A job well done.

Betty runs into my office. "Paul, you just got another messenger delivery. They stopped the man at the front desk. He says a guy in glasses and a base-ball cap stopped him in the lobby and paid him fifty dollars to deliver it."

"Let me see it," I say. "And get me Detective McDermott."

46

McDERMOTT STANDS alone in the interview room where Paul Riley sat thirty minutes ago.

"He ran back to his office," a uniform says. "He said you could call him there."

"He did, did he?" McDermott frowns at the officer, but Riley wasn't in custody, he was free to waltz out. He goes to his desk just as the phone rings, startling him. Why does that always happen to him?

"McDermott."

"Mike, Bentley just got back from whatever meeting he was in."

"Tell him to get his ass in here right now. Tell him right now, Tom, or I come to him, and it's not pretty."

"Okay, Mike. Listen, he won't be coming alone. He's got a lawyer."

A lawyer. "Paul Riley?"

"No, not Riley. Some other guy. Don't know him."

Now, that's interesting. Bentley isn't using Riley.

He places the phone in the cradle and it rings immediately. "Dammit." He lifts the receiver. "McDermott."

"It's Paul Riley."

"Oh, well, speak of—"

"He just dropped off another note. He stopped a messenger in the lobby, about ten minutes ago."

"Bring it to me," he tells Riley. "I'll get some uniforms over there."

"He was wearing glasses and a blue baseball cap. A button-down shirt and trousers," says Riley. "But he's probably in the wind by now."

"Yeah, thanks, Riley. Get the hell in here." McDermott makes a call, dispatches some uniforms to the scene, but he's less than optimistic.

SWITCH NOW, after dropping off the note at Riley's building, back to the parking garage, take the elevator to eight, get in the Chrysler LeBaron with state license plate J41258—the one they just described on the radio, be on the lookout, calling all cars, but, guess what, everyone—

Back out the car and drive down one floor to the beige Toyota Camry, another rental car, different rental company, he's not stupid, different rental company, different fake name, it's a good time of day to make the transfer, not first thing in the morning or quitting time, good time, not many cars, not many people, transfer the contents, transfer quickly, okay, good, that's done, that's done, now, one more thing, they always underestimate him, crazy Leo, he must be stupid, he'd never think of this—

Go to a secluded corner, a small alcove off the main strips of the parking garage, look at the cars parked against the cement wall, a sedan, parked nose in, but with a little space to maneuver between the front of the car and wall, enough space to duck in with a screwdriver, remove the front license plate, they'll never know, won't be looking at the front of the car when they get in, won't see it until later when it's way too late—

Take that license plate, exchange it with the LeBaron's plate, they probably won't search a parking garage, but, if they do, if they drive by and see a Chrysler LeBaron, they'll see the license plate doesn't match and move on, lazy, stupid cops, this is easy, he's smarter—

Pull out onto traffic and head toward the interstate. Almost done now.

I TAKE A CAB to the police station, carrying the manila envelope in a plastic shopping bag Betty gave me. I also bring the coded note I received on August 15, 1989, still encased in plastic. I give the cabbie a twenty and don't wait for change. McDermott is waiting for me at the top of the stairs and waves me past the desk sergeant.

"You just come and go as you please now?"

I hand him the shopping bag and follow him to his desk. Ricki Stoletti, at her desk nearby, comes over.

"Where's Gwendolyn Lake now?" she asks.

I tell her I have no idea. "I gave you her cell number."

"Yeah, and she didn't answer."

"I told her to call you," I say, but my focus is on McDermott, who is wearing latex gloves and opening the top of the manila envelope with a letter opener. He dumps out a regular-sized white envelope.

He nods to me. "What else is in here?"

I show it to him, the note I received from August 15, 1989.

"A job well done," he says, reading the Post-it I attached to it. "Any idea what a 'job well done' might have been?"

I clear my throat and tell him. The letter was referring to the dismissal of Cassie's murder from the case.

"Oh." He coughs out the word, like a laugh. "How's that Burgos case looking now, Counselor?"

"She had a secret," I say. "Whoever wrote this was glad it stayed a secret."

McDermott stares at me. "Y'know, Riley, for a guy who everyone says is so smart—"

"Open the note, McDermott."

He takes the white envelope and slices open the top, dumps out a single piece of paper, folded in three. With his gloved hands, he smooths out the paper.

I grab a notepad and pen off his desk as all three of us read it:

> *If For Years Others Urge Blind, Evil Hypocrisy And Vindicate Evil, Soon Heathens Engage Willingly. I Laugh, Love, Learn. I Vow Eternity To Other Opponents.*

I scribble it out as quickly as I can:

I-F-Y-O-U-B-E-H-A-V-E-S-H-E-W-I-L-L-L-I-V-E-T-O-O.
IF YOU BEHAVE, SHE WILL LIVE, TOO.

McDermott says, "If you—"

I brush past him and pick up his phone, dialing the numbers so quickly I mess it up the first time.

"Children's Advocacy Project."

"Shelly Trotter, please."

"Shelly—is not in. Can I—"

"Has she been in?"

"Has she—who am I speaking to?"

"This is Paul Riley," I say.

Voices in the background. I make out Rena Schroeder, the supervising attorney. Shelly's boss. I hear my name thrown out, then the phone changing hands.

"Paul, this is Rena."

"Rena, where's Shelly?"

"I was going to ask you that. She didn't show up today. She missed court, she missed our monthly—"

I drop the phone.

McDermott says, "Write down her address." Stoletti runs to get her coat. I scribble the address on the notepad and jog toward the exit, as I hear McDermott say into the phone, "Dispatch, I need all units to respond. We have a possible 401 in progress . . ."

THREE SQUAD CARS HAVE already double-parked in front of Shelly Trotter's brownstone when McDermott pulls up his sedan. For the third time he says to Riley, "We go in first," but before the car has even come to a stop Riley's pushing himself out of the passenger's door.

A couple of uniforms, standing at the door, look at McDermott. He points at Riley and shakes his head. He jogs toward the door with Stoletti.

"This is the governor's daughter, right?" she asks.

"It sure fucking is."

The uniforms block Riley, who struggles with them. "Paul, you can come up in a minute," McDermott says. "Let us do our job first."

"Shelly!" Riley is calling out as McDermott heads up the stairs. At the second-floor landing another uniform awaits them, shaking his head.

"I've never seen anything like it."

McDermott and Stoletti bound up the final sets of stairs and slow their pace as they walk through the entrance to the apartment. They step in and see another uniform standing next to a bloody chain saw.

They walk slowly toward the bathroom, pure dread filling McDermott's stomach. Wanting to do anything but—the damn *bathroom*, of all places—he sticks his head in, the putrid smell nothing compared to what he sees.

Blood spatters have reached well beyond the bathtub to the sink, the walls, even to the entrance. Inside the tub is a bloody mess, like remnants from a butcher shop.

"Mary, Mother of God," McDermott mumbles. He takes a careful step into the bathroom and looks in the tub. Stoletti looks in and draws an abrupt breath.

He caught her in the shower. The body appears to be naked, which is only to say there is no evidence of clothing. There is little to draw from the body because, as one would define a body—a torso with limbs, a neck, a head—there is no body anymore.

"He took his time with her," he says, trying to keep a clinical perspective. The body has been sawed into a hundred pieces at least. No arms, no legs, no neck, no head. Everything has been sliced through. Just little parts.

Trim-Meter chain saw cheerleader's brains all paint on the stained wall.

He hears commotion on the staircase. He steps out of the bathroom and moves to the doorway. Paul Riley looks like a running back trying to shed tacklers. Halfway up the final staircase, with two officers clutching at him, he makes eye contact with McDermott, still a trace of irrational hope on his face.

"I'm sorry," McDermott says.

"I want to see her." The struggle begins anew between Riley and the officers. McDermott takes a few steps down and grips Riley's arm.

"There's nothing left to see, Paul," he says. "I'm sorry."

Riley collapses on the staircase, crying out Shelly's name. McDermott looks back at Stoletti, who says to him, quietly, "We have to call the governor."

47

SEVEN O'CLOCK. Radio still mentioning his name, Leo Koslenko, wanted for questioning, armed and dangerous, Chrysler LeBaron, and now the new scoop, Trotter, Michelle Trotter, governor's daughter, daughter of the governor, might be a connection, wanted, dangerous, armed—

Guide the Toyota Camry off the interstate, follow the signs through town. New construction at this intersection, not what he's seen before, weird, feelings return, but the place looks different, he's never come back here, always stayed away, no reason to go back, but now he feels like he's back in every way, he's back to work, back in the game—

Mansbury College, welcome to Mansbury, where vision meets opportunity.

McDERMOTT TAKES ANOTHER REPORT from the neighborhood canvass, another report of nobody seeing anything. One neighbor did hear a chain saw earlier today, midday, but that was not terribly out of the ordinary in the summer, near the tree-lined park on the lake.

Midday, on a weekday. Koslenko must have subdued her while she was in the shower, getting ready for work, and then waited for the apartment building to clear before going to work on her. The guy may be crazy, but he isn't dumb.

The County Attorney Technical Unit and the medical examiner have nearly completed their work. They will run prints but everything was wiped down, and, anyway, they know who the hell it is. They just can't find him. They've had an all-points bulletin out on Koslenko and his car since this morning to no avail.

He takes a call on his cell phone from the squad room, where, apparently, Harland Bentley and his lawyer have had their fill of waiting for McDermott. They were there solely as a courtesy, his lawyer said, so they were free to leave.

"Albany left, too, Mike. We couldn't very well—"

"That's fine," he says. He has his hands full tonight. But he tells them to post a car at both houses, Bentley's and Albany's, and follow them if they go anywhere.

He looks into the living room, where Paul Riley sits on the couch, his face buried in his hands, his toes tapping on the carpet. They tried to get him into a squad car, but he refused. McDermott let him stay when he promised to keep out of the way.

Riley is wearing more than sorrow, more than shock on his face. He is wearing guilt. This is his fault, no matter what anyone tries to tell him. Over time, he'll work on the same rationalizations. He will tell himself that he did the best he could with Burgos's prosecution. He will tell himself that it was Leo Koslenko who killed Shelly, not him. But he won't accept any of that. He will put this squarely on himself.

McDermott knows that better than anyone.

He had the ability, the right, to have his wife institutionalized against her will. With a three-year-old child involved, he had more than that—he had the responsibility. How could he have left Joyce with Grace that day? After seeing her unglued the night before?

How could he do that to little Gracie?

She blames herself, the doctor said.

How could *she* do that to their daughter? No matter how sick, no matter how consumed by her illness—how could Joyce do that to Grace?

Get the shoe box from the closet.

Open it up.

Give it to Mommy.

He finds himself standing at the threshold of Shelly Trotter's bathroom. What happened in here was evil, whatever the face you paint on it, no matter that it was the product of mental illness. Death has no exceptions, only victims.

The angle. The crime-scene technician, thinking he was out of McDermott's earshot. Thinking that McDermott, devastated, clutching his three-year-old daughter, wasn't listening intently to every word from the next room.

The angle's unusual for self-infliction.

"Mike."

She would've had to hold the gun a couple feet away from her and aim it back.

"Mike."

Then that's how it happened, said Ricki Stoletti, his partner of four months at the time. *That's how it happened.*

Stoletti touches his arm. She avoids looking into the bathroom, but the situation is not lost on her. They've never discussed it, not even at the time. Back then, after that conversation with the technician, Stoletti had avoided eye contact with McDermott.

It's closed, was all she'd said to him. *Suicide.*

"Hey, Mike."

Thank you, he did not say out loud to her. Not then, not ever.

"The governor's here," she says. "Put on your game face."

I GET TO MY FEET as Governor Trotter walks into Shelly's apartment, in a suit and olive raincoat, his wife Abigail and a cadre of security detail close behind. He rushes up to me and grabs my hands, his own hands trembling, his eyes red but stoic. He is not crying. He's already done that.

"How—?" His eyes search mine for answers that I don't have.

"It's because of me," I say. "He killed her because of me."

He shakes his head, like he doesn't get it. Nothing about it makes sense. It won't make sense, maybe ever. Behind him, his wife is trying to get past McDermott to see Shelly.

"Abby, don't go in there," I say. "That's not Shelly any—anymore."

"How could this happen?" She turns to face me, looking years older than I've ever seen her. "What did you do, Paul?"

There's nothing I can say. McDermott comes over, takes the governor by the arm, and walks him and his wife into the kitchen to talk to them. The governor breaks free and looks into the bathroom, a deep, soulful wail soon following.

McDermott, distracted by the presence of the commander and the governor's staff, finally breaks away from them as they head to the station. It's approaching nine o'clock now. Second night in a row that he didn't put Grace to sleep. Could be the second night in a row that he won't sleep at all. He becomes aware of it, for the first time in hours, as his adrenaline finally decelerates. His brain is exhausted. His legs move painfully.

Susan Dobbs, the assistant medical examiner, is one of the few people left in the apartment now. The color has returned to her now; she seemed awed by the crime scene upon her arrival, hours ago, and that's saying something, working corpses in this city. "The governor needs to sign a DNA authorization," she says. "To verify identification."

"Nothing left of her." McDermott sighs.

She zips up her medical bag. "Just the one left foot."

"Oh, I forgot." McDermott snaps his fingers. "God, in all this flurry I—"

"Yes," she says, "it was there. A postmortem incision at the base of her fourth and fifth toes. He cut everything into pieces but the left foot. He wanted to make sure you saw it."

"Thanks, Sue."

She appraises him with sympathetic eyes. "When's he gonna be done, Mike? You said this was from those lyrics?"

McDermott nods, making a peace sign with his fingers.

"Two more kills," he says. "Unless I catch him."

Drive the car back on the interstate, north toward the city, pass the downtown, a motel would be best, one where he can hide the rental car in the back. No one's going to be looking for the Camry, but he'll be careful, be careful, he finds a place off the highway, uses his last fake identification, wears glasses and fake facial hair and a baseball cap, pays in cash, waits around the lobby but nobody's following, all clear, everything coming together now.

The governor's daughter is dead, all over the news, he sits on the bed and watches it, then turns it off and goes into the bathroom, empties the bag from the drugstore on the vanity—

He tapes Cassie's photograph on the bathroom mirror, traces the outline of her face with his fingers, pretty, so beautiful—

He uses the electric razor, shaves the front and top of his skull, no bald head, too obvious, not bald, just a bald spot, a patch of skin shaped like a horseshoe—

You look funny.

I know. But they won't notice me this way. They might expect me to shave my head, but not to shave a bald spot.

You still look funny.

Hair coloring will change from deep black to dirty blond, different color, different style, he looks at himself in the mirror, sees a middle-aged man with male-pattern baldness, light brown hair on the sides, glasses—

I'm scared.

I know you are, but the plan is working. Riley will help us now.

He drops on the bed, puts his head against the pillow, momentarily satiated but never expecting sleep.

ELEVEN O'CLOCK. The detectives' squad room is like a train station, the commander taking up residence in the lew's office, where he and Governor Trotter confer. The governor's son, Edgar Trotter, who is the chief of the state police, is in there, too, barking out orders and bringing in his top lieutenants in what appears to be a coup d'état. The younger Trotter stopped short of kicking McDermott off the case but made a point of saying the task force needed *more effective leadership* and suggesting that, if the slow-footed local cops had been quicker on the chase, maybe "this" wouldn't have happened.

Stick around, he told McDermott. *We might need you for details.*

Media relations is all over this, coordinating things with the governor's people, preparing statements, twisting and refining words so that they say just enough to give the appearance of sufficiency. The national press has arrived, too, lending a heightened sense of attention, if not panic, to the press people.

Panic, as he thinks about it, is not a bad way to describe the current state of affairs. There is unquestionably a defensiveness about the brass, a reaction, justified or not, to the feeling that the police are to blame for Shelly Trotter's murder. If that is ultimately the way this shapes up, there's no doubt who will take the bullet. It's unfair—Leo Koslenko got a tremendous head start on them, and they identified him within a handful of days of the onset of his murder spree—but fairness has never been an ingredient in the stew of local politics.

They all but tied an anchor to his foot. He's just a consultant on the case now, and when it's over, however it ends, who knows what he'll be doing?

It won't be foot patrol. That would be a level three. The union wouldn't stand for it. No, it will be a job at a desk—a desk in the basement, something that will force him to leave. When all is said and done, maybe McDermott will muster the energy to care.

He pops his head into the conference room and checks on Riley. Riley, he realizes, will take it harder than anyone. If this turns out the way it's looking, he either convicted the wrong man or failed to catch an accomplice, a coconspirator. If his client, Harland Bentley, is involved, the media will have their choice of motives—Riley obstructed the investigation either to hide his own negligence sixteen years ago or to protect his client.

But what the press, and maybe the county attorney, do to Riley will be nothing compared to what he will do to himself. This will never leave him. It will recede at times but return with violence, and without warning. It will temper every moment of happiness, color every scene.

McDermott knows it better than anyone.

Mommy did this, he would tell Grace, so many times he lost count. *It was Mommy. Mommy was sick and wanted to go to Heaven.*

He doesn't know exactly how it happened. He never will. He plays it out like he would revise a painful memory of his own, finding the path of least resistance: All she wanted from Grace was to get the shoe box from the closet; she was going to send Grace downstairs, so she wouldn't have to see it happen; she was going to call her husband first, to come for Grace; maybe she wasn't even sure she was going to use the gun. Maybe she was going to change her mind.

The gun went off. It was an accident. She *didn't* tell her daughter to pull the trigger. No, no matter how tormented her mind, she wouldn't put that on her daughter. It was an accident.

But he doesn't know. He never will.

Mommy did this. Hoping that the repetition would confirm the memory. Say it enough times and she'll believe it. Do three-year-olds even *have* memories? His earliest one, he was five. Sitting on a brick stoop by a fireplace, playing with toy animals and a barn. But *three*?

Dr. Sutton says no. *Only a very minimal chance* she would retain that information. *If* she ever appreciated it to begin with. *If* it even happened that way.

Riley is motionless in a chair, oblivious to McDermott's presence. His eyes are bloodshot and sunken into a washed-out face. His hair is a mess. His tie has disappeared. However this might end up, McDermott has made up his mind: Riley is guilty of no crime. He could play with the facts either way, but his gut has taken him pretty far and he trusts it. Why, after all, did Riley visit Gwendolyn Lake? Why did he go see Brandon Mitchum?

Because whether he admitted it to himself or not, he wanted to know if he missed something during the Burgos prosecution. He didn't let it go. He pursued it. He was willing to tear down the banner achievement of his professional career to get to the truth.

"Burgos fell into your lap," he tells Riley. "He had motive, he had opportunity, he had evidence all over his house. He confessed. I read the transcript. Anyone in your position would have stopped right there, with the guy in front of you."

It's as if Riley can't hear him. He is smoothing his hands over the table-top, like he's brushing away sand from an artifact. Like he's looking for words.

"I need your help, Riley. Your head clear enough to help?"

Riley says nothing. But McDermott's got nothing to lose. Maybe catching Riley off guard, defenses down, is a good play. Maybe it will be good for him, too, focusing on the case instead of the pain.

So he lays it out for Riley, though Riley probably knows or suspects much of it. Harland is Gwendolyn's father—something Cassie discovered near her death. Cassie was pregnant, and had an abortion, near her death—confirmed by Cassie's mother—and she'd been involved with Professor Albany. Cassie thought her father was sneaking around with her best friend, Ellie—again, near the time of both of their deaths.

He doesn't need to tell Riley that this points toward both Harland Bentley and Professor Albany. But if there's any doubt, he seals it with the note he found in Koslenko's possession, now confirmed by Albany: Harland made a trade with Albany—keep quiet about my affair, I keep quiet about yours.

Lots to lose. Wealthy wives, tenure-track positions. Lots to gain with the deaths of two young women.

Riley doesn't speak. Not a word from him yet. McDermott begins to wonder why he's even sharing this with Riley.

Riley pushes himself out of his chair. He walks to the corner of the room, staring off into space.

"Harland Bentley had his daughter whacked, Paul. And Ellie, too. He used a ranch hand with a history of mental instability and violence to do the wet work. He didn't keep his marriage together but his wife was too messed up to fight him, so she threw him a cool twenty million just to make him go away, and he took it. All told, not a bad deal for the guy."

Riley doesn't move. McDermott's just talking to himself.

"I don't know how Albany fits in yet. I think he helped with the other murders. He'd probably be able to get keys to the auditorium where the bodies were left. He'd probably be able to snatch Burgos's keys, too, to use his Suburban to get the women, and to get into Burgos's house. I'm sure it was his idea to use those song lyrics—I mean, Christ, who knew those song lyrics better than Albany?"

Riley puts a hand against the wall.

"The other murders covered up Ellie's and Cassie's. Made it look like a murder spree spawned by the song lyrics. And just to be sure about Cassie, they made you drop the charges on her murder. It all makes sense, Riley. It does. But that doesn't get us any closer to finding Leo Koslenko. I think this guy's off the reservation. Whoever was controlling him—Bentley, Albany—they're not controlling him now."

McDermott takes a breath. It's a lot to put on the guy, on top of finding his girlfriend in a hundred pieces tonight. But he doesn't have time for diplomacy. He senses that Riley will do whatever's necessary to catch Koslenko, and he needs that help now.

"Riley," he says quietly. "Everyone murdered this week—Ciancio, Evelyn Pendry, Amalia Calderone, and Shelly—every one of them had a cut between their fourth and fifth toes on their left foot. A postmortem incision. That mean anything to you?"

Riley is completely still. His lips move silently, like he's replaying what he just heard.

"I have to go," he says.

AT A QUARTER TO MIDNIGHT, I step out of the detectives' squad room, sleep-deprived and overloaded. The governor still has not left the police station. His press people gave out some statements earlier, but the media's still waiting for the red meat.

Beside me is a uniform, who is taking me home. I see the press barricaded from the police parking lot and from the front steps of the station house by wooden traffic horses, but I can hear them calling to me by name.

"Paul, did Leo Koslenko kill Shelly?"

"Is this connected to Terry Burgos?"

"Was Terry Burgos innocent?"

"Did Leo Koslenko kill the Mansbury Six?"

"Give me a second." I feel an adrenaline wave, after I'd expect to have nothing left. Maybe it's anger. Maybe it's fear. I break away from the cop and make my way to the reporters. Some of them, the veterans, are the same ones who interviewed me when I was prosecuting Burgos. How delectable this must be for them. How willingly their journalistic stomachs growl at the slightest hint of blood in the water.

"Did you prosecute the wrong man?"

"What did you say to Governor Trotter?"

"Was an innocent man executed?"

The cameras, the bright lights, the microphones all angle in my direction. They continue with the questions until it is clear I won't answer. Finally, the shouts subside, and they are ready to give me my moment.

"Leo Koslenko did not kill the Mansbury victims," I say as evenly as I can manage. "Terry Burgos did. What is happening now may bear some connection to the Mansbury murders. The police have asked for my help and I'm going to solve this. Give me a day or two, tops. I promise you, I will figure this out. But make no mistake. Terry Burgos killed those girls."

I pivot and walk back to the cop, the reporters shouting all kinds of follow-up questions to me. We hustle to the squad car and I jump in the back. I lay my head against the back cushion and close my eyes, drowning out the questions being thrown my way from behind the barricade.

WHENEVER SHE CAME *to the house, he felt a lift. She would always make a point of saying hello to him, maybe speak a few words of Russian to him.*

But not this day. She walked straight past him. He followed. She went up the stairs as Gwendolyn was coming down. Leo stayed back. Mrs. Bentley had been mad when he had overheard her conversation with Gwendolyn.

What did you say to my mother?

I didn't say anything she didn't already know.

You don't know anything about my father.

No, Cassie, I think you're about the only one who *doesn't* know.

Cassie gripped the handrail. She dropped her head. She was trying to control her anger.

Don't take my word for it, cousin. See where he goes. See who he's with. You might even see someone else you know.

She looked back up at Gwendolyn. She started to speak but, Leo thought, she was unable. She turned and bounded back down the stairs.

I can't wait to hear Uncle Harland's explanation, *Gwendolyn called out.* I'll bet he'll wish he hadn't signed that prenup!

LEO SNAPS OUT OF HIS FOG. The commercials are over. The all-news cable station has been covering the events live. He jumps from his bed as he sees the image of Paul Riley, speaking to reporters outside the police station. He yanks up the volume and holds his breath.

"Leo Koslenko did not kill the Mansbury women. Terry Burgos did."

He closes his eyes as the rest of Paul Riley's words play out.

"The police have asked for my help and I'm going to solve this. Give me a day or two, tops. I promise you, I will figure this out. But make no mistake. Terry Burgos killed those girls."

The sides of Leo's mouth curl. Almost a smile.

McDermott watches the television in the cafeteria, where he has come to refresh his coffee. On the television, live, is Paul Riley, standing outside the station, giving a statement to the press.

"What kind of nonsense is that?" Stoletti says to him. She was never a big fan of Riley, anyway, and it's been a supremely shitty day for the two detectives. Stoletti won't take the hit like her senior partner, but she'll still take it. " 'Burgos killed those girls?' 'The police want my help?' 'Give me a day or two, tops?' Does he know something we don't?"

McDermott nods absently, watching the news replay the sound bite.

The police have asked for my help and I'm going to solve this. Give me a day or two, tops.

Stoletti sighs. "I'm taking off, Mike. There's nothing left here for us. I've had my head kicked in enough for one night."

I promise you, I will figure this out.

"You gonna be here for the Bentley interview? He'll be in within the hour."

He shrugs.

Make no mistake. Terry Burgos killed those girls.

Stoletti walks up next to him, gesturing to the television, featuring Paul Riley's angry, flustered mug. "Oh, hell, I guess the guy's entitled to blow off some steam. Not exactly a banner day for him, either. But he's making himself look like an idiot." She raps him on the arm and leaves.

"Maybe," McDermott mumbles. Maybe he's acting like an idiot.

Or maybe he's "behaving."

Friday
June 24, 2005

48

I SIT IN THE HALLWAY on the top floor of my house, leaning against the railing of the staircase, staring at the alarm pad on the wall. The alarm is not set. It's not even hooked up to the police. But even disarmed, it covers five entry points to the house, plus motion sensors on the ground floor and along the final flight of stairs. If an entry point is breached, the number assigned to that position lights up. There will be no consequence—no shrill alarm, no call to the police—but at least I will know.

Zone One for the front door. Two for the sliding glass door. Three for the door from the basement. Four and five for windows on the ground floor.

My eyes close. My stomach is reeling, my head throbbing, my body beyond exhaustion. My eyes pop open after only a moment, I think, as I try to snap myself out of disorientation.

I look at the zone numbers on the alarm pad, still dark.

AT FIVE MINUTES AFTER one in the morning, Harland Bentley walks in with counsel. He'd been told to be here by one o'clock sharp, so he's late, and McDermott considers saying so. Could be a minor difference in clocks, but McDermott supposes Bentley was deliberate in his arrival. Bentley is wearing a navy tailored suit that no cop could afford with a month's salary, and he supposes that decision was intentional, too.

McDermott, now and from here on out, will be a spectator. At some point in the lieutenant's office after McDermott was excused, the commander, the governor, State Police Superintendent Edgar Trotter, and their staffs came up with the astonishingly bad decision that Edgar Trotter would conduct the interview with Harland Bentley, accompanied by one of his top aides.

McDermott walks into the central observation room, chin up—he's not bowing down to these idiots, not when he's done nothing wrong—and stands quietly next to the commander. Inside Interview Room One, Harland Bentley adjusts his coat and whispers to his attorney. The lawyer looks familiar. A large, handsome black guy done out nicely in a three-piece gray pinstripe. These two look immaculate, crisp, and well coiffed, for a hastily called interview in the middle of the night. No accident there. They are ready for the show.

They perk up as Edgar Trotter enters the room with his lieutenant. They are out of their chairs quickly.

"Harland," says Trotter. He nods to Bentley's lawyer. "Mason."

Mason. Oh, that's it. Mason Tremont—the man who until recently served as the U.S. attorney for the jurisdiction that includes the city. Not surprising that Bentley has brought in the heavy artillery.

They start in with the condolences. How are you holding up? How's the governor? How's your mother? Oh, this must be so tough on Abby.

McDermott looks at the commander with his eyebrows raised. This is quite the start to the interrogation. These guys are old friends. Harland Bentley has poured hundreds of thousands of dollars into Governor Trotter's campaigns, and Mason Tremont was appointed the top federal prosecutor by the Republican president at the request of the governor, who tapped Tremont, if memory serves, as a thank-you for his impressive ability to raise campaign cash.

And now the governor's son will question two of the governor's closest allies.

After they are seated, Mason Tremont asserts himself. "Of course, Edgar, of course we want to do *whatever* we can to help. But there"—he looks at Harland, almost laughs, as if incredulous—"there is a difference between being asked to help as a friend and being threatened as if Harland were a suspect. The officer—I think his name was McDermott—he left us with the impression that, somehow, there was suspicion directed—"

"McDermott's off this case," says Edgar Trotter. "You're talking to me now."

McDermott steels himself. He tries to resist the rising urge to see Edgar Trotter fail, to watch him flail about ineffectively until, with no other choice, he reluctantly taps his arm toward the bull pen and brings in McDermott to do this right. He can't deny the satisfaction it would bring him, but, more than anything, he just wants to know what the hell Bentley knows.

Trotter starts with the basics. He says them as suspicions, not fact: that Harland was sleeping with Ellie Danzinger; that Harland had fathered Gwendolyn Lake, in addition to Cassie; that Cassie had been pregnant and had an abortion near the time of her death. Leo Koslenko, he says, worked at the home belonging to Mia Lake and her daughter, Gwendolyn. "Information we have received," he calls all of it.

"Do you know where Leo Koslenko is, Harland?"

"I don't. Edgar, I'm not sure I can even recall who the man is. Certainly, I've not spoken to him, at least not any time I can recall."

Trotter slides the photograph across the table, the one found in Fred Ciancio's closet in a shoe box: Harland addressing reporters, Koslenko in the background.

"This man in the background, I suppose?" Bentley says. "You say he worked at Mia's house, not ours?"

Giving himself distance from Koslenko.

Trotter cocks his head. "You didn't help him get asylum in this country?"

Closing that distance a little. A good response, and well delivered, played just about right—he said it like he was curious, without threat.

"If I did, I don't recall that. I'd think that would fall more into Natalia's camp."

Trotter takes a moment with that. Nods his head slowly but doesn't speak. A good interrogation technique. Silence is uncomfortable in a conversation. Suspects like to fill the space. They usually elaborate, and often dig a deeper hole.

But Harland Bentley is no ordinary suspect.

"Shelly was a wonderful young woman," Bentley says. "I'd met her only recently."

Trotter listens to him, holds his stare, and says, "Were you having an affair with Ellie Danzinger around the time she died?"

Mason Tremont raises his hand from the table. "Edgar, I wonder if that's really necessary. We are more than happy to help you pursue any meaningful leads, but we're talking about something a lifetime ago."

"I appreciate that, Mason, I really do." He nods his head emphatically without making eye contact. "But Leo Koslenko didn't kill my sister because the past is irrelevant. So I'd like an answer, please."

The lawyer, Tremont, puts a hand on Bentley's forearm. "Edgar—"

"Either he's willing to answer or he isn't." Trotter drops the pen from his hand and sits back in his chair. "I'm waiting."

The temperature has dropped in the room.

Tremont adjusts his gold-rimmed glasses. "I've advised my client to limit his answers to things that are relevant. Personal smears are not relevant."

"What about Gwendolyn Lake, Harland? Are you her father?"

Tremont bows his head slightly. Seems to be a signal to his client.

"Yes, that's true," Harland says.

McDermott nods. Not surprising. And not surprising he'd admit that, either. Gwendolyn is still alive. A simple paternity test could answer that question. He's giving them something they could get without him and, in the process, appearing to be forthcoming.

Edgar Trotter removes a document from the folder in front of him. McDermott lifts himself with the balls of his feet to get a better look. It's the note they found in Leo Koslenko's bedroom. McDermott has a copy, too:

I know that you know about my relationship with Ellie. And I know about your relationship with my daughter. If you tell, so will I. But if you keep quiet, I will endow a chair in your name at Mansbury College. I need your answer right now.

Bentley leaves the note on the table, so that his attorney can read along. He reads in silence for a moment, then snatches it off the table to get a closer look. Tremont, who can no longer read it, gives his client some space.

McDermott watches Bentley's eyes move across the page. His mouth parts, his eyebrows tremble. Soon he is mouthing the words as he rereads it, his face contorting in mounting horror.

Something isn't sitting right. Something in McDermott's gut.

"My God," Bentley says.

"This note was delivered to Professor Albany," Trotter says without affect. "He's already admitted receiving it. And he's already admitted answering yes to the request."

The lawyer, Tremont, puts his hand on his client's arm.

Bentley pops out of his chair and paces in the corner of the room, a hand on his face.

"Maybe this would be a time for a short break," Tremont suggests.

Bentley spins and looks at Trotter. "You're telling me that—that teacher—and my daughter?"

Trotter doesn't respond to the question. Instead, he says, "We know that you kept up your end," Trotter continues. "You endowed a chair for Professor Albany."

"Well, *yes*, I—" Harland Bentley freezes in midsentence. His head moves slowly upward, his eyes dancing about, his lips moving almost imperceptibly, uttering something unintelligible.

"I'll need a minute with my client," says Tremont.

Something doesn't feel right here.

"Oh, that is rich," Bentley mumbles. "That is rich."

49

INTERVIEW ROOM ONE is silent. Harland Bentley continues to shake his head, even wearing an ironic smile at one point, but choosing not to speak for the moment. Edgar Trotter has made the decision to let this happen of its own course.

McDermott thinks again about Harland Bentley's reaction to the note. It wasn't like with Albany. Bentley read every word. And if he was bluffing by his look of surprise, he's as good a bluffer as McDermott has seen.

Harland Bentley did not write that note.

"I didn't write that note."

Trotter picks up his copy of the note and looks it over, or at least makes a show of doing so. "This note is describing someone else?"

"No," Bentley concedes. "This note is describing me. It's—it's true about Ellie Danzinger and me. I admit that. Yes. But I didn't write that note. I've never seen it before."

"So you endowed this chair at Mansbury College for the professor—"
"Yes."

"—but you're saying, it *wasn't* because of a trade-off with the professor."
"Correct."

"This is just a coincidence. Whoever wrote this note can predict the future?"

No, that's not what he's saying, either. If he's telling the truth, then whoever wrote that note knew about his affair with Ellie. And knew about Cassie's affair with Professor Albany.

And would have some ability to influence a decision like endowing a chair for a college professor.

And would know Leo Koslenko, who delivered the note to Professor Albany.

"Natalia," McDermott says aloud.

In the interview room, Harland Bentley shakes his head again, lost in thought. "When Natalia and I divorced—well, I could hardly blame her. She not only wanted out, but she wanted out immediately. She could have tried to enforce the prenup, fought me in court, but she gave me a lump-sum settlement. That told me everything I needed to know: she wanted me gone, and gone right away." He sighs. "She said the money was mine, with only one condition."

"The endowment for Albany," Trotter says.

He nods solemnly. "She said, he'd been a mentor to Cassie. Cassie had spoken so highly of him. And now, because of what that—that monster did, this professor would probably lose his job. He didn't have tenure yet. He'd never teach again." He clears his throat, steadies a hand in the air. "I was not unaware of my deficiencies as a husband. If Nat wanted that one favor from me, I was going to do it. If I'd known, if I'd even suspected that he'd put his hands on my *daughter*—"

McDermott glances at the commander, who remains silent. The cold shoulder. McDermott doesn't have a say anymore. For all he knows, the commander doesn't have much of one, either.

Fuck it. This is McDermott's case, like it or not. And it's just gotten more interesting.

It's breaking up for the night. It's close to two in the morning. A long day for the Trotters, for the cops, for everyone. Nothing more will be done tonight, other than the frantic search for Leo Koslenko's vehicle.

Natalia Lake had that note delivered to Albany. She didn't want her daughter's affair with Professor Albany to come to light. She didn't want her husband's affair with Ellie to come out. She divorced Harland only weeks after Cassie's and the other murders.

Why?

"Go home, Detective," the commander says to him.

McDermott says nothing but nods his head. There's nothing more for him to do here. It's time to leave.

But he's not going home.

TIME BECOMES THE ENEMY. I sit in the hallway outside my bedroom, swimming against the current, until five-thirty in the morning, nodding off and popping awake, checking the alarm pad on the top-floor hallway with blurry eyes. I pop a couple of aspirin and take a quick shower. I move about my house quietly, listening, anticipating. I force a piece of toast down my throat. I head out the back door, expecting it to happen there. But I walk undisturbed to my car. I open the garage door and brace myself, but there is nothing in there but my Cadillac and a few lawn and garden tools.

I get in the car and take a deep breath. It's time to go see Natalia Lake. It's time to learn how well I play poker.

50

WHEN I GET OUT of my car at seven o'clock, a woman dressed in all white awaits me, hands clasped behind her back.

"Good morning, Mr. Riley."

"'Morning."

She opens her body to the door. "Mrs. Lake is expecting you."

I follow the woman through one of the front doors into an elaborate foyer. She leads me into a parlor with a baby grand piano and antique furniture. It is a clean, elaborately designed room that screams of wealth and sadness.

"Thank you, Marta."

I turn to see Natalia Lake, my mind instantly flashing to long ago, when she'd just identified her daughter's body. She has aged well, by my estimation with some significant cosmetic surgery on the face and neck. The artificial tightness of her skin lends an unusually severe tinge to her expression.

"Thanks for agreeing to see me, Mrs. Lake."

"Oh, please, it's Nat." Nat is wearing a lavender blouse with three-quarter sleeves and white slacks. She takes my hand with both of hers. "After everything, it's Nat."

We sit together on a couch. The tips of her spindly fingers touch my arm. "This was a woman you were involved with? Shelly Trotter?"

I nod my head.

"Lang's daughter. Oh, my." She focuses on me. "Paul, please tell me that Harland is not responsible for any of this."

"Harland is not responsible for any of this."

She takes a breath. A reaction, but I don't know what kind.

"What has happened this week is a cover-up," I say. "And Harland has nothing to cover up. True, he did many shameful things. He slept with your daughter's closest friend. He fathered a child with your sister. But he didn't kill anyone back then, Nat. Which means he'd have no reason to kill anyone now. There's nothing for him to protect."

I let my comments sit, hoping Natalia might fill the silence. The line of her mouth adjusts into a frown. She is disappointed, I think, by my assessment, but I don't expect her to say so. She occupies herself with her cigarettes, opening the small pearl case, lighting up, and smoking in silence.

I'm not entirely sure what I'm looking for here. I know there's something. And I'm pretty good at digging.

"You know how to reach Leo Koslenko," I say.

"I certainly do *not*." But her response is too readied, too defensive in its delivery. She was prepared for the accusation.

"You're the one who brought him over, Nat. It was your family in the Soviet Union that was friendly with his. He was a sick, tortured man who was loyal to you and only you."

Natalia taps her cigarette into a marble ashtray. She has never, in her life, had to answer to anyone. She is not about to start now.

She will need some prompting.

"Leo Koslenko killed Ellie Danzinger," I tell her. "At your direction."

"Oh." A burst of amusement escapes her lips. She turns to me, holding that expression, a combination of disdain and delight. "And—is that all? Did I direct the murders of all of those girls? Including my own daughter, Paul?"

Her tone is patronizing, but her eyes have caught fire now. She leaves the cigarette burning in the ashtray and moves from the couch, adjusting a piece of art on the wall. It looked straight to me, which tells me she's getting uncomfortable, maybe stalling for time.

"You didn't want to kill your daughter," I say. "But you had no choice. Cassie figured out what you'd done to Ellie. And you knew she wouldn't keep quiet."

What I'm saying isn't true. At least, I don't think it is. But the best I can do is shake the tree. This feels like a pretty good tree to shake.

Something catches my eye to the left, a momentary alteration in the hallway lighting. Like a faint shadow.

Someone is in the hallway.

"You were the one who wanted the charges dropped on Cassie's murder," I say. "You were afraid of anyone taking too close a look at that. Or at her."

Natalia places her hands behind her back and nods slowly. "What you are saying is not only ridiculous, Paul. It is also something you could never prove."

"Don't be so sure." I open my shoulders toward the hallway without being obvious. I start to pace—again, to move closer to the hallway—and speak in that direction, with my back to Natalia. I want to make sure that both Natalia and the person in the hallway hear this.

"We'll start by exhuming Cassie's body," I say.

"That's a bluff," she answers to my back. "You've already convicted a man of—"

She stops, and I smile at the irony. Thanks to Natalia, *nobody* was convicted of Cassie's murder. Her case has never been prosecuted.

"That's a bluff," she repeats.

"It's no bluff, Nat. Governor Trotter intends to have me appointed as a special prosecutor to investigate Cassie's murder. My first official act will be to arrest you on suspicion of murder."

None of that is true, but it's believable, which is all that matters.

"Technology has come a long way in sixteen years," I advise her. "I can only imagine what we'll find on Cassie's body."

The truth is, I doubt there would be much to gain. But she doesn't know that. And in any event, that isn't the point.

"And you'll tear down everything you accomplished," Natalia warns me. "You'll destroy the banner achievement of your career."

It isn't a question, so I don't answer. I keep my eyes on the hallway.

Gwendolyn Lake makes her first appearance, stepping into the threshold of the parlor in a long T-shirt and gray sweats.

"Sweetheart—" Natalia comes forward, into my peripheral vision.

I nod to Gwendolyn.

"You're wrong," she says to me.

NEVER COME BACK, don't ever return, an order, must obey—

Never come back, never set foot in Highland Woods, take the money, more if you want, don't ever come back, no one can know—

The neighborhood looks different, some houses remodeled, some brand-new, nice neighborhood, Highland Woods—

Never come back. But there are exceptions. Like when Paul Riley visits Mrs. Bentley—now Mrs. Lake.

Leo passes her house, Mrs. Lake's house now, used to be her sister's, a quick pass, then he parks at the bottom of the hill. The maze of streets is a loop, all roads leading to Browning Street at the bottom. He will wait for Riley here, parked at a meter, with a cup of coffee and a newspaper.

It has been an endless week. But today will be the end.

NATALIA LAKE STEPS BETWEEN Gwendolyn and me. "No, sweetheart, no—"

"Aunt Natalia." Gwendolyn tries to move around Nat.

"No, honey—"

"Aunt Natalia. Aunt Natalia!" She takes Nat by the shoulders and looks at her squarely. "*Aunt Natalia,* I'm saying this. I know you want to protect Cassie's memory, but it's not worth *this.*"

After a momentary struggle, Nat finally relents, her posture easing. She walks past me, without a word or glance, toward the window.

I look back at Gwendolyn. In her long T-shirt and sweats, her sleep-flattened hair and tired eyes, there is an air of nakedness, candor, about her. I don't speak, for fear of stopping the momentum. Gwendolyn has come to me. She is rolling down a hill now. Shelly, I realize, ignoring the ache in my chest, had been right about her: She would tell me eventually. It just took some prompting from me.

"You're right about me," Gwendolyn says to me, her voice free of any affect. "Harland is my biological father. My mother told me before she died. She hadn't wanted to tell me, but she felt like I had a right to know." She fixes on Natalia, who is now staring out the window, motionless. "She was so horrified by her pregnancy, initially, that she flew to France. To our place at Cap-Ferrat. She was planning, I think, to have—well, to end the pregnancy."

I nod. Mia Lake changed her mind, obviously, decided against the abortion and gave birth to Gwendolyn on the French Riviera.

"I told Cassie about it," she concedes. "When I was in town that summer.

In hindsight, it wasn't a nice thing—I shouldn't have. I didn't know what Cassie was dealing with at the time. I didn't know any of that until it was too late."

Until it was too late.

"You're telling me that Cassie killed Ellie Danzinger," I confirm.

It was how I figured it. After everything I heard last night, I couldn't see any other way. But there are a few things I don't know yet.

"We found out later," Gwendolyn continues. "Cassie told us afterward. And, no, we didn't say anything. We didn't do anything. We just—well, I didn't know what to do."

"You left town," I say. "The Wednesday of the murder spree."

She nods. "I wasn't the type—back then especially—I didn't think I'd hold up under police questioning." She takes a moment, her breathing escalated. "You understand, we knew when they found Ellie, they'd come find Cassie. They were best friends. And I didn't want to have to answer any questions. I was just popping into town for a visit, anyway, so it would be perfectly natural for me to leave."

I look back at Natalia, standing immobile by the window, then back to Gwendolyn. Tears threatening her eyes, her skin now a ghostly shade, she nevertheless seems to be relieved.

"And then what?" I say to Gwendolyn—really, to either of them.

Gwendolyn shakes her head, blinks away the moisture in her eyes. "Then, nothing. I left. Aunt Natalia and Cassie just held their breath and waited for the police to come. But they never did. So they went on with their lives, and then Cassie was murdered."

I shake my head, like I'm still a few pieces short of the puzzle.

Gwendolyn shrugs. "Terry Burgos must have seen it happen. He was stalking Ellie, wasn't he? He must have seen it happen. And then he killed Cassie because of it. I mean, you tell me, Mr. Riley. It's anyone's guess."

Anyone's guess? I think not. Not to the two women in this room, at least. But I'd like to hear the rest of this, anyway.

"What about Leo Koslenko?" I ask.

"He knew, too. Cassie told the three of us."

I open my hands. "And?"

"And nothing." She shrugs. "He didn't do anything."

"We don't know why Leo's doing what he's doing now." This from

Natalia, who turns from the window. "In some way, we think he's trying to protect Cassie."

It's an unsatisfactory explanation, but it's not surprising. They know more than they're saying, but I wasn't expecting help from them on this point.

And I didn't come here for this story. I came here to accomplish two things. One of those things, I achieved just by showing up. And the other, I might be close to acquiring.

"So my first act as special prosecutor," I say, "is to formally acquit Terry Burgos of Ellie's murder and identify Cassie as the killer."

"Is that really necessary?" Nat approaches me. "Under the circumstances—"

"Under *what* circumstances?" I ask. "She planned a cold-blooded murder. It doesn't—"

"She didn't *plan* anything!" Gwendolyn's face becomes a glowing crimson. "She wasn't some calculated killer. She saw her father come out of her best friend's apartment, Mr. Riley. You can't imagine anything so revolting, so disgusting—"

She breaks it off, covering her eyes with a hand. Natalia's stoic façade begins to crumble.

I call on all my experience as a trial lawyer, trained to feign calm in the midst of surprise, taught to stifle emotion and maintain a cool front. My limbs begin to tremble. Sweat breaks out all over. I have to go. I have to get out of here. I don't think I can even speak, over the surge of adrenaline coursing through me.

I walk away from them, toward the door. Natalia calls to me, "Please think about this, Paul," or something like that. I can't hear her anymore. I am overcome now by hope, by a promise so consuming I have to remind myself to put one foot in front of the other.

They've told me a lot, much of it lies or misdirection. But between the lines they have told me something much more important than what happened sixteen years ago.

Shelly might still be alive.

51

HERE HE COMES. Here he comes. He's with us now. Back with us. He's talked to Mrs. Lake now. She fixed it. Now *he'll* fix it. Just like he did before.

Leo raises the newspaper as Riley's car passes, turning onto Browning Street.

What did she tell him? Does he know everything?

What's he going to do now?

Follow him now. But not too close. Wait and see.

WHAT DO I DO NOW? I move my car down Browning Street, unsure of my next step. The idea was that Koslenko might be following me. If my hunch about Natalia Lake was right—that she pulled the strings, with Koslenko as the puppet—and he saw me visiting her, he might think I am on his side now. That, plus the statements I made to the press last night at the police station—insisting that Terry Burgos killed the six Mansbury women—would have to be enough to convince him that I am his ally again, his *comrade,* in the cover-up.

Where is Shelly? Just asking the question, considering the possibility that I might be right about her, turns my stomach into a full-scale revolt.

So what do I do now? Wait for Koslenko to come to me? How do I make that happen? I've done everything I can, between my public comments and my visit to Natalia Lake, to reel him in. Is there something else I can do?

Shelly could be anywhere. Koslenko would have a million places to hide her. I'm going to have to see Koslenko face-to-face. I have to find some way to get him to tell me—

A football bounces into the street in front of my car, followed almost immediately by a boy, a young teen, scrambling after it. I slam on my brakes and stop about five feet short of him. He looks up at me like the whole thing is my fault.

Jesus, kid, I think to myself, adrenaline decelerating. *Don't you have school or something?*

But then I snap to attention, as the kid in the street gives me the finger, and I answer my own question.

God. Of course.

He doesn't have school. School's out for the summer.

RILEY'S CAR SCREECHES TO a halt. Leo slows his Camry, three vehicles back. But after a moment, after the kid in the street returns to the sidewalk, Riley's car guns forward like a rocket, passing one car and blowing a red light, multiple car horns sounding their objection.

No. No. No. Leo maneuvers his car and gets lucky with a green light. He wants to stay back but not too far back. And the way Riley's driving now, it won't be long before Leo loses him. No, no, can't lose him—

He's turning. Up ahead, two blocks ahead, his car maneuvers into the right-turn lane. Leo tries to make out the street, flooring the accelerator. Then he sees it.

Riley is getting on the highway, heading south.

YOU CAN'T IMAGINE *anything so revolting, so disgusting . . .*

I speed through the Mansbury College campus, the images surreal to me now, everything the same but everything so very different. The campus is largely deserted, as it was this time sixteen years ago. Next week will be the beginning of summer school. The question is, will they find another body?

Bramhall Auditorium takes up half the block, a dome-topped structure arising from a large concrete staircase, a threshold supported by granite pillars, with a manicured lawn to each side. I pull up to the curb and kill the engine. I reach under the car seat, pull up the carpet, and remove the ordinary kitchen knife, with the five-inch blade, that Terry Burgos used to remove the heart of Ellie Danzinger and to slice Angie Mornakowski's throat.

At least, that's what I thought. When I removed the knife from its encasing on the Wall of Burgos in my basement this morning, I had to admit that I was no longer sure about that.

Sixteen years ago, I emerged from a car very close to this precise spot. And my life changed.

Last time, the place was surrounded with police officers and technicians, residents of the town pressed against the police tape, and six dead women lay inside. This time, if I'm right, there is only a victim inside, and she's still alive. And there are no police. It's what Koslenko would want. I couldn't risk bringing in McDermott or anyone else.

If you behave, she will live, too.

I put the knife into the inner pocket of my sport coat. I don't own a handgun and couldn't get one on short notice. I could have brought any number of kitchen knives, but maybe, just maybe, this particular one will come in handy.

I say a quiet prayer to a God I have neglected and get out of the car. The building looks undisturbed, vacant. This week—the sixteenth anniversary of the murders—is one of the few weeks of the entire year that the entire Mansbury campus is shut down.

I turn, as if to look back at my car, and do the best I can to look around me. Is Koslenko here? Is he watching me? I will only have one chance to do this. I have to play this right.

Which means, ignoring the internal turmoil, I take the stairs slowly, with confident authority.

There are three entrances. Front door, a maintenance entrance on the east, and a service door for deliveries in the back—north—side. I try the massive front door. Disappointed, but not surprised, that it's locked.

I walk around to the east side of the building.

Leo pulls up to the north side of the auditorium—the rear side—leaving his car in the adjacent parking lot. He runs up a ramp and goes to work on the service door with his tension wrench and short hook. The dead bolt slides open and he pulls the handle, entering the darkness.

The east-side door has only an internal push bar. Nothing on the outside but a flat, rusted door. I couldn't open it with a cannon.

I walk on uneven, sloping ground to the rear of the building and freeze as I turn the corner.

There is a single car, a Toyota Camry, in the back lot.

I sprint with everything I have left, stifling emotions, toward the only door, at the top of a small ramp. I grab the handle, try again, with a prayer, and open it. I'm inside.

My eyes adjust to the dimness and sweep a spacious room, a storage area, large refrigerators and floor-to-ceiling shelving filled with boxes. I run through the room into a large kitchen, sinks and stoves and more refrigerators. To my left are a staircase and an elevator.

I rush up the dark staircase and push open the door into light on the ground level. A large, ceremonial room, draped in red and gold, with antique furniture, with sunlight filtering in through large windows. My heart skips a beat. I know this room. The reception area, the anteroom to the auditorium. Forgetting my role as the cool authority figure, I run through another door and I'm in familiar territory, next to the large stage and podium in Bramhall Auditorium, natural light pouring into the theater. I sprint through the aisle, passing the very chairs where Detective Joel Lightner and Chief Harry Clark sat with me, recounting the grisly details of six slaughtered women. I reach the foyer and look to my left, at the door that leads to the basement, to the janitor's supply room.

I reach the door, which I know for a fact is a dead bolt that would ordinarily be locked, and quietly open it.

He's expecting me.

52

LEO OPENS the last door in the basement. He passes the chain-link lockers on the short wall and the shelving units, heads to the large storage lockers on the far wall. He stops a moment and listens. He hears nothing. He opens the middle locker and looks down.

Shelly Trotter does not look up at him, but her bleary eyes show some trace of recognition. She has received two heavy doses of gamma hydroxybutyrate—GHB—enough to keep her in a thick fog since yesterday morning, when he first subdued her in the shower. Her wrists and ankles are handcuffed, with another set of cuffs linked to the wrist and ankle cuffs, contorting her body into a forced, rounded triangle and allowing her to fit, just barely, into this oversized locker that normally holds a snowblower, shovels, and the like. A locker that now holds only two things: Paul Riley's love, and a Barteaux heavy-duty, twenty-six-inch, high-carbon spring steel machete.

A painful body position, he knows, one they used occasionally in the Soviet Union to coerce the unwilling, to break the spirit through elongated periods of discomfort. But her pain is irrelevant to him. He had to leave her for extended periods and had to be sure she couldn't move. She has, in essence, been in a forced coma since he took her from her apartment.

Shelly Trotter, Shelly Trotter.

He can see, now, that she would not have been able to act, notwithstanding the handcuffs. The GHB has worked well. Her head bobs, she groans but is unable to speak. The sweatpants he dressed her in are soiled from her bodily functions, the pungent odor fighting the antiseptic smell of the cleaning materials. Her curly hair is flat against her head. Her lips move but she doesn't speak, a line of saliva falling from the corner of her mouth.

He unlocks the third set of cuffs, the ones that link the restraints on her wrists and ankles. Her body reacts, straightening out as best it can in the confined quarters. He slides her out of the locker. He will not remove the cuffs on her wrists and ankles. He debates, for a moment, whether he should give her a third dose of the paralyzing drug but decides against it.

He hears a noise, a faint echo in the hallway, the pitter-patter of footsteps on stairs. He stands quickly and freezes, controls his breathing, listening. He hears the creak of a door opening—the door at the end of the hallway.

He removes his gun and waits.

I FORCE MYSELF to a walk, a spirited but controlled gait, toward the last door in the hallway, the janitor's room, where the bodies were found. I pass the other storage rooms, knowing he might be in any of them, waiting to ambush me. But I have to assume Shelly is in the janitor's room. Any room, this time of year, with the school on vacation, would suit his purposes, but he's been smart. He tried to mimic the lyrics of the song to make the recent murders look like a copycat. He wanted to frame Albany all along, and it was the professor, after all, who knew these lyrics better than anyone. He'd want everything to be the same.

I reach the final door quickly, realizing I have no plan and no time to formulate one. I turn the door's lever and push it open, praying that I won't be greeted with a rain of gunfire.

But he's had plenty of chances to kill me.

I step into the room and a groan escapes my throat. Koslenko is squatting along the back wall against a locker, his gun trained against Shelly's head. Shelly is barely conscious, her skin deathly pale, wearing a T-shirt covered with grime and badly stained gray sweats. My knees weaken but I manage to maintain my focus, forcing out the images of what she has gone through.

This is the chance I prayed for. And it's only one chance. There is no rehearsal.

I force it to the surface, compel the corners of my mouth upward, expel a noise from my chest that sounds something like a chuckle.

"Okay, okay," I say. "We have work to do, Leo. Work to do. You and me."

Koslenko looks different. His hair has been shaved to give the impression of a heavily receded hairline, and the coloring is different, too—dirty blond. The glasses, too, but they don't conceal those eyes, or the half-moon scar beneath. Next to him is a cane.

Smart disguise. The balding forehead especially. When combined with a limp and a cane, he puts at least ten years on himself.

It's a good reminder for me. He might be insane, but he's not stupid.

I look at Shelly, watch the movement of her body, the rise and fall of her chest. She's alive. How close to dead, I don't know.

But I can't think about that. I can't show the emotion that almost brings me to my knees, that makes me want to beg him to trade my life for hers. I would make that trade, I realize, in an instant. But Leo Koslenko cannot work with weakness or pleading.

Koslenko looks at me with a quizzical expression. "How—how?"

"How—did I know to come here? You know how, Leo."

I'm keeping it vague, afraid that something too specific will pin me down. The problem is, I don't know the depths of his psychosis. I don't know if he hears voices. Does he see a tree and think it's a spy dressed in bark?

Crazy, not dumb. But how crazy?

Regardless, right now he's suspicious of me. I wait him out, like the answer's obvious. Koslenko struggles with it.

"Natalia told me, Leo. What do you think?"

"Missus—Missus—Bentley? Missus—" Koslenko looks down, but not at Shelly. He is struggling with something internally. "Does she—like?"

Does she like?

"Not—ma—mad?" he asks.

Okay. That tells me something. He's wondering if Natalia approves of what he's done this week. He's telling me that everything he's done this week, he did alone—not at Natalia's direction. "Mrs. Bentley," he called her. Yes. That hasn't been her name for years. But it was her name back when Cassie was murdered.

He hasn't talked to Natalia this week. And that gives me some room.

"No, Leo, she's not mad. You were just protecting Cassie."

He looks up at me. He doesn't say anything, but the look on his face reads pure anguish. This man, who has killed several people this week—and maybe some sixteen years ago—looks like he's about to cry.

"Nobody knows Cassie killed Ellie Danzinger," I say. "And I'm going to make sure it stays that way."

Koslenko's eyes cast downward. He looks like a kid who just found out his puppy died.

"So—scared," he says. "So scared, so—"

CASSIE, *so scared, trembling, crying at the kitchen table, taking Leo's hand,* I think I killed her—I think I killed Ellie, *she says.* It will be all right, *he tells her.* Mother, Mother, I have to call Mother. *She comes, Mrs. Bentley, Natalia, they go upstairs, Leo stays at the kitchen table, looks out the window into the darkness, he likes the darkness better, he decides it will be all right, okay, everything will be okay. He volunteers, Nat accepts. See if Ellie's dead, check on Ellie, see if she's dead. If she isn't—if she isn't—make her dead.*

An address. He knows the name: Terry Burgos. He knows it because of the thing in court, bothering Ellie, following Ellie, they'll find the body at Terry's house, he'll be the obvious suspect, Cassie will be safe.

Easy, so easy. He double-parks the car. The door is closed but unlocked. Ellie is lying on the bed, faceup, her eyes staring at the ceiling, her body cold and rigid. He carries her to the front door, looks out, no one there, into the car, drive to Terry's house, same thing, dark, no one awake, carries the body to the back door of Terry's house and runs back to the car.

Watch, *she's told him.* Watch.

He moves the car, doubles back on foot. Doesn't expect it the first night, but it happens, that night, near midnight, a figure, Terry, it's Terry, Terry carrying a body in his backyard, between the house and the detached garage. Terry enters through the garage's side door, then runs back to the house, comes back with blankets, a long bag.

Five minutes. Ten. Twenty. Forty. An hour.

Then the garage door opens, the Chevy truck backs out of the garage and leaves. He doesn't know why, he doesn't know what, he doesn't know how. He doesn't know where.

What is it? What has happened here? This man, Terry Burgos—what has he done with Ellie's body? Leo had anticipated many outcomes but not this.

He reports to Natalia. He doesn't know where Terry took her. Natalia is silent. She is thinking. She tells Leo nothing. He senses it then. He understands. Suddenly—of course—he understands. How did he not see this immediately?

Terry Burgos is one of us. He has disposed of the body.

I TAKE TWO steps forward, carefully transferring my weight, as Koslenko comes out of his fog. The revelations—no matter how garbled and rambling—are not lost on me. Cassie killed Ellie after seeing her father come out of Ellie's apartment. A single blow to the head, on Ellie's bed, where she proceeded to bleed out. But Cassie had already fled, not to her own home but to the one on the other side of Highland Woods—a house that was largely empty these days, with Mia Lake's death and Gwendolyn Lake's globe-trotting. Cassie told her friend, Leo Koslenko, what had happened, and then told her mother Natalia.

Natalia sprang into action. She dispatched Leo to remove Ellie's body and dump it at Terry Burgos's back door. It was a brilliant move. Burgos stalking Ellie was already a matter of public record. There was the restraining order, as well as Burgos's own history of mental instability. He was the perfect patsy.

And when Burgos disposed of Ellie—when he brought her to this very room in which we are standing—Koslenko took it as a sign that Burgos was working on his side—that Burgos was *one of us.*

Us. A team of spies. A team that included, at a minimum, Natalia Lake Bentley, Terry Burgos, Leo Koslenko, and me.

Ellie was a gift from God, Burgos had said. He'd meant it literally. God had placed this girl on the back porch of his house, dead from a blow to the head. God was telling him to begin the course of action Tyler Skye had spelled out. God had given him the woman he coveted, as the first of six victims. So he ripped out Ellie's heart, in accordance with the song, and moved the body to Bramhall Auditorium.

I consider how quickly I could remove the knife from my jacket and use it, if necessary. But I know that isn't the play here. I take another step toward Koslenko and Shelly and watch his reaction. His eyes are focused somewhere on the floor. He is reliving what happened sixteen years ago.

With his left hand, he wipes a stray bang off Shelly's face. His gun is pushed into her ear, his finger on the trigger. I can't tell how aware he is, but I can't risk it. He's shown his physical abilities to me before. If I rushed him, Shelly would be dead before I reached him.

And there's a better way. We are comrades, he and I. It may have taken me a while, in his eyes, to come aboard again—including, ultimately, using Shelly as leverage—but here I am.

"You've done your part, Leo," I say. "It's time for me again. Just like before."

I take another step toward him. With a little momentum, I could lunge forward and reach him. He watches my feet, then looks up at me.

"Burn Albany," I say. "I'll do it. There's nothing more you can do."

His eyes pinball about. He is lost again in his thoughts. But the gun is still planted in Shelly's ear. I can't risk it.

"You and Terry are heroes," I say.

"Te—Terry. Hero—heroes."

KEEP WATCHING, *Natalia tells him.* Keep watching Terry. Tell me what he does.

Leo obeys, he knows how to watch, knows how to follow, he likes it, another mission. Terry stays in the house all day Monday. Leaves in the Chevy Suburban at a quarter to six in the evening. Drives to a place called Albany Printing a few miles from the Mansbury campus. All the other cars are leaving, he's working alone, stays there until nine o'clock, then he pulls out of the parking lot, but he doesn't go home, no, not home, he goes to the city instead. Leo follows. The Suburban cruises around the city's west side, driving in a loop. Leo needs to be careful he won't be noticed.

But nobody notices Leo.

The Suburban pulls over to the curb, and a woman, a prostitute, walks up to his car, talks like she knows him, she gets in, he drives off, they go back to his house.

Same thing around midnight, same thing as last night with Ellie, Terry carrying a body out the back door and into the side door of the garage. Garage door opens, the Suburban backs out. This time, Leo is ready. He follows. The drive is short, not ten minutes, five-six-seven-eight minutes. Terry parks his car in front of some kind of theater, big building, fancy building. Leo stops his car a block away. Terry pops the trunk of the Suburban and removes the woman's body, wrapped in a bag, rushes up the stairs with her in his arms, uses a key to unlock the tall door. He comes out twenty minutes later. Leo waits for him to leave in his Suburban. This time, he will know everything. He pulls up where Terry pulled up. The front of the building says BRAMHALL AUDITORIUM. *He gets by the lock on the tall front door, he's inside, follows the dirty footsteps to another door, gets through that door, too, follow the footsteps, follow the footsteps.*

Follow the footsteps, they are both there, in the final room down the long hallway, Ellie and the new girl, both naked, Ellie's chest carved out, bloody gash, huge open wound, no heart, other girl's throat is slit, all the way across, torn open. He uses his switchblade to mark them, just like they marked their kills in the Soviet Union, where nobody would see it unless they were looking, a slice between the fourth and fifth toes, a sign that the kill was state authorized, authorized by the state, wrap it up, no questions asked, no questions answered, no answers questioned.

He tells Natalia. She is relieved. She is happy! A job well done, she says. His chest warms with her approval. He has done well. The operation is succeeding.

She sends him back to watch Terry. It happens again, the next night, Tuesday, a different part of the city, but otherwise like clockwork, out of work at nine, pick up the girl, take her back to the house, then, later, carry her to the garage, drive her to Bramhall Auditorium, and leave her in the basement.

Next day, Wednesday, he stops at the house, reports to Natalia, he sees Cassie through the crack of the door to the bedroom, oh, poor Cassie, torment washed across her face, no sleep, dried tears on her beautiful face, Natalia watching her carefully, She mustn't leave the house, don't let her leave, we have to protect her, *go Leo, go, go watch Terry, see if he does it again tonight—*

Hey, you. Hey! You!

He turns as he's leaving the house, after reporting to Nat, after seeing Cassie but not speaking to her, Gwendolyn—

Gwendolyn Lake, the cousin, her house, but she's never here, always overseas, but she's here, she's been here now over a week, the drinking and drugs, Ellie and a boy named Brandon and Gwendolyn and sometimes Cassie, and, here she is, Gwendolyn, expensive clothes and hair done up fancy, getting out of her Porsche, hiking her handbag over her shoulder, she has looks like Cassie but not gentle, not sweet, harsh, crushing a cigarette with her shoe and looking at him, she never looks at him, but she's looking at him—

Leo, right? You have any idea what the fuck is going on? In *my* house? What the hell is wrong with Cassie?

He doesn't answer, he rarely speaks, not out loud, he doesn't talk so well, he shrugs his shoulders and keeps moving—

Don't they have a fucking house of their own across town?

KOSLENKO LOOKS in my eyes. I nod, as if I knew everything he just said. Terry Burgos provided the ultimate cover for Natalia's plot to cover up Cassie's murder of Ellie—he went on a murderous rampage and killed four prostitutes. Nobody would suspect that Ellie had been murdered by some-one else, given what Burgos had done.

Maybe we would have looked at the final murder differently, if given the chance. But Natalia asked the county attorney to drop that murder from the case and the county attorney was more than willing to accommodate his heaviest financial contributor.

And I let him do it. It's something I will have to live with. But, for the moment, I need to use it to my advantage. Koslenko thought I did it because we were working together. He thought I was part of the cover-up.

"Under—stand? Underst—stand?"

I force a soft smile on my face. *Understand.* He wants me to know the full story because he knows I'm taking over for him.

"Fred. Fred," he says. "Under—under—"

"Fred Ciancio," I say. "The security guard. He let you into that building."

Koslenko's head pivots. He checks every angle around him. What he's looking for, I don't know.

"She said—don't—don't tell him. Keys. Just—keys."

"Mrs. Bentley," I clarify. That makes sense. A woman with money like that, and probably some connection to Russian money and influence here in the city, could find a way to reach out. It's never surprising when a former prison guard like Ciancio keeps in touch with inmates for less than virtuous reasons. And there were plenty of members of the Russian mafia—the *comradska*—in prison at any given time.

"You didn't tell Ciancio anything?" I ask. "Then—how did he figure it out?"

I say it with empathy, like I'm just as disappointed as Koslenko that Ciancio put one and one together.

"Po—lice. Cops. Cops after."

"He figured it out when the police came to the Sherwood building afterward."

Right. That makes sense. Of course.

"Listen, Leo—"

I stop, as I hear the same thing Koslenko hears. Noise above us. The sound of glass shattering. Someone breaking into the front of the building.

Shit. I look at Koslenko, then back up at the ceiling.

Koslenko, panicked, fixes on me, the gun pushed farther into Shelly's ear.

A door slams against a wall. The door to the stairway leading down.

"They don't matter," I say quickly. "They trust me, Leo. *They always have.* Look what I did before. I'll do it again. Natalia—Mrs. Bentley told me to do it again. I will. But not if you hurt Shelly, Leo. If you hurt her, I'll tell them about Cassie."

Koslenko's eyes ricochet about, a soft moan escaping his throat. He is mumbling something I can't hear.

No, I realize, just words I don't understand.

Footfalls on the staircase now. Less than half a minute before they storm in. All bets are off then. Shelly won't have a chance.

"I'll protect her, Leo. I always have."

"Protect. Protect."

"Always, Leo. Always."

But he's not listening to me, or to the sounds of the men rushing toward this room.

"It's your time, Leo. Just like it was Terry's."

"*Skoro,* Katrina," Koslenko says, as the door to the room kicks open, Detective Michael McDermott training his gun in our direction.

I close my eyes as the sound of a single gunshot echoes through the basement.

Saturday
June 25, 2005

53

I AWAKEN the next morning on a small cot, perpendicular to Shelly's hospital bed. She is in a large, private room, allowing Governor Trotter and his wife the neighboring bed. My head lifts with some difficulty. Doctors are looking over Shelly, who has recovered relatively well from the ordeal.

A tox scan showed that Shelly had been injected with gamma hydroxybutyrate—GHB—a depressant that acts on the central nervous system. They figure she was given two powerful dosages, spaced apart by twelve hours or so, that rendered her functionally paralyzed, almost comatose. But its effects are not long-lasting.

Other than the drugs draining from her system, she probably has a concussion, but nothing worse, from when she was subdued. She was not sexually assaulted. Leo Koslenko had no interest in her other than leverage.

Shelly came to around noon yesterday. She had suffered retrograde amnesia, so she remembered nothing. She didn't remember the attack. She didn't remember that day at all. I'm thankful for that. I figure he got her in the shower, where she would be vulnerable, because Shelly is no pushover physically.

I leave around noon. Her entire family is hovering over her, stroking and coddling her. They are lukewarm toward me, which is understandable. I found her, yes, but, then again, she wouldn't have been victimized at all had it not been for me. Regardless, I feel like an outsider at a family reunion. I kiss Shelly on the cheek and tell her I'll be back soon.

I use the emergency-room exit to avoid the omnipresent media surrounding the front of the hospital. When I step outside into the late-morning sun, I use my cell phone. I call information for the number. When I'm patched through, a woman answers the phone.

"Dr. Morse, please," I say. "This is Paul Riley."

"You need to make an appointment, Mr. Riley?"

"No. I just need one minute of his time. It's rather important."

I look around, to make sure I have my space, no reporters, no police, no anybody. I wait for Dr. Morse to take the phone, but I already know the answer.

I DRIVE TO the police station. They tell me McDermott is in the observation room, and, for some reason, no one has a problem with escorting me there. I find him there leaning on the ledge, looking into one of the interview rooms, his collar open, shirtsleeves rolled. He looks over at me with dark, lifeless eyes.

Inside one of the interview rooms, Natalia Lake sits composed, cigarette smoke lingering about her weathered face.

"Natalia here says Cassie killed Ellie." He nods at her.

I walk up next to him. I wasn't sure Natalia would say that. I know it wasn't her idea.

"But she doesn't know what happened after that. She says they were scared to death of the police coming, but it never happened. She figures Terry Burgos had seen what happened at Ellie's apartment and went in and removed the body. And she figures, Burgos killed Cassie later to retaliate."

That's the story she tried to sell me at her house yesterday. Cassie did kill Ellie, but the rest of what she told McDermott is a lie.

But I won't tell him differently. Not now, anyway. Maybe never.

"You believe her?" I ask.

He takes a moment, working his jaw. "I guess I don't know. I'm not sure I could prove anything different." He nods to me. "For what it's worth, it sure looks like Burgos killed the hookers."

He did. I know that from Koslenko. But what makes McDermott so confident?

"I put a rush on DNA tests for the Mansbury girls. Just got back the results. The prostitutes had his semen inside them, and his blood. The intercourse was antemortem, so it seems pretty obvious he did them."

Right. But the intercourse was postmortem with Ellie and Cassie. And he now knows that Cassie killed Ellie. So who, he's wondering, killed Cassie?

"You got DNA in a few days," I comment, trying to change the subject.

"It was high priority. Had to be." He hits my arm. "Should make you happy. It wasn't a total miss for you, Riley. At least he killed four of the women."

I underestimated McDermott. He had the right suspicions from the start. And he's right, I guess—I can't deny feeling some relief knowing that Terry Burgos wasn't completely innocent.

Innocent. Guilty. Such flimsy words.

"Makes me wonder about Cassie," he adds.

It isn't a question, so I don't answer.

"You got any thoughts on that subject, Riley?"

Now it's a question. I don't know what else to tell him but the easy choice.

"Terry Burgos killed her," I say. "I can't imagine who else."

He doesn't like the answer. I don't blame him. But the Mansbury murders are not his case. His job was to catch the recent killer, Leo Koslenko, and he did. His job isn't to solve Cassie's murder.

Good thing for him. Because Detective Michael McDermott could investigate that case from now until the end of time and not come up with the answer.

"Koslenko, he didn't tell you anything while you were in that basement with him?"

I shake my head no. I don't see the need to fill in the spaces for the police. Not now, anyway. And maybe never.

"How'd you know to go to Bramhall Auditorium?" I ask him.

He takes a deep breath. "Watching you on television, talking to those reporters," he says. "Stubbornly insisting that Terry Burgos killed all those girls. I didn't think you believed that. So, I figured, maybe you were trying to draw Koslenko to you. To gain his trust. To 'behave.' Only, when I went to your house the next morning, I could see you were already gone. So I got on the radio and had a lookout for your car. And meanwhile, hell, I've got nothing to do, I'm on a forced vacation, I hear it's lovely on Mansbury's campus in the summer."

I smile at him. Again, I underestimated him. He probably figured Koslenko was trying to act like a copycat killer, maybe he'd use the same locale. Hell, it was worth a shot.

"So what about Fred Ciancio?" he asks me. "You think getting access to that building was to steal abortion records? Or what?"

I play dumb. But I know that Cassie Bentley didn't have an abortion. She was never pregnant.

I suspect that Gwendolyn Lake did have a paternity test done, either at Cassie's insistence or on her own, for spiteful proof. Everyone now knows that Gwendolyn was Harland's daughter. Harland admitted as much. So I go with that choice.

"The paternity test results probably set Cassie off more than ever," I say. "So when she saw Ellie sleeping with her father, for God's sake, she snapped."

"And Koslenko, afterward, stole those test results because they'd be evidence of Cassie being upset?" He shakes his head. "Plausible but weak."

I throw up my hands. McDermott doesn't pursue it. The crime has been solved. Leo Koslenko is now dead from a single, self-inflicted gunshot through his mouth. There will be no trial. There will be no search for motive.

"Did you have any idea Shelly would be in there, alive?" he asks.

Of course I did. But I can't possibly tell him I knew that. Because then I'd have to tell him how I figured that out.

"No idea," I say.

He accepts that. No reason for him to think otherwise. I can see he's not done with questions.

"You think Koslenko acted alone?"

"I do," I say, relieved to make at least one statement that is true. "Natalia is no killer," I add, breaking my streak at one.

"And he does all this—Ciancio, then the reporter, everyone—just because he wants to cover up evidence of a stolen paternity test?" His eyes narrow. "That make sense to you?"

"The mind of a madman," I answer. "Who can say?"

It's a good cop-out here, an easy explanation for the unexplainable. Koslenko was crazy—who knew *what* he was doing? But it's not true. He was smart and organized. The premise of his world was nonsensical, but his actions within that world were not. He knew exactly what he was doing.

I think of McDermott's wife, her bipolar disorder and suicide, and regret using the word *madman*.

"So—who was next for Koslenko? He had the kitchen knife and the machete."

Right. In the auditorium basement where everything ended, the police found a machete identical to the one that I had kept from the Burgos case as a souvenir, a Barteaux heavy-duty, twenty-six-inch, high-carbon spring steel machete. I realize, with a shudder, that Leo Koslenko must have been in my house at some point, to get a good look at that machete so he could buy the same one. If he was a copycat, after all, he needed to play the part as best he could.

"My guess? Koslenko was going to kill Harland Bentley," I say. "Then finish with Frank Albany. It would make it easier to blame Professor Albany for everything if he wasn't alive to deny it. Again, my guess—he'd kill Albany but make it look like a suicide."

"Jesus." McDermott sighs. "This might seem odd coming from a cop, but I actually feel sorry for Koslenko."

"It doesn't sound odd at all. He was sick, Mike. He didn't know what he was doing."

McDermott raises his head, nods toward the interview room. "I was sure it was either Professor Albany or Harland behind all this."

That was Koslenko's intention. That was always the plan back then, if anything went south with Ellie Danzinger's murder. They'd put it on Albany. Instead, Burgos went wild after finding Ellie's body and pretty much insulated them by killing the prostitutes in rapid succession. If Ciancio hadn't gotten in touch with Evelyn Pendry and Leo Koslenko this week, none of this ever would have come to light.

"Ciancio had ties to the *comradska*," McDermott tells me. "We just found that out today. So I figure, that's how Koslenko would have gotten to him. Russian connections."

Yes, that's how the connection was made. But it wasn't made by Koslenko. It was made by Natalia. She had the money to reach far enough, through the right Russian circles, to make an arrangement with a security guard. I have no doubt that she kept her name out of it completely. And that she will continue to do so.

And I won't say differently. Not now, anyway. And maybe never.

I nod toward the window, toward Natalia Lake. "What's gonna happen to her?"

Natalia might be in some trouble. She covered up her daughter's involvement in the murder of Ellie Danzinger. And she might have abused the truth a little this week. But, in the end, from their perspective, she covered up the culpability of someone who became one of Burgos's victims, too. And they will have a hard time proving any of the things they suspect. They will have to prove that she knew Cassie committed Ellie's murder and that she played an active involvement in covering it up. How could they prove any of that?

"All we know is that her daughter killed someone sixteen years ago. She doesn't have to report it. Maybe she had Koslenko break into that building for the paternity tests, but we can't prove that. Koslenko and Ciancio are dead, and she's smart enough to know we have nothing."

"Right," I agree.

"She was protecting her daughter," he adds without prompting. "She may have colored outside the lines a little, but she was protecting her daughter. If it were up to me—"

He stops on that. Takes a long breath.

"She didn't hurt anybody," he says. "Her daughter did something, and she made the best of the situation. Is that so wrong?"

He turns to me, challenging me, emotion coloring his face.

"You telling me you wouldn't do the same thing if it were your daughter?"

I raise my hands in surrender, and I haven't even said a word. He's fighting with himself.

"Yes," I say, "I would protect my daughter, too."

He turns back to the observation window. "Sorry. Jesus."

"Been a long week," I say.

He stares at me for a long moment. Sleep deprivation and stress do wonders to a person. McDermott strikes me as a solid-as-rock sort of guy, but I wouldn't be surprised if he burst into tears right now.

"I meant what I said before, Riley. About Burgos. You had him dead to rights. And, look, he did kill four girls, maybe five." He hits my arm. "Hell, even his own lawyer took one look at the whole thing and pleaded insanity. He didn't fight you on the facts. It's not your job—"

"It *is* my job. I had discretion." I look at him. "Burgos was insane, Mike. He was the dictionary definition of insane. He thought God was speaking to him through a song."

"Yeah," McDermott counters, "but he knew what he was doing was a crime, right? He fabricated an alibi. He hid the girls in a basement. Would you change a single thing about your argument to the jury if you could do it over again?"

"One thing," I say. "I wouldn't make the argument at all."

I walk away from him. Yes, Terry Burgos was aware that a law in this state prohibited murder. And, yes, he took steps to avoid getting caught. He manufactured an alibi. He hid the bodies so no one would find them until his spree was finished. He picked victims from different parts of the city so he wouldn't have to go back to the scene of an abduction. And all of that means, he didn't fit the definition of insanity, as that definition was written up by a bunch of politicians who don't want to appear soft on crime.

"Leo Koslenko knew he was breaking the law," I say. "Oh, and he also 'knew' that he was a superspy, protecting the world from undercover enemies posing as prostitutes. He also 'knew' that *I* was a spy working with him for that secret world organization." I flap my arms. "So you're telling me Koslenko wasn't insane?"

McDermott shrugs. "You know better than anyone if you appreciate you're breaking the law—"

"Oh, come on, Mike. I'm not talking about the *legal* definition of insanity," I say. "I'm saying Burgos's head was in another galaxy. He thought he was doing God's bidding, and, if that's what you *really* think, why would you care about some silly state law?"

McDermott doesn't answer.

"He should have been incarcerated the rest of his life," I say. "And treated. But he shouldn't have been executed."

McDermott's in no mood to argue. He'll let me beat myself up if that's what I want. He walks over to me and shakes my hand. There was a time—really, only a couple days ago—when I'd have never thought it possible that we'd be parting on cordial terms.

"None of my business," he says. "But out of curiosity."

"Shoot," I say.

"You gonna stick with your million-dollar client, Mr. Bentley?"

A fine question. Harland's conduct back then was disgusting. But he didn't kill his daughter and didn't have anything to do with the cover-up, either. Still, it seems hard to imagine we can just go back to business like nothing has changed.

"Hard to say if I even want to be a lawyer anymore," I say.

He stares at me a moment, like he's waiting for the punch line. "Yeah, right." He waves me off. "Get lost, Riley. Take care of Shelly."

I look back at the interview room, where Natalia Lake sits motionless. They might prosecute her, depending on media pressure. Maybe I would be a witness, too, because I have learned a good deal of information from her, Koslenko, and others. That would be hearsay, of course, but you could argue for an exception, statement of a coconspirator's the best bet, if you could establish an overt act—

I catch myself. Listen to me, turning everything into an evidentiary question. McDermott's reaction was right. It's in my blood, the law. It's all I know. It's all I want to do.

I leave the police station and, this time, say nothing to the reporters.

Not now, anyway. Maybe never.

Wednesday
July 6, 2005

54

SHELLY AND I are spending a week in the presidential suite at the Grand Hotel, ordering room service and walking on the beach and seeing the sights and eating delicious, rich food. We've managed some time for intimacy, too, but we've put a modern twist on the phrase *sleeping together*. We have done just that. We have averaged ten hours of shut-eye a day.

Shelly is doing better now. You don't just bounce back from being attacked in your home and abducted, even if your memory of it is foggy at best. She has had to adjust, more than anything, to the concept of fear itself. We've walked into the town and strolled the beaches, but only during daylight hours. Without either of us acknowledging it, I've led her back to the fourteen-acre estate of the Grand Hotel every night. This, I've come to realize, is not about seeing the sights. It's about getting away.

On our fourth day here, I awake around nine. Shelly has just come out of the Jacuzzi and is wrapped in towels. I open my eyes and catch her looking at me, watching, and I see it in her eyes, a sense of reserve, apprehension. I say "Good morning" and she reciprocates, but with her eyes diverted.

There is a knock on the door and she jumps.

"Oh. Room service," she says, chuckling at herself without humor.

I throw on a shirt and answer the door. I tip the bellhop on his way out. I put the fruit and granola in my mouth, chew it, swallow it, but I don't taste it. She plays with a piece of toast and laughs appropriately at my jokes, but she is holding back. Shelly holding back is about as natural as the sun rising in the east. But now I feel it, more than ever, even more than when she broke up with me, because, at least then, I had hope that she'd return.

I shower and dress in a short-sleeve shirt and slacks. I walk her down to the spa, where I have arranged a day of beauty for her. Massage, facial, the works. She demurred initially, and positively scoffed at the notion of a pedicure until they explained that a foot massage is included. She is not looking for pampering so much as relaxation.

I walk her to the door of the spa, an act of chivalry, but she senses I'm being protective escorting her everywhere. She's right.

"What are you doing with your morning off?" she asks me.

"I'll think of something."

She nods and turns to the door.

"Shelly."

She looks back at me casually, then reads my expression. When the pause becomes more than momentary, when she watches me struggle, she senses what's coming and braces herself.

"Let's move up our flight," I suggest. "Let's take off tomorrow morning."

She looks into my eyes.

"You need to get back to your life," I add. "I need to get back to mine."

She struggles with that awhile, but, with every moment she doesn't respond, she is answering. I know Shelly Trotter better than she knows herself. I know the difference between wanting to be with someone and the fear of never being with anyone. I know the difference between someone loving me and someone being *in* love with me.

I retreat to my hotel room with that silence, painful but honest, hanging heavily.

I STEP OUT ONTO the veranda with a folder I brought from work. I have a multiple-defendant fraud trial four weeks from now. I've fallen behind, but I don't mind. The preparation is my favorite part, mapping out strategy and planning its execution. It's a game, a competition, something between a contact sport and theater. My client probably should be convicted, seems to me. At best, he buried his head in the sand while the executives around him were playing fast and loose with the Medicaid regulations. At worst, he specifically directed the illegal action.

But I think he'll walk. We will argue that he didn't know what was going on and couldn't have known. And their best witness, the flipper, the guy who cut the quick deal with the feds and agreed to testify against my guy, is on bad paper. He lied to the feds initially and admitted to doing so, and it looks like he had a bit of a gambling problem, too. I will tear him to pieces in front of the jury. I'll throw up enough smoke to blur the picture.

That's my job now, to smudge the picture, to mess with the prosecution's case, to make adverse witnesses unlikable and untrustworthy while my client sits peacefully, smiling gently and sweetly and silently. That's the game. It's about winning. It's not about truth. It's not my *job* to make it about the truth.

It used to be. But I'll never be a prosecutor again.

I lean over the veranda's railing, the warm wind curling under my T-shirt, the rays of the sun warming my face, images of Leo Koslenko and the Mansbury victims and, most of all, Terry Burgos swimming through my mind. I think of him strapped in the electric chair, chubby and disheveled, looking into my eyes as the prison guard called out that Burgos had no last statement.

I'm not the only one, he'd mouthed to me, his final words. Was he simply quoting Tyler Skye's lyrics? Or did some part of his brain know his words to be true?

I use my cell phone. The number has been programmed in, at the governor's insistence. I didn't plan on using it.

I get an aide, who patches me through quickly.

Governor Trotter's initial reaction is one of concern. I put him at ease, tell him we're doing well here, Shelly's enjoying the break, she's getting a massage right now. We do a little small talk, but neither of us thinks I'm calling to shoot the breeze.

There is a small pause, and I clear my throat.

"As you requested, Counselor," he says, "I put in a word for this detective, McDermott. I think he can be expecting a promotion soon."

"I appreciate that, Lang. Very much."

"But that's not why you called," he adds. "And it's not to ask me for Shelly's hand in marriage, either."

"No," I agree, not elaborating on just how correct he is.

"It's not to ask me to put in a good word for you with Harland, either."

He laughs. "From what it sounds like, he wants me to put in a word for *him* with *you*."

Before Shelly and I left for vacation, Harland Bentley showed up at my office. It was the first time he had ever come to me. He apologized for keeping information from me during the Burgos prosecution. He asked me to stay on as his attorney. He said he needed me and would accept any terms I demanded.

I don't kid myself that I'm the only lawyer who could handle Harland's legal work. I'm a good face to put at the top, and, when necessary, I step in, but there are many lawyers who could do the work, and who could grow into the necessary leadership role. I do believe that Harland values my contribution, but there's no question that his plea to me was born, in no small part, out of guilt. He feels like he owes me one.

I introduced Harland to Jerry Lazarus, who has been one of the lead partners I've utilized on his litigation. I told him Jerry, a young, aggressive, and smart lawyer, was the man he wanted. He agreed, mostly, I think, because I asked. So the firm will not be laying off lawyers. It will not lose Harland Bentley's business. The only difference will be the name on the law firm's door. Shaker & Flemming will be just fine.

"Vacations, getting away—it gives you space," the governor remarks. "Gives a man time to step back and think about his life. Think about the future."

I don't respond to him. But I smile.

"Don't be so hard on yourself, Paul. I was a prosecutor for many years. A man confesses to murder and has forensics all over his house. And he still killed most of those women. Hell, his own *lawyer* thought—"

"Thanks, Governor. I appreciate that. It's a little late, unfortunately."

"Is that why you're calling, Counselor? Because it's too late?"

He knows why I'm calling. I can't change what happened, no matter how much I wish I could. But I want to believe, I *have* to believe, that it's not too late to do some good.

"I suppose you heard—last week, Judge Benz announced she's stepping down," he says. "She was a credit to the federal bench. She'll need an equally worthy replacement."

Lang Trotter is a very smart man. A good one, too.

I thank him and close the cell phone.

I CATCH A TAXI outside the hotel and give the man the address. I rest my head against the seat and look out along the coastline, the magnificent beaches and the eternal, ice blue sea, as the cab navigates the narrow roads.

Leonid Koslenko, it turns out, had murdered his sister, Katrina, when he was fifteen, insisting to his family afterward that she was a spy bent on destroying their family and country. His parents had connections with the politburo and got him institutionalized instead of criminally prosecuted. And while accounts are still sketchy, it sounds like someone in the KGB became impressed with Koslenko's physical skills and, after he'd spent two years in a mental institution, recruited him for some dirty work. About two years after that, his disapproving family pulled some strings and cut a deal with the Soviet government—probably spreading around plenty of money in the process—that allowed Koslenko to leave the Soviet Union as a "political dissi- dent." It was, apparently, a fairly easy sell, because it was widely known that the Soviets locked up political enemies in mental institutions.

But Leo Koslenko was no dissident. He belonged in an institution.

In Koslenko's mind, his days as an assassin-spy never ended. The United States was just a new assignment, with Natalia Lake Bentley as his mother superior. He continued in treatment for paranoid schizophrenia and took his medications. No one knows what was in his mind during that time— whether he was awaiting orders or whether he was conducting "missions" of his own—but, as far as we know, he managed to stay out of trouble, living fairly comfortably at Mia Lake's home, working as a ranch hand, so to speak. He came to know Cassie, who was far and away the most approachable, sin- cere member of the Lake-Bentley clan.

But he was ready when his orders came—the day Cassie murdered Ellie Danzinger in a fit of rage and despair. When Natalia called on him, he sprang to duty.

From what he was mumbling to me about Burgos—*He was one of us*—it seems that, after watching Burgos dispose of Ellie's body so efficiently, he came to believe that Burgos was working with them, too. That, in his mind, was why Natalia had directed him to move Ellie's body to Burgos's house. He was another spy, a comrade. And when he watched his comrade Burgos kill the prostitutes, he came to believe that prostitutes were the enemy, acting out covert missions, using their occupation as cover.

No one knows how many prostitutes Leo Koslenko murdered after the Burgos affair. Streetwalkers disappear all the time and people rarely look very hard for them. The prostitute he'd been accused of murdering a few years back, it turned out, had the incision between her fourth and fifth toes on the left foot. Police have opened files on other hookers who were found dead; three of them so far have the same signature mark. Others, however, would have to be exhumed, and it's unlikely anyone will go to the trouble.

That's why he killed Amalia Calderone, the woman I escorted out of the bar. He thought he was saving my life. He wrapped my unconscious hand around the tire iron, the murder weapon, not to frame me but to get me involved, to wake me up to the fact that help was needed again. He also killed a woman from a hardware store who was not a prostitute but who was very attractive and provocatively dressed and whose tortured mind took to be a hooker—read spy.

He'd also used a Russian prostitute who went by the name of Dodya to substitute in as Shelly's double in the bathtub. Turns out, the *comradska* imported young Russian women into the city and kept them in a warehouse where anyone with enough cash could make use of them. Koslenko had purchased the girl outright for eight thousand dollars, killed her, took her to Shelly's apartment, and did what he did to her.

He'd been unhappy with me up to that point. I hadn't responded to his notes. I'd thwarted his attempt to kill Brandon Mitchum. I wasn't being a *comrade*. His trick in Shelly's apartment was intended to get me on board—I had a day or two, at best, before blood tests and other testing would have established that Shelly was not the woman in that bathtub. I think the idea was, if I didn't clean up the mess—if I didn't *behave*—in a day or so he'd kill Shelly for real. In the meantime, no one would be looking for Shelly because everyone—except for me—would think she was dead. He was sure I would know differently.

Natalia Lake, thus far, has escaped any criminal charges. The word is the county attorney is considering a charge for her role in covering up Cassie's murder of Ellie Danzinger, but I think that's just to placate the media feeding frenzy. It's not going to happen. There's no real proof that Cassie even killed Ellie—she did, of course, but knowing it and proving it are two different things—much less that Natalia actively covered anything up. And this is to say nothing of the fact that Terry Burgos has already been officially blamed, convicted, and executed for the murder of Ellie Danzinger.

Natalia's statement to the police, of course, left out the part where she directed Leo Koslenko to move Ellie's body from the apartment to Burgos's house and directed him to keep watch over Burgos and report back to her. And I haven't told the police any of that.

Not yet, anyway. And maybe never.

The taxi moves into a residential neighborhood, large estates built high up on the hills, with large fences surrounding them. I had thought about renting some estate for this week with Shelly, but hotels are much better in terms of security. Shelly didn't need to be sleeping in some giant house with creaks and groans in a place thousands of miles from home.

And, besides, a partner of mine in my law firm said if you stay in Saint-Jean-Cap-Ferrat on the French Riviera, you gotta stay at the Grand Hotel.

I pay the driver in euros sufficient to convince him to stick around. I walk up to a large gate, bordered by twin, white stone blocks, and push a buzzer embedded in a gold plate.

"*Bon jour*," a woman's voice says through a speaker.

"Paul Riley," I say, "for Gwendolyn Lake."

"Ah." She pauses to convert to English. "Mister—Riley?"

"Paul Riley, yes."

"You have an appointment?"

"No. Tell her I'm alone, please."

After a good ten minutes, a man walks down the long driveway toward me, looking tan and healthy and wearing all white. "Mr. Riley?"

"*Oui*."

"*Bon jour*." He opens a small gate and leads me into the estate. We climb endless, outdoor stairs, past well-kept, flourishing island plants and trees. The house itself is large but not monstrous, a two-level brick, full of windows that gleam in the bright sunlight.

Instead of taking me into the house, he leads me down a path that winds around the house, until we reach the back. There is a swimming pool as big as the one that was in my high school, a Jacuzzi off to the side, and a large deck area.

"Ms. Lake," the man says.

The last time I saw her, she was ragged, in bedclothes and with flat hair, pouring out the beginning of a story to me in the parlor of Natalia's home. Four hours later, she boarded an American Airlines flight, nonstop to De Gaulle airport in Paris.

Today, she is wearing a one-piece orange bathing suit with a white terry cloth robe over her shoulders, spread out on a lounge chair on the deck by her pool. Her skin is more tanned than the last time I saw her. Her hair has dried from a swim, hanging at her shoulders. She peeks at me over her sunglasses.

She says nothing to me, doesn't offer me a chair or anything else.

"I don't know what Natalia told you," I say, "but I don't see any charges sticking against her. She's lucky."

She places the book she's reading to the side and sits up in the lounge chair, putting her feet on the deck.

"I'm surprised she even told the police about her daughter killing Ellie. She didn't have to do that. I take it that was your idea?"

She remains still, looking off in the distance through her shades. I'm right, of course. Natalia never wanted anyone to know that Cassie killed Ellie. She'd have let Terry Burgos, Professor Albany—anyone else—take that blame.

"You told her if she didn't tell the police, *you* would."

Again, she doesn't answer, or even look at me.

"You ran away before," I say. "Back then. On Wednesday, the week of the murder spree. You flew to France."

We've already been over this. I'm bringing it up for a reason and she knows it.

"France doesn't extradite its citizens to the U.S.," I continue. "Roman Polanski can tell you that. Which, I assume, is why you left back then."

She doesn't answer.

"And why you're here now," I add.

She looks up at me.

"You understand," I say, "that the murder of Cassie Bentley remains unsolved. That case, technically, was never prosecuted. You know that, right?"

"I know that." Her voice is flat, defiant. "Of course I know that."

And yet she returned to the United States, anyway, albeit three years later.

"Do I have a clear picture of Cassandra Alexia Bentley?" I ask. "The destructive affair with her professor. The mood swings. Finding out Harland fathered the girl she thought was her cousin. Harland's affair with Ellie. And then she snaps. It's too much. She storms into Ellie's apartment, after seeing Daddy come out, and she gives her one on the brain. Is all of that true?"

A tear appears beneath the sunglasses. She wipes at her face, her mouth contorted into a snarl, but she remains motionless otherwise.

"Look at me," I say, "and convince me that everything I've just said is true."

She stares into the ground. She is choking up a bit, sniffling and clearing her throat. After a time, she removes her sunglasses and looks up at me with red, wet eyes.

"Okay," I say. "And there was no pregnancy. No abortion. That was a natural assumption. The break-in to the Sherwood Executive Center. Everyone thinks it was to steal a pregnancy test, or abortion records, or paternity records. That's all crap, right?"

She says nothing.

"But it's believable," I say. "Evelyn Pendry assumed it. The cops assumed it. Hell, I assumed it." I take a breath. "And then I fed it to you when I came to see you at the lake."

She's smart enough to stay silent.

"And once I put that idea in your head," I continue, "you took it and ran with it. You and Natalia, you got your stories straight afterward. The next day, you both came to us 'voluntarily' and told us how Cassie Bentley had been pregnant and had had an abortion. You wanted us to believe that. You wanted us to believe that because it made Professor Albany look guilty. That had been Natalia's plan all along, right? If anything went south? Blame Professor Albany."

Burn Albany.

"But that was all just a lie. Right?"

Her eyes drift off as she considers her answer.

"The truth," I demand. "You have to convince me that I'm doing the right thing."

She laughs with a tinge of bitterness. "'The right thing.' You think you know who killed Cassie—"

"No, that's not going to work," I say.

She watches me carefully, a slight tilt of her head, narrowing of the eyes. She's getting the picture now. The walls of this impressive estate are beginning to close in.

She gets out of the chair, turning in all directions as if seeking shelter from this. Finally, she turns to me, regarding me in a different light. Newfound respect. Maybe newfound fear.

"Did you like what Koslenko pulled with Shelly?" I ask. "The chain saw? The poor girl in the bathtub?"

She looks away. Otherwise, she doesn't respond, but she must have appreciated the irony. *Old habits die hard,* she must have been thinking.

It took me a while to figure it out, I admit. But I can connect a dot or two.

The murder in the bathtub—the unidentifiable mass of bones and tissue—was one.

Koslenko's note, for another: *If you behave, she will live, too.*

Too. As in, *also.* As in, *like others lived.*

And Koslenko's explanation about how Ciancio figured everything out: At the Sherwood Executive Center that night, Ciancio had given Koslenko the keys and left him to commit his burglary. Ciancio only figured it out afterward, Koslenko told me, when the police came to that building on the Burgos case.

But there was only one reason the police came to that building after the bodies were discovered.

"A couple weeks ago," I say, "I was talking to Harland. We were chasing this red herring about the Sherwood Executive Center. I asked him if his daughter's doctors were at that building. You know what he said?"

She freezes. She has no idea, of course, but it seems she's interested.

"I figured he'd have no idea about his daughter's medical care. But you know what? He did. He remembered taking her there to have a cavity filled when she was a little girl."

Her face contorts. A fresh tear falls. Her shoulders begin a slow tremble.

"You helped out, too," I tell her. "When you were describing Cassie's reaction, seeing her father walk out of Ellie Danzinger's apartment."

In the midst of her sobbing, she nods. I imagine, in hindsight, she realized that, too.

You can't imagine anything so revolting, so disgusting, she had said. A little too personal, too heartfelt, for a secondhand account.

"Natalia sent you off to Paris," I say. "Wednesday of that week. I assume it's not entirely different from how you described it—you were a mess. A basket case. You had no idea what was happening. You had no idea what was *going* to happen."

"Of course I didn't." She looks at me. "'Basket case' is a good description. I was confused and scared and, by that point, overmedicated. I was a zombie when I got on that plane."

I believe her. I can't imagine otherwise. "You didn't wonder about the passport?"

She shakes her head. "I—I probably should have—but, no."

And so there she was, safe in France, secure in the knowledge that a French national couldn't be extradited.

Natalia Lake, I see now, was quite masterful throughout all of this. She had Koslenko move Ellie's body to Burgos's house, she cut a quiet deal for mutual silence with Professor Albany, and she got lucky, very lucky, when Burgos began a weeklong murder spree.

But Natalia Lake did more than just cover up a murder. She also *ordered* a murder, an order that Leo Koslenko obeyed, beating the poor girl beyond recognition and planting her, like Ellie, on Burgos's back doorstep.

And then she had my boss, the county attorney, drop the charges on that murder so no one would take too close a look.

Cassie saved me, Burgos had said. He'd thought the final murder in the first verse meant he had to kill himself. That was what the lyrics suggested— *stick it right between those teeth and fire so happily*—and Tyler Skye had played it out that very way when he put a gun in his own mouth. But Burgos, clearly, didn't want to kill himself. He delayed the move for two days. Maybe he was never going to do it. But then, suddenly, God was giving him a reprieve: Terry found a badly beaten corpse outside his back door, the same place God had left Ellie Danzinger. He couldn't reconcile this development with Tyler Skye's citation to the Leviticus passage, so he leafed through the Bible until he found a verse relating to stoning, which was the most apt way to describe what had been done to the woman on his back porch. He crossed out the Leviticus passage on his list and wrote in the one from Deuteronomy. And then, as if to keep consistent with Leviticus and the lyrics anyway, he put a bullet through the corpse's mouth.

Like everyone else, Burgos thought that corpse lying on his back doorstep was Cassie. Why wouldn't he? Even with the beaten, crushed face, there was the driver's license and credit cards in her pants pocket belonging to Cassandra Bentley.

We didn't stop at identification found on the victim, of course. A family ID is the minimum we do. And Natalia, of course—not her husband—made that identification at the morgue.

Nor did we stop there. With a beaten face like that, and no fingerprints in a database to match, you go to the obvious next step.

You pull the dental records.

When I woke up in the hospital that Saturday after we found Shelly, I put in a call to my dentist, Dr. Morse. He explained that, in 1989, most dentists didn't have computerized or digitalized dental records. They simply had hard copies of the X rays sticking out of a pouch with a person's name assigned to them.

Yes, he agreed, back in 1989, if someone broke into his office in the middle of the night and switched dental records from one pouch to another—say, swapping one half sister's records with the other's—nobody would be the wiser. You might have to switch some labels around, but it would be easy, and no one would know.

Fred Ciancio, working his security post at the Sherwood Executive Center the week after the bodies were discovered, must have scratched his head when he saw the police march up to the dentist's office for the records of Cassie Bentley. Did that have anything to do with Koslenko? he probably wondered.

Then, shortly after that time, he saw a photograph in the newspaper of that same man—Koslenko—standing in the background with an eye on Harland Bentley. He put Koslenko together with the Bentley family and he was probably pretty sure of what had happened. He called the reporter covering Burgos, Carolyn Pendry, but thought twice about it and clammed up. Carolyn finally gave up on Ciancio, and the whole thing stayed quiet.

This June, something brought it all back for Ciancio. Probably it was the special he saw, Pendry's thing on television, expressing sympathy for Burgos. He managed to find Leo Koslenko and told him it was time for a second installment on the payoff. Somewhere along the line, he also called Carolyn's daughter, Evelyn. Who knows? Maybe he was debating between coming clean and getting some extra retirement money. He must have given Evelyn some kind of a taste—mentioning the Sherwood Center, probably—but didn't fully clue her in.

I wonder if Ciancio ever actually figured out the entire truth. Things must have looked hinky to him, but did he know exactly what had happened?

Koslenko, of course, had no intention of letting Ciancio continue breathing. He tortured him and got Evelyn's name. He tortured Evelyn and got Brandon Mitchum's name. Each of these people knew something that could point back to the truth.

The truth being that Cassie Bentley was never murdered. Instead, she got on a plane to Paris using Gwendolyn's passport, while Gwendolyn suffered a brutal death before being cast off as her half sister Cassandra after the switch of the dental records.

Cassie Bentley pulls her robe tight, watching me. "What now?"

"Gwendolyn's murder," I say. "Your mother should have to answer for that."

But the only way that happens, both of us realize, is if everyone learns about Cassie, living here in France under Gwendolyn's name.

"I don't approve of what Mother did." Cassie brings a hand to her face. "I would have stopped her if I knew. But she did it for me, Mr. Riley. She knew the police would come straight to me after Ellie was killed. She knew I wouldn't be able to withstand any questioning at all." She flaps her arms. "But if I'm dead, no one looks for me."

The same strategy Koslenko used when he put in a substitute for Shelly in her bathtub. If I behaved, he was telling me, she would live, too. Like Cassie lived.

I believe what she's telling me. Nothing I've learned about Cassie Bentley makes me think she could have been part of a diabolical plot. She was kept in the house after Ellie's death, like Koslenko told me, and then shipped off to Paris. She didn't know they were going to fake her death. She didn't know what was in store for Gwendolyn.

Gwendolyn, of course, was a natural choice. She didn't have any real family or any real home; she bounced from continent to continent so she wouldn't be missed. She looked like Cassie—they shared a father and their mothers were sisters—and her face was crushed, in any event. And Gwendolyn was probably a wild card, anyway. She couldn't be counted on to play along in a cover-up. A wild card. She was the perfect choice. Two birds with one stoning.

"Your mother had nothing to do with Ciancio, or Evelyn Pendry, or any of the recent murders?" Koslenko already told me he acted alone, but I want to hear her answer.

She is emphatic, showing much more resolve. "Mr. Riley, she hasn't talked to Leo in years. None of us has. After everything happened, she gave Leo enough money to live out his life, bought him a house in the city, and didn't speak to him."

Right. The police found a safe-deposit box for Koslenko with almost a million dollars in cash. Koslenko was off the reservation. He was acting alone. He was trying to protect the woman he loved, Cassie, from being discovered.

"Mother was in Tuscany, with friends, when Leo started killing. She had no idea until the police got hold of her in Italy. *I* had no idea. When you first came to see me at the lake, it was the first I'd heard of it."

That makes sense. But then she and her mother talked, they got their stories straight, and they gave it to the cops and me the same way. They gave up Leo, they gave up Albany.

But, in the end, Cassie—as Gwendolyn—came clean, at least enough to spare Albany and Harland. She had probably figured there was nothing she could do to save Leo at that point; he was clearly responsible for the murders of Ciancio, Evelyn Pendry, and Amalia Calderone, plus the failed attempt on Brandon Mitchum. But she *could* save Harland and the professor. She and her mother had us pointed toward both of them, but, that last day, she marched into that parlor and gave up Cassie—herself. She explained who really killed Ellie, to her mother's obvious surprise, and over her objection. She was trying to do the right thing while keeping her true identity out of the picture. She did the best she could. Her mother was willing to let Albany, or even Harland, take the fall, anything to protect Cassie, but Cassie, in the end, wouldn't let that happen.

That's why I've been silent on the whole thing, why I wanted to reserve judgment until I spoke to her. Cassie killed a girl, her best friend, but the circumstances are what they are. The law provides excuses—extreme emotional distress, temporary insanity—in a clumsy attempt to reconcile competing societal concerns, to strike a balance between retribution and compassion. I don't know what a judge would make of this. What a jury would decide. I have seen it better than anyone, the imperfect application of the law to the facts.

I didn't stop for a single moment to consider whether Terry Burgos was insane. I went to work immediately to dispel that notion, lining up evidence to beat his defense, telling myself that he had a lawyer, that there was a jury, that the system provided safeguards to ensure that the truth came out.

But I was a prosecutor. My job was about more than winning. Yet in every piece of evidence demonstrating Burgos's psychosis—and there was plenty of it—I saw only an obstacle to victory, a land mine to sidestep, something I had to discredit. I didn't care whether I was right. I didn't even ask the question.

Maybe, I will tell myself, what Burgos did was inevitable, that he had a short fuse that something, somehow, was going to light. If it wasn't Ellie's dead body setting him off, it would have been something else. Anyone provoked that easily was probably going to do it, anyway. Surely, I will remind myself, he should not be given a pass. He was a danger to society. He *did* kill four young women. It will be a debate I'll play out the rest of my days.

"Do whatever you're going to do," Cassie says softly, her eyes shining once more with tears. "I won't fight it. I'm—I'm so tired of running."

A prosecutor is given infinite discretion. He can decline to prosecute for any reason whatsoever. I am no longer a prosecutor, but the Mansbury murders were mine, and what happens to Cassie Bentley is entirely up to me, whether I like it or not.

"Good-bye, Gwendolyn Lake." I leave Cassie standing motionless, staring out over the horizon, wondering if she'll ever stop running.

ACKNOWLEDGMENTS

As always, I have relied on the talents and insights of others in helping create and shape this novel.

Bill Kunkle, a former colleague and the lead prosecutor in the matter of *People v. John Wayne Gacy,* was very generous in sharing his experiences and opinions on the prosecution of a schizophrenic serial killer. I wish I had a fraction of your war stories, Bill.

Dr. Ronald Wright, a forensic pathologist in Florida, again was liberal with his time and patience in answering technical questions and in helping make the discussion of dead people more interesting than I ever would have suspected.

My old law school classmate Matt Phillips was kind enough to lend me the brilliant mind of his wife, Dr. Wendy Phillips, who gave me an overview and some needed details on the subject of paranoid schizophrenia.

Jeff Gerecke gave me excellent direction and advice, as he has done for many years, and I am forever in his debt.

I rounded up two of the usual suspects to read the manuscript and offer anything that came to mind. Jim Jann, urban poet and leader of men, always manages to see things that I cannot and clues me in. Jim Minton, from minor details to plot flow to the big picture, always makes my books better. To this group I added Mike McDermott, who let me use his good name (literally) and whose comments on an early draft are greatly appreciated.

J. A. Konrath, who knows a few things about writing of serial killers and who has given me so much advice in my literary career, provided critical commentary, some advice, and a good jolt of encouragement, too. I owe him one—thousand.

Dan Collins, a federal prosecutor and a friend for life, was always there to answer my annoying questions about law enforcement. Or maybe that's just because I sprang for drinks.

Larry Kirshbaum, my agent, teaches me something every time he opens his mouth. His enthusiasm is infectious and his wisdom limitless.

It's not easy being my editor. But Brendan Duffy has been outstanding from start to finish in guiding this novel in matters big and small. This book wouldn't be the same without him. I'm lucky to have such a talented partner in crime.

And finally, my wife, Susan, who listens to my endless jibbering about my novels and who keeps me balanced and sane and deliriously happy. You still make my heart go pitter-pat.